THE
Love's Journey SERIES
IN SUGARCREEK

the
Sugar Haus
Inn

THE

Love's Journey SERIES

IN SUGARCREEK

the

Sugar Haus

Inn

BY SERENA B. MILLER

LJ EMORY
PUBLISHING

Originally Published by: *Summerside Press™ Minneapolis 55438*

Under the title: *Love Finds You in Sugarcreek, Ohio ISBN 978-1-60936-002-3*

Copyright © 2010 & 2016 by Serena B. Miller

Find more books by Serena B. Miller at *SerenaBMiller.com*

Find her on Facebook, *FB.com/AuthorSerenaMiller*

Follow her on Twitter, *@SerenaBMiller*

The town depicted in this book is a real place, but all characters are fictional. Any resemblances to actual people or events are purely coincidental.

Scripture references are from the Holy Bible, King James Version (KJV). The Holy Bible, New International Version®, NIV®. Copyright © 1973, 1978, 1984 by Biblica, Inc.™ Used by permission of Zondervan.

Most foreign words have been taken from *Pennsylvania Deitsh Dictionary: A Dictionary for the Language Spoken by the Amish and Used in the Pennsylvania Deitsh New Testament* by Thomas Beachy, © 1999, published by Carlisle Press.

Front cover photo by JD Schrock and Amish Leben, LLC.

AmishLeben.com and *FaceBook.com/AmishLeben* - Used by permission.

Author photos by Angie Griffith and KMK Photography

KMKphotography.com - Used by permission.

Photos of Sugarcreek provided by Bev Keller, editor of *The Budget*. - Used by permission.

Cover & Interior design by Jacob Miller

Published by L. J. Emory Publishing

For information about special discounts for bulk purchases, please contact L. J. Emory Publishing, sales@ljemorypublishing.com

ISBN: 978-1-940283-22-7

ISBN: 978-1-940283-23-4 (eBook Version)

To my Old Order Amish friends in Sugarcreek,
for sharing their wisdom, laughter, and homemade pie.

Be not forgetful to entertain strangers:
for thereby some have entertained angels unawares.

~HEBREWS 13:2 KJV

PROLOGUE

The leather on Rachel Troyer's gun holster creaked as she shifted her weight on the kitchen chair. Her three elderly Amish aunts shot wary glances toward the offending weapon.

"My niece." Bertha clucked her tongue with disapproval. "Carrying a gun!"

This was an old subject—thoroughly discussed and dissected over the years. Her aunts had made it abundantly clear that they disapproved of her profession as a police officer. Bertha, the old fox, was trying to distract her from the subject at hand, but Rachel was determined to not get sidetracked.

"That's *not* what we were talking about, Bertha, and you know it," she said. "It's time for the three of you to make a decision. You can't put it off much longer."

Square-faced and stolid, Bertha lifted her chin. "This old inn has been welcoming guests ever since your grandfather built it a hundred years—"

"I know the story," Rachel interrupted. "You've told it to me many times. He came from Pennsylvania to Sugarcreek, Ohio, with only a new wife, a mule, and carpenter's tools. He bought a

1

farm, built a six-bedroom house, filled it with four kids, rented out three of the bedrooms, built two cabins for extra travelers, and tapped the sugar maples he found growing on the place. He was also a bishop in the Amish church. I get it. Grandfather Troyer was a great man. The place has history."

"Which you do not value."

"I *do*. But I value the three of you more."

Frustrated, Rachel pulled her hair into a tighter ponytail. As their closest relative, it was her sad task to convince her aunts that they were too old and fragile to continue doing the heavy work necessary to keep the small inn running.

Unfortunately, they were of an entirely different opinion.

She had known it would be difficult. The Amish were not exactly known for their willingness to accept change, and Bertha was being especially pigheaded today.

"I'm only asking this because I love you." Rachel glanced around the table at their glum faces. "You *do* know that, don't you?"

All three averted their eyes. The phrase "I love you" was rarely heard in Old Order Amish households. It made them uncomfortable. In their world, one *showed* one's love rather than verbalize it. Yapping about "love" was something the "Englisch" outsiders did. The Amish put muscle behind the word instead of their mouths.

Rachel knew this, but she was desperate for anything that would impress upon them how strongly she felt about the issue of closing the small inn her grandmother had named the Sugar Haus.

Gentle Lydia, who was peeling a basketful of windfall apples from their small orchard, laid down her paring knife and repositioned a straight pin that was holding the waistband of her dark green work dress closed. A plain white choring kerchief covered her gray hair. At seventy-six, she was reed-thin in spite of the never-ending stream of sugar-infused cakes, cookies, and pies that flowed from her kitchen.

Her aunts' use of straight pins to hold their clothing together had annoyed Rachel for as long as she could remember. But nothing else was acceptable among the stricter members of their church district.

It was a puzzle to her. She could understand the church's traditional ban against buttons on women's clothing. Plain dress was part of their identity—and buttons, she supposed, could conceivably be considered fancy. She could even tolerate the restriction against zippers—which mainly affected the men who had to wear britches with buttoned flaps. But for the life of her, she could *not* understand their church's prejudice against the convenience of safety pins.

She caught sight of Anna's vulnerable bare feet tucked beneath her chair and winced at the thought of how many straight pins her sweetest aunt must have stepped on in her lifetime. She longed to protect her from pain of any kind. Anna's struggle with Down syndrome was difficult enough.

"The three of you need a break," Rachel pleaded. "You should enjoy the years you have left instead of half killing yourselves by waiting on guests."

"How?" Bertha gathered the long skirt of her brown dress to one side and eased her recently broken leg into a more comfortable position atop a footstool. An active seventy-eight, Bertha had been robust until taking a tumble down the stairs one week earlier.

"How what?"

"*How* should we 'enjoy' ourselves?" Bertha stuffed an errant strand of gray hair beneath her white prayer *kapp*. "How should we spend all this *frei* time you say we need?"

"However you want. Travel. Quilt…"

"I have already traveled everywhere I wish to go," Bertha said. "And I do not enjoy quilting. Quilting is what Lydia does."

"Maybe you could get caught up on your reading." Rachel had made up her mind not to budge on this issue. As painful as this discussion was for all of them, they had to face the facts.

"After I have read and Lydia has quilted"—Bertha snagged an apple slice from Lydia's bowl and took a bite—"what then? Are you going to put in electricity and make us watch television all day long like your *Englisch* friends?"

"I quilt *goot*," Anna piped up.

Anna, at fifty-seven, was pushing the odds of longevity for someone with Down syndrome. She was, in fact, one of the main reasons Rachel wanted her aunts to close the inn. With Anna's insistence on being part of every activity, she worked too hard for someone who, like so many with Down syndrome, struggled with a weak heart.

Rachel could not bear the thought of living without Anna's unquestioning love or Lydia's gentleness or Bertha's strength of character. She wanted her aunts to live forever. They were all she had.

"You do quilt goot." Lydia patted her younger sister's hand, and Rachel's heart ached with love for these good women. She knew for a fact that Lydia frequently stayed up after midnight removing Anna's lengthy and disorderly quilting stitches—and then redoing them by lantern light. This was a closely kept family secret they all conspired to keep from Anna forever.

"And you want us to live on Victoria's money." Bertha spat out the words as though they tasted of poison.

For the first time, Rachel realized that she had underestimated the pain Bertha had endured because of her younger brother's marriage to a local Englisch girl. In her aunts' eyes, it had been this marriage that pulled their only brother into a job that had taken his life—a profession Rachel now shared.

"Yes," Rachel said flatly. "I do. Now that I've turned thirty, the trust fund my mother left me is accessible, and this is what I want to do with it. I have looked forward to helping you for a long, long time. There is no reason the three of you need to keep working so hard."

"You have no obligation to do this for us," Bertha said.

"No obligation?" Rachel shook her head. "You have been my surrogate mothers ever since the day I was orphaned at eleven. You went without sleep when I was sick. You made special meals for me when I was hungry. You sewed clothes for me to wear. You gave me a happy life—even though I chose not to accept your traditional faith. I've wanted to do this for you ever since I learned I would receive an inheritance."

"Taking care of you was not so hard." Bertha waved a dismissive hand. "You were an obedient child. You owe us nothing."

"Please, Bertha. Don't be stubborn about this," Rachel said. "It's time you started receiving instead of giving all the time."

Bertha cocked her head. "And are *you* going to 'retire' from your work now that you have this money?"

The question took her by surprise. She had focused so much on her aunts' needs that she had not considered the possibility of quitting her own job. Now that she thought about it, the idea terrified her. Who would she *be* if she was no longer a cop?

"No. I won't retire. I—I like my work."

Bertha's eyes narrowed. "You did not like it so much when that bad man in Cleveland put you in the hospital."

Rachel swallowed against a sudden wave of nausea. She still battled flashbacks of the beating that had almost ended her life.

"We're not talking about me right now. Will you, or will you not, stop taking in guests?"

Bertha frowned. "What do *you* think, Lydia?"

Lydia rose and dumped the bowl of just-sliced apples into the large cooking pot she had positioned on the kitchen stove. Widowed and childless, she was the quietest of the three and in many ways the most fragile. It made Rachel cringe every time she saw Lydia wrestle the heavy pots and pans with her arthritic hands, as she created huge breakfasts and mounds of fresh-baked sugar cookies for their guests.

Rachel hoped for Lydia's support. If *anyone* had earned a rest, it was her middle aunt.

It didn't happen.

Lydia shook some cinnamon into the pot, added a couple of cups of sugar, and turned on the propane flame. "Who will I cook for," she asked, plaintively, "if we have no guests?"

Rachel stared at the surface of the old oak table and fought to gain control over her emotions. She was trying to give them a *gift*, for crying out loud. She was trying to take care of them—just as her father would have wanted her to do.

She had imagined them getting misty-eyed with gratitude and relief. She had dared to hope they would be pleased with her generosity. Instead, they were acting like bewildered children who were being punished when they had done nothing wrong.

"I think we can still take care of our guests," Bertha said brightly. "My leg will heal. Anna's heart is strong enough to gather eggs for breakfasts. I can use a stool to help Lydia in the kitchen. We can hire a nice Amish girl to do the laundry. We will manage."

"You have been promising to hire a 'nice Amish girl' for the past five years. Somehow it never happens."

"We did not need help before this."

"Really?" Rachel arose, put both hands flat on the table, and leaned forward. "You fell down the steps carrying a chamber pot from the upstairs bedrooms, Bertha!" she exploded.

"True." Bertha chuckled. "Fortunately, the chamber pot was empty."

Anna sniggered then looked at Rachel's face and sobered.

"Bertha was something, she was." Lydia, still smiling, was gathering another lapful of apples into her apron from the bushel basket beside the table. "She went down the steps—*kershlammy!* I found her at the bottom, wearing the lid like a hat."

Bertha laughed out loud at the image Lydia had painted.

"That is *not* funny." Rachel couldn't believe her aunts could find humor in the situation. It had scared her witless when she had learned that Bertha was on her way to the hospital. "How can you laugh at such a thing?"

"*Ach.*" Bertha made a rueful face. "At our age, if we do not laugh, we will shrivel up inside."

"*Dess lacha behayt sich zu veina!*" Rachel said sharply. "'Excessive laughter turns into crying.' *You* were the one who taught me that proverb, Bertha." She took a deep breath and plunged on. "You could have broken your neck. It's time to stop doing all this—this needless work." She gestured around the enormous kitchen unadorned by modern conveniences.

Anna innocently continued to smile, but Lydia and Bertha reacted as though Rachel had slapped them.

"Honest labor *iss* from *Gott.*" Bertha's Germanic accent deepened as she crossed her arms over her chest. "We are used to our ways."

Lydia began to peel another apple, but not before Rachel saw the hurt reflected in her eyes and knew that she had gone too far. Her aunts considered the work of running the inn a calling—not an act of drudgery.

She adored them, but these three women were going to be the death of her. Even giving them the use of her mother's money wasn't going to keep them from working until they dropped.

Unlike some Amish business owners who found ways to compromise in order to thrive in the modern world, her aunts ran a strictly Old Order Amish establishment. No electricity. Flashlights and kerosene lamps at night. Gravity-fed plumbing. Everything they did was labor-intensive.

The problem was, tourists might *think* they wanted to experience the simplicity of Amish life—but not if it involved sleeping without air conditioning, sharing a single downstairs bathroom, waiting for the low water pressure to refill the tank, or eschewing television and wi-fi.

Most of the guests who were willing to put up with a complete lack of modern conveniences did so for two reasons only—her aunts' low rates and Lydia's generous cooking.

She had watched the quality of her aunts' clientele drop in recent years and was afraid that if they didn't make some changes soon, the Sugar Haus Inn would turn into a flophouse for deadbeats with no money. Her aunts, tenderhearted and easily taken in by a sob story, were barely scraping by as it was.

Anna gently touched Rachel's face. In one of her surprisingly insightful moments, she gazed at her with understanding and sympathy. "You are 'fraid for us?"

A lump rose in Rachel's throat. "Very afraid."

"'Cause you *leeva* us?" Anna said.

"Yes, because I love you."

Anna leveled a look at Lydia and Bertha. "*I* don't want Rachel 'fraid."

It was rare for Anna to take a stand. Rachel thanked God that she had chosen to do so now.

"I know Lydia's not as strong as she used to be," Bertha grumbled. "And Anna is taking heart medication now. I am not much use until this leg heals. I *know* we have slowed down—but what you are asking is a hard thing."

"I know," Rachel said. "I'm sorry."

Bertha remained silent for a long time as everyone awaited her decision. Finally she released a sigh that came from the depths of her soul. "Even though it is hard to accept...you are right. We will close the Sugar Haus Inn to paying guests. We will accept the use of Victoria's money. But I insist on one thing."

Rachel's heart grew lighter as she realized she might have won the battle. "What's that?"

Bertha pointed to an old wooden plaque hanging on the wall beside the kitchen door. It had defined her aunts' philosophy of life for as long as Rachel could remember. It read:

BE NOT FORGETFUL TO ENTERTAIN STRANGERS: FOR THEREBY SOME HAVE ENTERTAINED ANGELS UNAWARES. HEBREWS 13:2

"*If* we have reason to believe that Gott Himself has brought a stranger to our door, we will not turn that stranger away."

"But—"

"That is scripture, Rachel, and I will not compromise on doing the Lord's will."

Rachel respectfully bowed to the older woman's convictions. She knew she had achieved as much as possible. Bertha was no pushover. The older woman had endured shunning in order to train as a nurse. She had worked in a Haitian orphanage for twenty years, until her parents had fallen ill. Then she had come home to kneel before the very Amish congregation that had banned her, asking for forgiveness and returning to the stricter religion in order to be allowed to care for her ailing parents—and Anna.

Bertha might be nearing eighty, but she had a spine of steel when it came to doing what she believed to be right.

Rachel pulled a savings passbook out of her back pocket and laid it on the table. "This should be enough to keep you comfortable for several months. Tell me when you need more. I don't want you doing without a thing."

"*Dank*," Bertha said with dignity. "Thank you. Our church will be blessed not to part with alms for us, and we will be glad not to have to receive them. I will go to my room now, to pray over this."

Doubt filled Rachel's mind at her aunt's words. "I thought you had already made your decision."

"Yes, of course." Bertha waved a hand. "We will do as you say. We will no longer give *The Budget* our advertising dollars, and you may take down the sign at the end of the road. But I will ask Gott to give us wisdom so that if there is a stranger He wants us to minister to—we will not blindly turn an *engel* away."

"Agreed." Rachel resolved to add her own prayers to Bertha's— that there would *be* no more strangers, no more demanding guests. She believed in God, but she didn't buy into the whole "angels unaware" thing.

Her aunts had earned a much-deserved retirement, and she was going to see to it that they got one. Whether they wanted it or not.

CHAPTER 1

I t had been miles since Joe Matthews had taken the time to
truly notice his whereabouts. Images of the towns he had
driven through during the past few months blurred together like a
child's sidewalk chalk sketch in the rain. If he didn't start paying
attention, he was afraid he would end up driving into the Atlantic
Ocean with no memory of how he had gotten there.

He was fairly certain that he and his little boy, asleep in the
booster seat beside him, were still in Ohio. He had a vague
memory of driving through Columbus a couple of hours ago.

His back hurt from too much driving, his right shoulder ached
from too many years of physical punishment, and his eyes were
inflamed from the strain of watching mile after mile of road pass
beneath his wheels.

Where was he?

A lone oak tree near the road beckoned, offering some shade
from the unseasonably warm September sun. He pulled his blue
Ford pickup beneath it, turned off the engine, and unearthed his
dog-eared road atlas from behind the seat. As he studied the map,
he rolled down the window to let in some fresh air.

Silence, in the form of a veritable ocean of ripe, golden corn-fields, surrounded him. This was an alien land, a strange universe, the other side of the moon from his home in Los Angeles.

As the dappled shade of the giant oak played over his wind-shield, he glanced at his four-year-old son. The simple serenity of sleep on his child's face clutched at his heart.

He, too, longed for rest—a short break from the reality that had been thrust upon him. Hoping for a catnap, he leaned his head back against the headrest and closed his eyes.

Bobby immediately stirred. "Are we home yet, Daddy?"

The question felt like a knife twisting in his gut.

"Not yet, son. Try to go back to sleep." He adjusted his headrest. Those few seconds of shut-eye had felt so good.

"I gotta pee."

"Can it wait?"

"Daaa–ddy…" The little boy jiggled up and down. "I gotta go. *Bad!*"

Bobby did not have good bladder control, and the last thing either of them needed right now was a drenched seat. Joe sprang into action.

"Hold on, buddy."

The long, straight road was empty as far as the eye could see. He ran with his son behind the oak tree and pointed him in the general direction of the cornfield. He had just pulled up Bobby's minuscule jeans when he heard a vehicle approach. A low bass *thump, thump, thump* from the driver's music grew louder as a bottle green truck with jacked-up wheels hurtled down the road. A blast of wind from the truck hit Joe in the face as it passed.

The monster truck seemed out of place in this lovely rural setting. As it whizzed by, two teens in the front seat made obscene gestures before roaring on down the road.

"I don't like that truck, Daddy."

"Me either, buddy."

In the wake of the giant vehicle, it seemed strange to hear the gentle *clip-clop* of horse hooves. A black buggy with an elderly bearded man in a simple black hat, white shirt, and cloth suspenders drew up beside him. Unless Joe was mistaken, this man was a member of the Amish faith. Up until now, he had only seen pictures.

"Whoa." The man pulled back on the reins and the horse pranced at the sudden stop. "Are you having *druvvel*—trouble?"

"No." Joe laid his hand atop Bobby's head. "My son just needed to use the bathroom."

The man, who appeared as if he had time-traveled straight from the 1800s, nodded as though he found Joe's statement to be profound. "Little boys—they are bad about not waiting. I had eight." He frowned at the horizon where the truck had disappeared. "None turned out like them *dummkopps*, thank Gott! They almost ran me over." His gnarled hands, holding the reins, were still shaking, as though he'd had a bad fright.

"I'm sorry." Joe surveyed the fragile buggy. The old man had good reason to tremble. The buggy would stand no chance against a truck of that size. Or any size. "I'm glad you're all right."

"It is Luke Keim's twins." The man shook his head in dismay. "They should plow a field in the hot sun all day. That would cool them off plenty goot."

"Boys that age aren't known for having good sense."

The old man made a clucking sound in the back of his throat. "Their *daett*—their father—should have better control of his *shtamm*—his family."

He peered at Joe's out-of-state license plates. "You are a tourist?"

"I'm just passing through. How far is it until the next town?"

"You do not know where you are?"

13

"Not exactly."

The Amishman pointed straight ahead. "Sugarcreek—two miles that way." He slapped the reins against the front of his buggy. "Giddyap!" The buggy abruptly veered back onto the road.

Joe scratched his head as he watched the horse trot down the road. His meager store of knowledge about the Amish came entirely from the movie *The Witness*. It felt surreal to be nearly blown off the road by a souped-up truck one moment and discussing potty breaks with an Amishman the next.

Wait a minute.

Joe mentally rewound and replayed their brief conversation. Had that man said *eight* sons? As he buckled Bobby back into his car seat, he tried to imagine raising that many children—and couldn't. It was taking everything he had to care for *one*.

As many times as Bobby had asked if they were home yet, Joe had asked himself the same question. He didn't know the answer, but he *had* to believe that there was a place of sanctuary for them somewhere. His son deserved a better life than this. Bobby needed home-cooked meals, his own bed, and friends to play with.

The question burning a hole in Joe's heart was—where?

Rachel was fighting a losing battle.

Kim Whitfield, a new police academy graduate, was putting in volunteer hours manning the Sugarcreek Police office—and Kim liked to chat.

Unfortunately, her presence was driving Rachel straight up the wall.

Normally, Sugarcreek's five full-time and five auxiliary police officers were well able to deal with the everyday problems that arose in this rural township, but the week of the famous Swiss Festival was another thing altogether.

Years ago, the local cheesemakers had joined forces with local winemakers to create a fall festival that would attract new customers. Their plan had worked even better than expected. Thousands of tourists now descended on the picturesque town every fourth weekend after Labor Day, tasting and voting on the various cheeses and local wines. They danced the polka and participated in the parades and other events—and strained the small police force to the limit.

Unfortunately, in addition to the responsibilities of the Swiss Festival, Rachel also had a pile of reports to finish. In her universe, desk work ranked somewhere below locking up drunks and cleaning out the squad car. However, she definitely needed to get her desk cleared before the crunch of the Swiss Festival hit with full force on Friday morning.

As she worked her way through the stack, Kim wandered over to peer curiously at the report she had just finished.

"A DUI?" Kim asked.

"Yes."

"But...it says here that the DUI was a horse and *buggy*."

"Uh-huh." She really didn't want to be drawn into a conversation right now. There was way too much work to do.

"How could you even tell the driver was drunk if he was driving a horse and buggy?"

"The horse ran a red light."

"You're kidding."

"Nope."

"Maybe the driver just wasn't paying attention."

Rachel turned around to look at Kim. It was obvious the girl wasn't going to leave her alone until she got the whole story.

"You're right. The driver *wasn't* paying attention. He was passed out dead drunk on the seat. The good horse was taking him home. Unfortunately, the horse didn't know enough to stop at a red light. Both the horse and the driver could have been killed."

"You mean, the driver was *Amish?*" Kim was not from Sugarcreek. Her voice told of her disbelief. Like many outsiders, she seemed to be under the impression that all the Amish lived unwavering, righteous lives—as though old-fashioned dress and transportation somehow made them immune to human failings.

"The buggy driver was an Amish teenager enjoying his *rumspringa* a little too much."

"Rumspringa?"

"It's their 'running-around' time, those years when Amish young people want to taste the outside world before settling down and becoming faithful members of their church."

Kim chomped a piece of gum as she thought this over. "I always thought they just grew up and turned into carbon copies of their parents."

"Some do. A few go off the deep end, but some don't go through rumspringa at all." Rachel turned back to her work.

"Being a cop here is different from other places, isn't it?"

"People are people no matter where they live," Rachel said. "They all struggle with problems. We're lucky in that Sugarcreek inhabitants are just a little nicer than most."

"I like it here."

"I'm glad, but I need to get these reports finished...."

"I won't bother you anymore."

"Thanks."

Unfortunately, Kim just *had* to talk. She immediately began a running commentary on the tourists walking past the police station's street-level window.

"Whoever told *that* woman she looked good in shorts should be shot." Kim blew a bubble and snapped it. "And those shoes. Hello! Four-inch heels were never meant for a woman her age."

Rachel glanced out the window. The woman Kim was targeting couldn't have been a day over thirty—her own age. Kim seemed competent enough, and she had gotten high marks from the academy, but the girl's mouth was getting on her last nerve. Having her working here was turning out to be a whole lot more bother than being shorthanded.

"Um—I'm trying to concentrate here," Rachel said pointedly.

"Oh." Kim whipped around, her long auburn hair flipping over one shoulder. Her big brown eyes were round and innocent. "Sorry."

Rachel felt a stab of remorse. The girl really did mean well. It had been unprofessional to snap at her. Kim had done nothing wrong.

"It's just that I have all this work to do and…"

The phone rang and Kim answered, her eyes still glued to Rachel as though she were trying to puzzle out why Rachel was annoyed with her. She covered the mouthpiece with her hand.

"This lady says she's your aunt Lydia. Do you want me to tell her you're not here?"

"Why on earth would I want you to do that?"

"I don't know." Kim shrugged her perfectly toned twenty-two-year-old shoulders and made a face. "Because she sounds, like, you know, really *old*?"

Rachel tried to excuse the girl, but the comment bugged her. Kim was from an upper-end suburb outside of Cleveland and had no idea how hard it had been for Lydia to gather enough courage to walk out to the phone shanty, unlock it, and dial the number to the police station. The shanty, the phone, and the answering machine were Bertha's province. Lydia used it only in emergencies. The last time she had done so had been the day Bertha had fallen down the stairs.

Something was wrong. Rachel just knew it. Her pulse raced as she reached for the phone. "Lydia? What's happened?"

"Rachel?" The elderly woman's voice quavered. "Is that you?"

"Yes, Lydia—it's me."

"I am making your favorite foods for our *ohvet essa*, our evening meal. Will you come?"

Her heart ached at the uncertain tone in her aunt's voice. Lydia *did* sound old. "Of course I'll come. Thank you so much."

Lydia, unused to phone etiquette, hung up awkwardly and abruptly.

The invitation struck Rachel as sad. Normally she was a frequent guest at her aunts' table. They seldom called to formally invite her, but she had been so involved in preparations for the Swiss Festival that she had not seen them for over a week. With no guests to care for and all their Amish relatives preoccupied with harvests and canning everything from apple butter to piccalilli from their orchards and autumn gardens...they were probably feeling a little abandoned right now.

"Is something wrong?" Kim asked, as Rachel stood staring out the window with the phone in her hand.

"No." Rachel replaced the handset. "My aunt was calling to tell me that she's cooking my favorite meal tonight."

"So—what's she making?"

"Mashed potatoes, roast, homemade egg noodles with cabbage, green beans, and sugar cookies flavored with orange rind. That has been my favorite meal since I was a kid."

"Wow. You are *so* lucky. I was raised on TV dinners. Mom didn't like to cook."

At the look of envy on Kim's face, Rachel felt a small, guilty jolt of satisfaction. The girl's comment about not answering the phone

18

because Lydia was old still rankled. How *dare* she judge the woman's worth by her age?

Rachel shoved away her negative thoughts and hurried to finish her desk work so she'd be on time for supper. A couple of hours out at her aunts' farm beckoned like an oasis in what she knew would be a crazy two days. Neither she nor any other town official would draw a free breath until Sunday when the Swiss Festival would be over.

The sign said: WELCOME TO SUGARCREEK, THE LITTLE SWITZER-LAND OF OHIO.

Joe didn't care if it was the *real* Switzerland as long as it had a decent mechanic. His truck had suddenly developed a loud and disturbing noise. He desperately scanned the various businesses, looking for a place that might be able to fix it.

Finally he noticed what appeared to be a small, working garage. At least he *hoped* it was a working garage. Oddly enough, it was housed in a building designed to resemble a Swiss chalet, and it shared space with a craft store. Tires and tools leaned against the outside of the building. Nearby sat an eye-catching, ancient jalopy, developing multiple layers of rust.

As he nosed up to the open bay, his truck shuddered to a stop. From the sounds coming from beneath the hood, he feared the stop might be permanent.

"Are we home yet, Daddy?" Bobby craned his neck to see out the window.

Joe sighed. The never-ending question. "Not yet." He tousled his son's blond curls. "Our truck's not running right."

"Did it break?"

"I don't know, but it's got a bad cough."

He knew that Bobby understood coughs—the little guy had been fighting one ever since yesterday morning. Joe was starting to get worried. The over-the-counter cough syrup he had bought had given Bobby little relief.

He climbed out of the cab and lifted the hood, hoping that whatever was wrong with his vehicle would be easy to fix.

"Daddy! Catch me!"

He peered around the hood. Bobby had both arms stretched toward him and was leaning out of the open window—*too* far out.

"Watch out, son! You'll fall." He caught Bobby just as he toppled from the window. "Careful, buddy. Don't do that again. I might not catch you in time."

Bobby stuck his thumb in his mouth and mumbled around it. "Don't 'eave me!"

Thumb-sucking was something Bobby had outgrown two years ago. Now it was back.

"I won't leave you. Ever. I promise."

Bobby dug his face into Joe's chest. "'kay."

With his son's arm looped around his neck, they checked out the engine—as they did everything these days—together.

"Need some help?" A man dressed in blue coveralls walked toward them, wiping his hands on a rag.

"My truck's acting up," Joe said.

"I heard. Sounded like a blown head gasket." The man stuck his head beneath the open hood. "Looks like it too."

Joe's heart sank.

The mechanic stepped back from the front of the truck and glanced at the Texas license tags. "You're not from around here." He made it sound like an accusation.

"Just traveling through." There was no need to explain that although the truck was from Texas, he and Bobby were not.

"It'll take a day or two to pull the engine head and resurface it.

And another day to put it in, maybe two." He stuffed the rag into his right back pocket. "I could order the part before I go home tonight. You want me to do the work?"

"I'd appreciate it."

The man considered. "I'm a little backed up. It might be a couple days."

"I suppose we have no choice." Joe shoved a hand through his hair. "How much?"

"Depends. The parts and resurfacing aren't too expensive, but there's a lot of labor involved. Probably run you around five hundred. Maybe a little more." He looked him over doubtfully.

Joe knew the mechanic was evaluating his ability to pay, and who could blame him? The scruffy beard Joe had affected and the worn clothes he had picked up at Goodwill had not been chosen to inspire financial confidence. If anything, the exact opposite.

"I'll need a deposit if you want me to order it."

"Sure." Joe shifted Bobby and groped his back pocket for his wallet—but it wasn't there.

Frantically he searched his other pockets. No luck.

"I'll be right back." He rushed to the truck and tore the cab apart. The only thing he found were a couple of stray twenty-dollar bills and some change he had tossed into the console earlier in the week. Desperately, he tried to remember the last time he had seen his wallet.

Then it came to him—the truck stop where he had filled up with gasoline this morning.

He had gone into the restroom, carrying Bobby in his arms. Two men had jostled him as they passed in the doorway. He had not felt the hand slip into his back pocket, but he would bet money —if he had any—that one of them had lifted his wallet. It had contained several hundred dollars in cash, a credit card, and the card accessing his bank accounts—his lifeline.

He felt the blood drain from his face.

"You okay?" the man called. "You don't look so good."

"I think someone stole my money." He ran a hand over his face and realized that he'd broken out into a cold sweat. "Could I leave my truck parked here until I can figure out what to do?"

"I suppose. There's a place in back I can store it for a couple of days."

"I'd appreciate it."

They maneuvered Joe's vehicle to an empty spot behind the station while Bobby watched with wide, frightened eyes from the cab. His little forehead was furrowed with worry, his gaze glued to his father's face. Joe wondered when it would end, when his son's fear of letting him out of his sight would cease.

After what Bobby had been through, maybe it never would.

Bobby coughed—a wrenching sound that made Joe wince.

"I thirsty, Daddy," Bobby said.

Joe set the emergency brake and pulled Bobby out of the truck, rubbing a smear of dirt off his son's cheek with his thumb. He dredged a juice box from a cooler in the back. It floated, alone, in a puddle of lukewarm water. The ice had melted hours ago.

He tore off the attached plastic straw and its cellophane, inserted it into the box, and handed the drink to his son, wondering when he could afford to buy more.

As Bobby slurped the juice, Joe nervously dug at an itch beneath his chin. He hated growing a beard—but it helped to hide his identity.

"Is there a really cheap place in town to stay?" he asked.

The mechanic choked out a laugh. "There isn't even an *expensive* place to stay in town right now. Let alone a cheap one."

"Why?"

"You don't know?" The man stared at him in surprise. "I figured that's why you were here. This is Swiss Festival weekend. Everything in town has been booked for weeks. The place is crawling with visitors."

"I've got some camping equipment. Is there a state park or public land close by?"

"There's a campground up ahead." The man shrugged. "The Wally Byham Airstream Caravan Club is probably already set up there by now. They come every year." He pointed down the road. "Turn left on Edelweiss and keep going. You'll see it."

"How far?"

"It's a bit of a hike." The mechanic hesitated. "I'd take you, but like I said, I'm kind of backed up here."

"Thanks anyway." Joe set his son on the ground and pulled a small tent and a duffel bag out of the truck. "Come on, partner; we're going camping."

"I wanna go *home*, Daddy." Bobby's voice was plaintive.

"I'm sorry, son. We don't have a choice."

The mechanic disappeared into the depths of his garage as Joe walked toward the outskirts of town with Bobby hanging onto his belt.

He considered the odds of getting enough money together to fix his truck in the next couple of days. Without his credit cards and ID, they weren't good. By now, his money would be enhancing someone else's lifestyle, and his empty wallet was probably residing at the bottom of some dumpster. Fortunately, the code to his bank card would be near impossible for a common thief to break.

What should he do?

He turned onto Edelweiss, and what appeared to be miles and miles of cornfields lay ahead.

"Carry me, Daddy," Bobby demanded.

Joe was already lugging a tent and a duffel bag. Carrying forty solid pounds of little boy would be difficult.

"Daddy needs for you to walk, buddy."

Bobby, at the end of his emotional rope, plopped himself down on the asphalt road and began to cry.

Fearful that a car might come, Joe scooped up Bobby. The child's sobs stopped. The baggage, in addition to Bobby's weight, tugged at Joe's bad shoulder. Pain shot down his arm.

So many operations over the past two years—all from the best surgeons in the world. None, however, had been good enough to turn him back into the well-oiled throwing machine he had once been.

Instead of a car, once again he heard the *clip-clop* of horse hooves. Turning around, he saw the same old Amishman who had stopped to talk to him outside of town. Joe wondered what the old man must be thinking now—finding him and Bobby on foot.

"*Wie geht's.*" The man pulled back on the reins. "Hello. Where is your vehicle?"

"It has a cough," Bobby reported importantly.

"Ach." The old man's eyes danced with amusement. "That is a pity. Perhaps you should buy a goot horse and buggy!" He slapped his knee and chuckled at his own joke.

Joe shifted Bobby in his arms. "Right now, that sounds like a pretty good idea."

"Put the *boovli*—the little boy—in here." The old man shoved a box of apples toward the back. "I can take you a piece further."

Gratefully, Joe eased Bobby onto the buggy seat and wedged himself in next, putting the tent on the floor and holding the duffel bag on his lap.

"Giddyap!" the old man said. The horse took off with a start, throwing Joe against the back of the seat. He automatically reached for a safety belt before realizing the vehicle didn't have one.

He felt exposed and vulnerable riding inside the buggy. It

swayed with every movement. Visions of that monster truck surfaced.

"I am Eli Troyer. And this"—he nodded toward the sleek brown horse—"is Rosie."

The horse acknowledged the introduction by raising her tail and depositing a steaming pile of fresh manure on the road. She followed that by passing gas—loudly.

Bobby was wide-eyed as he stared at the horse's rear end.

Eli seemed oblivious to Rosie's faux pas. "My Rosie was a racehorse," he said. "Can you not imagine her on the track as a young mare?"

"I'm sure she was something else," Joe said.

He had visited a racetrack a few times with friends. Never had he dreamed that any of the powerful horseflesh there could end up pulling an Amish buggy.

A low-slung red car zoomed past, rocking them in its wake. Rosie shied and danced a few steps to the right, into the gravel.

"You must get tired of all the tourists," Joe said.

"That was no tourist. That was a local." Eli steered Rosie back onto the blacktop. "The tourists are usually polite and careful. They stay far behind us when they follow us up a hill. It is our locals who lose patience." He clucked for Rosie to pick up her pace. "The worst are the ex-Amish who have chosen to 'jump over' into the Englisch world. Some act angry when they pass us. It is as though they are saying"—Eli raised a fist in the air and shook it to demonstrate—"'Get out of my way, old man! I am so smart to leave the church!'"

Eli pointed at the car disappearing down the road. "I know him." His voice was filled with sadness. "He used to be one of our people."

Joe had no idea what to say. This wasn't his battle.

Eli changed the subject. "What is your boy's name?"

"This is Bobby, and I'm Joe Matthews." Joe noticed that the buggy's rocking motion was causing the tent to edge toward the open door. He secured it with his foot.

"It is goot to meet you. Do you have shtamm—family—here?"

"No," Joe said. "No family here. The mechanic back in town said there's a campground up ahead."

"Sure is. But it is not so big, and it will be full."

"How do you know?"

"It is Swiss Festival time."

Everywhere Joe turned, it seemed he was hearing about the Swiss Festival. Obviously, he could not have come to this town at a worse time. Where would he and Bobby sleep tonight? Joe looked at the huge cornfield they were passing and wondered if the farmer who owned it would mind if a man and a small boy pitched a tent at its edge.

A deep cough racked Bobby's small body.

"Your son is ill," Eli pointed out.

"He's had a cough for a couple of days."

"And you have no vehicle and no place to stay?"

"That's pretty much it."

"Do you have *geld*—money?"

Joe felt embarrassed, but it was a fair question, under the circumstances. "Not much."

"I know a place," Eli said. "It is not far."

"A place to camp?"

"No. A sick child should be under a roof at night. I will take you to my cousins. It will be all right. You will see. But first I need to make this delivery of apples."

Eli seemed so confident about everything being okay that Joe allowed himself to be lulled by the gentle rocking of the buggy. Bobby, enraptured by the novelty of riding behind a horse, sat quietly, pressed tightly against his side.

After Eli dropped off the box of apples at a young Amish housewife's home and accepted payment, he drove Rosie back past the garage where Joe's broken truck sat. They made a couple of left turns and then crossed over a small creek before trotting past an IGA grocery store that had also been constructed to resemble a Swiss chalet. Buggies were tied up at hitching posts at the end of the parking lot. Across the street from the IGA was a large restaurant also constructed with a Swiss chalet appearance.

"Beachy's has goot food." Eli pointed to the restaurant. "My granddaughter, Mabel, works there. She is a hard worker, that girl."

They turned onto Sugarcreek Road and the village fell away as rolling farm land once again took precedence. When they topped a hill, a large, two-story white farmhouse with a blue metal roof appeared.

"My cousins have closed their inn," Eli said, "but I think they will make room for a father and his little boy."

Joe noticed two tiny white cabins dotting the yard to the east. A much smaller replica of the larger house sat directly behind the farmhouse. A lone horse grazed in the pasture. Multicolored chickens pecked at the grass. It was a pretty scene, and his heart lifted at the sight.

As they turned into the driveway, he noticed a shedlike structure directly to his right. It reminded him of an old-fashioned outhouse, but for the life of him, he couldn't imagine why it would be there. Were the Amish so accommodating that they constructed toilets by the roadside for travelers?

"You will be wondering what that little building is for, I betcha," Eli said.

"I was."

"It is a telephone booth." Eli glanced at Joe's face to gauge his reaction to this news. "We do not have telephones in our homes, but we have them nearby for emergencies." He pulled back on the reins to slow Rosie as she trotted down the gravel driveway. "We are very modern around here."

Joe shot the man a sideways glance to see if he was joking and caught a telltale twinkle in Eli's eye.

From his perch beside the buggy's door, he spied a weather-beaten sign lying on the ground near the fence. It read SUGAR HAUS INN.

"Wait here," Eli said. "I will see if it is all right for you to stay."

A face flashed momentarily in the window of the residence as the buggy stopped. Eli secured the reins to a hitching post before disappearing into the house.

"I'm hungry," Bobby announced.

Joe had a few snacks in his duffel bag, but he wanted to dole them out slowly, hoping to get his son through the evening if he could.

"Let's wait. I want to see if we're going to be staying here or not."

Instead of hunger, worry gnawed at Joe's belly. When he'd left Los Angeles, he had never, in his wildest dreams, imagined that he would end up stone-broke in a strange place without so much as a roof over his head.

"My cousins have an empty cabin for you," Eli called, waving them in from the porch. "Come."

Joe climbed from the buggy and dragged out his baggage, laying the tent and duffel on the ground before reaching for his son.

"I must go," Eli said as he came near and untied Rosie. "It is past time for milking. My cousins will take goot care of you and your child."

Eli made clicking sounds as he coaxed Rosie to back up. Then, with a wave, he drove down the driveway and out onto the road.

Joe and Bobby mounted the steps. A short dumpling of a woman, neatly dressed in a wine-colored dress with a white cap and black apron, stood waiting for them. She bore the unmistakable features of <u>Down syndrome</u>.

"<u>I'm Anna!" she announced</u> happily.

"I'm Joe Matthews." He laid his palm on Bobby's head. "This little guy hiding behind my legs is my son, Bobby."

"Wie geht's!" Anna squatted and peered around Joe's knees at the little boy. "We have cookies!" she sang.

Joe shifted beneath the weight of the gear he was carrying. "Eli said you have a cabin?"

"Uh-huh." She put her hands over her eyes, peeked through her fingers at Bobby, and said, "Boo!"

She giggled while Bobby dug his face into his dad's leg.

Joe cleared his throat. "How much do you charge for your cabins, ma'am?"

She stood up, frowned, and chewed her lower lip as she concentrated. Then her face lit up as she remembered. "Forty-five dollars."

"I don't have quite that much. We don't mind sleeping in our tent."

"You can stay anyway." Anna's almond-shaped eyes were as innocent and trusting as a child's. "Bertha says."

"We only need a piece of level ground and access to a water spigot," Joe said. "I'm not looking for a handout."

"Bertha says!" She frowned and stomped her foot but then brightened and stooped to the boy's level. "We have kitties. Wanna see?"

Bobby slid out from behind his father's legs and nodded.

"C'mon." Anna slipped the little boy's hand into her own.

Bemused, Joe marveled as Bobby grabbed Anna's hand and

trotted off beside her. She was the first person Bobby had trusted since...since...

After all these months, it was still difficult for him to place his lovely wife, Grace, and the word "death" together in the same thought. His mind shied away from it like a skittish colt. As he walked toward the cabins, he tried to focus his thoughts entirely upon having miraculously found safe shelter for his son. For now.

CHAPTER 2

As Rachel pulled into her aunts' driveway and climbed out of the squad car, her stomach growled in eager anticipation of Lydia's cooking.

On the way here, she had ticketed the Keim twins again. Those two boys had enthusiastically and single-mindedly embraced the worst of the Englisch world during their rumspringa.

She knew that their parents, good solid Amish farmers, were ashamed of the boys. Their grandparents were, as well. And yet since the twins were not yet baptized believers, the church could not discipline them with threat of the Bann. The whole community was watching and shaking their heads with dismay as the boys went on their merry and destructive way.

She couldn't count the number of speeding tickets she had issued to them in the past two years. They had even spent several days in the county jail for drunk and disorderly conduct. Unfortunately, they had *liked* it there. Television and free meals. No farm chores. The county sheriff had released them early—not for good behavior, but because they were enjoying themselves too much.

In some ways, she understood their need for rebellion. Had her father not left the Amish faith, she would have had to. She was not a woman who was cut out for wearing dresses 24/7 or obeying without question the stricter tenants of the *Ordnung*—the rules each church district set forth to govern the dress and lifestyle of its members.

As much as she respected certain aspects of her Amish heritage, she could not imagine never having gone to high school or to the police academy. She could not imagine never watching a movie, listening to music, driving a car. Or carrying a gun.

Fortunately, she had not had to be the one to make that break. Her father had made it for her when he had chosen not to join the church. Since she was considered part of the Englisch world instead of being a rebellious Amish woman in need of discipline, she could be welcomed into her aunts' home without her aunts being admonished by the bishop.

It was rare for an Amish family not to be large, but somehow big families had passed theirs by. Bertha, busy caring for others, had never married. Lydia, now widowed, had endured a succession of miscarriages, which had produced no living children. And Anna was, well—Anna was Anna.

Rachel's father and mother had produced only one child—her.

Even though both her parents had been taken from her early, Rachel had never felt orphaned. Instead, she'd always felt as though she had three mothers looking out for her. In spite of what she saw and experienced as a cop, the world never felt like an evil place while she was sitting in one of their front porch rockers, helping shell peas or string green beans. And seeing Anna's delight in a budding flower or a newly born calf was always a salve to her soul.

As she rounded the corner of the house, she stopped short. The sight of a small boy swinging from her old tire swing surprised her. Anna, beaming, was pushing him.

Rachel leaned against the tree and watched. "Who've you got there, Anna?"

"Bobby." Anna stopped pushing to better concentrate on her words. "He wants the white kitty—so you can't have it."

The cherubic little boy was gorgeous. Curly blond hair, pink cheeks, innocent blue eyes.

She walked over and squatted to greet him. "Did you give the white kitty a name?"

His Dresden-blue eyes met hers as his feet dragged the ground to slow the swing. "Uh-huh. Gwacie."

"Gracie?"

The little boy nodded.

"That's a nice name. Why Gracie?"

"It's my mommy's name." Bobby's lower lip trembled. "She's in heaven."

Rachel and Anna shared a concerned glance over his head. Anna shrugged, letting her know that she, too, was ignorant about the child's mother.

Lydia stepped outside at that moment. "Food is ready!" she called.

Anna helped the little boy out of the swing. "Come."

He slipped his hand into Anna's and glanced up at her with utter acceptance. Rachel had seen this before—small children always trusted Anna.

"Where is his father?" Rachel asked.

Anna pointed to one of the small cabins. "Bobby's *daett* has no money."

Rachel cocked an eyebrow. The cabins had no running water or electricity. The child's father must, indeed, be down on his luck.

A screen door slammed and Bertha limped out of the cabin, leaning heavily on her walker. The stranger had to duck his head as he followed her. The doorways of the cabins were six feet high. Rachel judged the man to be nearly three or four inches taller.

Her practiced cop's eye scanned and evaluated him in less than three seconds. Even dressed in ill-fitting clothes, she could tell that he was built like an athlete—someone who had obviously spent much time working out.

Many men developed that sort of muscle definition while in prison. They beefed up with weights out of boredom—or for sheer self-preservation. She hoped that was not the case with this man— her aunts' first guest since she had exacted their promise to close down the inn. Based on that promise, Bertha must be of the opinion that this stranger had been sent by God.

Rachel had her doubts.

He wore torn jeans and a faded T-shirt and had wild-looking, dirty-blond hair worn down to his shoulders. He also sported a full, unkempt beard.

It was the beard that bothered her the most. Old Order Amish men with untrimmed facial hair were merely telling the world that they were members of their church. And that they were married. Non-Amish men who wore a full beard, in her experience, were frequently hiding something...or hiding *from* something. The psycho who had put her in the hospital had been heavily bearded. It made her a tad prejudiced.

The stranger had the same startling blue eyes as the little boy. Not a kidnapping, then, unless it was domestic. No markings on his face or forearms. She glanced at the webbing between his thumbs and fingers where gang tattoos were frequently placed. Nothing there. No earrings or visible jewelry. No piercings.

Her eyes fell to his shoes. Shoes could tell a lot about a person. What in the...?

This man, in worn clothing, who supposedly had no money, was wearing a pair of new Saucony ProGrid Paramounts—one of the most expensive tennis shoes available. She had longed for a pair herself.

"Hello, Rachel." Bertha, who had made her way across the short expanse of yard, huffed from the exertion of it. "This is Joe Matthews. Joe, this is our niece, Rachel. She works for the Sugarcreek Police Department."

"Pleasure to meet you, ma'am," he said.

Rachel caught his split-second sweep of her uniform as his hands curled into fists at his side. The man was visibly uncomfortable in her presence.

He had a deep voice, unaccented in an area where a Germanic lilt flavored many people's speech. The polite ease of his words belied his rigid stance. He held his breath, as though awaiting her reaction.

She reached to shake hands with him and evaluated his grip. Firm handshake...but his palm had none of the roughness she associated with men who worked outdoors for a living.

"Glad to meet you. Um, 'Joe' did you say?"

He released his breath, almost on a sigh. "Yes, ma'am."

The stranger looked her square in the eye and held it—a little too deliberately. Few people did that when they first met a uniformed cop, even those with a reasonably clear conscience. Her instincts went on full alert. This guy was hiding something, and it was her job to find out what it was.

"What's your business here, Joe?" she asked. "Are you a tourist, or are you just passing through?"

"Just passing through. My truck broke down. I'll be moving on as soon as I can get it fixed."

"Uh-huh." She allowed silence to settle over them. People with something to hide usually kept talking. Silence was something she had used many times to get people to reveal more than they intended.

Unfazed, he waited out the silence. It was impressive. And it was something else he might have learned in prison.

"What do you do for a living, Joe?" She watched his eyes as he answered.

"Construction." He blinked a couple times as he answered, a tip-off to her that he might be lying.

Interesting.

"I hope you get your truck fixed soon, Joe."

"So do I, ma'am."

She decided that if this man spent the night, she would be sleeping in one of her aunts' guest rooms. It wouldn't hurt Joe Matthews—if that was his real name—to see a squad car parked outside this Amish home.

Lydia rang the dinner bell impatiently. Her food was ready, and no one had come.

"We should go in now." Bertha began her slow progress toward the house and everyone followed.

When they arrived at the kitchen door, Joe politely stood back and held open the screen door, allowing Bertha, Anna, and Bobby to enter. All had to pick their way over a broken back step. Rachel made a mental note to fix it as soon as the Swiss Festival was over.

Joe waited for her to enter as well, but there was a long pause while she silently refused. She had absolutely no intention of allowing this stranger to maneuver himself behind her. Her hand lay lightly on the butt of her gun while she stood, feet planted far apart, and gestured for him to go ahead.

Reluctantly he entered, while she weighed her chances of taking him down if he tried something. Her estimation was that subduing Joe would be quite a struggle, if not impossible.

She deeply regretted her promise to Bertha to allow them to take in "angels unaware." Unless she was badly mistaken, this man was no angel.

Her aunts seemed to be oblivious to the direction her thoughts were taking. Instead, they were acting as if they were delighted to have a table full of company again.

Much to-do was made over piling a bundle of old newspaper copies of *The Budget* on a chair to elevate Bobby. Joe was automatically given the position of honor at the head of the table. Rachel chose the seat at the far end, where she could observe Joe's every move.

After everyone was seated, the aunts bowed their heads in their customary silent blessing.

The little boy, seeing the adult heads bowed, clasped his hands beneath his chin and began saying his own prayer out loud. "God, thank You for this food and my new kitty and for making my daddy stop driving. I'm tired of being in Daddy's truck. Amen."

Everyone's eyes lifted in surprise—except Joe's. He stared at his plate.

Lydia cleared her throat. "Do you like mashed potatoes, Bobby?"

"Are they like my mommy's?"

"How is that?"

"With a pond in the middle."

Lydia whisked the child's plate off the table, built a gravy pond in the middle of the fluffy white mound, and set it in front of him.

"Is that all right?"

"Oh, yes!" He dug into the mashed potatoes with a spoon.

"*Nau ess du.*" Anna added some pot roast and vegetables. "Eat."

The child ate even the vegetables without protest. He seemed grateful for everything on his plate.

Joe closed his eyes as though trying to regain his composure after Bobby's sad little prayer. Then he took a deep breath, shook out his napkin, and placed it on his lap.

Rachel was surprised by the elegance with which he used his

eating utensils. She noted that he held his fork in his left hand and his knife in his right—a European style of dining in which most Americans were unpracticed. Definitely *not* a habit learned in prison.

It was obvious that both he and Bobby were hungry, but Joe took small bites and chewed slowly. She got the impression that he was forcing himself to hold back.

"We weren't expecting a gourmet meal when we asked to pitch our tent, ma'am," he said to Lydia when the silence had stretched out a little too long.

"Dank." Lydia ducked her head. Compliments were something with which she had never been comfortable.

"This tastes better than McDonald's," Bobby said.

"High praise from this guy." Joe tousled his son's hair. A deep cough racked the little boy's body.

"Is he all right?" Bertha asked.

Joe laid the back of his hand against his son's forehead. "I think so. He's had this cough for a couple of days, but no fever so far. We've been traveling with the windows down some of the time. I'm hoping it's just allergies."

Partially mollified, Bertha returned her attention to her plate but glanced often at Bobby.

"I don't want to ride in the truck anymore, Daddy," Bobby said.

"We'll stop soon, son."

"Can we live here?"

"This isn't our home, Bobby. We have to move on."

"I don't wanna! I want to live here!" Tears began to course down the tired little boy's face—much to the consternation of Lydia and Anna, who fluttered around, offering him everything from cookies to more mashed potatoes.

"Will you excuse us?" Joe said. "I need to talk to my son." The aunts nodded in unison. He arose, took Bobby by the hand, and led him out onto the porch.

Rachel slipped over to the window. If Joe laid one angry finger on that sweet child, she'd have Social Services on him so fast it would make his head swim.

Instead, he sat down on the porch swing, gathered the sniffling little boy into his arms, and talked to him in a low voice. She couldn't make out the words through the glass, but they sounded kind.

"Rachel," Bertha hissed. "Come away from that window. Give the man some privacy."

Rachel backed away as Joe arose and headed toward the door.

"My son is very tired," he said as he came through the door. "I think it would be a good idea if I put him to bed now."

Lydia rushed off to gather two flashlights from the kitchen. Anna stuffed cookies into a baggie. Bertha hobbled to the gas-powered refrigerator and filled a thermos with cold water.

"I'll carry those." Rachel took the flashlights upon Lydia's return. "Joe can take the cookies and the thermos. I'll help settle them into the cabin."

"That's not necessary," Joe said.

Rachel gave him the steely-eyed look that had cowed many a bad guy. "I insist."

She could feel her aunts' gaze behind her and could almost sense them begging her not to be rude as she followed Joe outside. She had no intention of being rude, but she did intend to be direct.

The walk to the cabin wasn't long. "There's the outhouse," she said, pointing the flashlight at a small, narrow building off to the side. "And there's a pump for water near the kitchen door if you need it."

She flashed a light around the inside of the one-room cabin as Joe tucked Bobby into bed. Taking the second flashlight from

Rachel, Joe handed it to Bobby to play with. The space was tiny but clean. One of the aunts—she guessed Anna—had put a small vase of wildflowers on the little table between the twin beds. Freshly washed quilts filled the small shelter with the smell of sunshine. For Bobby's sake, she was glad that her aunts had made things nice.

"Thank you, Officer," Joe said. "We'll be fine now."

"I want to talk to you outside for a moment."

He glanced at Bobby. "Will you be okay by yourself, buddy?"

Bobby, enraptured with the flashlight, nodded.

"I'll be right outside, son."

As soon as the door closed behind them, Rachel let Joe know exactly what was on her mind. "Mister, I don't know who you are or what your story is, but if you touch a hair on any of my aunts' heads—if you so much as steal a petal from Anna's flower garden—I'll be on you so fast, you won't know what hit you."

Instead of shock or anger, there was an expression of stalwart acceptance on his face.

"I understand."

"I'm not a person who makes empty threats."

He sighed. "You don't know me, Officer, and I don't blame you for thinking the worst. But I'm no thief, and I would never hurt someone as kind and gentle as one of those ladies. You and your aunts can sleep easy tonight. There's no reason to be afraid."

Joe had the sort of voice that made a person want to trust him. But she didn't. Not for a second. Ted Bundy had been a likable guy too, a real charmer—until he was arrested for serial murders.

"Actually," Rachel said, "I don't intend to sleep at all tonight. So don't try anything, Matthews. My aunts may be innocent, but don't make the mistake of thinking that I am."

She had hoped her speech would intimidate him, but somehow it misfired. Instead of him being cowed, amusement flickered behind his eyes. "I'd never make the mistake of thinking you were innocent, Officer."

Without waiting for a response, he stepped back inside the cabin and firmly closed the door in her face.

She stalked back to the house, her cheeks burning at his remark. How dare he turn her threat into a double entendre! She was definitely going to find out who this jerk was—and exactly what he was hiding.

Bobby refused to sleep in the bed the aunts had made up for him. After a dose of cough medicine, he'd opted to sleep on Joe's chest instead. Joe didn't mind. The feel of his son's sturdy little body, the sound of his breathing, was a tonic for the soul. He had lost everything he valued in life except this sleeping child. His love for Bobby had been the only thing keeping him from losing his sanity during the past few months while his world fell apart.

Now, every breath he breathed, every step he took, was for his son. Every bit of intelligence and strength he possessed, he intended to use to keep Bobby safe and to carve out some sort of life for him. It was all he had left to give. It was all he could figure out to do.

His own life, to all intents and purposes, was over.

As he struggled to sleep, his thoughts turned to Rachel. She was not as glamorous as his actress-wife, Grace, but in her own way, Rachel was an attractive woman. Straight, no-nonsense, shoulder-length brown hair. No makeup covering the freckles scattered across her sunburned nose. That nose, he'd noticed, was slightly crooked, as though it had been broken in a fight. And without intending to, he had seen that she had a figure nice enough to pull off wearing that off-the-rack policeman's uniform of dark blue slacks and a light blue shirt.

It was her eyes that he recalled most vividly. They were alive with intelligence. He had watched them sum him up in a glance and then quickly narrow with suspicion. He respected her for taking his measure, for evaluating the potential danger of allowing him in her aunts' home. He had watched every nuance of the evening reflect in those confident dark brown eyes.

In spite of her suspicion of him, he was impressed with her fierce protectiveness of her aunts *and* the direct way she had spoken to him when they were alone. She was a strong woman who would fight for her family and herself.

With all his heart, he wished his wife had possessed the suspicion and ability to engage in battle that he had seen in Rachel tonight. Maybe then Grace would have survived.

He would do his best to fly beneath Rachel Troyer's radar until he could get out of here. The last thing he needed was to capture the undivided attention of a police officer—or anyone else, for that matter.

CHAPTER 3

B*am! BAM! BAM!*
    In one smooth motion, Rachel slid her service revolver from the top of the bedside table, rolled out of bed into a semi-crouch, and aimed it at the door.

Then she woke up.

She lowered the weapon and cocked her head to listen. It wasn't gunfire she was hearing. The sound that had triggered her combative reflex was a hammer slamming into wood somewhere outside the house.

She carefully laid the gun on the floor, sat back on her heels, and rubbed her hands over her face—shaken by the realization that she had been a hairbreadth away from blowing a hole through her aunts' guest room door—with no knowledge of who, or what, might be standing on the other side.

She shouldn't be trusted with a weapon.

She didn't know how to live without one.

Bam! BAM! BAM!

She flinched at each sound, her temples throbbing in unison.

She had stayed up most of the night, watching to see if Joe

Matthews would decide to take a midnight stroll to the house—but he had never left the cabin. Before dawn, once her aunts were awake and moving about, she had allowed herself a quick catnap.

BAM!

Who would be using a hammer this early in the morning? Glancing at her watch, she was aghast to see that it was almost eight. She had been asleep for a good three hours and was now late for work. So much for that catnap!

She decided to run past her house anyway. After sleeping in her clothes, a fresh uniform was a necessity.

Rising from her crouch, she gasped from the sudden pain in her back—another reminder of the battle that had ended her career as an inner-city cop in Cleveland. She had managed to lock that psychopath behind bars, but not before he had laid her out in the hospital for a month *and* sent her scurrying back to Sugarcreek afterward, where her biggest challenges so far had been traffic tickets, DUIs, and convincing Amish kids to keep their rumspringa parties in check.

Bam! BAM! BAM!

She glanced outside and saw nothing except the yard, the barn, and the rolling hills beyond. Shoving her face close to the window, she angled her eyes downward. The noise seemed to be coming from directly below her, but she couldn't see who was making it.

Perhaps Eli had finished his milking and come to repair that broken step. If so, she would try to make it up to him. Now that she was once again living in Sugarcreek, her aunts were her responsibility, not Eli's. He had enough to do in keeping his own farm running.

After the Swiss Festival was behind her, she would be able to spend more time here, get more done. She needed to trim the yard again, for one thing, and lug that heavy sign at the end of the driveway into the barn. The fact that she had not fixed that broken

44

porch step yet shamed her. It should have been a priority. Her aunts couldn't afford another accident.

Retucking her shirt and straightening her uniform, she finger-combed her hair and strapped on her utility belt. If Joe Matthews was still in residence after today, she would bring a change of clothes and come back tonight. There was no way she was leaving her aunts alone with him for any length of time. In fact, she intended to swing by the farm as often as possible today just to let him know that she was keeping an eye on him.

A lone bottle of aspirin sat on the dresser. Grabbing the glass of water she had carried up to the room last night, she tossed back a couple of pills. Too late, she remembered to check the date. Just as she had suspected—it was several months past expiration. Her aunts, bless their hearts, needed more watching with each passing year. She made a mental note to go through the rest of the house and toss any other expired medications as soon as possible.

As she clumped down the stairs, she saw that all three aunts were gathered around the kitchen window, craning their necks, fascinated with something outside.

"What's going on?" Rachel rested her hand on Lydia's shoulder as she asked the question.

Lydia moved aside. "Joe is fixing that bad step." Her voice soft-ened into wistfulness. "And Bobby is helping."

"Joe is *nice!*" Anna said.

Rachel immediately saw what had so riveted her aunts' atten-tion. Joe, in jeans, T-shirt, and tool belt, would cause anyone to stare. She couldn't remember ever seeing a man so perfectly formed.

Visions of the potential harm those muscular arms and hands could do swam in front of her. She had experienced firsthand the damage a man could inflict on a woman—even a woman trained in self-defense. Her precious aunts wouldn't stand a chance. They couldn't even call for help without first stumbling out to the phone shanty.

Unfortunately, there were some outsiders who were under the mistaken impression that the Amish had lots of money. She had overheard people say, resentfully, that the Amish *must* be rich because they didn't have to pay taxes. She always spoke up when she heard that nonsense. She knew for a fact that they were required by law to pay all taxes except Social Security—from which they were excused because the Amish took care of their own.

If this homeless guy thought that her aunts were sitting on a pile of cash, they could be in terrible danger.

However, in spite of her distrust, she had to admit that father and son made an arresting picture. Bobby sat cross-legged on the porch floor with a crumpled paper sack in his lap, concentrating on handing his daddy one nail at a time. Joe thanked the child politely for each nail he accepted from his son.

Then she noticed that the red-handled hammer looked familiar. So did the handsaw. And the tool belt...

Rachel put her hands on her hips. "Who gave that man permission to use Dad's tools?"

"I did." Bertha pulled away from the window. "Joe offered to do some repairs to pay us for the use of the cabin. I told him to help himself to anything he needed."

Rachel bit back a sharp retort. The aspirin was too weak to diminish her headache, and her irritation over her aunts' gullibility rendered her nearly speechless.

Her dad's tools were good ones. Expensive too. Frank Troyer had believed in buying the best he could afford and caring for his tools properly. They were stored away in the old workroom inside the barn. Now she was afraid that if she didn't keep a sharp eye out, they would find their way into Joe's possession when he left.

Rachel gritted her teeth with frustration and glanced at her watch.

"Look. I'm uneasy about this guy. Something is off about him. Trust me on this. Don't let him back into the house unless I'm here. And please promise me you'll ask him to leave after he's repaired the steps."

Bertha stumped over to the rocking chair and fell into it. "No," she said.

"No?"

"I will not send that child away. You should not ask me." She stared pointedly at the wooden plaque beside the door.

Rachel closed her eyes and willed herself to have patience with that "angels unaware" thing—again.

"At least promise you won't let Joe move into the house while I'm gone," she said.

"We promise," Lydia said. "But will you get angry if we let Bobby play with your old toys from the attic?"

Angry? She was coming off as angry to her aunts? She was simply trying to protect them, for pity's sake. Lydia's comment hurt, and tears stung the backs of her eyes.

"Of course I don't mind. Let Bobby play with anything he wants." She grabbed her keys off the kitchen counter and headed out the door. "If Joe and his son are still here when I get back, I'll be spending the night again."

"That is fine, Rachel," Bertha said calmly. "You know you are always welcome."

She avoided the back step—and Joe—by stepping directly off the porch. Unfortunately, she misjudged the distance and landed in the middle of the flower bed. It had rained during the night, and the earth was soggy. Gathering her dignity, she extricated herself from the muddy soil.

"Have a good day, Officer." Joe lifted her father's favorite hammer in a wave.

Unable to speak past the lump in her throat, she ignored him. Even if he skipped town with her dad's tools in his possession, she hoped the man would be gone before nightfall.

Of all the scenarios Joe had anticipated when he chose to leave his identity behind in LA, being broke was not one of them.

For the first time in years, getting ahold of some cash was a major issue. One option was to find temporary work in town. A few days of—what? Waiting tables at Beachy's Country Chalet? A short-lived construction job?

Even assuming he could find work, what would he do with Bobby?

One thing he knew for sure: he needed to make himself invaluable to the Troyer sisters. He hoped that if he kept doing odd jobs for them, they wouldn't kick him out quite yet. For now, they were his best hope of keeping Bobby fed and sheltered until he could figure out how to survive without being tracked down by the people determined to find him.

"Are you finished?" Bertha hobbled to the edge of the porch.

"Yes, ma'am. This is my last nail." Joe gave it a whack and slid the hammer back into the leather tool belt.

She peered down at the newly repaired steps. "You know carpentry pretty goot?"

"My dad liked to build. He taught me the basics."

"Ach." She nudged Bobby with the walker. "Helping your father. That is how a boy learns."

Bobby looked up at her with his innocent blue eyes. "Daddy says I'm a good helper-boy."

"*Da ayya lowb shtinkt,*" Bertha said with a smile.

"Excuse me?" Joe asked.

"It is an Amish proverb," Bertha said. "It means, 'He who praises himself stinks.'" She shrugged. "We try to keep our children from thinking too highly of themselves."

"I see."

Actually, Joe didn't. It was his opinion that children needed every drop of confidence they could get. Fortunately, Bobby didn't seem to have been affected by Bertha's proverb.

Her eyes narrowed as she gave Joe an appraising look. "Wouldja mind trimming the yard a bit?"

"I'd be happy to."

She smoothed her hand over Bobby's hair. "You come with me, boy. Lydia has some toys you will be wanting to see."

Bobby handed his father the bag of remaining nails and obediently followed Bertha inside. Just before the screen door closed behind them, Bertha called over her shoulder, "The fence rows could use a few whacks too. The scythe is hanging in the barn."

Fencerows? Scythe?

It had not been his intention to spend the entire day doing odd jobs for the Troyer sisters. Not that he minded helping them out; they had been kind to him and he was grateful, but he needed to be finding a way out of this situation. And considering the suspicious nature of their niece, he needed to find a way out fast.

He considered various possible plans as he carried the hand tools back to the barn and put them away. None of the ideas worked for him.

It was quiet in the barn—and peaceful. It was also the first time he had been away from Bobby since they had begun their journey. He felt guilty over the momentary relief he felt at this short breather from his son and the constant little-boy questions. He loved Bobby desperately and completely, but the stillness inside that old barn was healing.

Dust motes danced in a slant of sunlight inside the barn. He remembered his father once saying that God was aware of everything—each speck of dust and grain of sand—even down to knowing the number of hairs on his head.

The silence and dignity of the old Amish barn enveloped him. It almost felt as though he had entered the sanctuary of a cathedral. He suddenly felt himself acutely missing the comfort of his father's faith.

Although he had taught Bobby to say grace before meals, personal, heartfelt prayer was something to which he had allowed himself to become a stranger. Formerly wrapped up in his hectic schedule, there had never seemed to be enough time. And after Grace's death, he had become so angry and hurt that he had rebelled against the very thought of a loving God who would allow such a tragedy to occur.

He knew better. Much better. He knew that Satan was also a factor in the world—one with which Joe had wrestled and lost.

The slice of sunlight illuminated a stack of hay bales in the center of the barn. As though his legs had a will of their own, he approached the bales and kneeled in the loose straw and dust scattered across the floor. As he leaned his elbows on a hay bale and bowed his head, the sliver of sunlight warmed his shoulders like a grace note from God.

He had no words. He could form no prayer. Instead, he simply rested in God's presence, acknowledging the fact that he was totally beaten and had been for a long time. As he knelt, absolutely still, communing silently with the God he had once served, a gentle warmth began to fill him, thawing areas of his heart he had not realized were frozen. It was the first relief he had felt since he had discovered his wife's broken body.

With renewed inner strength he arose, determined not to worry, at least for now, about the future. He would concentrate on the task at hand—cleaning out Bertha's fencerows—while trying to allow God to lead the way. His own original plan, to hide himself and his son away by constantly traveling upon the back roads of America, was not working out particularly well. He hoped God had a better one.

He found an old-fashioned scythe hanging from a nail beside the workbench. The curved wooden handle came nearly to his chest. He carried it outside and took a few awkward swipes at some weeds near the barn.

"That is *letz*—wrong."

He was surprised to discover Eli watching him. The Amishman was wearing a battered straw hat with a flat brim, faded gray pants, and a stained blue work shirt with suspenders.

The old man reached for the scythe. "I will show you."

In Eli's capable hands, the scythe cut through the weeds like a knife through warm butter.

"Twist at the waist and keep the blade level with the ground." Eli wiped his forehead with a handkerchief. *"Du broviahra."* He thrust the scythe toward Joe. "You try."

Joe did as Eli instructed and was amazed at what the long, curved blade could accomplish when properly wielded.

"Better, *jah*?" Eli nodded his approval.

"Jah." Joe was impressed with the tool. "I mean—yes."

"Come, I will teach you how to sharpen it. Then you can finish on your own." The old man found a whetting stone on the workbench, sat down on a hay bale, and began to hone the blade.

Joe dropped down close beside him to better watch the expertise of Eli's hands. The old man immediately scooted away, increasing the distance between them by a full foot. Joe made a mental note to be more respectful of Eli's personal space in the future.

"Where will you go when your vehicle is fixed?" Eli rubbed a thumb along the scythe blade, testing it.

"I haven't decided yet."

"To your family, I betcha."

"I don't have any—except Bobby."

Eli looked at him in surprise. "No family?"

"Not on this continent."

"You have been driving around with no destination?"

"Pretty much."

"You Englisch." Eli's voice was puzzled. "I will never understand you."

Joe was surprised to find that the old man's opinion mattered to him. He didn't want Eli to think his journey had been frivolous.

"My wife—died. I—I felt the need to get away for a while."

Eli stared hard at him. "When was this?"

"Six months ago."

"It is hard to lose one's woman, but it is not possible to run away from grief." Eli's eyes filled with empathy. "I, too, have felt the sting of losing my mate."

"I'm sorry," Joe said. "How long?"

Eli looked down at the whetting stone he now held motionless in his hand. "Four years—today."

"How have you stood it?"

The old man suddenly stood up and went toward the door of the barn. Fetching a tin of water from the pump outside the barn, he returned and poured a trickle over the scythe.

"Work is a gift from Gott for those who are grieving, so I work hard." The whetting stone rasped gently across the blade. "I pray often for the healing of the pain—and I try to take the affection I had for my wife and give it to others in small ways."

Joe plucked a loose straw from the bale of hay and shredded it with his thumbnail. "How?"

Eli shrugged. "A wooden toy whittled for a grandchild. A word of encouragement for my daughters-in-law." He glanced at Joe from beneath shaggy eyebrows, a smile quirking his mouth. "A much-needed buggy ride to an overburdened stranger."

"Does it help?"

"Giving to others is a joy to the giver," Eli said.

"And this 'giving to others' takes away the pain?"

"No." There was a great sadness in Eli's voice. "But it helps you keep breathing."

He arose and handed the scythe to Joe. "You should stay with us awhile, Englischer."

"I'd like that." Joe grasped the wooden handle. "But Officer Troyer has made it clear that she wants me out of here."

"Oh, that Rachel." Eli shook his head in dismay as they walked outside and down the hill together. "She should be married by now with a *haus* full of *kinder*. It is not good for a woman to spend her life chasing crooks."

"If marriage and a house full of kids is what she wants, I agree, but what if the woman loves her work?"

"Our Rachel does not love her work. She thinks she must do it."

"Why?"

"It is not my story to tell." The old man glanced down at the ground, making it clear that he was finished with the subject.

Joe didn't press. "Thanks for teaching me how to use a scythe."

"My cousins will be glad for your help," Eli said. "Bertha likes a neat farm. I will be getting back to my own now."

As Eli headed toward a path that skirted the pasture, he stopped and turned back. "Have you ever milked a cow, Englischer?"

"No."

"I have fifteen I milk by hand. If you stay and are willing to help, I will teach you tomorrow morning. I pay pretty goot. My sons are good boys, but they have their own work and families. My farm is over the hill. This path will lead you there. You may bring the boy—he is old enough to watch and learn."

Joe's spirits lifted. Even if Eli's idea of good pay wasn't on the same scale of his own, *anything* would be a help right now. "I'd like that, Eli. How early do you want me?"

"Oh, don't worry, Englischer. I sleep very late."

Joe was surprised. He had expected Eli to be an early riser.

Eli walked backward a few steps, watching Joe's face. "Jah. I like to sleep in very late. Be at my barn at four thirty tomorrow morning."

Joe caught the twinkle in Eli's eye. The dour-looking Amishman was teasing him.

"I'll be there!" Joe called back.

Rising early had never been a problem for him, and it would be a blessing to be able to bring Bobby. Tomorrow morning would be interesting—for both of them.

That is, *if* the sisters didn't turn him out and *if* Rachel didn't run him out of town first. The image of the pretty cop haunted his mind once more. What had Eli meant when he said Rachel didn't love her job? And why was a woman as attractive as Rachel still unmarried?

He shoved aside his curiosity and turned his attention to mastering the skill of using the scythe. Tomorrow, evidently, he would learn to milk. His life had taken an interesting turn when he had broken down here in Amish Country—and he was grateful to God for the respite.

CHAPTER 4

J oe attacked the overgrown fencerow with vigor. Soon he had mastered the knack of twisting at the waist while skimming the scythe level to the ground, mowing down all the weeds in his path. He discovered a rhythm and the work went quickly. The movement didn't seem to put any extra stress on his damaged shoulder, a fact for which he was grateful.

He soon finished the perimeter of the yard and went after the fence along the small pasture beside the barn, only stopping long enough to tie a handkerchief around his forehead to keep the sweat from pouring into his eyes. The temperature was mild, but he was working hard, and the sun was bright in the cloudless sky.

Feeling the autumn sun on his shoulders, using his muscles in this timeless, rhythmic ballet of man and scythe, glancing around from time to time at the rolling, peaceful fields...he felt as though he were sweating out the toxins of the past two thousand miles of road. He was glad for the work, even if all he was getting out of it was a place to sleep and some food. Eli was right. Hard work when one was grieving was, indeed, a gift from God.

"Boo!"

He glanced up to see Anna holding a quart of water in a Mason jar and a napkin filled with the sugar cookies he had enjoyed at supper the night before. He smiled, pleased at her thoughtfulness —but her face registered disappointment at his reaction. It took him a second to realize that she had been expecting him to be frightened. Obediently, he slapped a hand against his chest and gasped.

"Anna! You scared me!"

She beamed and giggled at the success of her trick.

"Did you bring that water and cookies for me?"

She nodded happily.

He gratefully drank the water and wolfed down the buttery cookies while she watched. "Thanks, Anna." He handed the jar and napkin back to her.

She smiled, clasped them to her chest with both hands, and plodded back to the house. He reminded himself to act frightened the next time she tried to scare him.

He finished the work on all the fencerows then went back into the barn and carefully oiled the scythe and hung it on its nail. He felt strangely at peace for someone who was, at the moment, broke and homeless.

Work, Eli said. Work was healing.

He was not unaccustomed to hard work. He had built a career out of nothing but raw talent and dogged determination. He knew what it was like to strain every muscle. But it was a different feeling to be quite literally earning his "daily" bread. He had found himself repeating that phrase of the Lord's Prayer with each swing of his scythe.

It was the line about "forgiving those who trespass against us" that gave him pause. He wasn't ready for that one yet. Probably never would be.

That reminded him—with Bobby occupied and out of earshot

—this would be a good time to check with the private detective he had hired. Assuming, of course, he would even have cell phone service out here.

He pulled the phone out of his pocket and checked. Three bars. Service to spare.

He dialed a number, and a gruff voice answered. "Grant here."

Joe pressed the phone closer to his ear. "Do you have any news for me?"

"Yeah. There's a lot of people hunting for you."

"I'm aware of that. Anything else?"

"Not much. The police seem to be preoccupied with figuring out how you managed to kill your wife while signing autographs a hundred miles away."

"The police never told me I was a suspect."

"That's because they don't have a case against you—but some of them would be thrilled if they did. It would tie things up neatly, and it would make the media *so* happy."

Joe's legs felt weak. For a few hours he had escaped this nightmare. Now it came crashing back. "I didn't kill my wife."

"*You* know that, and *I* know that, but the public wants a story and a quick resolution. They want it wrapped up and served to them with a big ribbon on the eleven o'clock news…and the powers-that-be want to give it to them."

Joe rubbed a hand over his face. "What should I do?"

"Keep doing what you're doing—whatever that is. So far it's working. The media haven't found you yet, have they?"

"No."

"I don't want to know where you are, but you and Bobby *are* okay, right?"

"We've found a safe place—for now." Joe bent over and plucked at a stray piece of hay. "Henrietta is still making those payments I promised you, isn't she?"

There was a pause.

Joe crushed the piece of hay in his fist at Grant's silence. "Tell me."

"The economy is going through a tough time."

"So?"

"So, your business manager had to cut me off. Henrietta said that what with all the expenses…"

"What expenses?"

"She said that big house of yours is burning a hole right through your cash."

"There was more than enough in my accounts to take care of things—including your salary."

"It doesn't matter. The clues have dried up. The cops aren't sharing. Unless someone comes forward for that reward you offered, there's not much I can do. Besides…I have some newer cases I need to be working." Grant hesitated, as though he realized how hard all this must be for Joe to hear. "I–I'll keep an ear out for you, though."

"Thanks, man." Joe felt sick. Grant was giving up?

"Keep your head down. Take care of your son."

"I will."

Joe disconnected and shoved the phone back into his pocket. Should he call Henrietta? Find out why she couldn't manage to pay the detective he had hired?

He didn't want to talk to her. Not yet. He knew that if he called, she would insist he come home. Henrietta, who was both his business manager and public relations manager, was also his friend—one who had been dead-set against him and Bobby leaving.

It was tempting, though, to call and ask her to wire him some cash. But even though he knew he could trust her with his money, he wasn't sure he could trust her with his location. Henrietta had always loved the limelight, even when it was only secondhand. It was one of the things that made her an excellent PR person. It would be impossible for her to keep it quiet if she knew where he was.

In the distance, he heard Lydia calling him to their noon meal—a meal he had earned several times over this morning. That call to Henrietta could wait until he knew for certain that he and Bobby couldn't survive without it.

Rachel sat down at the computer in the break room at the police station and thought about her day. She had managed to keep the 2 p.m. Kiddie Parade moving in spite of the route getting clogged by a fender bender. Then out-of-town tourists had made the mistake of trying to pet a horse attached to an Amish buggy. It had spooked, big-time, but Rachel and its owner had finally gotten it under control.

A woman had gone into sudden and extreme labor downtown, directly in front of the Alpine Museum, and Rachel had helped to open a path through the crowd for the ambulance, hoping all the while that she wouldn't have to personally deliver the baby in the middle of the sidewalk.

All this drama played itself out against the continual background of the *oompha! oompha!* polka music at the pavilion. She had watched as a group of teenagers, inspired by the happy music, formed a conga line and wound their way through the serious polka dancers, cavorting and acting silly. Since the elderly couples actually dancing the polka didn't seem to mind the impromptu conga line, she left it alone.

The grinding, mechanical sound of a small carnival competed with a yodeling contest. Small children tried their hand at milking a life-sized mechanical cow while their parents waited in line at the fire station to sample some of the best Swiss cheese in the world.

In the crowd, girls in Amish dresses, crisp prayer kapps, black hosiery, and tennis shoes had jostled against people wearing ornately embroidered Swiss costumes. This was the cultural mix into which Rachel had been born, and she felt completely at home. The sound of accordions, yodeling, and the booming harmonies of long-necked alphorn instruments was in her blood.

It was not, however, a good weekend to have a wreck—or give birth or bring a high-strung horse into town. It also wasn't a good time to have an unwanted guest at her aunts' home.

Their farmhouse was less than a mile from the heart of town, so she had been able to drive by every time she had an extra ten minutes. Each time she had passed, Joe Matthews had been outside engaged in some sort of project. He had patched a cabin roof, weeded the large vegetable garden, mowed the yard, and cleaned out all the fencerows surrounding the home. At one point, she had seen him picking the final apples from the small orchard beside the house. He had even carried away the heavy sign she'd left lying in the grass beside the fence. The man was a working machine and obviously desperate for a place to stay.

She knew that she should be relieved to have all those chores off her to-do list, but she was more concerned about Joe's presence in her aunts' lives than ever. She knew them well. They would be so thrilled with him after today that they would probably offer him a key to the house. *Not* that they ever remembered to lock the doors anyway—or saw the need to. No matter how many times she reminded them.

"What are you doing?" Kim Whitfield said from directly behind her.

Rachel disliked having someone read over her shoulder, but Kim had been a real help today. Her quick dispatch work in getting the ambulance to the middle of town had kept Rachel from having to deliver a baby.

"There's a man staying at my aunts' place. I'm trying to find out who he is."

"Did you get his name?"

"Yes." Rachel paused. "He gave me *a* name."

"You don't believe him?"

"I don't know." Rachel clicked a button, and a list of Joe Matthewses from across the country filled the screen. "Maybe. Maybe not. That's the problem."

"I can help if you want. What's he done?"

"The only thing he's *done* is spit and polish my aunts' farm today."

"And that's a bad thing?"

Rachel swiveled around in her desk chair. "It's a bad thing when my aunts believe in 'entertaining angels unaware.'"

Kim cocked an eyebrow. "This guy is no angel, huh?"

"Who knows? Perhaps I'm being prejudiced because he has a beard, long hair, no money, and no transportation."

"That describes my last two boyfriends," Kim said. "I tend to fall for losers."

"I wouldn't exactly describe him as a loser—he has a confidence about him that is at odds with his situation. There's something 'off' about this guy, though. I can feel it."

Kim grabbed a notebook and pen. "Tell me everything else you know and I'll see what I can find."

"He has a child with him named Bobby, and his wife died awhile back. Her name was Grace. He's wearing old work clothes, but his tennis shoes are top-of-the-line."

"That's it?"

"That's it. Except for one other thing."

Kim stopped scribbling in her notebook. "What's that?"

61

"He uses his fork in his left hand and his knife in his right. That tends to be something only people from other countries do."

"Is he European?"

Rachel stood up and leaned back against the desk. "He doesn't have an accent. I can't detect a trace of any particular locality at all. That in itself bothers me."

"We don't have a terrorist right here in Sugarcreek, do we?" Kim looked troubled. "That sounds a little nutty."

"I doubt it's anything that exotic, but I'm not going to relax until I know who this guy is."

Kim sat down in the chair Rachel had vacated. "I'll noodle around with it and let you know if I find anything."

For the first time, Rachel decided that Kim had possibilities.

It had been years since he'd done any yard work. Back in LA, he'd had gardeners to do all that. But it was worth all the sweat and blisters to see Bobby so contented and happy. During supper, Joe got to hear about Bobby's day and playing with Anna. His son showed him all the pictures he had colored. Anna wanted Joe to admire *her* pictures too, upon which he lavished praise.

It felt good to be part of a little community of gentle people, especially people who expected nothing more from him than repairs and yard work.

It would be nice to stay here awhile longer, but he was getting uneasy again. Rachel's squad car had driven past the farm at what seemed like regular half-hour intervals all day.

"If you would like to stay a few more days," Bertha said, "we would be glad to have you. No one is using those cabins."

"I appreciate that, ma'am, but I'll be moving on as soon as I can get my truck fixed."

"Look, Daddy!" Bobby came running over to show off a multi-colored construction-paper chain Anna had placed around his neck.

He lifted Bobby into his arms, being careful not to crush the chain. Bobby smelled like crayons, paste, and sunshine.

"You could walk into town and see the festival tonight, Joe," Bertha commented. "Bobby would probably enjoy it."

She was right. Bobby would enjoy the lights and music. As much as he appreciated the Troyer sisters' hospitality, sitting in the dim light of kerosene lanterns all evening didn't hold a lot of appeal.

"What do they have at the festival?" he asked.

Bertha picked up the schedule from the newspaper and consulted it. "Let's see…it's only six thirty. The firehouse will still be open for cheese sampling."

"I'm stuffed from Lydia's cooking. I couldn't eat another bite."

Lydia looked up from a new piecrust she was forming and smiled.

"There are several polka bands performing tonight," Bertha read. "Oh—*here's* something you might be interested in."

"What's that?"

"The competition of the Steinstossen."

"Steinstossen?"

"'Stone tossing,'" Lydia explained. "Men toss a big rock. Women throw one too."

"How big of a rock?" Joe asked.

"Do you remember the weight, sister?" Lydia asked.

"Not exactly. It is over one hundred pounds. The women throw one that weighs less."

"That's it? They just throw a rock?" Joe said. "That seems like a pretty simple competition."

"Some people take it very seriously," Bertha said.

63

"Well, what do you say, buddy?" Joe asked. "Want to go to the festival?"

"Will we be gone a long time?" Bobby looked longingly at Anna, who, having been convinced by Joe's praise that she was a talented artist, was busy coloring a new picture.

"Nope."

"Will we come right back?"

"Absolutely."

"And I will have an apple pie waiting for you," Lydia said.

"That's my favorite!" Bobby said.

"I guess we'll go check things out then," Joe said. With Bobby riding on his shoulders, he made the short walk to the village.

The sounds of the merry-go-round reached him first, and then he smelled the enticing aromas of fried onions and sausages. As he saw the strings of food booths, he was grateful they had just had a good meal; otherwise Bobby would have been begging for a taste of everything—which they could no longer afford.

Polka music filled the air as he asked directions to the Stein-stossen event. He soon found a large paved rectangle with a white line painted across it and a sandpit at the far end. A crowd had gathered on blankets and folding chairs on the hill above. Several men were lining up to register for the event.

"Where's the stone?" he asked a middle-aged man standing near him.

The man pointed to a large, oddly shaped rock. "There it is," he said. "One hundred and thirty-eight pounds. It's kept under lock and key down at the fire station all year long so no one can tamper with it."

Joe took a closer look at the huge rock. He could see nothing all that special about it. "What's the prize for first place?"

"For the men? Seventy-five dollars, but if a guy beats the record, he gets another hundred."

One hundred and seventy-five? That should be enough to pay for parts for the truck. Maybe he could barter some work around the garage to pay for the labor.

"You're a big guy." The man peered at Joe. "You thinking about trying it?"

"Maybe. What's the record?"

"A local man threw it fourteen feet six inches back in 2005. The record still stands."

Before his shoulder surgeries, Joe had routinely bench-pressed his body weight of 240 pounds. On good days, he could bench-press more. How hard could it be to toss a 138-pound rock a few feet?

He glanced at the men in line. Most were shorter and stockier than him. Some looked as though they would have trouble lifting it even a few inches off the ground. Unless he missed his guess, there were going to be a lot of sore backs tonight.

This could be his way out.

He queued up and registered for the event. The one thing in life he had always been able to depend upon was his superior strength and athletic ability. With any luck, he might excel in this sport, as well. The adrenaline rush from his desperation to get his hands on some cash wouldn't hurt, either.

CHAPTER 5

Rachel unlocked her front door and felt a measure of pride. This was the first real home she had ever owned. In Cleveland, unwilling to make a commitment to a mortgage, she had lived in a succession of rentals.

But not here. Sugarcreek was her home. Once she moved back, she had no qualms about signing the papers that made her the legal guardian of this two-bedroom, one-story cottage.

She tossed her keys onto the tiled kitchen counter and filled a watering pot at the kitchen sink. Growing up in her aunts' home had given her a need for the presence of flowers.

The insides of most Amish homes were strictly utilitarian. Their lives, even down to the particular type of hardware allowed on their buggies, were unified and simplified by the rules laid down by their mutually accepted Ordnung—upon which each member had a vote.

But their flower gardens were their own to create, and they were magnificent. It was rare to see an Amish home without flowers and decorative wrought-iron trellises shouting out to the world the Amish woman's love of color and beauty.

Carefully, she began the lengthy process of watering every living thing in her home. Many of her potted plants were cuttings she had taken from the flower gardens out at the farm.

It was so lovely here in Tuscarawas County. The tourists who made their pilgrimages here saw the small, rustic towns and rural back-road lanes and sighed with envy. They saw the ruddy-cheeked children dressed in simple Amish clothes and watched the Plain people driving their slow-paced buggies and thought that at least here, in this idyllic place, was peace and serenity.

To some extent, they were right. There was much peace here. But to some extent they were mistaken. Satan was alive and well, even here. There were problems creeping in. Problems that weren't present when Rachel was growing up. Drug dealers had learned to target the vulnerable Amish teenagers during their wild rumspringas. Teenage drug and alcohol abuse was as great a worry to the Amish parents as it was to their television-watching Englisch neighbors.

The crime they did have was, for the most part, brought in by outsiders, people who thought they could put something past the Amish residents with their eighth-grade educations.

They were wrong, of course. The Plain people were plenty smart, but they were nonviolent, and those who were not sometimes took advantage of that fact.

Rachel was not at all nonviolent. Her philosophy was simple: she watched out for her own—whether protecting her township, her fellow officers, or her aunts.

Her father, Frank Troyer, had taught her to have respect for the Amish ways—but to be ready to fight if necessary. Tonight, with Joe Matthews still in residence, she would keep vigil out at the farm once again.

After caring for her plants, she tossed a few things into a canvas bag and locked the front door, grateful that she could leave with no more effort than the turn of a lock. There was little in her home she would be upset about if it were stolen, and she preferred it that way.

She did, however, allow herself one personal extravagance— her 1966 silver blue Mustang. It made her smile every time she drove it. In fact, one of her special pleasures was driving in the retro "Fabulous Fifties" parade of over five hundred classic cars that arrived in Sugarcreek each June.

As she pulled out onto the road, she wondered if Joe was any closer to leaving.

Speak of the devil.

Her foot came off the gas pedal as she spied a familiar-looking man with a small boy on his shoulders. Yep, it was Joe and Bobby. What were they doing in town?

Curious, she parked and followed Joe as he wove his way through the crowd. She was surprised when he stopped and registered at the Steinstossen pit. Then he found a place on the hill with the other spectators and settled down with Bobby to wait.

He was going to compete? That was interesting. Joe had the muscle mass to do well, but she knew it took more than sheer strength to heave that stone the distance it took to win. The rock was misshapen and hard to handle. It took some forethought as well.

The first man to throw was badly out of shape. He managed to get the rock up past his large belly and balanced against his chest, but when he tried to hoist it above his head, the rock slipped from his grasp.

There was a gasp from the crowd as the rock fell. Rachel took an involuntary step forward. She had helped put more than one Steinstossen contestant into an ambulance when the rock slipped. There had been plenty of concussions and broken feet in the past.

Fortunately, this guy hopped out of the way a split second before the boulder thudded to the ground.

Apparently not willing to risk injury in trying again, he bowed to the crowd with good-natured humor and wandered off to be consoled by his buddies.

She saw Joe relax and lean back on one elbow.

The second man was short but built like an ox. He expertly grasped the rock, lifted it to his belly, then rolled it onto his chest. From there, he got a secure hold and lifted it high above his head. He wavered for an instant under the weight but then found his balance and ran toward the white line, heaving it as far as he could into the awaiting sandpit.

Rachel knew that most newcomers believed the Steinstossen event to be about brute strength alone. But she had watched it for years and knew that it took skill and expertise in addition to strength. Charging the foul line gave a contestant the impetus needed to hurl the stone far, but sometimes it was impossible for the runner to stop in time. There was a delicate balance to be maintained—running fast, but not so fast as to be unable to stop. Stopping before the foul line, but not so soon that the toss fell short. This man had done well.

Two auxiliary policemen watching the foul line measured the distance of the throw with a tape. Then they removed the stone with a dolly and raked the sand smooth as the announcer shouted out the distance. "Eight feet, ten inches."

A respectable distance, but beatable. She saw Joe sit up and take the man's measure.

Then, a local contractor, whom she knew to be well past sixty, took a try. In impressive shape for a man his age, he strutted over and picked up the stone. He was strong, but not strong enough to get the rock above his waist. He duck-waddled to the foul line and tossed it over. It landed mere inches past the line. He grinned and lifted clasped hands above his head in a mocking victory salute while the crowd applauded his game attempt.

One after another, the contestants fought the rock up their chests and above their heads, some tossing much farther than others. Some gave up and dropped the stone where they stood. Some were frustrated and disappointed at discovering they were not as strong as they thought. Others seemed surprised at how well they did.

At one point, the name of a distant cousin of Rachel's was called. Even within a family of strong men, he was famous for his strength. With an air of indifference, he strode over to the rock, lifted it with apparently little effort, and hoisted it above his head without so much as taking a chest rest.

She knew that Joe stood little chance of beating him and was surprised that she felt disappointed at the knowledge. She supposed it was because she always tended to root for the underdog.

The cousin seemed bored with the event. His throw of thirteen feet seven inches was no record, but she doubted anyone here could beat it. He nonchalantly walked off the court.

Joe, having arrived only minutes before the final event started, was the last contestant to be called. He was making his way through the crowd, carrying his son, when he spotted her.

"Would you watch Bobby while I throw?"

"Sure."

As Joe transferred the little boy into her arms, his hand accidentally grazed her bare skin. The sheer warmth of his touch unnerved her in a way she didn't entirely understand. Trying to ignore her sudden physical awareness of Joe, she held Bobby close. As she did so, the little boy gave her a hug and a kiss on the cheek. The sweet gesture melted her. Bobby was adorable.

While Joe toed up to the stone, the little boy confided in her ear, "Miss Lydia's makin' apple pie for when we get home."

Home? Joe and his son had only been here one full day. Already the child was calling the farm "home"?

"Let's watch your daddy, honey," she said, pointing.

Bobby watched his father with interest. "My daddy's strong."

"Yes." Rachel once again tried to dismiss from her mind the memory of Joe's touch. "He is."

Unlike most of the contestants, Joe squatted to grasp the boulder instead of bending over. Then he heaved himself up by his legs with the stone cradled against his chest. He hesitated a moment, gathering his strength as he got a better grip on the rock. Then he jerked the stone above his head in one smooth motion.

The veins in his forehead didn't bulge at the effort like with many of the men. So far, he was managing to make it look fairly easy, but she could tell by the white around his lips that it was costing him to keep the stone balanced above his head.

He took one step backward and then plunged full force toward the foul line. She couldn't help but admire the powerful way he moved.

She was afraid that, as a novice, he would make the mistake of stepping over the carefully watched line, but he didn't. He stopped and cleared it with a clean throw that looked as though it had, astonishingly, flown even farther than what her cousin had achieved.

The crowd clapped and whistled their approval.

"Your daddy did good," she told Bobby.

"I know." Bobby was matter-of-fact, as though he were used to his father excelling. "Can we go home and have pie now?"

"In a minute."

Rachel watched as Joe made his way back through the crowd to her while the judges measured his distance.

"Good job." She transferred Bobby, being careful not to touch Joe as she did so. She noticed a few abrasions on his outstretched arms from the stone.

"Thanks. It was a little tougher than I was expecting."

"Fourteen feet, six and a half inches!" the announcer called. "A new record!"

"You won!" Rachel said. "Congratulations, Joe. How in the world did you do that?"

"Probably because I need the money a whole lot worse than the other guys. I'm hoping it will be enough to put a deposit on that truck part," he said. "I do plan on leaving as soon as I can."

"Better go collect it," she said. "I'm headed out to the farm now. I'll drive the two of you back if you want."

"Thanks."

After watching Joe receive his prize money and accept congratulations from half the crowd on his record-breaking throw, Rachel led them to her car and strapped Bobby into the backseat of her Mustang.

"Nice ride," Joe said as he climbed into the passenger seat.

She stroked the immaculate blue upholstery. "I try to take good care of her."

Bobby coughed a deep, wracking cough, and she saw Joe's fingers grip the door handle.

"That child needs to see a doctor," she said.

"He'll be fine."

"Maybe." She kept her eyes on the road as she pulled out onto the street. "What is your story anyway, Joe? Were you fired from your job or something?"

"I wasn't fired."

"Are you running from the law?"

"No." He turned to look at her. "Do you think I would be sitting here with you if I were?"

"Then I suppose you wouldn't mind letting me take a peek at your driver's license."

He rested his left ankle on his knee and draped an elbow out the open passenger window. "Have you seen me break the law in any way?"

"Not yet."

"I was under the impression that I had a constitutional right not to be unlawfully searched."

He was right, of course, but it irritated her that he was resisting her very reasonable request to see his driver's license.

"And I have the right"—she lifted a finger—"no, I am compelled by law to call Social Services if I think a child is being endangered in any way."

Joe sat up straight. "You would take my son away from me for not producing my driver's license?"

"That wasn't my point. I would take him away if I thought you were unable to care for him."

"Daddy!" A sound of sobbing erupted from the backseat. "Don't leave me!"

"I won't leave you, buddy." Joe reached behind the seat to pat and comfort his son.

Rachel cringed at the fact that Bobby had overheard her harsh words. She wasn't used to being around kids. She had forgotten that they listened to everything.

Joe shot her a venomous glance after Bobby calmed down. "I don't *have* a driver's license. Someone stole my wallet. If I had it, and the money that was in it, I wouldn't be stuck here taking charity from your aunts or busting my guts trying to throw a stupid stone."

"Sorry." She felt sick at having upset the child. "I didn't realize Bobby was listening."

"Obviously, he was."

"You could have just told me about the wallet."

"The last time I checked, a person in this country is innocent until proven guilty. I guess that doesn't apply in your township?"

"I said I'm sorry."

She stopped in front of the farmhouse. Bobby was still sniffling. Joe got out and swung him up into his arms.

"It's okay, buddy. Nobody's going to take you away from me." He glared at Rachel. "*Nobody.*"

"Aren't you hungry, child?" Lydia asked, when Bobby ignored the apple pie.

Bobby had been listless ever since they had gotten back from town. Joe hoped Rachel's thoughtless threat had not caused this reaction.

Bobby leaned his head tiredly against Joe's arm.

"His face is flushed," Bertha said.

Joe touched his forehead. "He feels hot."

"Anna," Bertha said, "bring my medical bag."

"Medical bag?" Joe asked.

"I used to be a nurse. Still am, I suppose."

Anna brought the black bag to Bertha, who took out a thermometer, shook it, and put it into Bobby's unresisting mouth. She read it and her lips tightened.

"What?" Joe asked.

"It's 104 degrees. Do you have any Children's Tylenol?"

"Not with me. I do have some in the glove compartment of the truck. I could go get it."

Suddenly, to everyone's shock, Bobby stopped breathing and began to convulse in a bone-jarring seizure.

"Dear God, what's happening?" Joe caught Bobby before he fell off the chair.

"It's a febrile convulsion." Bertha immediately took command. "Lydia, fetch a basin of water. Anna, clear off the table. Joe, get him undressed. Rachel, get towels and washcloths."

"Shouldn't we call an ambulance?" Rachel asked.

"Later," Bertha barked. "Right now we need to get that temperature down!"

Everyone rushed into action. In seconds the unconscious child was cushioned on a thick towel in the middle of the table with Bertha and Joe sponging him off with cool water. He had begun to breathe again, but his legs, arms, and face continued to spasm.

"I called." Rachel clicked off her cell phone. "But there's been a three-car accident on State Route 93. Both ambulances are on their way to the hospital."

"Hold on, buddy," Joe crooned, as he smoothed a cool washcloth over his son's face.

Bertha wrung out another washcloth. "His fever is coming down." She grabbed a bottle of adult Tylenol capsules out of her medical bag. "Take one of these, Rachel, and dissolve half of it in a bit of warm water."

Rachel glanced at the date on the bottle.

"Don't worry," Bertha said. "I bought it two weeks ago." She caught a look on Joe's face. "What?" she asked.

"Nothing. I guess I just figured the Amish would use herbs or something."

"We do and we could," Bertha said. "We could find an echinacea plant, dig up the roots, grate them into a pile, and boil them into a glycerin-based tincture. Or we could make a tea out of catnip, which I do not have. Or"—she shot Joe a look—"we could use something that works quickly and efficiently like Tylenol. Do you have objections?"

75

"No."

"Bertha really was a nurse," Rachel assured him as she hurried back with the dissolved fever-reducing medicine and handed it to him. "And a good one."

"I believe it."

"Bertha also ran an orphanage in Haiti for many years."

Joe caught a hint of pride in Rachel's voice as he began dribbling the liquid into his son's unresisting mouth. The color slowly came back into the little boy's face as he groggily regained consciousness.

"Are you feeling better, buddy?" Joe asked.

Bobby nodded weakly.

The child put up no resistance as Bertha checked his ears with an otoscope from her bag and palpated the outside of his throat with her fingers.

"Ach." Bertha made a clucking sound. "This *bobli* has an infection in both ears and swollen throat glands. No wonder he has been coughing. I am surprised he has been able to play at all. He needs antibiotics to fight this sickness."

"There's an urgent care clinic that stays open late in Dover," Rachel informed him. "I can drive."

"Thanks. I'd appreciate it."

"Get that Children's Tylenol from your vehicle too," Bertha said. "It will be safer if I can judge the dose."

Bobby's eyelids feathered downward and stayed closed. His even breathing reassured Joe that he would be all right—at least until the fever medication wore off.

"Go get my purse, Rachel," Bertha said. "Joe will need to buy medicine."

"No," Joe said. "I think I have enough."

Bertha looked puzzled.

"Joe won the Steinstossen," Rachel explained. "He has prize money."

"Ah," Bertha said. "I am not surprised."

"Can we go?" he asked Rachel. "I don't want to waste another minute."

The drive to Dover was strained. Rachel tried to concentrate on driving instead of on her awareness of Joe's presence in the backseat, where he sat watching over Bobby.

At the clinic, the doctor confirmed Bertha's diagnosis and wrote out a prescription. Rachel held Bobby while Joe shelled out nearly half of his prize money to pay for the visit.

At the nearby CVS, Rachel, who had never purchased antibiotics for a child, was stunned when the medication took most of the rest of Joe's cash.

"What will you do?" she asked. "There's nothing left to repair your truck."

He shrugged. "I'll give my son his medicine and thank God I had enough to cover it."

She had known some dedicated family men—her father had been one—but this man seemed to live for his child and his child alone. And yet, unless he had resources she didn't know about, he could barely buy Bobby a Happy Meal with what he had left in his pocket.

As she followed him back to the car and began driving west toward Sugarcreek, she wondered what lengths the man would go to care for his child. In her estimation, if he wasn't already a criminal, being penniless with Bobby to care for could very well make him one.

She wondered what *she* would do under the same circumstances. She suspected there was almost nothing she wouldn't do if it was the only way she had to feed her hungry child—or get him medical treatment.

As much as she was growing to admire Joe's dedication to his son, she also believed it was that very dedication that could put her aunts at risk if he grew desperate enough.

And although she'd dabbled in it before, discovering who he was had just become her number-one priority.

"Could we stop and get Bobby's Tylenol out of my truck?" Joe asked.

"Sure."

In a few minutes, they were parked behind Joe's broken vehicle. With Bobby asleep in the backseat, Joe unlocked the truck and extricated the fever medicine. He caught her shining a penlight on the license plate.

"Texas?" she asked.

Joe slammed the truck door shut. "Yes."

"You're from Texas?"

"I'm from a lot of places."

"Where did you get the truck, Joe?" She aimed the penlight straight at him.

"Get that light out of my eyes, Rachel." His voice was menacing. For the first time, she fully comprehended that she was alone in a back alley with a large man, a stranger she had just witnessed tossing a 138-pound rock across the width of a good-sized room. She weighed eight pounds less than that rock. Goose bumps raised along her arms.

She backed up, automatically reaching for a gun that wasn't there.

"Don't act like I'm going to attack you," he said. "I'm not a monster. I'm not a thief. I'm not a criminal. I'm not going to hurt you or your aunts. I just want to get my child back to the cabin, give him his medicine, find some way to get my truck fixed, and then get *out* of here."

He covered his eyes with one hand. "But in the meantime, would you please quit pointing that LED light at my retinas!"

His voice sounded more exasperated than menacing. She clicked off the penlight. "You didn't answer my question."

"I did not steal the truck, if that's what you're worrying about. It's on loan from a friend. If you run the tags and talk with him, he'll vouch for me."

"I'll do just that."

"Fine."

"Fine."

Joe held up the bottle of liquid Tylenol. "We could stand here all night sounding like junior high kids fussing at each other, or we could get my sick child into bed. Your call, Officer."

"Put Bobby's booster seat in my car and get in."

CHAPTER 6

R ain splattered against the Mustang's windshield and scattered festival visitors as Joe and Rachel drove through town. Lightning flashed in the sky directly overhead.

"It's going to be a bad one," Rachel observed as they pulled into the farmhouse driveway. "I hope all the festival tents hold."

When they arrived, Lydia held the door open and illuminated their way with a flashlight, as they ran through the rain and onto the porch.

"How is the boy?" she asked, as they entered the darkened house.

Joe automatically grappled with the wall inside the front door, searching for a light switch.

"You may have this, if you like." Lydia handed him the flashlight.

He immediately realized his error. Of course this nonelectric house had no light switches.

"Sorry," he said.

"All Englischers do that," Lydia said. "When the inn was still open, we were always washing fingerprints off the walls."

Rachel, used to visiting her aunts in the evening, had already turned on the LED penlight with which she had blinded Joe. Lydia led them into the front room, where Bertha helped him get bubble-gum-scented medication down a resistant Bobby.

"If I can borrow an umbrella, I'll take my son out to the cabin now," Joe said.

He was passionately looking forward to being back in the private little cabin, where they could be alone. He had spent more than enough time this evening with Rachel watching his every move.

"No," Bertha said. "The child should stay in here. With us."

"In the house?" Rachel said.

Joe heard a world of worry in that one question, and he resented it. "I'd prefer to take him to the cabin."

Bertha had other plans. With her leg propped on a footstool and her white prayer kapp askew from having dozed with her head against the back of the chair, she made her proclamation.

"Bobby might get chilled in the cabin, and you would not have us near if his fever spiked again. Bobby will sleep on one couch. You will sleep on the other." Bertha's voice was firm. "Lydia has already set out quilts and pillows. We could put you upstairs in a room, but this way you will be right outside my bedroom if you need me."

"I don't want to impose any more than I already have."

"This is not about you, Joe," Bertha said firmly. "It is about your child."

He could tell from the look on Rachel's face that she was not a bit happy with Bertha's decision. What she didn't understand was, neither was he.

"Do not argue." Bertha glanced at Rachel. "Either of you. I have made up my mind." She folded her arms over her chest.

Joe now knew exactly what Anna meant when she punctuated a

statement by "Bertha *says*." The whole household seemed to think that Bertha's word was law. Perhaps it was just as well. If it were not for this woman, he would be sitting in a tent in the rain tonight with a convulsing little boy.

This situation *had* to stop. He had to get his life back in control. It was time to call Henrietta. He would have done it long before now if he had any guarantee that it wouldn't result in a flood of reporters streaming to this village and destroying what fragile anonymity he had obtained.

Before going to bed, Bertha took Bobby's temperature one more time. It had dropped to within a normal range.

After everyone had left, he threw a pillow on the floor and laid himself down beside Bobby's makeshift bed. The other couch beckoned, but he wanted to be able to reassure his son with a touch if the little guy awoke during the night. He also wanted to check him every few minutes for a return of the fever.

As he tossed and turned on the hard wooden floor, he wondered if, after what she had seen tonight, Rachel would make good on her veiled threat to call Social Services.

Would *he*, if the roles were switched?

He honestly didn't know. The one thing he *did* know was that he couldn't allow that to happen. Bobby had to stay with him, no matter what.

He stared into the darkness as he tried to figure a way out of this mess. The money he had intended to help get them out of here was now gone—transformed into a bottle of pink, life-saving liquid.

The weight of the rock with which he had won first prize had not done his bad shoulder any good. He'd felt a slight tear deep within it the moment the massive stone had left his hands.

Getting his career back someday was looking less and less likely.

The thunderstorm passed as he lay mulling things over. When the thunder and lightning ceased, he noticed a multitude of stars through the window.

It had been a long time since he had really noticed the night sky. He remembered watching the endless panorama of the stars a lifetime ago, while sitting outside a hut in Western Africa with his father's arms wrapped securely around him. There, with no light pollution, the stars had seemed close enough to touch.

He closed his eyes, savoring every detail—the feel of his father's broad chest against his back, the familiar sounds of the African bush, the small crackling fire behind them, his brother and mother asleep in the hut.

It had been a rare moment, an evening when he'd had his father all to himself instead of surrendering him to the beck and call of the mission churches he was forever establishing.

Joe had been six. They had celebrated his birthday only two days earlier. He had received a genuine-leather, American-made baseball for his birthday, along with a homemade bat that had been hand-carved by an African craftsman employed by his mother. Both gifts lay close beside him. He had been guarding them all day from his younger brother, who had a penchant for losing things.

His father had pointed to the stars. "Did you make those?"

The stars shined so bright in the dark sky that they seemed to hover directly above Joe's head—almost within reach.

"No, Daddy." Joe laughed at the silly question and with the joy of being in his father's arms. "I didn't make them."

"Hmm," his father said. "Isn't that strange? I didn't make them either. Who do you suppose did?"

"God?" Joe was proud of knowing the answer.

"Why, I believe you're right. He's the only one *I* know of who is big enough and smart enough to make them. Why do you suppose he did that?"

"I dunno."

"Me either."

Joe turned to read his father's face. He'd thought his dad knew *everything* about God.

His dad chuckled at his surprise. "I don't know all the reasons why God made the stars, but I suspect that one reason was as a present to us—just so a little boy and his daddy could talk about how much God loves us and is always watching over us."

"Like you watch over me?"

His father hugged him. "Like I watch over you, except much, much better."

Bobby suddenly flailed his legs, kicking off the covers. Joe leaped to his feet, checking for signs that the fever was returning. The child's forehead was warm, but not hot—and Joe breathed a sigh of relief when Bobby snuggled more deeply into his pillow, breathing quietly and evenly.

Joe lay back on the floor and was surprised to discover that his own pillow was soaked with tears. He turned it over and once again lay staring out the window—longing for his father and the security he had known as a child, leaning against his father's chest and being convinced that God had created the stars and the moon just for him.

It was the sound of rocking that awakened him, along with the melody of a hymn being softly hummed. For a moment he was disoriented, and then he realized he was lying on the floor of an Amish farmhouse. Bertha sat in her rocking chair with his son in her arms and her walker next to her chair.

"Bobby awoke when I took his temperature," Bertha said. "I

rocked him back to sleep. He was sweating. I believe his fever has truly broken."

"That's good." Joe sat up and leaned against the couch, watching Bertha in the dim moonlight. Her bare foot pushed against the floor, making the chair rock. She wore a simple robe, and her gray hair was in a long, loose braid and hung over one shoulder. This was the first time he had seen her without her prayer kapp, and although she was completely modest, it made the moment strangely intimate.

"Aren't you tired?" he asked. "Do you want me to take him?"

"No." She smiled down at the sleeping child. "I am enjoying this."

Joe saw so much character and integrity in the old woman's face that his concept of beauty was suddenly redefined in that moment. He wished he had a camera to forever capture the image of Bertha rocking his sleeping child.

"When I worked at the orphanage, it seemed as though I always had a lapful of children," she said. "I miss it."

"Those children were blessed to have you."

"I was the blessed one." She began again to hum the tune that had awakened Joe.

"I wish I knew how to thank you for all you've done."

"The Holy Scripture says to treat all strangers as though they were angels. Are you an angel, Joe?"

Her question so took him by surprise that he almost choked on his reply. "Far from it."

"Our niece agrees with you. She thinks you are hiding something." Bertha hummed some more. "I think she is right. In Haiti, we had men who pretended to want work, only to steal from the orphan children. I quickly learned to distinguish bad men from good. It was a matter of survival—for me and for the children. It is very hard to fool me, Joe."

85

"Fooling you was never my intention."

She traced the delicate wings of Bobby's eyebrows with one finger. "I am not someone who has to tell the things I know in order to look important. This need is like a sickness in some, but God saw fit to give me strength in that area. If someone confides in me, it stays with me. Do you believe me when I tell you this?"

"Yes. I believe you."

"Then I want to know why it is that when you were cutting weeds behind the barn and Bobby could no longer see you, he wet his pants from fear that you would not come back."

"He did that?" Joe felt sick.

"We dealt with it." Bertha rocked faster and clutched Bobby tighter. "I do not care who you are or what you are running from. Oh, yes," she said in answer to his questioning glance. "I know you are running. But all I care about is this sick child and how to help him. If you will trust me with the answer to why you are running, I will better know how to help you."

"We aren't your responsibility, Bertha. I'm sorry we have become a worry to you."

"You became my spiritual responsibility the moment I allowed you to come under my roof. I believe I have earned the right to know why this child I hold in my arms weeps in his sleep…and why his father groans in his."

Joe leaped to his feet and leaned over Bobby. Sure enough, the little boy's cheeks were wet with tears—the evidence of yet another bad dream.

He collapsed onto the couch. For once he was grateful for the lack of electric light in the house. It was easier to talk with nothing but pale moonlight in the room. He searched for words to describe the unspeakable.

"My wife was murdered," he said. "While I was gone. Someone locked Bobby inside his room. He was there for hours before I returned. He doesn't seem to have seen or known anything, except that his mommy wouldn't come for him when he called."

"Do you know who did this terrible thing?"

"No. That's the problem. No one has any idea."

Bertha rocked and rocked as she digested this. "And what were you doing that was so important to take you away from your family?"

"I was in another city, tending to business. It seemed important at the time. Believe me, if I could go back in time and change things, I would."

"Why are you running?"

How could he explain? His life in LA was so different from her simple, rural Amish lifestyle. He knew he could never truly explain, but she deserved some sort of an answer.

"I–I'm someone who has been in the public eye for many years. When my wife died, I couldn't even hear the minister at her graveside for the sound of news helicopters. People took pictures of me and my son as though they thought the funeral were entertainment. I shielded Bobby the best I could, but no matter how much I asked for privacy, they wouldn't leave us alone. Finally, I just headed out. To grow this beard and keep moving from one place to another was the only thing I could think of to stay out of the public eye." He rested the back of his head against the couch. "It's probably impossible for you to understand."

Bertha leaned forward. "You think I do not know what it is like to be the object of another's curiosity?" Her eyes were blazing. For a moment, he got a clear picture of the fierce young woman who had faced down thieves in order to protect the orphan children.

"When my father died, Englischers took forbidden pictures of our people. When my uncle Isaiah was hurt in a buggy wreck, Englisch passersby grabbed pieces of the broken buggy for souvenirs." She settled back again. "As individuals, we may not be as famous as you are, but we deal with intrusiveness every day of our lives. For us, just to go to town for a spool of thread during tourist season means stares and Englisch children pointing at us. This is our life too, Joe."

He felt chagrined. These peaceful people endured more prying into their day-to-day lives than he had ever realized. "How do you stand it, Bertha?"

"God gives us strength," Bertha said. "And once people look their fill, they grow bored. They see that we are not so interesting after all, but just people living our lives. Then they leave us alone and we buy our spools of thread in peace."

"You are a wise woman, Bertha."

"No." She waved a dismissive hand. "But I have lived longer. Now we must decide what to do with you. Do you have a plan?"

"Not really, but a roommate from college has an old hunting cabin in West Virginia. Up in the mountains. He told me a long time ago that if I ever needed to get away, it would be available. I've been thinking of going there when I get my truck fixed."

Bertha thought this over. "It would be better for Bobby if you stayed here."

"I don't think that's possible."

"Why?"

Joe hesitated. "Because of Rachel."

"Ah yes. Our Rachel. She is a suspicious one, that girl."

"I've noticed."

"Do not judge her too harshly." Bertha shook her head. "She has been through much."

Joe found himself more curious about Rachel than he would have guessed a mere twenty-four hours earlier. "In what way?"

"She lost her mother when she was young, and then there was her father, my little brother...." Her eyes took on a faraway gaze. "He was always fascinated with guns. Even as a boy, he was constantly out in the woods target practicing with our father's hunting rifle."

"Your people own *guns*?"

Bertha looked surprised. "Of course. How do you think we protect our livestock from predators?"

"I had no idea. Please go on."

"After Frank chose not to join the church, he became a policeman, but he worried about keeping his weapons in the same house as his little girl. Children are fascinated with forbidden things, so as soon as he thought she was ready, he brought Rachel out to the farm and did target practice with her, over and over. Lydia and I grew tired of hearing the shots."

"Rachel wanted to do this?"

"Oh yes. She was a natural. On her eleventh birthday, she and her father went to the bank for money to celebrate. A man was robbing the bank when they entered. My brother went for his gun, but the robber was faster."

"I am so sorry, Bertha."

"Rachel was standing next to her daett when he was shot. It is not something a young girl—or anyone—should ever experience."

For the first time, Joe got a glimmer of why Rachel was so serious and grim. Now he knew. She, too, had experienced the evil that resided in the world.

"People who were there at the bank," Bertha continued, "said that as her father went down, Rachel bent over him. They thought she was bravely trying to protect her father with her own body, but when she stood back up, she had both hands wrapped around his revolver—and it was cocked."

Joe swallowed. "Go on."

"She pointed the gun straight at the robber, even though he already had a gun. They said her hands were steady and her finger was on the trigger, but tears were streaming down her face."

"Oh, Bertha." He knew at that moment that he would never look at Rachel in the same way again.

"The bank robber didn't know what to do. Having a little girl in a frilly, pink birthday dress pointing a handgun at him was not something he had anticipated. A male customer tackled him from behind while he hesitated."

"What about Rachel?"

"One of Frank's deputies had to talk to her for a long time before she handed the gun to him." Bertha shook her head. "She never wore pink again."

"I see."

"I also see, Joe. I see your kindness toward us and your love for this child. I think you are a good man who needs our help. You are welcome to share what we have for as long as you need to stay."

Her words were like a gift. Who would ever have believed that his shattered faith in mankind could be resurrected by an elderly Amish woman?

"Thank you. That means more than you can know."

Again she waved that dismissive hand, as though her offer were of no importance. "You are welcome. I will deal with Rachel."

The wind-up clock in the kitchen chimed four o'clock.

"I promised Eli I would help him with his milking this morning in half an hour."

"That is most interesting." She peered at him over her glasses. "Eli is fussy about who touches his cows. Have you ever milked before?"

"No."

She chuckled. "Then you will be learning much. Help me get this big boy back onto the couch. I will stay with him while you help Eli. I think you will be needing some breakfast before you leave. I will show you where things are."

Quietly, Rachel crept back upstairs in her stocking feet. The house was sturdily built. Long-gone Amish carpenters had seen to that, and the stairs did not creak. She was especially grateful now for those ancient carpenters, because she did not want Joe and Bertha to know that she had been listening.

Unfortunately, after coming downstairs to use the bathroom, she had heard only a few snatches of their conversation—something about a murder and the child being in the house with his mother.

She now had something to go on. A partial story to research. License tags to trace. And the water glass that Joe had held to the little boy's lips. It was in a plastic bag now, readied for fingerprinting tomorrow morning.

She had the tools to discover the true identity of the man her aunts were so innocently harboring.

CHAPTER 7

"Das iss goot." Eli nodded his approval of Joe's full pail of foaming milk.

Joe felt as proud of his accomplishment as if he had won a trophy. Spending the early morning hours helping Eli milk the cows had proven to be a study in humility. If he had a shred of pride left after everything he had been through during the past few days, it would have dissipated the moment he walked into this Amish farmer's barn.

He had never felt so clumsy and less skilled in his life. Manually milking a cow was no walk in the park. Had there been machinery involved, he might have been able to redeem himself, but Eli milked the old-fashioned way—head against the side of the cow and hands on udders that had been soaped and rinsed off in early-morning darkness dispelled only by lantern light.

Eli had been in high good humor as he instructed Joe in the fine art of milking, watching with a solemn expression that occasionally slipped into a goofy grin while Joe repeatedly and unsuccessfully tried to coax a stream of milk into a pail. Once he had achieved a minimal amount of success, Eli had proceeded to strip the milk from three cows to every one of Joe's.

It was becoming apparent that Eli did not need the help as much as he needed the company *and* the entertainment that watching a novice provided. Joe figured he had inadvertently become Eli's own private Saturday morning cartoon show.

It didn't bother Joe in the least. He had received enough public adulation to last him several lifetimes. The realization that he was giving the old Amishman so many reasons to chuckle into his beard had pleased him.

And yet there came a moment when he finally figured out how to make the milk ring in strong streams against the inside of the metal bucket. The chore settled into a peaceful rhythm as he watched the fresh, pure milk rise in the bucket.

The sounds of the farm awakening around him had the soothing impression of classical music, as the patient cows munched their fodder and the roosters at both Eli's and the Troyer sisters' farms competed in an early morning crowing contest. The sound of horses' hooves clip-clopping down the road as Amish men and women went to work created a sort of counter-beat to the barnyard symphony.

Eli had splashed part of Joe's earlier milking into a round pan that was immediately ringed by a barn cat and her six kittens. Joe was surprised to hear the tiny kittens growling at one another as they lapped the warm milk. One by one they staggered off, drunk on the richness of fresh milk.

Joe suspected that this was an early morning ritual between farmer and cat, as he watched the mother feline contentedly cleaning her bemilked whiskers as her comically satiated babies, their bellies distended and drum-tight, flopped down in the loose hay and promptly fell asleep.

Eli forced a crumpled twenty-dollar bill into Joe's hand as soon as they finished the milking, processed it, and cleaned up. Joe knew he hadn't been worth even that. He knew Eli was simply being kind.

"Tomorrow morning, jah?" Eli said.

"You still want me?"

"Oh, sure." Eli nodded emphatically. "Many hands make quick work."

"Clumsy hands make *long* work."

"Maybe not so clumsy tomorrow."

"I'll be here."

The sun had just begun to rise as they left the barn. Eli blew out the lantern. "Do not come too early. Remember, I like to sleep late." Eli jauntily walked toward his house, chuckling over his joke.

Walking home was a pleasure. Joe stopped for a moment to breathe in the unpolluted air while he admired the silent beauty of the sunrise. Everything felt so fresh and clean this morning. No LA smog. No traffic. Even with little sleep, it had been a long time since he'd felt so alive.

He knew they would soon have to leave this place, but his desire to get back on the road had dissipated in the short amount of time they had been here.

When he entered the kitchen and found Lydia bustling about, fixing a second breakfast for him, it felt strangely as though he were truly coming home.

"Watch me, Daddy!" Bobby ran through the kitchen wearing nothing but underwear. He climbed onto a kitchen chair and prepared to jump off. "I'm Superman!"

"Off the furniture, buddy." Joe looped an arm around his son's stomach and flew him around the kitchen. Bobby stretched his arms straight out and made swishing sounds with his mouth.

The medicine and the God-given healing properties of a child's body had worked an overnight miracle. Bobby's fever was gone and he was now practically bouncing off the walls.

With a start, Joe realized that Bobby had awakened to find him gone and had been okay with that fact. Apparently *very* okay.

Lydia, in her neat prayer kapp and long lavender dress, flipped bacon with a nonchalant air as though she were quite used to having small children flying through the air. He supposed she probably was, after having run an inn for so many years.

"Boo!"

This time, Joe had the presence of mind to gasp and pretend to almost drop Bobby in surprise, before he turned around to discover Anna. "Goodness, Anna. You scared me!"

She clutched both hands behind her back and rocked back and forth on her bare feet, beaming with delight at the success of her joke.

Out of the corner of his eye, he saw Lydia nodding with approval at his reaction. "Breakfast will soon be ready," she said.

Joe set Bobby on the floor. "Let's go get your clothes, buddy. I think we'll give Lydia and Anna a break from Superman."

"'kay." Bobby whooped and galloped into the living room, now pretending to be a horse, until he weakened and allowed Joe to put on his clothes and tennis shoes. The medicine was good, but it was apparent that the little boy hadn't completely recuperated yet.

Joe had a strange feeling when he reentered the kitchen. Breakfast was waiting on the table, but all three aunts were looking at him with overly bright eyes. They kept glancing at one another, as though sharing a great secret.

After a silent prayer, in which Joe participated by thanking God in his heart for this wonderful—if temporary—home, Bertha passed him a dish of crisply fried potatoes. "We have been talking…"

Anna put a couple of slices of bacon on Bobby's plate, and Lydia poured Joe a cup of coffee.

"...and we have a business proposition for you," Bertha finished.

Lydia passed the cream. Anna clasped her hands beneath her chin and waited.

"You do?"

Everyone wore serious expressions. Even Bobby knew something was up and looked from one adult to another as he munched his bacon.

"We happen to know of a job opening," Lydia said.

"I'm listening." Joe's voice was cautious.

"It is time we hired some help around here," Bertha stated.

Anna nodded happily. Lydia watched him over the brim of her cup of coffee.

"We're offering you a job," Bertha said. "Here. Helping us. We would like to reopen the inn next spring, but there are many repairs and much cleaning that must be done. Our home needs to be painted. We can no longer take care of the yard. I need a new clothesline."

"You could live in the *daadi haus*—the grandfather house." Lydia's voice was eager. "It was where our father lived for many years."

"The salary won't be large," Bertha continued. "But it would be enough to live on and..."

Anna bounced up and down in her seat as she finished her sister's sentence. "Bobby can stay!"

It sounded wonderful to him after the long, lonely weeks on the road. "Are you women serious?"

"Yes," Bertha said. "As Rachel has pointed out to us many times, we are not as strong as we used to be."

Joe toyed with his fork. "Eli told me this morning that his eight sons have given him thirty-four grandchildren and ten great-grandchildren. Why would you hire me, a stranger, when you have relatives who would help you?"

"You are right," Bertha said. "We have many people, and they would help. But all who are old enough to be of any use have their own homes and families and jobs. More importantly"—she placed both hands flat on the table and leaned toward him—"the day you arrived, I was in my bedroom praying that Gott would allow us to show His love to one more stranger before we died. When Eli knocked on our door and I saw you and Bobby in his buggy, I knew that Gott had brought you to our door, Joe."

"All that happened was that my truck quit and Eli was kind enough to pick me up. I doubt God had anything to do with it."

"Gott created the world." Bertha cocked an eyebrow. "You think He cannot break a truck motor?"

Bobby, who had been helping himself to one slice of bacon after another, understood at least part of what the ladies were saying. He stopped eating, climbed onto his father's lap, put both hands on the sides of Joe's face, looked him directly in the eyes, and said, "I don't want to ride in the truck anymore, Daddy."

Joe's heart shattered. The three women had no idea how long he had been dragging his son around the United States and how tired he was of it.

Despite his misgivings about spending even one more day in the same town as the lovely, suspicious-eyed Rachel, he silently bowed to the Lord's sense of humor. Becoming a handyman to three Amish women and an old dairy farmer would never have occurred to him as an option for his life—but it was looking pretty good at the moment. He had no transportation. He had no money. Unless he resorted to crime—or called Henrietta—his choices were practically nonexistent.

One thing that was *not* an option was going back to LA and the life he had once lived. He simply couldn't take it anymore, and Bobby couldn't either. In his estimation, every normal, nontraumatic day his little boy could spend with these gentle women was a godsend.

Flashes of *The Witness* came back. Being deep in Amish Country had thwarted the discovery of Harrison Ford's character by the bad guys, at least for a while. Perhaps it would confuse those who were trying to find *him*, as well.

"I appreciate the offer, ladies," Joe said. "More than you know. Thank you. I'll try to do a good job."

"Of course you will do a good job. What else would you do?" Bertha frowned. "Bobby, do you not want some scrambled eggs to go with all that bacon?"

Bobby accepted a spoonful of eggs, but his mind was on more important things. "Can I keep the white kitty cat now, Daddy?"

"Maybe."

"You will need to get the daadi haus ready," Bertha said. "It has long been sitting empty. There will be much work."

Rachel entered the kitchen at that moment. "How's Bobby this morning?"

"Much better," Joe answered. "Aren't you, buddy?"

Bertha glanced disapprovingly at Rachel. *"Da kee shvans is immah shpoht!"* she said.

"What?" Joe asked.

"Bertha just told me that the tail of the cow is always late." Rachel made a wry face as she helped herself to a cup of coffee. "It's something Amish mothers say to children who come straggling in."

"Do you want some breakfast?" Lydia asked.

"Sorry, I can't stay," Rachel said. "Bertha's right. I *am* late." She shot a glance at Bertha. "Although I don't think that exactly makes me a cow's tail." She took a sip of her coffee. "What was that I heard you saying about a job, Bertha?"

"We have hired Joe to be our handyman." Bertha's voice had steel in it, daring Rachel to disagree. "He will be moving into the daadi haus."

Rachel nearly choked on her mouthful of coffee. She carefully set the cup down on the counter. "You did *what?*"

Anna whispered loud enough for everyone to hear. "Rachel's mad."

Kim was hard at work on the computer when Rachel came in from overseeing yet another fender bender. These roads were not meant to handle the heavy traffic of the Swiss Festival. And the fact that it was a gorgeous fall Saturday with the clarity that came after a thunderstorm had brought people out in swarms.

"Did you find anything about Joe Matthews?" Rachel asked.

"Sure," Kim said. "There are *hundreds* of Joe Matthews in the United States. Take your pick."

"Try in Texas. That's where his tags are from. We really need to find this guy."

Kim clicked a few keys and the computer screen filled with names. "Looks like there's at least fifty. You're going to have to give me something more to work on."

"Try seeing if there are any whose wives were murdered in the past year."

"Whoa." Kim turned to look at her, eyebrows raised. "*That* should narrow it down. How did you find out?"

"It's not important." Rachel didn't want to admit that she had been eavesdropping.

"Is he a suspect?" Kim turned her focus back to the computer screen.

"I hope not," Rachel said. "My aunts have hired him as their new handyman."

"I'll see what I can do." Kim kept her eyes glued to the computer as she clicked keys. "Any luck in running his tags?"

"The truck belongs to a car dealership owner in Dallas, Texas. When I called, he said he had let Joe borrow it."

"Did he give you any other information?"

"Nope. It was like talking to a wall. When I tried to get some personal information out of him, he clammed up. Said he had a customer and hung up."

"Tough luck."

"I suppose. It would have been even tougher if I had found out the vehicle was stolen. I'm not *wanting* to tell my aunts the man they just hired is a bad guy. I just want to make absolutely certain he's not."

"Gotcha."

"I need to get over to the Swiss cheese judging in a few minutes." Rachel checked her watch. "I think I'll check in with Ed first."

She stuck her head inside the police chief's office. "Have you gotten word about those fingerprints?"

"Not in the system." Ed Spencer looked up from his desk. "Sorry about that. I know you're disappointed."

Ed was thin and of medium height—which was why criminals tended to underestimate him until they were facedown on the ground. He was a good boss and a better cop, and Rachel respected him.

"There's no need to be sorry, Ed. Joe's prints not being in the system is a good thing."

"You think?"

"It proves that the man living at my aunts hasn't been arrested."

"It also proves that he's never applied for a government job or gotten a driver's license in Texas, California, or Florida, the three states that require fingerprints."

No Texas driver's license? Interesting. Joe had driven to his car dealership buddy's from some other state. Eliminating those three states narrowed it down a little. Only forty-seven to go.

"Are you done with the man, Rachel?"

She moved from the doorway into Ed's office. "I'd like to know who he is and where he came from."

"Maybe he's Joe Matthews, like he says. A decent man who's down on his luck. A *lot* of good people are having a hard time these days." He fiddled with a pencil. "Have a seat."

She slid into a chair.

Ed dropped the pencil, clasped both hands, put them behind his neck, and leaned back. "Do you know what the difference is between being poor and being homeless, Rachel?"

"No."

"It's *family*."

She had to acknowledge the truth of that statement. After she had been released from the hospital in Cleveland, she'd sheltered with her aunts until she had recuperated enough to hire on with the Sugarcreek police force a year and a half ago. What if she'd had no one?

"Maybe this guy is just a decent man who doesn't have anyone he can turn to," Ed said.

"But he's hiding something. There's something *off* with him, Ed. I can feel it."

"'Off' as in being a psychopath, or 'off' as being half a sandwich short of a picnic?"

"Neither." Rachel drummed her fingers on her knee. "If you cut his hair, dressed him in a business suit, and put him in a board-room, he'd dominate the meeting. He has a presence about him that simply doesn't fit someone who is in his present circumstances."

"You're impressed with him?"

She glanced down at the floor. "How can I be impressed with someone who is living off the charity of my relatives?"

"I thought you told me that he'd been doing work around the farm. That doesn't sound like a man looking for a handout. It sounds like your aunts have simply worked out a barter arrangement. The Amish do it all the time."

"He *is* a hard worker," Rachel said reluctantly.

"You're dogging a man who has done nothing illegal, is taking care of his child the best he can, is trying to pay your aunts back with repairs around the farm, and whose only crime is that his truck broke down in a strange town and he doesn't have the money to repair it."

"It's not quite like that."

"It's *exactly* like that. What's really eating at you, Rachel?"

"Nothing. I'm just trying to do my job."

"There's more than that going on." He sighed. "Okay. We've tiptoed around it ever since you got here. Are you ready to talk about what happened in Cleveland?"

"There's nothing to talk about."

"You saved the life of a woman and her three children."

"I screwed up."

"That's how you see what happened? A screw-up?"

"I should have called for backup earlier. I shouldn't have tried to deal with the situation alone."

"You made a judgment call. None of us can read minds."

"I lost control of a situation."

"You fought a mentally ill man three times your size and gave his wife and children time to escape to safety. You could have been killed, but you protected them anyway."

"I could have handled it better."

Ed arose and walked over to a bookcase beside his desk. He returned with a framed picture of a man in uniform and handed it to her.

"Your dad was the best cop I've ever known. He hired me fresh out of the academy because he saw something he thought he could use."

She traced her father's face with her finger.

"I chose you for this job out of twenty-four other qualified applicants. All of whom were bigger than you."

"And male." She pointed out.

"Yes."

"Don't tell me you hired me because of my dad."

"I did, but not for the reasons you're thinking. If Frank Troyer were alive, he'd have my hide if he thought I put you on the police force simply because you were his daughter."

"Then why did you?"

"Frank always said there were four kinds of people who go into law enforcement. Some crave the power over others they think the job entails. Some want the respect they think comes with the uniform. Some simply like the adrenaline rush of chasing down bad guys—they think it will make them feel like heroes. All are eventually disillusioned. But there are the others—the fourth kind —who simply have a heart for protecting the weak and the helpless."

He took the picture from her and set it carefully on his book-shelf. "You were born with that kind of heart, just like your dad. *That's* the reason I hired you."

It was true. That's all she had ever wanted—to protect the weak and helpless. Even if it had meant drinking her dinner through a straw in the hospital for a month while her broken jaw healed.

"You're a good cop, Rachel. One of the best. But I'm worried about you. A person needs some balance in life. You can't be a cop twenty-four hours a day, seven days a week. You have to hang up your gun from time to time and just be a person, or you aren't going to last in this job—even here in Sugarcreek. You'll burn out. I think you are already beginning to."

"I have my aunts."

"But do you have any friends your own age? Do you have any hobbies? Any other interests? Do you ever just let down and go to the movies or bowling or, I don't know, church activities of any kind?"

"I have a good life."

"You need more in your life than a gun and a badge."

"No offense, Ed, but what can it possibly matter to you what I do when I'm not at work, as long as it isn't illegal?"

"Because I drove out to the farm and visited with your aunts. I talked to Eli. Met Joe. Watched him interact with his son. He seems like a decent man to me. Eli likes him. So do your aunts. I think you're seeing boogeymen where there are none. I think part of it is because of what happened in Cleveland and part of it is because you never, ever, unclench your emotional fists. You see danger everywhere you look. That's not healthy. You have to realize that sometimes all you're looking at are people just getting by the best they can."

His words hit her like a slap. "I don't know how else to be."

"Then you'd better learn." Ed picked up the papers he had been working on. "Because I wouldn't want to let go of one of the best cops we've ever had."

CHAPTER 8

The milking went quicker the second day. Lydia awoke in time to stir together some oatmeal for him and then sat on the front porch to listen for Bobby in case he happened to awaken. With Bobby feeling better and the weather mild, Joe and his son had spent the night in the cabin. It was a relief to no longer be camped out in the aunts' living room.

Joe, pleased at his growing proficiency in milking, found Bobby still asleep when he returned from Eli's. Grateful for the chance of a quick catnap, he lay down beside his little boy.

It was the bell that awoke him from his second slumber. A church bell rang out over the hills and valleys of Sugarcreek, and he realized with a start that it was Sunday.

He lay in bed, thinking about the days when getting up and dressed for worship was as natural to the rhythm of his life as breathing. His mother and her two boys would walk the short distance to meet their father, who would invariably already be at whatever African church he was in the process of establishing.

In spite of having an advanced degree in Bible, his father had always deliberately preached on a level that a child could understand. Even when Joe had been quite small, it had never been a chore to listen.

That is, not until the day Joe had informed his dad that he had chosen a different path than the Bible degree his father had sacrificed to pay for in the States. His father had dreamed of a father-and-son mission team.

Joe had a very different plan.

There had been harsh, hurtful words. Joe waited for his father to apologize. His father waited for Joe to apologize. There were over three thousand miles between them—and telephone service in the African bush was spotty. By the time Joe contacted his father about his marriage to Grace, the rift was permanent. His father had been quite vocal in his disapproval of Joe's alliance with a Hollywood actress who was not a Christian.

Joe had been resentful of his father's judgmental attitude toward a woman he'd never met. His father had too forcefully reminded him of the biblical warning against being unequally yoked with unbelievers.

Suddenly his father's religion had seemed antique and of no use in Joe's modern and affluent world.

They had no more contact until Bobby was born. Joe had sent pictures of the newborn who bore his grandfather's name, hoping it would soften his father's attitude toward him. A Bible inscribed with Bobby's name had traveled the miles between them—a sample of his father's idea of an appropriate baby gift. There had been no letter or note. Just that small, hand-tooled, leather Bible sitting on Bobby's little dresser like a visible accusation.

Grace had been puzzled by it all. In her world, people did not care who married whom. And they seldom gave Bibles as baby gifts. Joe had known it was his father's private way of reminding him where and to whom he belonged. His father could hardly breathe without preaching the gospel. Virtually anything else was a waste of time to Dr. Robert Mattias. Joe seethed at the judgmental implication.

Now he was glad he had chosen, at the last minute, to stuff Bobby's Bible into the duffel bag. For some reason, the presence of that small leather Bible was a comfort to him.

The bell continued to ring. Bobby awoke and blinked at him from the other cot.

"Good morning, sleepyhead," Joe said. Then he realized that those were exactly the same words that had come out of his own father's mouth every morning.

Bobby scrambled out of bed, ran the few steps between them, and snuggled into Joe's arms. His sturdy little body warmed Joe's heart.

"Are you hungry, buddy?"

"Mmm-hmm."

Joe chuckled. "Are you even awake yet?"

Bobby sat up and cocked his head to one side. "What's that sound, Daddy?"

"It's a church bell."

"Why is it ringing?"

"To tell people it's time to get up and go to church."

"Are we going to church?"

Joe hesitated. "Do you want to?"

"My friend Ricky goes to church. He gets cookies."

Joe searched his mind for a Ricky in Bobby's life. If he wasn't mistaken, he was one of the little boys in Bobby's play group back in LA.

"Not today, buddy." In spite of teaching Bobby to say his prayers, he had never actually taken him to church. Grace had not seen any use in it, and there were always schedule conflicts. Besides that, it was awkward and embarrassing to attend worship only to be asked to sign autographs.

Bobby's lower lip protruded.

It occurred to Joe that he wouldn't have to worry about being asked to sign autographs now. He could enter a church and be completely anonymous. A powerful longing to once again participate in worship grew within him.

Perhaps he would just go and find out where that bell was coming from after all.

———

Rachel heard the church bell while she was getting ready to take a shower in her aunts' downstairs bathroom. She picked up a straight pin lying on the rug and deposited it into the trash can before she stepped into the stall. From painful experience, she was now always on guard for those things.

The water was sluggish, the aunts depending on gravity-fed water, but there was enough pressure to help wake her. She lathered with the handmade, sweet-smelling glycerin soap her aunts had bought from a local woman—reminding herself as she did so to buy some for own home. Now that she had her mother's money at her disposal, she could afford a few small luxuries.

Then she realized that she *had* finally come into her trust fund and the best luxury she could come up with was some homemade soap. Maybe Ed had a point.

As she rinsed, she felt hope rising. Today was her first day off in two weeks. The Swiss Festival was over. It was a beautiful day— a perfect day to do something wonderful.

The problem was, now that Joe was taking care of the farm, she couldn't think of a single thing to do—except go back to work.

That was just sad. Ed was right. She needed to get a life. A friend. A hobby. A...

The church bell kept ringing.

Hadn't Ed said something about church? Before her mother's and then her father's deaths, they had always gone as a family to the very one that was now ringing the bell.

Something stirred within her. There was nothing to keep her from attending worship. Even as a child, she had felt cleaner and happier on Sundays. If she hurried, perhaps she could make it to the service.

As Rachel headed out the door, she passed Lydia, who was reading the latest copy of *Keepers at Home*, an Amish homemaking magazine.

"Where are you off to, Rachel?"

Rachel halted, her hand on the doorknob. "I thought I might go to church this morning."

"That's nice. Joe and Bobby just left for church. Maybe you could pick them up."

"Maybe."

"We will be leaving soon too," Bertha said from where she was sitting near the window. She had a thick copy of *The Budget*, the world-renowned Amish newspaper published right in the heart of Sugarcreek, in front of her.

"Where are you going?" Rachel asked.

"Eli is taking us out see Daniel's Katherine. She has felt poorly since the baby was born. Lydia baked more apple pies last night for her family."

"That's nice. Have a good time."

"We will." Both Bertha and Lydia went back to their reading. Sunday, a day of rest, was one of the few days in which they indulged in the various magazines and papers that came into the home.

Knowing Joe was also going to church dampened Rachel's enthusiasm a little, but she braked the Mustang when she saw him walking down the road with his son and a Bible in hand.

"Need a lift?"

Joe had brushed his long hair into a low ponytail and looked neater than she had yet seen him. He was dressed in a white shirt that defined his broad shoulders and dark jeans. Bobby had on a little blue shirt and khaki pants.

Joe stopped. "Where are you headed?"

"Church."

"Us too!" Bobby jiggled up and down.

"He thinks they give out cookies," Joe explained.

"If he gets Marge Jones as a teacher, he just might," Rachel said. "I had her when I was a kid. She was the best Sunday school teacher in the world."

A cloud passed over Joe's face. "I'd prefer to keep him with me."

"They won't tear him out of your arms, Joe."

"I know that." The cloud disappeared, replaced by a killer grin. "Are you, by any chance, headed to the church that was ringing that bell?"

"That's the one."

"We'd appreciate a ride."

"Well, seeing that I still have Bobby's booster seat in my car," she said, smiling, "get in."

It seemed strange to enter the church of her childhood with Joe and Bobby beside her. Of course, it would have felt strange entering alone too. All in all, she was grateful to have some company—even if it was the mysterious Joe Matthews and his son.

There was only one song book in their pew, which forced her and Joe to share a copy. Joe surprised her with his good voice and familiarity with the hymns. When the preacher spoke, she noticed that Joe didn't fumble with the pages, instead turning to the cited biblical passages with no hesitation. This was not a man walking into church for the first time.

After services, as she spoke with people, she kept an eye on Joe

—and was impressed that he seemed totally at ea
perhaps, than herself. The man's manners were f'

She was a little surprised to discover that Joe w.
creature. He genuinely seemed to enjoy talking with t..
members. Because of this, she and Joe were among the last
leave.

"I enjoyed that," Joe said as they left the building and walked
toward the car.

Rachel pulled the car keys out of her purse. "I would never have
picked you as a churchgoer, Joe."

"Haven't been, for way too long." He buckled Bobby into his
booster seat and climbed in. "By the way, where are your aunts?"

"This is a no-church Sunday for them." Rachel checked for
traffic as she got into the car and backed out of the parking lot.

"A what?"

"A no-church Sunday. The Amish only have church every other
week."

"Really. My brother and I would have loved *that* as kids."

"Me too." She laughed. "For the Amish, it is—as much as
possible—a day of rest. They eat sandwiches instead of cooking,
and they do no housework. Sometimes friends and family drop by
to visit, or they go visit others. It's a pleasant day for them. Today
my aunts are visiting some cousins over in Holmes County."

"But where do they have church on the Sundays when they go?"

"Each Amish family takes a turn with having it in their home.
That's why their houses tend to be so large. Not only do they have
big families, but they also build houses that can hold approxi-
mately two hundred people. Once a church district gets bigger
than that, they create a new one."

Joe thought this over. "If they meet in one another's homes,
how do they keep track of where they are going? With no telephones, how do they pass the word around?"

ou'd be surprised at how organized they are. They mail a ,etin several pages long to every family. Each church district is sted, along with each bishop and minister. 'A' districts meet on one Sunday. 'B' districts meet on alternate Sundays. The bulletin tells who will be hosting."

"So they never have the expense of church buildings."

"No. Nor do they have the expense of a paid staff. Each church has one bishop and three ministers—all chosen from within the church by a sort of combination voting process and casting of lots. When a new bishop is needed, one is chosen from the three existing ministers."

"If they don't have buildings or paid staff, what do they do with their contributions? They do take up a collection, don't they?"

"Only twice a year, when they have their communion and foot-washing ceremony. As to what they do with the money, that's simple—they take care of their own. It's called 'alms,' and the church votes as a body on who receives it."

"So who receives it?"

"Primarily widows and orphans. Or families that have fallen on hard times because of illness. Of course, if there is farmer who can't work his crops because of illness, the other men will help him out."

"It sounds like a good system."

"It's worked for hundreds of years."

He turned to look at her. "Why did you choose not to accept your aunts' religion?"

"I am like so many others who have grown up in this area." She chewed her lip before she continued. "I respect the connectedness of the Amish, the network of support, and the integrity of their beliefs, but there is a dark side to the Amish religion as well. It is not all dumplings and prayer kapps, as my father used to say."

"A dark side?"

"If one doesn't comply with all tenants of the Ordnung, one can be shunned into obedience. I find it hard to accept a religion where a woman as brilliant as Bertha was banned by her church because she wanted more than an eighth-grade education. I am no biblical scholar, but even I know the difference between man-made traditions and actual scripture. The Amish try so hard to have unity in all things that it seems they sometimes lose sight of the spiritual reasons behind the rules they create."

"You've given this a lot of thought."

"It would be impossible to live in Sugarcreek otherwise."

"So Lydia doesn't cook on no-church Sundays, huh?"

She smiled. "Hard to imagine, isn't it?"

"I went to church," Bobby piped up from the backseat, "but I didn't get any cookies."

"Are you getting hungry, buddy?" Joe asked.

"Uh-huh."

"You know what?" Joe turned toward Rachel. "I have two of Eli's twenty-dollar bills burning a hole in my pocket—and the promise of permanent employment. How about we go to that Homestead Restaurant over in Charm? Eli tells me they make the best chocolate pie in the world. I'll pay. You can consider it my peace offering to you for being here."

She ignored his comment about a peace offering. "Homestead's pies are wonderful, but that restaurant isn't open today."

"No?"

"It's Sunday, Joe. This is Amish Country. Most family-run businesses are closed."

"What about Beachy's?"

"Beachy's is closed too."

"Interesting." He thought this over. "It's a different world here, isn't it, Rachel?"

"You have no idea."

"I like it, though." He gazed out at the rolling countryside. "It's peaceful."

"I try to keep it that way."

"So, do we just go home or what?"

She thought that over. Going back to an empty house with Joe didn't seem like such a good idea. She *could* just drop him off at the farm and go back to her own empty cottage...but that didn't hold a lot of appeal, either.

Ed's words came back to her. The fact that her boss had met this guy and decided he was legit gave her pause. Maybe she *should* take this chance to actually get to know him.

"I suppose we could drive to New Philadelphia or Dover. There are restaurants open there. Or..."

She looked at the sky. It was a gorgeous fall day. "We could stop at the IGA here in town. They're open on Sundays. We could pick up some lunchmeat and have a picnic. There is a table beside the creek, near where the buggies tie up."

"That sounds really good." He turned to look at his son in the backseat. "Do you want to have a picnic, Bobby?"

"Yay!" the little boy answered.

Rachel smiled. For an hour or two today, she was going to obey Ed and hang up her mental weapons and enjoy herself. A picnic with Joe and Bobby sounded surprisingly appealing. Especially since they would be out in public. She still didn't feel entirely comfortable being alone with this man, but perhaps if she spent some time with him, she would learn something about him.

She was impressed that even though he had so little, Joe insisted on paying for their simple meal. They carried the grocery sack out to the empty picnic table beside the creek and set out the bread and bologna while Bobby threw rocks into the shallow stream from the small footbridge.

"Is that the famous Sugar Creek?" Joe asked.

"The one and same."

He seemed much more relaxed around her than he had the previous two days. Maybe it was because she was no longer in uniform. Or maybe it was because he now had a paying job and a roof over his head. She wasn't thrilled with the fact that it was probably her mother's money funding his new job, but it *was* a relief to have some of the responsibility of the farm off her shoulders.

She wondered if his newly relaxed state might somehow pay off for her. Perhaps he would let down his guard and let something slip about his past if he could forget she was a cop for a moment.

You're looking for boogeymen, Rachel.

Ed's words came back to her. Okay, so she was doing it again. She willed herself to relax. She had the right to enjoy this day off with the autumn sun on her face and a handsome man sitting across from her.

Whoa. Handsome?

How could she think Joe was handsome when she couldn't even see his face for the beard?

It was his eyes, she decided. It was the way they lit up every time he looked at Bobby. The way they crinkled at the corners when someone said something funny. The way they followed Anna with such compassion. Yes, there was a lot of depth in those gorgeous blue eyes.

Gorgeous? She sat up straight at the direction her thoughts were taking her. She didn't know this man. She didn't even *want* to know this man. Not really.

Unfortunately, the sad fact was, having this impromptu picnic with Joe as they watched Bobby throw rocks into the stream was the most fun she'd had in months. Or had it been years?

Ed was absolutely right. She definitely needed more in her life than police work.

Joe had had one goal and one goal only, when he'd suggested they go out to eat. If he was going to stay here awhile, he wanted to normalize things between himself and Rachel. Bobby needed some stability in his life, and Joe was willing to do almost anything to keep his son in the middle of this oasis of gentle people—even if it meant making friends with the resident cop.

During the church service, he had decided to be charming enough—and engaging enough—that Rachel would drop her suspicions and leave him alone.

He had not expected to enjoy it.

Dressed in a rust-colored sweater and khaki slacks, she seemed like an entirely different person than the one he knew when she was in uniform.

He liked how well she answered his questions about the Amish. He was finding her to be an intelligent, thoughtful woman. He also appreciated the way she cut Bobby's sandwich into little squares and took off the crusts without being asked…as her hair shone in the autumn sunlight in shades of light brown to reddish gold.

Sitting at the picnic table, enjoying what Rachel informed him was a sandwich of the delicious, locally made Trail bologna, he realized with surprise that he was having a really good time.

And he wasn't at all pleased about that.

He sternly reminded himself of Grace and the grief he had been carrying. He told himself that he had no business enjoying the company of another woman.

Bobby ate a few bites of his sandwich and a handful of potato chips then immediately went back to splashing rocks in the water.

"How did the creek get its name?" Joe asked. "Is the water especially sweet, or does it have white, sugarlike sand somewhere?"

"Some people say it got its name when a farmer from

Ragersville came to town for groceries and accidentally d
couple sacks of sugar into the creek when his wagon tippeu ᴗ
the bridge. Some people think it more likely that it got its name
from all the sugar maple trees that grew around here. Of course
the town took its name from the creek."

"Was Sugarcreek a good place to grow up, Rachel?"

She smiled at the memories. "It was a *wonderful* place to grow
up. Practically no crime, everyone watching out for one another.
Have you noticed how Main Street has that long, steep hill? They
used to block that off on snow days when the weather was just
right for sledding, and every kid in town would show up. It was so
much fun. Once when I was little, my dad grabbed a toboggan, and
he and my mom and me slid down the hill together, over and
over."

"Was your father shunned for leaving the church and becoming
a cop?"

"No. Dad left before he was baptized into the church. Bertha
left to get her nursing degree after she joined. Baptism is the line
of demarcation for the Amish."

"Why?"

"It's what they were martyred for back in the 1500s. The state
church was baptizing babies, and the Amish believed in adult
baptism only. They were hunted down and burned at the stake for
their beliefs. Baptism is a *very* big deal to the Amish. Their ances-
tors died because of their belief in its necessity."

"They were burned at the stake for a point of doctrine?"

"A scriptural point of doctrine considered a matter of salvation.
Don't *ever* think that because they are a pacifistic people they are
pushovers. My father's people are strong. They've endured perse-
cution, withstood the pressures of progress, lived daily with the
world's ignorance of their ways, preserved their culture, and are
presently doubling in size every twenty years—even though their

lives are not easy or convenient. Many wrest a living out of the soil using not much more than a horse and plow, while non-Amish farmers with giant farm equipment are giving up."

"No wonder you are the way you are."

She glanced up at him. "And how is that?"

"Tenacious. Loyal. Hardworking. Self-sacrificing."

"There are worse attributes."

"Absolutely—but what traits did you get from your mom's family?"

"Oh, Mom's folks were Swiss cheese makers. My grandfather on my mother's side bought lots of land around Sugarcreek during the Depression...and sold it later at a profit. They were frugal people. Invested and saved what they had. Dad and Mom met when she was clerking at a grocery store near here. Dad always said that for him it was love at first sight. Mom said he bought so many candy bars, trying to court her, that she had to go out with him."

"So both parents were homegrown Sugarcreek kids."

"My roots go deep. What about you? What kind of childhood did you have?"

He watched Bobby struggling to unearth an especially large rock. The little guy succeeded and tossed it into the creek with a satisfying splash. The antibiotics were doing their job. His son was immeasurably better.

"Joe?"

"Excuse me?"

"What kind of a childhood did you have?"

How much should he reveal? "We traveled a lot."

Rachel began to clear the picnic table. "Overseas?"

"Yes."

"I thought so. You handle your knife and fork like a European."

"I picked up that habit in boarding school. Never lost it."

She walked over and tossed the crumpled papers into a trash can near the creek. "Is your mother still living?"

"No."

"What about your father?"

"I think so."

"You *think* so?"

He sighed. "We've been estranged for years."

"Why?"

Joe traced around a knothole in the picnic table with his finger. "He had plans for me—plans I didn't go along with."

"What were they?"

Joe hesitated for a long time. "He wanted me to become a preacher."

Rachel sat down directly in front of him. "You could not possibly have said anything that would have surprised me more."

He pretended offense. "You can't see me in the pulpit?"

She seemed to consider the idea. "You might look more the part with a haircut and shave."

"Maybe they would accept me into the Amish church. I have the beard for it," he teased.

"You'd never make it as an Amishman, Joe."

"And why not?" He drew himself up. "I can milk cows with the best of them now. Give me a straw hat and suspenders, and I could pass."

"Joe, you could speak fluent Pennsylvania Dutch and dress in handmade Amish clothing, but no Amish person would *ever* mistake you as one of them."

This interested him. "Why?"

"You don't move or stand like an Amish person, and you never will. I've seen outsiders attempt it. They always fail. One of my aunts' Englisch guests once wanted to try Amish dress. She put her hair in a bun and put on Lydia's clothes. Everything was technically correct, but everyone could see that the woman was not Amish. It's impossible to describe the difference, but you just know. Anyone around here would know."

"Then I won't ever try to disguise myself as an Amishman."

"Good idea. Especially since you're *already* wearing a disguise."

Her words jarred him, which had likely been her intention. "It's the shoes, Joe. Their price doesn't match the rest of your clothing."

He lifted one foot and regarded it sadly. "I've always loved these shoes."

"Are they as comfortable as I've heard?"

"More so."

Rachel looked him straight in the eyes. "Who are you hiding from?"

"Honestly? Pretty much everyone."

"Why?"

He looked over at Bobby. "I'm just trying to give him some normalcy."

"The past three days have been normal?"

"Compared to the life we were living, yes."

"You aren't going to tell me any more than that, are you?"

He scraped a thumbnail into the seasoned wood of the picnic table. "No."

She sighed and gathered her purse. "I had convinced my aunts to close down their inn until you showed up."

"I don't think they were *ever* convinced it was the right thing to do."

"Stubborn old women."

He laughed. "In fifty years, you'll be exactly like them."

A grin grudgingly spread across her face. "I sincerely hope so."

CHAPTER 9

The daadi haus was a modest two-bedroom cottage attached to the farmhouse by a short, well-worn path. When Bertha opened the door, a musty smell assailed them.

"It would probably be best to stay at the cabin until you get this aired and cleaned," she advised.

Joe set the bucket, scrub brush, soap, and rags Lydia had given him on the floor. Dark brown, cracked leather furniture was pushed against a smoke-stained wall. The small living room was dominated by a large, blackened fireplace.

"My father lived here after our mother passed on. He had lost patience with all the hustle and bustle of guests. In his later years he lit a fire every day, summer or winter. He said it helped his arthritis." Bertha's voice held a note of apology. "I never had the heart to rent it out before we hired you."

The kitchen was only slightly smaller than the living room, and not as dark. A silent gas-powered refrigerator sat in a corner. Joe opened an oak cabinet hung high on the wall. Ancient, thick china plates were stacked neatly inside. Another cabinet revealed a few drinking glasses and cups. A small gas cookstove sat beside the sink. And an oak table with four chairs rounded out the sparse kitchen furnishings.

"There are two bedrooms and a study," Bertha said, "as well as an attic for storage."

"I don't have much to store," Joe said, as he took stock.

Abraham Troyer didn't appear to have collected any clutter. With soap, water, and some paint, these rooms would be quite livable. The wooden floors were scuffed, but they would shine up nicely. Joe's spirits lifted. With a few days of hard work, this cottage could feel like a real home.

The two bedrooms were as sparsely furnished as the kitchen and living room—bare mattresses on twin beds in each, along with a chair, a kerosene lamp, and a bedside table. Nothing else. Abraham could have been living in a monastery, for all the comfort he had afforded himself.

"This is my father's study." Bertha led him to the back of the house. "Daett spent a great deal of time back here."

Joe was pleasantly surprised when they entered the room. There was a wooden desk facing large, bare windows. The windows overlooked a tangled rose garden and the pasture where the sisters' one horse stood munching grass.

He wondered if his duties would ever include harnessing and hitching this horse to the buggy he had seen in the barn. If so, they were all going to be in a world of trouble. He had no earthly idea even how to even ride a horse, let alone hitch one.

Joe turned around and took an involuntary step backward. The entire wall opposite the bank of windows was filled with shelves, and on those shelves, he estimated several hundred volumes to read.

"Daett liked his books," Bertha said.

"Liking books" was an understatement. Joe approached Abraham's personal library with reverence.

"Alfred Edersheim's *Life and Times of Christ*," he murmured, pulling the dusty volume off the shelf. He ran his finger over the spine of another. "*Strong's Exhaustive Concordance*." He pulled a three-inch-thick title off the shelf. "Philip Schaff's *History of the Christian Church*—all eight volumes." He glanced up at her. "Your father was a scholar, Bertha."

There was confusion on Bertha's face, and he realized that she was wondering why her handyman was so familiar with these religious books. In his excitement with coming face-to-face with these old friends, he realized that he had let down his guard.

"My father was a preacher," he explained.

It was true. It didn't even scratch the surface of the whole truth, but it was true.

Bertha smiled, pleased with his answer. "Your daett was a preacher?"

"Yes."

"My father was too, most of my young life," Bertha said. "Then the Lord chose him to be the bishop of our church."

"I thought the Amish didn't believe in advanced education—even biblical. How did your father come to possess all these?"

"My father's collection is quite unusual for an Amish bishop. There was a regular guest with whom he became close friends—a professor of Bible at a small Christian college. They had many discussions about religion over the years. My father shared his own copies of Amish works with his friend, and they spent hours together comparing his German Bible with Englisch translations. The professor brought my father gifts of books every time he came. The friendship spanned decades."

"And your father read all these?"

"Cover to cover. He never desired the position of bishop, but he took the heavy mantle Gott chose for him very seriously. He struggled to gain wisdom."

"Why did he accept the position of bishop if he didn't want it?"

"When a young man is baptized into the Amish church, he agrees to serve in whatever position Gott might choose for him. Our belief is that, if chosen, Gott will give him the strength to carry out his responsibilities."

"Did he get into trouble with the others for all this study?"

"It was not something he discussed with the others." She looked beyond him through the window, as though seeing into the past. "I doubt anyone outside our family knew. The Amish believe there is a risk in much study. Even of the Bible. There is a temptation to be proud of one's ability to quote Scripture or know where certain passages are. My father did not tout his scholarship; instead, he took the knowledge deep into his soul and allowed it to come out only in ways that helped him lead his flock."

"He sounds like a great man."

"No!" Bertha looked alarmed at his praise of her father. "He was a humble man—as Gott willed."

Joe plucked another well-thumbed book off the shelf, J. Gresham Machen's *The Virgin Birth of Christ*. A classic.

"You can read them if you want," Bertha said. "I haven't known what to do with them. It would not be appropriate to give them to someone in our church. Few would understand."

Joe reverently put the book back on the shelf and dusted off his hands. This room could be glorious with a little work and a comfortable chair. Strangely enough, he found himself longing to be lost in Abraham's books.

It had been years since he'd had the desire to study. Now, after all he'd been through, he found himself eager to dig into the Word of God and these classic works of biblical scholars.

"Do you mind if I paint the walls?"

"No, I would be delighted. I will pay for the supplies."

He felt more than a glimmer of hope. No one would ever

expect to find him here in Sugarcreek, Ohio, living in an Amish daadi haus and working as a handyman. It was practically the last place on earth anyone would look. It would be so good for Bobby, as well as for himself, to have a place to come home to each day.

That is—if Rachel continued their unspoken truce. He thought they had done pretty well together yesterday at their little picnic. He'd done everything he knew to put her at ease.

"If you think you can live here," Bertha said, as though reading his thoughts, "without missing too much the electricity and the television—I think you can have a good life. Bobby will give all of us joy, and we can help you watch over him. You will have no more need to run." She smiled. "I do not think anyone would ever suspect that someone famous would be living here at our humble farm."

"I am more grateful than you can know. But I hate having to accept pay from you."

"The Bible says that a workman is worthy of his hire. We have enough money to pay you. Rachel has seen to that. Although I do not think she quite had this in mind."

Before he could inquire about *that* interesting piece of information, Bertha clumped out of the daadi haus, shaking her head and chuckling at some inward, private joke. Then she turned back with a grin so wide it warmed his heart.

"Welcome home, Joe."

It was Monday, and once again Rachel had a day off—and she had no idea what to do with herself. What did regular women do on their days off—women who had normal jobs and didn't tote guns? Did they visit friends? Do their nails? Shop for clothes?

Shop.

Not something usually high on her list, but today it seemed like an intriguing idea. She had done nothing at all with the inheritance she'd received, except to turn a portion over for her aunts' use.

She deserved to buy at least a little something for herself. Maybe some new clothes. Or something for the house. Serious shopping would require a drive to New Philadelphia and the New Towne Mall, but the day was gorgeous and New Philly not all that far away.

A bubble of excitement rose within her at the thought. As she went to her closet to get dressed, it occurred to her that this shopping trip was actually seriously overdue. Her wardrobe was functional but sparse. Half of her attire consisted of her basic blue-on-blue uniforms.

She was going to spend some money today, and she was going to enjoy every minute of it!

Five hours later, she staggered back into her home, footsore, eyes glazed, and laden with bags. The only thing in the world she wanted was to soak in a hot tub until the ache of mall-walking drained away with the bathwater.

Fortunately, she had just the thing. A trip to Bath and Body Works had bagged a citrus-ginger bubble bath and shampoo that had caught her attention the moment she'd sniffed the sample. Refreshing. Light. Perfect. She had also purchased some candles of the same scent, which she'd lit and placed around the bathroom.

She had never been one for scents, but there was something about this one that made her want to close her eyes, inhale, and smile.

Which was exactly what she did after she pinned her hair up and stepped into her seldom-used, claw-foot bathtub.

Pampering herself felt a little strange. She was half-embarrassed by indulging in such luxury.

Her final act of indulgence had been picking up a new mystery novel at Waldenbooks. She loved mysteries. Loved her ability to solve them long before she'd turned the last page—but for the life of her, she couldn't remember the last time she had allowed herself the joy of reading one.

Ed was right. She needed to loosen up a little. Quit being a cop all the time. Quit feeling responsible for her aunts all the time. Quit—

The phone rang. And rang. And rang.

Her first instinct was to ignore it, but her responsible nature got the better of her. She dragged herself, dripping, out of the warm, sweet-smelling water.

Three minutes later, the tub was draining and Rachel was toweling off. Aunt Bertha had called. Joe was preparing the daadi haus for habitation, and Bertha wondered if Rachel couldn't come and help. Bertha felt it would be best for Bobby's health if they could move in quickly.

Rachel had no choice. She pulled the hairpins out of her hair and shook her head. The haircut she had received a few hours earlier during her shopping spree fell easily into place. As she dressed in her newly purchased, better-fitting jeans and an apricot T-shirt, she wondered if Joe would notice anything different about her.

Not that it mattered or anything.

She wasn't going over there to impress Joe. She was going because her aunts had asked her to.

She told herself that Joe's being there had absolutely nothing to do with the fact that she was wearing her new clothes to go help clean the daadi haus.

With Bobby happily "helping" Lydia bake cookies, Joe set to work heating water on the stove. The moment it was hot enough, he added some cold water, rolled up his sleeves, and plunged his hands into the now-warm soapy water. The daadi haus wasn't so big that he couldn't scrub down most of it by nightfall.

He was whistling a tune, down on his hands and knees, and scrubbing the kitchen floor when he heard a noise and looked up. Rachel had entered the house. Once again, she was not in uniform —and she looked absolutely stunning.

"Hi," she said.

He concentrated on wringing out the rag he had been using. "Hi, yourself."

"You're really going to do this? Move in here?"

"I really am."

"You will miss having electricity." Rachel dropped into one of the kitchen chairs.

"I doubt it. I've lived without it before."

"Oh?"

His unusual childhood had been a matter of much discussion in the media at one time. He had no intention of discussing it any further.

He noticed she was not wearing her habitual stark ponytail and had gotten a new haircut that framed and softened her face. She had the features of a true beauty, the fact of which she seemed utterly unaware.

"Aren't you working today?" He glanced away, afraid to spend any more time thinking about how lovely she was. The last thing he needed was to develop an attraction to a nosy cop.

"Nope." She crossed her long, denim-clad legs. "Bertha asked me to help you."

Her T-shirt fit her perfectly, and those jeans accentuated curves he had never noticed when she was wearing her uniform.

He stared hard at the floor he was mopping. "Why?"

"She thinks the sooner you move in here, the healthier it will be for Bobby."

He went to the sink to dump the dirty water. As he passed by her, he noticed a scent so enticing it made him want to bury his nose in her hair and inhale.

Not a good thing to have on his mind right now.

He busied himself by pouring out the bucket of water and refilling with fresh. "Bertha's probably right."

"She usually is. Drives me crazy sometimes." Rachel stood and looked around the half-cleaned kitchen. "So—what can I do to help?"

Joe felt a little strange about allowing Rachel to help him; he still didn't know if she considered him a friend or a foe. But Bertha had sent her over here, and it wasn't his place to send her away. He just wished he wasn't suddenly *so* aware of her as a woman.

"I was planning on scrubbing down the study next," he said.

"All those windows will need polishing. I could do that."

"You're dressed too nice."

She seemed startled that he had noticed. "I—I went shopping today."

"I can tell."

Was it his imagination, or was Rachel starting to blush?

"I have some work clothes upstairs in the farmhouse," she said. "I'll put something else on."

"Might be a good idea."

Strangely enough, she didn't move. Nor did he. They stood in the middle of the wet kitchen floor, staring at each other. Aware of each other. Only inches apart. As though truly seeing each other for the first time.

It was awkward...and intense. The air grew heavier, making it difficult to breathe.

As though drawn by a magnet, Joe's hand lifted and touched a strand of her silky hair.

She didn't move.

His index finger moved to her cheek, and he gently caressed the curve of her jaw. Her sudden intake of breath at his touch broke the spell that had fallen upon them.

Joe turned away first, avoiding her gaze, busying himself with heating fresh water...angry with himself for doing something so stupid.

Rachel hesitated, as though trying to process what had just happened. Then, without a word, she ran into the farmhouse.

She came back with Windex and paper towels, wearing a flannel shirt with the sleeves rolled up—and determinedly acting as though nothing at all had just transpired between them.

Joe was relieved that she looked ready to work instead of ready to walk into a lonely man's dreams.

Unfortunately, she still smelled like a mix of ginger and oranges—a scent he was determined to ignore as they carried their cleaning supplies into the study.

"I remember my grandfather reading in here," Rachel said as she sprayed the window cleaner on a dingy pane. "He kept peppermints in a drawer and always gave me one when I came to visit him. I would sit on his lap, and he would tell me stories about our people."

Joe pulled an armload of dusty books off the shelves and laid them on the desk. "You must have loved that."

"I did. He was kind to me."

Rachel was so engrossed in her task that she didn't notice him watching her as the late afternoon sun made the natural highlights of her light brown hair shine like burnished gold. She didn't notice as his eyes traced the curves of her body. She didn't notice as he forced his gaze away from her.

Rachel was not the type of woman he had ever thought he would be interested in—and he didn't want her in his life now. Not as things were.

But he couldn't help thinking about what a ferocious and wonderful mother this half-Amish girl would make some lucky child. What a strong companion and loyal wife she would be to some fortunate man.

Joe fought against the fantasy of him and Rachel together. He fought against indulging in the dream that he was an ordinary man who could build a simple life for his son in the sweet Ohio town of Sugarcreek. Dreams like that weren't for people like him.

CHAPTER 10

Joe applied one last stroke of off-white paint over the dark paneling in the living room. Yesterday, with Rachel's help, he had finished the kitchen with the same color.

Based on what he had seen within the aunts' farmhouse, the Amish preferred plain white walls. Fancy colors were studiously avoided—with the exception of their quilts, dishes, and exuberant flower gardens.

However, with Bertha's permission, he had chosen a light blue for Bobby's bedroom, one close to the shade his wife had used in his son's old bedroom back home. Grace had called it "desert blue" and had insisted on having the other twenty-two rooms of their home professionally painted in what she had called "Navajo colors."

Joe had hated the extravagance of that house but had purchased it because Grace wanted it so badly. He loved simplicity. Always had. Grace's need for show had been a struggle for him to accept.

This Spartan daadi haus suited him perfectly. The austerity of it reminded him of the bare, windswept huts he had known as a child.

Finished with the living room, he took his painting supplies into Abraham's study, which, as a small treat for himself, he had saved for last.

He laid a few newspapers on the floor and opened another fresh can of paint. He had never realized how the simple act of smoothing paint onto walls could feel so cleansing. He loved this task of covering the years of stains and smudges with the bright, light paint. It satisfied something deep within his soul. It felt as if he were making his own life new again with each stroke. Each finished room felt like a small rebirth.

If he could just hold on here for a while longer, perhaps he could manage to live the simple life he craved. Maybe he could blend in and become that average guy no one took notice of. An ordinary Joe, living an ordinary life, in an ordinary town, doing an ordinary job. No pressure. No press. No one hounding him for an autograph or an interview.

It was a vision entirely too good to be true. The most he could hope for was a respite. He knew that somehow, some way, it would eventually come out that he was here, and then the nation's ravenous curiosity about him would be fueled by those who wrote the news.

Abraham's desk was so heavy when he tried to move it more into the center of the room that he pulled drawers out to lighten it. The top drawer held old-fashioned pump fountain pens, a bottle of ink, two yellow pencils that had been carefully sharpened with a pocket knife instead of an electric sharpener, and a more recent book than the ones on the shelves. He reached in and drew out a hardback copy of *Forty Years Preaching Christ on the African Plains.*

It was, Joe knew, written by a famous African missionary, telling the stories of a life spent building congregations in some of the poorest villages in the world.

He turned to the back cover, where there was a full-page

picture of the author, Dr. Robert Mattias. His father's familiar, craggy face stared up at him. Joe had read the book, of course. His dad had been a master storyteller, and the book was good—part adventure and part hard-core evangelism.

It had been a small publishing success in the Christian book market a few years earlier. Joe would bet his life that every penny of royalties his father received had gone into the stomachs of his people and the drilling of more wells for fresh water in the war-torn countries where his father had labored.

That was the kind of man his father was.

The book included some stories of himself as a small boy. His father's love for him had shown through, in spite of the rift now between them. He felt a pang as he pictured his father bending over a desk, penning page after page. How amazing that it had somehow touched the life of an old Amish bishop, and possibly in the very place Joe would soon be residing!

Joe knew that some people would call this a coincidence, but his father had never believed in coincidences. He had taught Joe that God watched over every aspect of the lives of those who served Him.

The problem was, both men, Abraham and his father, had lived lives dedicated to serving the Lord, filled with integrity and sacrifice.

And he...well, he hadn't.

Joe put the book back in the desk, poured the white paint into a roller pan, and began covering the years of accumulated nicks and stains on the walls. He wished it were as easy to renew a damaged life as it was to repaint a stained wall.

Rachel yanked at her thick hair with the delicate hairbrush Lydia had left for her in the bathroom. Once again, she had spent the night at her aunts'. The problem was, it was no sacrifice to do so anymore. No sacrifice at all. For the past week, as Joe had worked on the daadi haus, she had found herself drawn to the farmhouse like a moth to light every free minute. She had tried to convince herself that she was merely coming over to help.

The fact was, she had never felt so conflicted in her life. There had been that moment when she and Joe were alone together in the daadi haus, when both of them had felt the electricity crackling between them. Neither had acknowledged it in any way. It was too bizarre to contemplate.

And yet, several times, as she cleaned the rest of the windows, or trimmed out the baseboards, or dipped the roller in the fresh paint, she had sensed Joe staring at her—but when she turned, he had immediately glanced away. Several times she had caught herself doing the same thing.

This could not continue. This could not be. He was a stranger, a drifter, a man without a past or a future. She wanted him gone.

No, she didn't. Yes, she did. Didn't she?

Her mind slowly revealed once again—as though pulling a jeweler's polishing cloth away from a rare stone—that breathless moment when they had stood motionless in the kitchen, looking into one another's eyes, nearly paralyzed by the unspoken and shocking realization that there was a powerful attraction between them.

Who would have guessed that simply cleaning a house together could have such an effect?

This was crazy. She had to put up her guard...defend herself against this guy's charm. And his smile. And the kindness and understanding she read in his eyes.

She chided herself. She couldn't let her attraction to him blind her to the need to be on her guard for her aunts. Regardless of Ed's evaluation that Joe was simply a good man fallen on bad times, she still needed proof.

But his fingerprints had not been in the database, Kim had found nothing in her computer search, and the license plate had been a dead end. She had even attempted other calls to the used-car salesman who had lent Joe his truck, but his secretary kept saying he was out.

All she knew for sure was that men who lived decent, honest lives didn't drive into a strange town with no job, no connections, no friends, and no money.

It was imperative that she keep reminding herself of this fact, or she would be a goner with one more look into those incredible blue eyes.

She gave up on her hair and laid the brush on the bathroom sink. Today she had been pressed into service yet again by her aunts. They were determined to help Joe put the finishing touches on the daadi haus.

He hadn't asked for any help, but the aunts just couldn't keep their noses out of his business. Having made him their personal project, they were bent on turning the daadi haus into a real home for him and Bobby.

The daadi haus was nearly finished and the aunts had been gathering many useful things together as a housewarming surprise.

She couldn't wait to see the look on Joe's face when Lydia, Bertha, and Anna took over his home today.

She found Lydia and Bertha in the kitchen, each armed with housekeeping paraphernalia.

"Is everything ready?" she asked.

"Just a few more things," Lydia said. "Anna decided that her collection of seashells would look good in Bobby's room."

At that moment, Anna came down the stairs clutching an old shoe box. If Anna was giving Bobby her seashells, this was a serious sacrifice. She had gathered the shells on her one and only visit to see relatives in Sarasota, Florida, twenty years ago and had shown the shells to everyone who came to visit ever since.

Rachel knew that there were exactly 143 seashells. Everyone in the family had the number memorized, after hearing Anna count them over and over again through the years.

"Bobby and Joe are gonna be *so* surprised!" Anna jiggled the shoe box. "I can't wait!"

"Me either." Rachel meant it. She couldn't wait to watch what happened today.

Joe met them at the door with a paintbrush in his hand and a bemused look on his face as they bustled in, carrying various boxes and bags. Bobby was delighted about having company and proceeded to jump up and down on the old couch as he screeched and made faces.

"Whoa, partner." Joe laid the paintbrush on an old newspaper and grabbed his son in midair. "I don't think the couch can take too much of that."

Anna set her box of shells on the scarred coffee table and exclaimed, "We're gonna make your house nice, Joe!"

Joe hesitated only an instant before he smiled. "Thank you, Anna. Is there anything I can help carry in—or is that it?"

Rachel crossed her arms and leaned against the door frame. "Oh, there's a lot more, Joe. They still have a ton of stuff over in the kitchen."

"I don't deserve such kindness."

Strangely enough, he sounded as though he meant it.

"That's exactly what I told them"—she softened her comment with a smile—"but they wouldn't listen to me. Come help me carry the rest of it."

She and Joe went for the final load while the aunts unpacked the things they had already brought.

In the aunts' kitchen, Rachel picked up a box. "I'd appreciate it if you'd try not to hurt their feelings today. They have good intentions."

"You still don't get it, do you, Rachel?"

"Get what?"

"Those three ladies could hang pink polka-dot curtains in the living room and a giant velvet picture of Elvis on the wall and I'd still be grateful."

"They're Amish, Joe. They don't do pink polka-dots or velvet Elvis pictures."

"You know what I mean."

Rachel searched his eyes one more time to see if there was a criminal behind the gentle voice and unruly beard. Ed was right. The criminal she had imagined simply wasn't there.

From one box, Joe lifted a garish calendar imprinted with bright pink Victorian-style cabbage roses. He held it at arm's length and gave her a lopsided grin. "Isn't this a little fancy for an Amish home?"

"Pink cabbage roses are Anna's favorite. The only wall decorations most Amish have are Scripture plaques or old-fashioned calendars. A few will hang jigsaw puzzles of farm scenes and landscapes when they're finished working them."

"If it makes Anna happy, I'll go nail this up in the kitchen right now."

"That would definitely make her happy."

Through the open door, they heard Bertha singing a hymn.

"Let's go see what the ladies are up to." Joe's eyes twinkled with amusement.

"Brace yourself. I overheard them making plans last night."

"I can't wait to see."

As they entered the daadi haus, Rachel saw that one of Lydia's handmade quilts had been spread over the old brown couch. It had transformed the couch into a work of art. She wondered if Joe had any idea what that Amish quilt would be worth at auction. Probably not. She wasn't entirely certain that Lydia did.

Cushions covered with the same pattern had been placed on the two armchairs. A wooden bowl of nuts and fruit sat in the center of the coffee table, along with several out-of-date but brightly colored and much-treasured *Countryside* magazines.

Through the kitchen doorway, she saw Bertha and Lydia absorbed in their transformation of that room. A plain dark green tablecloth had been laid catty-corner on the square Formica kitchen table. Green crockery from the aunts' own kitchen was lined up on the counter. Bertha, seated at the table, happily threaded white curtains onto empty curtain rods.

She could hear Anna chatting merrily with Bobby in his room. Suddenly, as though Anna had told a joke, they heard Bobby belly laughing.

"Do you hear that?" Joe said. "I've gone far too long without hearing that kind of laughter coming from my little boy."

"It's a nice sound," Rachel agreed.

They went back to Bobby's bedroom and glanced in to see what was going on. Anna was dancing her seashells, one by one, across the shelves of a small bookcase.

"I'll be right back." Joe's voice sounded raw and choked. To Rachel's surprise, he abruptly turned and walked away.

Rachel followed and found him pacing in the yard outside.

"I thought nothing they could do would upset you," she said.

"They are so kind and giving, sharing what they have with me, a stranger—they break my heart."

"Which is why I've tried so hard to protect them," Rachel said. "An unscrupulous person could destroy them."

"The first night we met, I told you I would never hurt them. I meant it."

"With all my heart, I've hoped that's true." Rachel sighed. "Look, Joe, it's no secret that I've been less than thrilled with your being here...but helping you and Bobby is making my aunts happier than I've seen them in ages. I'm not going to mess with that. I don't want you to either. So go hang Anna's calendar, help Bertha put up the curtains, and tell them thank you when they're finished. They believe they are doing God's will."

"I know."

As she turned to leave, Joe put his hand on her shoulder. It was the first time he had done that, and she wasn't prepared. Startling her into a combat reflex, she whirled into a crouch, her eyes snapping and her fists clenched.

"Oh, Rachel, I wasn't trying to hurt you." Joe drew his hands back, palms up. "I just wanted to say one more thing before we went inside."

"Sorry." She unclenched her fists and took a deep breath. "I'm a little jumpy these days."

"For Bobby's sake, I need this chance at building a quiet life. At least for a while. Please allow me that chance."

Rachel chewed her bottom lip. "Tell me what you're running from."

"That would require trust, Rachel." There was a deep sadness in his eyes. "And trust is something I'm very low on these days."

"But I'm supposed to trust *you*." Her frustration was intense. Didn't he realize how completely trustworthy she was?

"I know it's a lot to ask."

Still unnerved by her reflexive reaction to his touch, she felt a strong desire to lash out at him. "I checked your prints."

He cocked an eyebrow and waited.

"They came up clean."

Joe nodded, as though he'd been certain they would.

"I ran your tags."

A slow smile spread over his face. "How *is* Buzzy?"

"Less than communicative."

"A good sort of friend to have."

"How did you do that, Joe? How did you talk a used-car salesman into letting you drive a perfectly good truck off the lot that didn't even belong to you?"

"I made a trade."

"What kind of trade?"

"The kind that left him driving a vehicle worth ten times the one I borrowed."

"Really?"

Joe crossed his heart. "Scout's honor."

"That makes no sense whatsoever." She put her hands on her hips. "Okay. Treat my aunts right, keep out of trouble, and I'll leave you alone."

He grinned that killer smile again. "You don't have to leave me alone."

She looked him square in the eyes, determined not to acknowledge his attempt to flirt. She dare not let him see that she was weakening toward him. "Step out of line even once, and our agreement is off."

His smile faded. "I wouldn't expect anything less of you, Officer Troyer."

CHAPTER 11

With the painting and cleaning completed, and with Joe and Bobby living comfortably in the daadi haus these past three days, Rachel had no excuse to spend her nights at her aunts' home anymore. Her own house, which had once felt like a well-ordered sanctuary, now simply seemed vacant and empty when she went home to it. She longed for the farm, for the comforting companionship of her aunts, and—if she was being totally honest with herself—what she missed most was the presence of Joe and his sweet son.

Rachel was exhausted. Her day at work had been especially brutal. If ever she had *needed* to spend some time at her aunts' farm, it was this evening. Deciding she had stayed away long enough, she drove over to check on how things were going with the aunts and their new handyman.

Spotting Joe on a ladder, scraping paint off the side of the farmhouse, gave her pause. It seemed strange, seeing a man constantly working around her aunts' farm, but she had to admit— the farmhouse had been in dire need of a fresh coat of paint. Thank goodness he was the one doing it and not her. Scraping paint was one of those things that set her teeth on edge, like fingernails on a chalkboard to others.

"What are you doing?" she asked as she approached the porch.

"Building the Sistine Chapel. What are *you* doing?"

"Okay, so that was a dumb question. Sorry."

"I have to admit," he said, "I didn't realize how tedious the prep work would be." He glanced down from his perch on the next-to-the-top rung. "Can't beat the view, though."

"Is supper ready?"

"Close, I think." He climbed down the ladder and laid the scraper on a windowsill. "Lydia kicked me out of the kitchen. She said she was making something special."

"That's Lydia for you." Rachel grinned and leaned against the porch.

"Since Bobby and I now have a kitchen, I attempted to cook a meal at noon today." He smiled crookedly. "Bobby brutally informed me that Lydia's cooking tastes better than mine." He placed the palm of one hand flat against his chest. "I was crushed."

"Well, as you pointed out last night at supper, Lydia is a genius in the kitchen. After that comment, she's probably half killed herself cooking for you today."

"I hope not. For women their age, all three of them work too hard as it is."

"I know. That's why I was trying—until *you* came along—to make them give up the idea of running an inn."

"I'm sorry about that. Bertha keeps coming up with more projects I need to complete before they open in the spring."

"She's almost eighty," Rachel grumbled. "Any normal woman her age would be gearing down, not restarting a labor-intensive business."

There was a pause as he studied her. "You sound worn-out, Rachel. Has something happened?"

The genuine kindness in his voice shattered her. She felt a lump rise to her throat as the tragedy of her day flashed through her mind. His question made her wish she had someone with whom to share daily events—someone besides her aunts, whom she tried to protect as much as possible from the harsh realities of life.

"What's happened, Rachel?" he prodded.

"A car wreck." She stared down at her boots.

"How bad?"

"Bad." The memory rose as bitter as bile. The child had been so terrified, so hurt. Rachel felt as though she'd explode if she didn't talk about it to someone. "We had to life-flight a little girl to the Children's Hospital in Akron."

"Will she survive?"

Rachel shrugged. "I don't know."

"How old is she?"

"Three. Her parents didn't have her in any kind of safety seat. She wasn't even wearing a seat belt. They were just dumb kids themselves, and they were high on something. Neither of them was badly hurt, which I suppose is a blessing. Maybe if the little girl survives, they'll decide to grow up and take better care of her." Rachel rested her head against the porch column and closed her eyes. "I don't understand what's *wrong* with some people."

His voice was quiet, intimate. "The people around here are blessed to have you watching out for them."

She opened her eyes. "Thank you for saying that. Sometimes I wish I'd become, oh, I don't know, a rocket scientist or a brain surgeon or something. You know"—she joked, wiping away a stray tear—"something easy."

"You'd be miserable doing anything else for a living."

"I don't know about that. Sometimes I think I should quit my job and help my aunts run their inn."

"Are you serious?" He looked at her closely. "They would be thrilled."

"Can you imagine me making muffins for breakfast?"

"Actually—yes. I can."

Wonderful smells wafted out of the window, and her stomach rumbled. Had she eaten any breakfast? No. Lunch had been a stray mint she'd found in her desk drawer. The only thing fueling her right now was black coffee. The caffeine and adrenaline were wearing off, and she was beginning to feel weak and light-headed.

"Where's Bobby?" She sank down onto the top step.

"Holding court in the kitchen last I saw. Anna had unearthed an old wooden high chair, and Bobby was sitting at the table making a tower out of Dominoes."

"It's probably my high chair. I think it belonged to my father and aunts too. Bobby's a little big to be using it."

"Not when he's pretending to be Anna's baby doll."

"You're kidding."

"I am *not* kidding." He grinned. "I have totally lost control of my son!"

"Boo!" Anna poked her head out the door and waited with a look of eager anticipation. Joe and Rachel gave the requisite jump and frightened gasp. Anna giggled with pleasure. "Bertha says—come eat!"

"Thanks, Anna."

Joe rinsed his hands beneath the hand pump after Anna left. "Do you have any idea why she does that 'boo' thing?"

"None of us really know what goes on inside Anna's mind. All we know is that saying 'boo' is her little joke and even the smallest cousins know to respond to it."

"She's a sweetheart."

"Yes, she is. By the way, please don't mention the injured child at the supper table. I try to protect her from sad things. She's not wired to deal with them."

"I'm pretty good at keeping secrets," he said.

"You *think?*"

Somehow Joe's laughter ringing out as they went into the house didn't irritate her. In fact, she liked it a lot. It almost scared her how easy it was to have this man in her life.

After supper, Eli arrived and announced that it was time to initiate Joe into the fine art of buggy driving. Joe was less than enthusiastic.

"If you are going to be helpful to the Troyer sisters, you must learn how to drive one of these." Eli patted the black buggy sitting in the yard.

"Um...that would first mean hitching it up."

"Jah. That is a problem?"

"Eli," Joe said, "I don't even know how to catch the horse, let alone hitch it up."

"Catching the horse is no problem."

"Maybe not for you, but it won't even let me pet it. I've tried."

"But Nellie is a gentle mare."

"I don't mind walking into town."

"True. But the sisters like to get out from time to time. Next Sunday is church Sunday, and they would like to go."

"Can't they go with you?"

"Why would they do that when they have a hired man to take them?"

"Because, oh, I don't know, they like to live?" Joe sighed. "I wish I had my truck."

"And how is that truck faring?"

"I should have enough money for it to be fixed in a week or two."

"Ah. Then that means you have your license back?"

"No." Joe kicked at a clump of grass. Not having a driver's license was a sore point with him. He had always been able to go when and where he wanted, usually much faster than the law allowed. It was hard not to go too fast when one owned cars that were famous for their speed.

"A buggy is not so bad when it is all you have," Eli said. "But first, I want to see you catch Nellie and put a bridle on her."

"How much time do you have, Eli? Decades?"

As Joe had expected, Nellie had her own agenda—and being hitched to a buggy was not on it.

"How do the aunts do this?" Joe asked, after Nellie had frisked away from him for the tenth time.

"They don't."

"What do you mean?"

"Bertha says 'Come,' and Nellie comes. Bertha says 'Back up,' and Nellie backs up. Bertha says 'giddyap,' and Nellie 'giddyaps.' Bertha says 'Whoa,' and Nellie..."

"I get it." Joe held up a hand. "What if Bertha isn't around? Does Lydia do it?" he asked hopefully.

"*Nein*. Lydia is afraid of horses."

"Why?"

"She was kicked in the side once. It left a bad memory."

"Oh *really*." Joe was not exactly thrilled with the idea of getting kicked, either.

As he halfheartedly chased the horse around the pasture, Nellie acted coltish as she scampered just out of reach. He tried hiding the bridle behind his back. He tried tempting her with an apple and then with sugar. Nothing worked. If Joe hadn't known better, he would have sworn she thought they were playing tag.

147

It didn't help that, for the most part, Eli spent his time clutching a fence post and giggling so hard he was nearly crying.

"Ach. Goot. Goot," Eli said, wiping his eyes. "Don't stop. Keep trying."

Joe looked at Nellie. Nellie looked at him—with every muscle tensed to prance away the minute he approached her. He could swear that had it been possible for a horse to do so, she would have thumbed her nose at him.

His face was gritty from running around the pasture chasing the silly animal—and he was getting a little tired of listening to Eli laughing.

"*COME!*"

He whipped around and saw Bertha, propped on her walker, standing near the fence. She frowned at the horse.

"*NELLIE. COME! NOW!*"

Nellie obediently walked over, lowered her head, and stood in front of Bertha.

"*STAY!*" Bertha said. The horse stood as still as a stump. "Go put the bridle on her, Joe. Eli, you help him." Then Bertha slowly inched her way back into the house.

It was humiliating—the woman was practically an invalid.

Obediently, Eli and Joe got the bridle fastened onto Nellie.

"What just happened here?" Joe asked, as they led the horse to the buggy.

"Did you not hear? Bertha said, 'Come' and 'Stay.'"

"*I* said 'Come' and 'Stay.' I said 'Come' and 'Stay' a *lot*."

"Jah, but you did not say it in German."

"Bertha didn't say it in German, either."

"No. But she *thought* it in German."

He saw amusement playing in Eli's eyes. "Okay, I'll bite. How did she 'think' it in German?"

"Could you not tell? Bertha was thinking, 'Come, you silly horse. Come and stand still and let Joe bridle you, or there will be no more oats or good fresh hay for your stall for the next month, and I might have to sell you to someone who will make you work for a living instead of frolic in the pasture all day...you big bag of lazy bones.'"

"Bertha was thinking all that, huh?"

"Jah. And the horse knew she was thinking that. It makes a difference."

"And what was I thinking?"

"You were thinking like an Englischman." Eli's voice grew high and mincing. "You were saying, 'Come, pretty horsey with the big hooves that might kick me. Come and stand still, or I will walk away and do nothing but cry because you are so much bigger and stronger than me.'"

"You have been having way too much fun at my expense, Eli."

"I am a very old man," Eli said sanctimoniously. "And I would like to live many more years to watch over my family. The Bible says that laughter is good medicine. You have already added several months onto my life span today." He chuckled and clapped Joe on the shoulder. "I will now teach you how to hitch Nellie to the buggy."

"You need a television, Eli," Joe grumbled as they split apart and walked down both sides of the horse. "With a great big flat screen. Messing with me is too amusing for you."

"Jah," Eli admitted happily. "That it is."

Rachel watched the interaction between Joe and Eli from an upstairs window. Eli had his hand on Joe's shoulder and was chatting with him as they walked Nellie toward the buggy. She knew that Joe was still too ignorant of Amish ways to appreciate the significance of the gesture.

There was a huge difference in personal space between the Amish and Englisch. The Englisch hugged—a lot. Sometimes hugging complete strangers...which was unfathomable to the Amish.

The Amish preferred to nod politely from a safe distance.

A local inside joke said that when Amish women got together, the *real* reason behind the use of their ever-present straight pins was to keep the too-affectionate Englisch from hugging them.

Rachel thought back to the day her father died. Even though she had been only eleven, she had never forgotten how the Amish arrived at her aunts' house and stood respectfully at the edges of the yard, paying quiet homage to her father, the man who had watched over and protected their people, even though he was no longer one of them. By their silent and unobtrusive witness, they had shown her that they shared her great grief.

And then the food began to arrive. Quiet, strong Amish women had kept a steady stream of food coming until the funeral was over and the guests had returned to their homes. No hugs. No tears. No clumsy words of condolence. Just hours of labor over homemade comfort foods during a time when the family was most desperately in need of comfort.

That was the Amish way. It was one of the many things Rachel respected about her father's people. They showed their love in practical ways. Physical affection was reserved for close family members—in private, if at all.

Eli's hand on Joe's shoulder meant that he had accepted Joe almost as one of his own.

This staggered her. What was it that Eli saw in the man?

Even worse, what was it that *she* saw in him? Her eyes, as though having a will of their own, automatically sought him out even when she was pretending otherwise. While here, helping Lydia strip beds, she couldn't keep herself from checking out the window every few minutes to catch a glimpse of the man.

Her prayer life had never been her strong suit, but she breathed a heartfelt plea now: *Father, whoever Joe is, whatever he's done, let him be a good man. It will break Eli's heart and my aunts' if he isn't.*

She paused before acknowledging the truth of things. *It'll break mine too.*

CHAPTER 12

"Am I a good helper, Daddy?" Bobby clutched the plastic sack of copper pipe fittings tightly in his hands as they drove Nellie home from Holmes Lumber, the local hardware store.

Joe was concentrating hard on driving the buggy. Nellie was swinging her neck back and forth in obvious irritation at her harness.

"You're a great helper, son," he said, absentmindedly.

This had been a short practice run, and things were not going well. Nellie wasn't happy. Joe wasn't happy. The horse was still stubborn about being caught unless Bertha was present. But they *were* progressing, and none of the harnesses had fallen off. Yet. His respect for the Amish who used this mode of transportation daily rose even higher.

"Lydia says I'm a hard worker just like you."

"You are."

Joe remembered dogging his father's footsteps as a child. His dad had always been patient with him as he repaired the various homes they had occupied. Dr. Robert Mattias was a rarity—a scholar who could work with his hands as well as with his mind.

The training Joe had received at his father's elbow was coming in handy these days.

So far, in addition to scraping the farmhouse, he had replaced some rotted wood he'd found beneath the old paint, washed all the windows, and was now involved in fixing a minor plumbing problem. This evening, if he had time before the sun set, he would replace some rusted guttering.

When they arrived home, he let a relieved Nellie into the pasture, ate a simple lunch, and then repaired the toilet, as Bobby watched raptly.

"What should we do next, buddy?" Joe asked once he finished.

"You said we could make the floors shiny."

"Shiny floors it is, then." Although he had scrubbed the wooden floors clean, they did need a good polishing. He tore rags for both of them, and they went to work.

Bobby soon lost interest and began to play with a marble he'd found wedged into a corner. The wooden floor had a slight slant—just enough to make an interesting game to a small boy.

The repetitious task of rubbing lemon-scented oil into the heavy oak was satisfying as he watched the dull grain take on a luster. The long-standing wood soaked up the polishing liquid as though it were parched.

There was a feeling of peace in this old house, especially now that the large multipaned windows were cleaned of the grime. The late afternoon sun streamed in, bouncing off the cream-colored walls and filling the room with light. One thing he had learned was that the Amish preferred plenty of windows in their houses. With their dependence on kerosene lights, they tried to eke out as much daylight as possible.

His son made spluttering car noises as the marble turned into a race car. He remembered doing the same when he and his brother were small.

His brother—another ache in his heart.

They had slept in the same bed as kids, eaten the same food, fought over the same toys, and been each other's shadow. But Darren had turned into someone he didn't know—a dreamer who dished out new business ideas as easily as Lydia dished up mashed potatoes. He had talked Joe into funding more than one of his get-rich-quick schemes. When Joe had stopped bankrolling his failed business plans, Darren had moved on to other potential "clients."

"Suckers" is what Joe called them.

It wasn't possible to be close to Darren anymore without getting burned. Darren thought that getting rich was the only way to happiness. Joe knew firsthand that it wasn't.

One of their father's favorite Scriptures from the New International Version came to mind—a prayer from Proverbs.

"'Give me neither poverty nor riches,'" Joe said aloud, savoring the sound of the ancient words echoing in the sparkling clean house, "'but give me only my daily bread. Otherwise, I may have too much and disown you and say, "Who is the Lord?" Or I may become poor and steal and so dishonor the name of my God.'"

"Are you praying, Daddy?" Bobby scrambled under a chair to retrieve his marble.

"I guess I am, son." He was bemused by the fact that Bobby had noticed. He wondered what else his son had picked up on when he thought he wasn't paying attention. Probably a whole lot more than he had realized.

His little boy deserved at least as good a childhood as he and his brother had enjoyed. It was high time he got serious about living an open life of integrity. Time he got serious about church attendance too. He was looking forward to going back to that church he had attended with Rachel.

Rachel. The woman was intruding on his thoughts more and more often. He had even dreamed about her last night—a pleasant dream. They were picnicking beside the Sugar Creek again. He had found himself missing her when he awakened.

A noise on the porch broke into his thoughts. He glanced up and saw all three Troyer sisters standing outside on the little porch, looking at him through the screen.

"Come on in," he said, standing.

They bustled in.

"The floor looks wonderful," Bertha commented.

Anna sniffed the air. "It smells good!"

"It does," Bertha said. "What are you using on that wood?"

"A man at the lumber store suggested I use a combination of olive oil and lemon juice."

"I like the smell of lemon," Lydia said.

Joe felt a small measure of pride. The daadi haus *did* smell and look good.

"Can I do something for you ladies?" he asked.

"We need to talk to you," Lydia said.

Bertha sank into one of the chairs and placed her walker at her side. Lydia and Anna perched on the couch.

"We have received a letter from an old friend of mine who is helping out at one of the many orphanages affected by that terrible earthquake in Haiti," Bertha said. "The children there are in need of so many things, but she has specifically asked if my sisters and I could manage to send them a sewing machine. The two sewing machines they had were ruined by a roof that collapsed. She says that the children need clothing, but they also need occupation. The plan is for the older girls to once again begin making clothing for the younger children as well as for themselves."

Lydia leaned forward, her brow knit with concern. "Can you *imagine* not having a sewing machine?"

Joe could imagine it very well, but he knew that a world without sewing machines was probably inconceivable to Lydia.

"We were wondering…," Lydia began.

"…if you would mind helping us…," Bertha said.

"…have a bake sale…," Lydia continued.

"…at our house!" Anna finished.

"I think we could make a fair profit on my baked goods." Lydia scooted to the very edge of her seat in her eagerness.

"One bake sale would pay for a new sewing machine?" Joe wasn't sure how much one would cost, but he thought they might be overly optimistic.

"No, no, no." Bertha shook her head. "It is impossible to purchase a good *new* treadle sewing machine anymore. The new ones are cheaply made and do not hold up. Eli has promised us his wife's old one. We are simply trying to make enough money to ship it."

"Eli said he would oil it and make certain it is in good working order." Lydia's eyes were dancing with enthusiasm.

"The need is extreme," Bertha concluded. "Some of the children have little but rags to wear."

"I'd be happy to help."

"Dank," Bertha said.

"What do you need for me to do?"

"Some open shelving in the kitchen would be most helpful. We need a place to display our baked goods. I will give you money to purchase lumber. It does not have to be fancy, just sturdy."

"I can do that."

"We will also need many supplies purchased." Lydia pulled a list from her pocket. "I will need much flour and sugar."

"No problem."

"And spices and lard and eggs."

"Of course."

"And milk and raisins and nuts."

"I'll get everything you need, Lydia."

Lydia handed him the list, her face aglow with happiness. "Oh, Joe, just think. Those young girls are going to get a sewing machine!"

Rachel had never been able to leave a puzzle alone. In fact, she had learned to not even begin a jigsaw puzzle unless she had several uninterrupted hours in which to finish it. She was simply unable to stop until every piece fit neatly together.

At the moment, she was entertaining herself by trying to piece together a very different sort of puzzle. It was a slow night at the station, and she was researching unsolved murders involving married women in the past year. She had searched for those by the name of Matthews, looking for one that had a child with her when discovered. The last part was especially important.

But she was having no luck. Joe had either lied about the crime, or Grace Matthews was not his wife's real name.

Was there some other piece of the puzzle she was missing?

She rose from her seat, poured herself a cup of coffee, and sipped it while pacing the floor. Then she pitched the empty Styrofoam cup into the metal trash can and sat back down at the computer.

Her nickname at the academy, based on her inability to let go of a problem, had been "Bulldog." An instructor had said that her tenacity was her greatest strength, but if she didn't watch out, it could also become her greatest weakness.

Sometimes, he said, a good cop had to know when to throw in the towel and concentrate on something else—like a case that actually had a chance of being solved.

With no crime on the books, she knew it was probably ridiculous to keep digging for answers to this puzzle. Most other cops would have lost interest in Joe Matthews long ago. But she wasn't wired like most cops. She *couldn't* let go. Somewhere, somehow, she would find the key to who he really was.

Unfortunately, her need to know had expanded completely out of proportion in comparison with her desire to protect her aunts. The man had begun to occupy nearly every waking thought. Something she had never experienced before.

She was searching for answers now…to protect her own heart.

CHAPTER 13

The carefully lettered homemade sign was staked on the edge of the Troyer sisters' front lawn.

FUND-RAISER BAKE SALE
TODAY 8-2
HAITIAN ORPHANAGE

The sign had required much discussion on the part of the ladies, as had every loaf of bread and every cake, pie, and cookie displayed on the new shelves Joe had created.

Even though the sign was now wet from an early afternoon rain shower and the words written in black Magic Marker had begun to blur, buggies and cars had arrived in a steady stream all day.

"How can such a small sign bring in so many people?" Joe asked Rachel when she arrived.

"Word spreads fast among the Amish," Rachel explained. "Especially for such a good cause. And Lydia's baking is legendary."

"I'm a little worried about your aunts. They worked all day yesterday and were up long before dawn this morning."

"I know. And here I had hoped they would slow down a little if they closed the inn. That was the whole point." Rachel sighed. "Do you suppose there's anything left in there to buy?"

"Last I checked, there wasn't much."

They entered the kitchen, which was still redolent of serious baking. The shelves were completely bare...and the sisters were ecstatic.

"Look at this!" Bertha dumped money out of a shoebox crammed full of crumpled bills. She gathered them into a stack, licked her thumb, and began to separate the bills into stacks. "Even if we take out the cost of supplies, I think we made enough."

"Just imagine," Lydia said, "all the things the girls will be able to make!"

"What about material?" Anna asked.

Lydia's and Bertha's mouths made perfect Os. "They will need material!" they said in unison.

"We could have another bake sale next week!" Lydia said.

Rachel started to object, but Bertha interrupted.

"Think of how much fun it would be for the girls to open up a big box of beautiful fabric."

"Can it have flowers?" Anna asked wistfully.

Once again, Lydia and Bertha looked at one another—this time with narrowed eyes, as they considered. Only the Mennonites and Englisch people wore patterned clothing.

"Probably not," Bertha said. "Flowered material is not Plain."

Anna's brow wrinkled. "The children are Amish?"

"No," Bertha said. "They are just themselves."

"They could have flowers," Anna pointed out.

"Maybe a small, conservative print." Lydia held her fingers close together.

"Maybe. When we have enough from our bake sales," Bertha said, "I will call a driver and we will go shopping. Maybe my cast will be off by then."

"Oh…" Anna clapped her hands in glee. "A Yoder Toter!"

"A Yoder Toter?" Joe asked.

"It's what the Amish call the fifteen-passenger vans that local drivers use to transport Amish. They use them when they need to go farther than the ten or so miles a horse can take them," Rachel explained. "Since so many Amish around here are named Yoder, calling those vans 'Yoder Toters' is kind of a local Amish joke."

Joe was relieved that he wouldn't have to drive Nellie for their shopping trip, but he was curious. "Isn't a fifteen-passenger van sort of overkill for three people?"

"You don't know the Amish," Rachel said. "Bertha will make a few phone calls and tomorrow there will be another dozen Amish women going along. They'll share the cost, everyone will bring snacks, and they'll have a picnic in the van and catch up on family news while they drive around. It's quite a party."

"Sounds like fun."

"It is!" Lydia exclaimed.

Rachel smiled. "Want to hear another Amish joke, Joe?"

"Sure."

"How many Amish can you pack into a Yoder Toter?"

"Beats me."

"One more." She held up a finger.

"I don't get it."

"You will when you see. The drivers charge by the mile. The Amish are frugal. They really pack those vans."

Bertha folded the money and put it into her purse. "You are not angry with us for doing this, Rachel?"

"Of course I'm not angry, but I'm worried. You three worked yourself to a frazzle yesterday and today."

"We enjoyed every minute."

"I know you did, but—"

"You cannot wrap us up in cotton and put us on a shelf," Bertha said. "I know you are trying to take care of us, but we have lived our lives by trying to be useful. When that possibility is gone, we will no longer have a reason to rise in the morning."

"But I still worry about you."

"You do not understand. Being trained as a seamstress can make the difference between life and death to a girl in Haiti. She can support herself with that skill. If one of us were to die while mixing enough pie dough to make that happen—what does it matter?"

"It matters to me," Rachel said.

"This is not about you," Lydia said softly.

What is it, Joe wondered, *that creates such a strong work ethic in the Amish?* He saw it even in old Eli, who was still trying to care for all those dairy cows when his strapping-strong sons and grand-sons would have happily allowed him to rock on the porch all day long.

His heart went out to Rachel as she absorbed Lydia's words. He watched as she bowed her head a moment. When she looked at her aunts again, there was a look of resignation on her face.

"You're right, Lydia. It's not about me. How can I help you make this happen?"

After helping her aunts tidy the kitchen and prepare for the next baking marathon, Rachel strode out to the barn and climbed the ladder to the hayloft. Since childhood, the hayloft had been her spot to contemplate, pray, or have a good cry. The huge, high window beckoned with a view of the valley that always inspired her. She sat down and scooted to the edge of the window, allowing her legs to dangle. Her heart was heavy, and she needed to unburden herself to Someone who would understand.

"Father," she said aloud, "my aunts are driving me crazy. They act like I'm punishing them by trying to get them to slow down." She stopped and contemplated her life. "My back still aches from the beating in Cleveland. Bertha allowed Joe to become a permanent resident—over my strong objections."

She hesitated. "And while we're talking, Father, what is it with Joe, anyway? I don't even know who he really is, and yet I feel myself drawn to him. There is something about the way he talks and moves and cares for his child that keeps me awake at night, replaying it in my mind."

She kicked her foot against the barn with her face lifted toward the sky in prayer. "I'm a mess, Father. And I'm really, really tired of being the responsible one around here."

It had been too long since she'd prayed like this. It felt as though a weight rolled off her shoulders as she finished. She scooted backward and lay on the scattered hay of the loft, watching a wisp of a cloud drift over the brilliantly colored fall trees. It was so quiet up in the hayloft that she was startled when she heard voices below.

"Can we play now, Daddy?" Bobby asked, holding up a plastic baseball set. He had chosen it for himself with the small "salary" Joe had given him for being such a good helper.

The rest of Joe's first pay from the sisters had gone into groceries and getting his truck fixed. He had given the mechanic a little extra to drive it to his house. With Rachel knowing he didn't have a driver's license, he wasn't about to risk being caught behind the wheel.

Still, it felt good having the truck parked out front in case of an emergency. The horror of the night that Bobby had gone into a febrile convulsion lingered. He had never felt so helpless in his life.

He hadn't yet figured out what to do about that missing driver's license. How could he replace it without revealing his identity to the local DMV people?

"Come on, Daddy, pleeease?"

Bobby was acting like any other impatient four-year-old these days. He hadn't sucked his thumb for over a week now. He was sleeping in his own room. There had been no potty accidents.

"Pretty, pretty, pretty please?"

Joe was delighted to see the healthy changes in his son. With Bertha's permission, he had even allowed the white kitten a one-night sleepover in the daadi haus. So far, so good. In another week he would probably allow the kitten to move in with them. With the next paycheck, he could afford cat food.

"You got it, buddy." He scooped up the little boy in his arms and ran into the pasture behind the barn, Bobby giggling all the way.

"Okay." He set his son down with the barn as the backstop and placed the plastic bat in the boy's hands. "Hold it like this."

"Like this?" Bobby let the bat sag.

"Close." He positioned the bat for Bobby again. "Here. Like this. Now stand right there, and I'll throw the ball to you. When it comes, you hit it. Okay?"

"'kay."

Joe threw, and Bobby swatted at the ball and missed. He threw again; Bobby missed again. Joe watched his son's lower lip start to quiver.

"It's hard the first few times, buddy." He tossed it as slow and as

164

straight as he could. Bobby missed again. "You have to keep trying. Nobody gets it the first time."

"Not even you?"

"Not even me. It took me a long, long time to hit the ball the first time." That wasn't entirely the truth, but he didn't want his little boy to get discouraged.

"'kay, then." Bobby took another stance, swung, and missed again. He threw the bat down, dropped to the ground, and folded his arms across his chest. "I quit!"

"You don't want to do that, son. Here, let me—"

"Hi."

It was Rachel, perched above them in the upper window of the barn. His heart leaped at the sight of her.

"You look like a kid playing hooky." He deliberately kept his eyes focused on Bobby. "Don't you have to work?"

"Not this afternoon, but I should be leaving soon. There's a baseball game I'm supposed to be at in a couple of hours."

"Baseball? In the fall?"

"It's something Ed cooked up. He's talked some of us over at the police station, as well as some of the guys at the fire department, into playing against Sugarcreek's Garaway High School baseball team. It's kind of a community-relations thing. He thinks it'll maybe create some bonds with the kids, make them realize we're regular people and not just here to arrest them when they drive too fast."

"My daddy's the best baseball player in the *world*," Bobby said. He had been distracted from his impending tantrum by the spectacle of Rachel appearing above his head.

"You don't say." She chuckled at the little boy's boast. "Do you play, Joe?"

"A little." He shrugged. "It's been awhile."

"I found out this morning that we're short a player. It would help if you could step in."

"I promised to play with Bobby."

Bobby kicked his bat. "I don't want to play ball. I don't like it." A thought seemed to strike him. "Will there be hot dogs at the ball game?"

"Absolutely," she said. "If you can talk your daddy into playing, I'll buy you all the hot dogs you want."

"Yay!" Bobby danced in place. "Hot dogs, hot dogs, hot dogs," he sang as he galloped off across the field.

"I'm coming down." Rachel grabbed a rope tied to the gabled end of the barn and swung herself to the ground.

"Neat trick," Joe said. "No Tarzan yell?"

"Not today. When I was ten, however, you would have been impressed." She dusted her hands off on her jeans and picked up the toys Bobby had abandoned. "Maybe if he sees you on the baseball field, he'll change his mind about liking the game."

"I doubt it."

"It doesn't matter if you aren't all that good. I'm sure the high school team will thoroughly enjoy beating us 'old guys.' I'd consider it a personal favor."

Joe considered. It might be wise to do a favor for Rachel. Ever since she had helped him clean the daadi haus, she had seemed to soften toward him. Joe flexed his shoulder. It was feeling a little stronger. He should be able to throw a ball around. Of course, he would have to dumb down his game. A lot.

"Sure." He took the ball and bat out of Rachel's hand. "I'll help you out."

Rachel introduced Joe to the rest of the team, several of whom voiced gratitude that he could fill in.

Bobby tugged at her hand while Joe chatted with the men on her team. "Can I have my hot dog now?"

"Absolutely." Although she would have preferred to stay and see how Joe got along with the other players, she bought Bobby his coveted hot dog, a soft drink, and some cotton candy, for good measure.

Then she sat him down beside Carol, a wife of one of the firemen who had a child near his age. They watched as Carol's son shared a toy car with his new playmate. The two children immediately started creating tiny roads together in the graveled dirt.

"Who is this little guy?" Carol said.

"Bobby. His daddy is helping us out today."

"I'll keep an eye on him for you."

"I'd appreciate it," Rachel said. "If he gets upset, let me know."

"You bet."

The men were laughing now. Apparently Joe had told a good joke. She hated that she had missed it. She was impressed that Joe had already been accepted by men she respected.

"Bobby's fine," she told him as she walked up to the group. "He's playing with a new friend. I bought some cotton candy, but I'm afraid it's going to get a little dusty before it's consumed."

"A little dirt never hurt anybody." Joe took an awkward practice swing with a bat. "I'm afraid it's been awhile since I played."

"That's okay," Rachel said. "Just do your best."

She left Joe to warm up while she approached their coach, Sam, who was a dispatcher for the fire department. Sam had once made it as far as a Cincinnati Reds farm team.

"Where did you find the new guy?" he asked.

"He works for my aunts."

"Can he play?"

"I have no idea, but he was available."

Sam watched Joe fumble a catch. "We'll put him in right field, where he can do the least damage."

"That would be my call too."

"What part of the infield do you want?"

"Is second base okay? I'll try to cover for Joe."

"You got it." He made a mark on a clipboard. "It's going to be tough giving these boys a respectable game. I don't know about you, but I could have used a little more time to get ready for this."

"Yeah, but we'll make them sweat a little."

"What I wouldn't give to be eighteen again."

"Not me," Rachel said. "It was tough enough going through that age once."

Sam laughed. "You weren't a guy."

CHAPTER 14

The cop/fireman team won the coin toss and took the bat first. The high-school pitcher, a boy with red hair who looked a little like Opie from the *Andy Griffith Show*, had a great curve ball and struck out the first two team members.

"You're up next, Matthews," Sam called.

Joe grabbed the bat he had liked the least, toed up to the plate, and purposely swung wild on the first two pitches.

"That's okay," Rachel called. "You can do it, Joe. Just take your time."

He glanced back at the dugout, where Rachel was trying to encourage him.

He didn't want to embarrass her for inviting him to play, so he clipped the third pitch hard enough to make the ball wobble forward a few feet. The trick was to play just well enough not to disappoint but to hold back so that no one would guess his true skill level.

While the Opie kid scooped up the grounder, Joe's toe touched base. A split second later, the ball hit the glove of the first baseman.

Rachel was up next. She connected with a line shot that took one bounce and hit the fence in right center. With Joe running ahead of her, she managed to pass third and tag back before the schoolboys threw it. In the meantime, Joe had slid into home. He gave her a thumbs-up as he brushed himself off.

"Beginner's luck," he called, pointing to himself.

The next batter struck out, causing the cop/fireman team to take the field.

"You're playing right-center field," she said as she handed Joe a borrowed glove. "There's only one left-hander on the boys' team. When he's up to bat, move closer to the line."

"Got it," Joe said.

It felt good being on a ball diamond again, even though he couldn't allow himself the pleasure of playing well. Actually, it felt good *because* there was no pressure to play well. At least not the kind of pressure he'd experienced in past years.

He checked to see how Bobby was doing. His son was happily playing in the dirt with another little boy with a vigilant mother watching over them.

No reporters. No news cameras. Just a small-town baseball game. The crisp fall weather was invigorating. The sound of the bat smacking into leather was almost hypnotic. Even the familiar smell of the dust on the baseball field gave him a sort of autumn high.

The teams were neck and neck. As the game continued, he could tell that Rachel's team was doing better than she had expected, and she was getting excited over the chances of winning.

Her team was up one run going into the top of the last inning when the cop/fireman team took the field, hoping to hold the boys and make that last turn at bat unnecessary.

"Watch out, Joe," Rachel called. "Keep an eye on that lefty I told you about."

He saw her backing up, playing her position deep, hoping to

cover anything in short right field and handle second base too. He smiled inwardly, wondering what she would think if she knew for whom she was trying to cover.

He had allowed himself the pleasure of stopping a couple of grounders that had gone through the infield during the game, but overall he had deliberately played with such mediocrity that he knew she had little confidence in his ability to field a ball.

The first batter took a walk down to first. The second batter hit a pop foul behind third base. The third baseman made a great catch but couldn't keep the runner from getting to second. The third batter laid a bunt down the third baseline.

While trying to field the bunt, the catcher accidentally kicked the ball. The batter ended up on first and the runner slid safely to third. One out, one man on third, and one man on first. The top of the batting order was up.

The lead-off hitter knocked some dust off his cleats and stepped into the batter's box. It was "Lefty," the hitter Rachel had warned him about. If the boy hit it to Joe and Joe missed the catch, the boys' team would tie it up and be in an excellent position to win the game.

"Heads up, Joe!" Rachel shouted, backing up farther.

Lefty whiffed the first pitch, took the second, tipped the third, and then slammed into the fourth pitch, drilling it toward the right-field line.

Joe got the same rising feeling of excitement in his stomach that he always did when he saw a well-hit ball flying toward the fence. That left-handed kid could hit!

The small-town crowd rose as one to their feet. Rachel started running, but she was too far away to make it. There wasn't anything anyone on the field could do about that clean extra-bases hit—except Joe.

His eyes lingered on the ball as it arced its way toward him, high, high against the blue autumn sky. It was apparent to all who watched that the ball was going to sail right over the fence.

The sight of that white ball was mesmerizing. Not once did it occur to him to let it go. Years of training and instinct came into play. Before he could check himself, Joe had a lock on the ball and was moving toward the section of the fence where the ball would go out. Without conscious thought, his legs coiled beneath him and he leaped high into the air, using every inch of his superior height and catching the ball over his shoulder right at the fence.

Lefty was out, but out of the corner of his eye, Joe saw the runner on third tagging up and heading for home.

"Throw it," the crowd roared. "Throw home."

⸺

She knew it was futile. Even though Joe had somehow made an ESPN-level catch, he was still at the fence, and there was no way he could keep the runner from sliding into home. No one on the team had that kind of arm—not even Sam.

She checked behind her. Ed, who was acting as the catcher, hovered hopefully over home plate. Then she glanced back at Joe. Her jaw dropped when she saw Joe launch a low, sizzling rocket straight toward home plate. She involuntarily ducked as the ball hissed past her head.

Ed squatted, held his catcher's glove directly in front of his chest, and was nearly knocked backward off his feet from the impact of the ball. Dust flew off his mitt, but he made the tag.

"Out!" the umpire called.

There was total silence on the field. Rachel was not the only one with her mouth hanging open.

Stunned, Ed stared down in disbelief at the ball embedded in his catcher's glove. Rachel and the rest of the team began trotting in from the field.

Sam nudged her with his elbow as she walked by. "I thought you said the man wasn't all that good."

"I didn't think he was."

Joe handed Rachel the baseball glove she had lent him. He seemed in a hurry to leave. "Thanks for letting me play," he said.

"How—how did you…" Her shock was so great, she couldn't find the words to finish her sentence.

"It was a fluke," Joe answered. "Sheer luck." He seemed distracted. "Where's Bobby? I lost track of him during that last play."

She pointed toward Carol, who was talking to some of the other mothers. "Over there."

"Right." Joe nodded. "I'm going to grab him and head on back to the farm. I have some grout work to do on the tile in the bathroom."

She watched him collect his son near a cooler of juice boxes Carol had brought to the game. She saw him thank Carol for watching his boy, and then his tall, lean body started walking home with Bobby seated firmly on his broad shoulders.

She shook her head in disbelief. Baseball players *lived* to make a throw like that. If it had been any of the rest of them who had made the play, the whole team would be going out to celebrate right now.

Her aunts' handyman, from deep right field, had just thrown a baseball on an arrow-straight line over 335 feet.

No one could do that. No one except a few elite pro baseball players had *ever* done that. Regardless of what Joe said, luck had nothing to do with it.

Who *was* this man?

"Wow." Ed came up beside her. "Joe can play on our team anytime he wants."

"I agree."

"You up for pizza? I'm buying for the team."

Joe was a speck in the distance by now, but he still held her complete attention.

"Thanks, but I need to get back to the office. I have some work to do."

She desperately wanted to access a computer. She was certain there was a story behind that magnificent throw—and she couldn't wait to find out what it was.

CHAPTER 15

J oe ran a bath for Bobby. The little boy was filthy from the combination of blue cotton candy and gravel dust. It was obvious he'd had a marvelous time. Joe sat his son in the bathtub and tenderly rubbed baby shampoo into his curly hair.

"You play ball good, Daddy."

"Thanks, buddy."

"Can we play together tomorrow? I'll try harder."

"If you want to."

Joe was being gentle with his son, but he was furious at himself. What had he been *thinking*, making a throw like that?

He knew exactly what he'd been thinking, and it disgusted him. There had been that moment when he saw Rachel backing up to cover for him. He knew what she was thinking—that he couldn't possibly make the catch...or the throw—and his stupid male pride had gotten the better of him, overridden his months of carefully orchestrated anonymity, and allowed his training and skill to take over.

It was, he conceded, an understandable emotion. He'd been homeless, penniless, and humiliated in front of her. She'd treated him like a criminal when he wasn't. For one split second, the desire to be himself in front of her—his *real* self, the athlete who had brought fans to their feet in awe—had been overwhelming.

He had regretted his decision the moment his fingers released the ball.

He should never have played at all. *How* could he have fooled himself into thinking that he could play badly, when playing well had been his life's breath for so long?

It had been heady, that sensation of being on a ball field again. The feel of a baseball glove against the palm of his hand and the sound of a bat cracking against a leather ball had felt like coming home. There had been the laughter, the camaraderie with other players, and then that soaring, addictive surge of power as he'd thrown a ball straighter, faster, and farther than anyone else in the world.

It had taken the gasp of awe from the watching crowd to bring him back to his senses.

Sick at heart, he muttered a curse beneath his breath.

"That's a bad word, Daddy." Bobby's eyes were wide with shock.

Joe was so ashamed, he felt like crawling into the closet and closing the door. "I'm so sorry, son. I didn't mean to say that word. I'll never say it again. Ever."

Bobby's shocked expression melted into forgiveness. He patted his father's forearm as Joe knelt on the bathroom floor beside the tub. "It's okay, Daddy. You made a mistake. You don't get mad at me when I make mistakes."

"You don't make the kind of mistakes that your daddy does."

"That's okay. You're bigger than me."

Joe was humbled by his child's instant forgiveness of his "mistake." Such a *huge* mistake—cursing in front of his son. This whole day, from the moment Rachel had shown up at the barn, had been one big mistake.

Why hadn't he been able to resist the desire to impress her this afternoon?

Unfortunately, he knew the answer to that question. Part of him wanted to run the opposite direction whenever Rachel came near him. The other part of him wanted to grab hold of her and never let go.

The problem was, he liked everything about the woman—the way she moved with such grace and purpose. The way she looked the world, and him, straight in the eye. She was the kind of person who would fight to protect even strangers who needed her help. He knew she would fight even harder for the people she loved.

Yes, he'd willingly trust Rachel with his life. The problem was, he wasn't certain he could trust her with his secrets. Coming face-to-face with someone famous did weird things to people and made them act strange. He had experienced that awkwardness over and over when people discovered who he was. He didn't want it to happen with Rachel. He couldn't bear to think of it happening with Rachel.

Now he just hoped that his momentary lapse on the baseball field hadn't destroyed the fragile normality of the life he had been beginning to live with his son.

Rachel stared at her home computer screen.

Finally, she knew exactly who Joe was.

She had tried to convince herself that he was nothing more than a charming, down-on-his-luck loser, but her gut had kept telling her there was more to the man—and her gut had been right.

It all fit. The ever-so-slightly changed last name. The fabulous throw. A deceased wife whose private, non-working name was Grace.

What didn't fit was the beard, the hair, the broken-down truck, the homelessness, the worn clothes, and the poverty.

Days earlier, she and Kim had searched the databases for some sort of criminal who would fit Joe's profile. Not once had she considered the possibility that he might be the exact opposite.

The name *Mattias* glared out at her now as though in neon lights. People frequently chose a form of their real name as an alias when they were trying to hide. Joe had done the same. His real name was Micah Joel Mattias—easily transformed into the nondescript and common *Joe Matthews*.

She already knew the story. Practically everyone in the country who followed baseball knew the story. Joe had started his athletic career in an unusual way. He had been studying for the ministry, paying his way through a midsized Bible college with a baseball scholarship. Then, during his junior year, he had taken his college team to an NAIA national championship. At that point, he had been discovered by a talent scout who was very impressed with this young man who could pitch *and* catch.

They'd tagged him for one of their farm teams and watched his lightning-like progress, and during one memorable game, he was thrown into the spotlight when a case of food poisoning and a broken ankle took out two major players in close succession. Joe was called up at the last minute to cover one of the open spots.

The rookie's coolness under pressure caught the world's attention. He was dubbed "Miracle Micah" as he brought home a victory by pitching a no-hitter against some of the best players in the world.

His childhood as a missionary's son only added to the mystique. The team's public relations firm churned out stories of an impoverished childhood in Africa, where they maintained that

Joe had developed his throwing arm by lobbing stones at small animals for food for his family's table. His good looks, skill with a baseball, genial personality, and unusual background made him an overnight media darling.

Offers for product sponsorships came rolling in, and Micah never looked back. As his fame, salary, and ego grew, he embraced the parties and the high-rolling lifestyle, eventually marrying Grace Plonkett, aka May Hunter—a former Miss Texas runner-up and a girl from a baked-earth trailer park in western Texas who had gambled on a perfect face and figure and won.

The resemblance between the young blond bombshell and Marilyn Monroe was too tantalizing for the press to ignore, especially after she married the world-famous baseball player. The press, playing on the relationship between Marilyn and Joe DiMaggio, dubbed them "The New DiMaggios." For a while after their wedding, they had been the most photographed couple in the world.

A baby boy was born. Grace had a difficult delivery, and while she was recuperating, her career tanked. There were thousands of younger actresses hungry for the few parts Grace would have gotten had it not been for her extended maternity leave. Joe was frequently absent from home as he traveled with the team.

Joe sustained a shoulder injury, which had kept him out of play last season. There were rumors that the team's owner was considering trading him. He had been playing pro ball for ten years—a long run for a baseball player. At thirty-two, he was considered the old man of the team.

Then the tragedy in their home happened.

Rachel felt sick to her stomach, knowing what came next. Joe had discovered Grace that fateful night and then desperately searched the house for his son.

With sworn alibis from his teammates, the cops did not list Joe as a suspect, but the press licked their lips and took him to court in their own way—hounding him every step of the way while he tried to assist the police in their search to find his wife's killer.

Every detail of the family's life was examined in the tabloids—from the cost of their house to their favorite restaurants to the number of shoes Grace owned. Even the measurements of the poor woman's body were touted in the tabloids, having been obtained from her Miss Texas competition resume.

Snippets of videos of Grace's vocal solo, which she had performed in the Miss Texas pageant, were played and replayed on TV, as though her singing ability could help the police solve the case. It had been a media-feeding frenzy.

From what Rachel gathered, when Joe couldn't take any more, he had walked away, and no one had known where he went. The various tabloids had tried for months to find him. His friends and his team had been interrogated and offered large sums for information about his whereabouts, but no one seemed to have any idea where he and Bobby had gone.

That is—until his truck broke down in Sugarcreek and he ended up sleeping on her aunts' couch.

Rachel clicked off the computer, shoved her feet into her tennis shoes, and walked the two blocks to the library, where she dug through stacks of *People* magazine. Six months ago, Joe's and Grace's pictures had been on the covers for five solid weeks.

She sat at a desk and leafed through the pages as their lives unfolded before her. The press had a lot to work with. Grace was a true beauty, with her dazzling smile, perfect body, and mane of platinum hair. Rumors were that the color was natural. Having seen Bobby's light-colored curls, she believed it.

As Rachel flipped through the various issues, she saw a picture that made her fists clench. It was of Joe fighting through a sea of reporters with Bobby in his arms. The little boy's face was buried in Joe's shoulder. The article said that Joe, determined to keep his son's face out of the limelight, had thrown a punch at one of the more aggressive photographers.

Crank calls became an issue at the Mattias house. A few were threatening. Some, which the cops tried to follow up on, called to confess to the murder and then spun sick fantasies about how they had done it.

The last magazine, the one before Joe's family drama drifted onto the back pages, said that Joe and Bobby had disappeared.

And that is where it all ended, except for several supposed "sightings" of Joe and his son. As far as the media was concerned, "Miracle Micah" had dropped off the face of the earth. But they were ready to pounce the moment anyone gave them a good tip.

She dropped her head to her hands in shame, remembering some of the things she had said to the man when he first arrived. That's all Joe had needed—a small-town cop trying to intimidate him into leaving town. So much for those instincts about which she had been so confident.

If only he had confided in her.

Would *she* have confided in him if their positions had been reversed?

Probably not.

Rachel gathered up the stack of magazines and approached the librarian.

"Can I check these out?" She laid them on the counter. The librarian, a woman for whom Rachel had once recovered some stolen property, glanced at the dates.

"Why don't you just take them?" she said. "They're going to end up in next month's book sale anyway. We don't have room to keep everything."

"I appreciate that. Thanks." Rachel left, hoping the librarian hadn't noticed that each copy had pictures of a certain famous athlete emblazoned on the front page. As far as Rachel was concerned, she would help keep Joe's identity a secret forever. *No one* deserved to experience what he had been through.

But first she owed him an apology.

Joe put the final dish in the drainer to dry. The macaroni and cheese Bobby had requested as a bedtime snack hadn't turned out half bad.

Yeah, Mr. Big Shot Ballplayer, his mind taunted. *So you managed to boil water and throw in some pasta, did you? You couldn't manage not to show off at the ballpark today. What's the matter? Didn't you already have enough attention in your life? You needed more?*

Still sick at heart, he dried his hands on one of the yellow dish towels Lydia had given him and then draped it over the faucet to dry—like he'd seen his mother do hundreds of times.

He missed her. She had been a rock of common sense and spiritual strength. He still grieved the fact that she had not lived to see her grandson. She would have loved Bobby, and he would have loved her.

Nothing had been the same since her death. She had been the glue that held everyone together, even when they were on separate sides of the ocean. If she had been alive, perhaps his father wouldn't have disowned him.

He glanced at Bobby, playing with a little truck at his feet. How could a loving father disown his own flesh and blood? Was there anything Bobby could ever do that would make him stop loving him?

Of course not.

But *had* his father stopped loving him? He honestly didn't know.

He shook his head in exasperation. Fathers all over the world would have killed to boast of having a pro baseball player for a son.

But not Dr. Robert Mattias.

He had to pick the one dad in the world who would be disappointed in him. Didn't his father realize that he had never been cut out to be a minister, let alone a missionary? Couldn't his dad understand that?

The next question was: had he stopped loving his father?

No.

He had been furious at him. He had been hurt by him. But ultimately, he knew he still loved the man who had held him in his arms and told him that God had made the moon and the stars just for him.

If his mother were still alive, she would have fixed things. He and his father would have both complained about how unreasonable the other was being, and while they were blowing off steam, she would have somehow fixed it.

"Can I watch the video now, Daddy?"

"Sure, buddy. You've got half an hour before bedtime."

He had found a small battery-operated DVD player at a garage sale on the edge of town today, along with two barely used Veggie-Tales DVDs. Quite a treasure. Oddly enough, he had enjoyed making that purchase more than he had enjoyed the last two homes he and Grace had bought.

He had no more than gotten his son set up in the living room and entranced with the adventures of Larry Boy, when he heard someone pull into the driveway.

His stomach tightened with worry as he glanced out the window. Rachel's squad car. She wasn't coming to visit her aunts tonight. She was headed straight for his house.

As she strode across the yard, he couldn't help but admire the way she walked—shoulders back, head straight, long, purposeful strides. Rachel took the straightest route to wherever she wanted to go—whether from her car to his front door or telling him she didn't trust him as far as she could throw him.

She was frowning as she mounted his steps. He hoped she hadn't come over to interrogate him about his actions at the ball game. He was so weary tonight of carrying his load of secrets that he was afraid he might just break down and tell her everything.

CHAPTER 16

Rachel had thought she would be able to do this with no emotion, but she was wrong. Joe had recently showered, and his wet hair was combed straight back. His blue work shirt hung open, and his chest and his feet were bare. He smelled good, and he looked good.

But he was no longer Joe Matthews, a man with whom she had a tentative, if very guarded, friendship. He was "Miracle Micah," someone who was known and admired around the world.

It made relating to him difficult. She had never known anyone famous.

How cramped this cottage must feel to him after the mansion he and Grace had shared, how measly the salary her aunts were paying him compared to what he had earned playing ball. And that ball game today—how silly it must have felt to play with such amateurs.

But he hadn't acted like any of it was beneath him. He had acted as though he was…grateful.

What a complicated man.

"Come in, Rachel," he said as he opened the door. "What can I do for you?"

She swallowed hard and stepped into his living room. Bobby was sitting on the floor, enraptured by a video that involved a dancing pickle.

"Can we talk privately?" she asked.

"Sure." He turned to Bobby. "Rachel and I are going to my study to talk, son. I'll leave the door open. Will you be okay?"

The little boy nodded without taking his eyes off the DVD screen.

"I think Bobby has a serious VeggieTales deficiency," Joe said as he ushered her toward her grandfather's old study.

Rachel said nothing. It wasn't Bobby she was concerned about right now.

The first thing that she noticed when she entered the room was that the musty smell she always associated with it had disappeared.

"What did you do?" she asked, playing for time to get her nerves under control. "This room doesn't smell like mildew anymore."

"Oh." Joe looked at the wall filled with books. "I wiped down all the book covers with alcohol."

"That must have been a job."

"Not so bad," Joe said. "Actually, it was a pleasure. I used to help my dad do that when I was a kid. He had a lot of books too."

There it was again. Joe and his gratitude. How could cleaning old books possibly be a pleasure for someone like him?

She decided it was time to stop beating around the bush. She had to face this thing and deal with it. She grabbed a straight-backed chair, turned it around, straddled it, and crossed her arms across the top slat as she faced him.

"That was some play you made today."

"Yeah, well." He shrugged it off.

186

"Have a seat, Joe. I've got a few things I need to say."

Joe reluctantly sat down behind the desk. "You sound serious, Rachel. Is this the place where you tell me it's time to get the heck out of Dodge?"

His tone was lighthearted, but his eyes showed real concern.

"No." Rachel's voice was soft. "I'm not going to ask you to leave —but Lord help us all if you stay."

"What are you saying?"

"I know who you are, I know why you're here, and I came to apologize for the way I've treated you."

She could almost see the shutters come down over his eyes. "What do you mean?" His voice was low and intense.

"Micah Joel Mattias. Age 32. Older son of Dr. Robert Mattias, a renowned missionary and author," she recited. "Graduated from a South African boarding school. Fluent in three different African dialects as well as in French and English. Left Africa to attend a Christian university in the States with the intent of obtaining a degree in Bible. The plan was for you to return and complete your father's dream of a father/son evangelism team."

She cocked an eyebrow. "How am I doing so far?"

He folded his arms across his chest. "I'm listening."

"Your mother, now deceased, once played on a highly ranked women's softball team. Because of the training she gave you, along with a good coach at the boarding school, combined with your uncanny natural ability, you won a baseball scholarship to college. During your junior year, your expertise was discovered by a scout, and you dropped out and signed with the Dodgers."

She paused again. "Do I have it correct so far?"

"Yes." He sighed. "Go on."

"Married to Grace Plonkett aka May Hunter. One child, Robert Douglas Mattias, born five years later."

"I don't want my son to hear this." Joe stood, walked over to the door, and closed it. His hand lingered on the knob, as though he wished he could walk away from this conversation. "What was it that gave me away?"

"No amateur can make a throw like that."

He shook his head. "I should never have agreed to play."

"I'm glad you did. Otherwise I might never have known."

Their eyes met and held. She saw a question in his that she answered. "You can trust me." She stood up. "I've got your back on this, Joe. I'll tell no one."

"If *anyone* had to know, I'm so glad it was you." He held his arms out to her.

It was only a hug. Just a hug between friends. She knew he didn't mean anything by it, but she wasn't prepared for the flood of emotions that being held by him triggered. She lifted her face to his. He stared down at her, his eyes dark and intense. His head began to descend, slowly. She could almost taste the kiss she thought was coming. It was a surprise to discover how much she hungered for it....

"Daddy." Bobby opened the door and peeked around it.

Joe abruptly pulled away and put his hands into his pockets. "What is it, buddy?"

"Can I watch the other video now?"

"Absolutely, son." Joe cleared his throat. "I'll be right back, Rachel."

She was grateful that Joe had to leave the room. By the time he returned, she had managed to pull herself together. The moment for a kiss was gone. She didn't know whether to be disappointed or relieved.

"All I know is what I've read," she said as she leaned against the desk. "What really happened that night?"

Joe hesitated, as though evaluating her mood. The moment of

intimacy between them seemed to have dissipated. It was, she decided, just as well.

"We don't know for sure. All we know is that someone locked Bobby in his room while he was asleep, and then—well, you know what happened then. The strangest thing was that whoever killed Grace left snacks and drinks for him."

"They left snacks? That's odd."

"The water and juice bottles had the seals already broken, and the lids had been loosened so Bobby could open them by himself. When I found my son, he was terrified at having been left alone, but he wasn't hurt or hungry."

Joe's eyes grew haunted. "The minutes between discovering Grace and finding my son were the longest of my life."

"Thank God he was unharmed."

Joe fell into the desk chair and thrust both hands through his hair. "I'm hoping that our disappearance will buy Bobby enough time to heal and grow up enough so that he can better deal with it. I love the fact that there's no electricity in your aunts' home. There's no TV or radio here. Frankly, I don't care if I never see a news program again."

She began to pace the room, her mind in overdrive as it worked on the puzzle of the crime. "Have there been any more recent developments?"

"As of yesterday, nothing." Joe laced his hands behind his neck. "There was this private detective I hired for a while. He's not actively working the case anymore, but he keeps an ear out for developments. I check in with him from time to time."

Rachel stopped pacing. "With so much media attention, I would think the cops would be working around the clock. I'm surprised this mystery hasn't been solved yet."

"They had little to work with. The killer left nothing behind."

"That's not possible."

"Whoever it was wore gloves, and no murder weapon was ever found. No unusual cars were noted. No visitors to our house were seen. Frankly, we lived in a neighborhood where people don't spend a lot of time watching the street. I posted a large reward before I left, but nothing of value came from it."

"Was there anything else the cops kept back?"

"Only one thing. I'd just had a new security system put in. Grace evidently disengaged it right before her death. Her finger-prints were the only ones on it. Bobby told us that somebody rang the doorbell while Grace was putting him to bed. She left him to go answer the door, and he fell asleep."

"Would she have opened the door to a stranger?"

"No. Grace was raised rough, and she wasn't stupid. She wouldn't have let someone in that she didn't know. Especially at night."

"Then it was someone she knew and trusted." Rachel pondered this information. "Did the police check that out?"

"Oh yes. When I started trying to make a list—and the cops definitely asked for one—it appeared that Grace and I knew half the people in California *and* Texas. There were hundreds of people she could have known well enough to invite in."

Rachel let that sink in. "Is there any chance that Grace might have been the one who locked Bobby in his room that night?"

"That's been discussed. One of the cops theorized that Grace might have somehow sensed danger and managed to fix it so Bobby wouldn't come wandering out. We may never know for sure."

Rachel hated to ask Joe the next question, but she was a cop, and the vagaries of the human mind held few surprises for her.

"What was your wife wearing, Joe?"

"A bathrobe."

"Anything else?"

"No." He picked up a pencil and traced circles on a notepad. "I know what you're thinking, Rachel. But Grace had a routine when she was at home, and she seldom broke it. She took a bath every night at ten o'clock. Then she would read a romance novel for half an hour before she went to bed. She told me that sleep is good for the skin, and she tried to get plenty of it. There was nothing unusual in the way she was dressed. My wife was not having an affair, if that's what you're wondering."

"Are you certain? If she intended to be entertaining someone, it would explain why Bobby was so well-provisioned."

"That's another angle the police kept hammering at. Lonely, beautiful wife, absent husband. I could tell they were determined to frame the murder as some romantic interlude gone wrong—and they probably still are."

"Can you be absolutely certain it wasn't?" Rachel asked.

"Yes, actually." Joe lifted his head. A ghost of a smile hovered on his lips. "I can."

"How?"

"She wasn't wearing any makeup."

"Pardon?" His statement made no sense to Rachel, who seldom used more than a slash of lipstick.

"Grace was a pageant queen, and she took her movie-star status quite seriously. She was a sweetheart, but she was a vain woman. She would have no more entertained a date without putting on makeup than she would have gone to the store wearing curlers in her hair."

"I see."

"That's everything I know." He drummed his fingers on the desk. "It's not much."

They sat in silence, each digesting everything that had been said.

"So," he said half-jokingly, "are you sure you don't want to call the tabloids now?"

Rachel blinked. "Why in the world would I do that?"

"Bobby and I are a hot topic. There'd be good money in a tip like that."

"I would never do anything to put you or Bobby in danger."

"I can take that as a promise to keep my secret?"

"I already gave you my word, Joe."

His voice softened. "Which, from what I've seen, is worth a lot."

"Like I said before"—she looked him square in the eyes—"I've got your back."

CHAPTER 17

Joe watched from the front door as Rachel got into her squad car and drove away. In some ways, it was a relief having Rachel know his identity. Life would be much easier without having to sidestep Rachel's suspicions. He was proud of her for not getting all weird and fawning when she discovered who he was.

On the other hand, someone else knowing his identity was a worry. Although he desperately wanted to trust her, he had no real assurance that she would not confide in someone else. It would only take one slip of the tongue.

He closed the door behind her and locked it. Unlike the Troyer sisters, he felt strongly about locking doors. Then he scooped up Bobby, who had fallen asleep in front of the DVD player. He carried him into his bedroom, tucked the covers around his sleeping child, and then wound up Abraham's old Regulator wall clock that he'd brought from the kitchen to Bobby's room. Its *ticktock* and hourly chimes seemed to soothe the child.

It was only seven o'clock. Too early to go to bed and too late to work outside. With Bobby asleep, an entire evening stretched before him—plenty of time to finally delve into Abraham's library. He was surprised how much he was longing to do so.

He went into the study, lit a lamp, and stood before the bookcase, deciding what volume to choose. A fat tome on biblical archaeology caught his eye. Archaeology had been a favorite subject of his back in college. He pulled the book off the top shelf and lost himself in uncovering the layers of Jericho.

For a few blessed minutes, his mind escaped the memories of Grace and his worries about the future. He was in ancient Jericho, hearing the trumpets blasting and the shouts of the Israelites, and experiencing the triumph of the Lord. He turned the page...and stopped. Between the pages lay a worn twenty-dollar bill.

Had someone used it as a bookmark? That seemed odd. He started to lift it out and discovered a minuscule drop of rubber cement holding it to the page. He removed the money and rubbed off the rubbery substance with his thumb. Had Abraham deliberately glued money to the page?

At that moment, he heard what sounded like a scratching noise coming from near the window. He glanced up and saw nothing there. Then he heard the noise again.

An animal? A branch?

There weren't any branches touching the windows, that he had noticed. He blew out the kerosene lamp and went over to the window hoping to see what was making the noise.

In the moonlight, he could make out the figure of someone standing near the wooden bench in the rose garden. It was a young girl, and she appeared to be pregnant.

He opened the back door and stepped outside.

She jumped, startled by his sudden appearance, and, in spite of her pregnant bulk, she quickly put the bench between them.

Her hair was long and falling into her face. Her eyes were huge, staring at him in what appeared to be near-terror.

He stood very still. "Can I help you?"

"Are—are—you Amish?" She took two steps back, putting even more distance between them. "Amish don't hit people, do they?"

She was terribly young, no more than fourteen or fifteen. He hoped she wasn't younger. She held her arms protectively around her stomach.

"The women who live in the farmhouse are Amish," he said. "I'm just the handyman, but I don't hit people either."

Her panic was evident. She cast glances around her as though preparing to flee.

Joe used his gentlest voice. "I'll help you if you'll tell me how."

She shook her head, as though dismissing the idea of help from him.

Her face was swollen and bruised. There were black and blue marks up and down one arm. He felt a slow rage building but was careful to hide it. Anger of any kind, even anger on her behalf, would send this girl running off into the night—possibly back to whoever had done this to her.

He remembered a young dog that had come into his yard once, abused and half-starved. It had craved help but had kept its distance. It had taken several hours before the dog trusted him enough to let him pet it. He had won that trust by slow movements, a low voice, and food. This girl's actions reminded him of that abandoned dog.

"Are you hungry?" he asked.

Her eyes darted to the window and then back to him. She nodded, slowly.

"Why don't you sit on the bench. I'll fix you a sandwich and"— his mind searched his refrigerator—"some milk. Maybe you'd like some cookies?"

She stared at him, longing and fear warring in her eyes.

195

"I won't come near you," he promised. "I'll just bring it out and set it down."

She hesitated but nodded again.

He went back into the house and rushed to the refrigerator, afraid the girl would disappear while he was inside.

He considered running next door to the aunts but was afraid the girl would bolt at that too. Besides, they retired early. He was also reluctant to bring such pain into the aunts' lives.

Rachel could handle the situation, though—and well.

He checked his cell phone. The battery was low, but there was enough to make a phone call or two. He made a mental note to start the truck and recharge his phone with the truck battery before the night was over.

He dialed Rachel's number, holding the phone between his ear and his shoulder while he slapped Trail bologna on bread and poured a glass of milk.

"Come on, Rachel, pick up. I need you," he muttered.

"Hello?"

The sound of her voice made him close his eyes in relief. "I have a pregnant, abused girl over here behind the daadi haus. She's scared to death, and I think she might run if I get near her. Could you come over? She might trust a woman more. I hate to involve your aunts in this unless I have to."

"Where did she come from?"

"I don't know, but she said she had heard that the Amish don't hit people."

"I wish that were always true," Rachel mused. "I'll be right there."

"Thanks." Joe didn't have a tray in his kitchen, but he did have a wooden cutting board. He put the girl's sandwich on it and added a handful of chips along with some of Lydia's sugar cookies and a large glass of milk.

He balanced the cutting board against his chest as he opened the back door and eased out into the garden. The girl was still there. She had seated herself on the bench but half rose as he approached her.

He stopped. "If you want to move away while I lay this on the bench, I'll understand."

She scooted to the very end of the bench, as far away from him as she could get without falling off.

He set the food down and stepped back while she fell upon it. She gobbled the sandwich, devouring it in four bites. He eased down onto the far side of the bench as the girl lifted the glass of milk and drained it without taking a breath.

"My name is Joe," he said.

The girl crunched a potato chip and seemed to think that over.

He tried again. "What's your name?"

She took a bite out of a sugar cookie. He knew she was debating whether to tell him anything. He waited in silence, letting her sort it out.

"Stephanie." She brushed a wisp of hair out of her eyes. "Those are really good cookies."

"I think so too. Stephanie is a pretty name."

She peeked through her long bangs at him. "I was named after my papaw."

"Where *is* your papaw, honey?"

At that the girl began to cry. She cried like the child she was, with total abandon.

He was afraid to touch her, to comfort her. And yet it seemed calloused not to. It was a relief to hear Rachel's car pulling into the driveway.

The girl's head lifted at the sound, like a little animal preparing to run. With all his heart, he hoped Rachel wasn't in uniform. He didn't think she would be, but he wasn't sure. She hadn't mentioned if she'd be working tonight. He also hoped she hadn't driven her squad car. He felt that any sign of authority would terrify this girl.

"Don't be afraid," he said. "I called a friend of mine to help you. She's very kind."

The girl's eyes were huge as she waited for Rachel to appear—but she didn't bolt.

"Thank You, Jesus," Joe whispered when he saw Rachel. She wore old, ripped jeans and a soft-looking lavender sweater. Her hair was down, and she wore sneakers. She looked as though she could be anyone's big sister.

"Hi, sweetheart," she said to the girl. "My name is Rachel. Looks like you could use a friend."

It was exactly the right thing to say. Stephanie immediately fell into Rachel's arms. Rachel rocked her and smoothed the girl's hair with her hand.

"It's okay," she crooned. "It's going to be okay."

"He threw me out of the car," the girl said. "Like I was garbage. He said he loved me. He said he would take care of me. He had a place over in Pennsylvania where we could be happy."

"Who did this to you, sweetie?"

"Last night?" The girl answered her with what sounded like a series of questions. "We got into an argument? And he hit me and then he stopped the car and made me get out? Then he drove off…."

She buried her head in Rachel's shoulder, tears streaming down her face.

"We need to get you to a hospital," Rachel said.

"No! I'm fine." She had cried so hard that she began to gag. She doubled over, put both hands on her knees, and retched.

"Shh, it's all right." Rachel patted her back. Her eyes locked onto Joe's. Pity and concern for this girl formed a palpable bridge between them.

"Where's your folks, honey?" she asked when Stephanie had calmed down.

"I—I don't have any."

Once again a telepathic look passed between Rachel and Joe. Maybe the girl was lying. Maybe she was telling the truth. The one thing both of them were certain of was that she was so upset, she was on the verge of going into a complete meltdown.

Rachel looked into her eyes. "I'll tell you what," she said. "I have a really good idea. Why don't you come home with me? I was just getting ready to watch a movie and was wishing I had someone to watch it with. We'll make some popcorn, you can take a bubble bath, I'll let you sleep in my guest bedroom, and we'll sort all this out in the morning after you've rested. Okay?"

"A movie?" There was longing in the girl's voice.

"I probably have a couple of Snickers in the fridge too. Looks to me like you could use some chocolate. I've heard that chocolate makes happy babies. When are you due, honey?"

The girl shyly laid a hand on her protruding stomach. "I don't know. I haven't seen a doctor."

Another look of concern passed between Rachel and Joe. She turned her attention back to the girl.

"Okay, then. Joe, do you have a shirt or something she could wear to sleep in? I don't think any of my tops will fit her."

"Absolutely." Grateful for an errand, he ran into the cottage and grabbed one of his extra-large T-shirts. As petite as the girl was, he thought his shirt would envelope her—even pregnant. He came back out as Rachel was tucking the girl into her Mustang.

"Here." He handed the shirt to Stephanie through the window.

"Thanks." She struggled to buckle the seat belt around her stomach.

"You're welcome." He reached in and held the belt strap out away from her until she could fasten it. "I'm glad you came to my house for help."

"Me too." She gave him a shy smile.

He ducked his head lower so he could see Rachel. "I'll call you later."

She glanced up at him with her hand on the ignition key. "I'd appreciate that."

As he watched the silver blue Mustang drive away, he thought about how well it matched its owner. Classic, quick, sleek, unique, dependable. And although he would never have believed it the first time he met her, he was enormously grateful to have Rachel in his life.

CHAPTER 18

Stephanie nibbled on a hangnail and stared out the car window as they drove through Sugarcreek. Rachel could see that the bruises on the girl's face and arms were fresh. By tomorrow they would be even deeper colors. She would take pictures in the morning to use against the creep who had beaten her.

If they could find him.

"Does your boyfriend have a name?" she asked.

Stephanie looked up from her hangnail and blinked.

"Uh-huh. Mack."

"Mack who?"

"I don't know."

"You don't know your boyfriend's last name?"

"He said it wasn't important."

Rachel's heart sank.

"How long have you known him?"

"Since the spring fair. He ran the booth where you throw darts at balloons."

Rachel's heart sank even further. A "carney" with no last name. The chances of finding him were slim.

"What's *your* last name, honey?"

Stephanie looked out the window. "I don't remember."

Rachel was skeptical. "Really?"

"I—I think I have amnesia or something. I saw that once on a soap opera."

"Tell me more about Mack."

"He stayed behind after the rest of the guys left. He was sweet to me at first, but he couldn't find a job, so he decided to go back on the circuit. He didn't want me to go with him." The girl laid her hand on her stomach. "But I'm having his baby! What else could I do?"

About a hundred other things, Rachel thought.

"How old is this 'Mack'?" she asked.

"Twenty-two." Stephanie nibbled again at the hangnail. "I think. Maybe a little older."

Probably pushing thirty, Rachel thought. If she looked past the bruises, the tearstained face, the tangled hair, and the pregnant belly, Stephanie was a beauty. Her eyes tipped slightly at the edges, her lashes were lush and long, and her skin was slightly tinged with olive. She had an exotic beauty that had probably turned more than one man's head.

The childlike quality that also clung to her, in spite of the pregnancy, broke Rachel's heart.

"How old are you, honey?"

Stephanie looked out the window. "Eighteen."

Rachel was silent. They both knew that Stephanie was lying.

"You sure about that?"

Stephanie slid her gaze toward her, sighed, and confessed. "I'll be sixteen in October."

Fifteen. Jailbait. No wonder "Mack" dumped her. Rachel was surprised he'd stuck around as long as he had.

"What make of car was he driving?"

"Red."

"You don't know what kind it was?"

Stephanie picked at her fingernail polish. "I don't know a lot about cars."

"Was it old or new?"

"Kinda old." Stephanie brightened. "He stole it. Does that help?"

"It could." Rachel mentally wagged her head at the girl's ignorance. "Do you remember who he stole it from, or what city?"

"What movie are we going to watch?" Stephanie asked.

She was either tired of the conversation, protecting "Mack," or simply acting her age. Probably a combination of all three, Rachel decided. Rachel hoped that popcorn and frozen Snickers would loosen Stephanie's tongue.

"We're here." She turned off the ignition when they arrived at her house.

"There's a cop car in your driveway," Stephanie whispered. "Are you in trouble?"

"Nope." Rachel answered. "That's mine. I'm a policewoman."

"You *are*?"

Rachel hoped Stephanie wouldn't try to run. She really didn't feel like chasing a pregnant teenager down the street.

"Yes."

"A girl cop? Like in *Charlie's Angels*?"

"Kind of."

"That is *so* cool!"

Stephanie's reaction pleased her. "I think so too."

"Do you know kung fu and all that stuff?"

"Some. Enough to protect myself. Usually."

"Wish I did," Stephanie said.

"It's good knowledge for a woman to have."

"Maybe after the baby comes, I could take a class or something."

"Wouldn't be a bad idea," Rachel said. "Let's get you inside. You can take a bath and we'll clean up some of those cuts."

Stephanie gingerly touched a cut on her forehead.

"Did he hit you in the stomach?" Rachel asked.

"No. Just my face and arms. I—I tried to protect my baby."

"Good for you."

"He didn't want to hit me. He's really a good guy at heart. He just wanted me to get out of the car, and when I wouldn't, he had to make me."

"Yeah. Okay." Rachel sighed as she unlocked her door and ushered Stephanie inside. Making excuses for the abuser had already started. The chance of Stephanie testifying against him, assuming they ever found him, wasn't good.

"Oooh. This is pretty." Stephanie looked around.

"Thanks. What do you think? Bath first, then the movie?"

"Yeah. That would be nice," Stephanie said. "What movies do you have?"

"Since you mentioned *Charlie's Angels*, how about that one?" Rachel would never admit it, but she had watched that particular DVD at least ten times. She knew it was all Hollywood, but still— Lucy Liu had some amazing moves.

"I'd like that. Can I have butter on my popcorn? My grandma always puts melted butter on it."

"No problem." So she *did* have relatives. "What's your grandma's name, honey?"

"Um, I don't remember. I think it's that amnesia acting up again."

"Uh-huh. What does your boyfriend look like?" Rachel asked. "Can you describe him?"

"He has a tattoo and a pierced tongue and blue eyes. Does that help?"

"Not much."

"Look," Stephanie said, "I know I shouldn't have done what I did, getting pregnant and running away and all, but it's just that… I fell in love."

"Perhaps your memory will return after a good night's sleep. You think that might happen?"

Stephanie toed the ground. "Maybe."

Rachel showed her to the bathroom, helped her start the bath water, gave her a bathrobe and towels, and left the child in privacy.

She went into her bedroom, where Stephanie couldn't hear. Pacing the floor, she called the county sheriff's office, letting them know the small bits of information Stephanie had given her and asking them to be on the lookout for a stolen red car or bulletins for a missing girl by the name of Stephanie.

She had just hung up when the phone rang.

"Hello."

"Hi. This is Joe. Are you okay?"

She hadn't expected what the sound of Joe's voice would do to her knees. She sat down abruptly on the edge of the bed.

"I'm fine."

"What about our girl?"

"She's taking a bath," Rachel said.

"Did she tell you anything?"

"Not much. Evidently she lives with a grandma but can't seem to remember the woman's name. I'm hoping popcorn and soda will loosen her tongue."

Joe chuckled, and she smiled at the sound. Now that she knew who he was, she allowed herself to acknowledge what she'd resisted for so long—Joe was an amazing man, and she enjoyed his company tremendously.

"Never heard of popcorn and soda loosening anyone's tongue before, Officer," he said. "But I'm sure you know what you're doing."

Somehow that title on his tongue sounded intimate—a private joke between them.

"Actually," Rachel said, "I'm kind of making this up as I go along. I might have to use my ultimate weapon."

"What's that?"

"Frozen Snickers."

"Did they teach you that technique at the police academy?"

"It was in all the handbooks. They taught us to never *ever* underestimate the power of chocolate on a female."

"Is that so?"

"If someone had waved a Hershey bar in front of Bonnie at the right time of the month, she'd have given up Clyde in a heartbeat."

This time he laughed out loud. Her heart warmed at the sound. She couldn't remember hearing him truly laugh before. Perhaps knowing that someone else understood his situation was helping him relax a little. He'd been alone with Bobby and his secret for so long.

"Thanks for calling me when you found her, Joe."

"I'm grateful that I had you to call. You handled the situation beautifully. I was afraid she was going to run away if I made the slightest move."

"She probably would have."

"What are you going to do?"

"I'm going to be kind to her, let her get some rest. She's only a kid. I'm betting she'll let down her guard by tomorrow. I've made a call to the sheriff to keep a watch out for the guy who did this. There's not much to go on, though. Tomorrow I'll take her to the clinic—that's my first priority." Rachel sighed. "She's only fifteen, Joe."

"What will happen to her if she won't tell you who she is or where she came from?"

"Let's hope it doesn't come to that."

"Rachel?" a young voice called. "Rachel?"

"In here, Stephanie," Rachel called. "Gotta go, Joe."

"I'll see you tomorrow."

"Bye."

A wave of tropical scents hit Rachel as soon as Stephanie entered the room. The girl had obviously helped herself liberally to the inexpensive bath salts Anna bought Rachel each and every Christmas. They'd been accumulating for a while. Rachel figured she'd finally found a good use for them.

"Feel better?" she asked the girl.

Stephanie's eyes sparkled. "Yeah. I'm ready for the movie now."

Rachel tucked her into the corner of her couch with an afghan and started the movie. Stephanie divided her attention between the movie and detangling her mass of curly black hair.

The girl is beautiful, Rachel thought as she went to make popcorn. As she waited for the microwave to finish, she glanced into a mirror over the kitchen sink. What she saw when she looked in the mirror was…just okay.

She knew she could attract more male attention if she bothered with makeup or a fancier hairstyle, but most of the time she'd rather spend her free time at the shooting range.

Joe's wife, however, had been truly gorgeous. A woman didn't become a Miss Texas runner-up without knowing her way around a mascara wand. Grace probably wouldn't have been caught dead in the clothes Rachel habitually wore.

Caught dead. Was she jealous of a dead woman?

Grace was evidently the kind of woman Joe preferred. She was probably the kind of woman who had her nails done on a regular basis and owned shoes to match every outfit. She probably even wore underwear that matched—every day.

Rachel's mouth quirked at that thought. Her underwear matched. It was white. All of it.

The microwave's bell went off, and she dumped the contents of the bag into a large bowl.

She was who she was. A small-town police officer whose beauty routine consisted of soap, water, and whatever shampoo was on sale when she ran out. She kept her nails short and her shoes low, and her off-duty clothes—even with the new ones she had just purchased—could fit into a large suitcase with room to spare.

She put a half stick of butter into a bowl and watched it melt in the microwave.

Joe's good looks had probably made a whole lot of women's hearts flutter. He was probably accustomed to women falling at his feet. She'd have to make certain their relationship stayed on a friendship-only basis. Not a problem for him. More of a problem for her.

Someday he would leave Sugarcreek and go back to his former life. Just because he was keeping a low profile and she was the only woman his age in his life right now, it wouldn't be smart to start thinking she could ever be anything more to him than a friend. Men like him probably had to fight women off in every city they went. They married movie stars and fashion models. They did *not* fall for women who carried guns and locked up drunks for a living.

Although, deep down, she wished they did.

She squared her shoulders. So, okay. She would value their new relationship for what it was—a friendship—and when she was in her dotage, she'd be one of those old people who would tell people who didn't really want to hear how she had once known the great baseball player Micah Mattias.

She saturated Stephanie's popcorn with melted butter and then popped a low-fat bowl for herself. Her figure wasn't a huge factor in her decision to forgo the calories, but her speed and endurance as a law officer were. As a woman, she had to have every advantage she could—and staying at peak form was part of the tools of her trade.

She would *need* to be in peak form if she was going to watch Joe's back as she had promised. A man like him couldn't hide from the public forever.

Joe stared at the book on archaeology that lay open in front of him. Slowly he turned the pages. Once again, on the twentieth page, was another twenty-dollar bill. A small pile grew as he leafed through the book. Over five hundred dollars had been secreted between its heavy pages, all stuck with a dot of rubber cement.

He pulled another book off the shelf, this time one at eye-level, and leafed through it. Nothing. He pulled another one out. Again, nothing. He stepped back, far enough away that he could see the entire wall of books at one time. There was something odd about the configuration, but he couldn't quite put his finger on what was wrong.

Then he realized that the largest books were shelved on the very top. That made little sense. Most people would choose to put the largest books on the bottom shelves. Especially for an aged man like Abraham.

Joe pulled another book off the top shelf, settled down at his desk, and turned to page 20.

Another twenty-dollar bill.

Page 40. A ten.

Again and again, he found the books on the top shelf meticulously filled with either a ten- or a twenty-dollar bill.

And there were at least fifty volumes on the top shelf. He checked a few more at random. Each one held cash.

If his estimate was correct, here was several thousand dollars of the old man's savings that apparently no one but him knew about.

He stared up at the books, wrestling with his conscience.

With this money, he could hide away with Bobby for months in the hunting cabin his college roommate had offered. He wouldn't have to contact Henrietta or anyone else for help. It wouldn't exactly be stealing because he would pay back every dime—eventually. His truck was right outside. Rachel was distracted by Stephanie and wouldn't notice him quietly rolling out of town.

Even though they had grown apart over the years, he trusted his old roommate, Aaron, as much as anyone. If he could just remain anonymous a few months longer, perhaps it would buy enough time for the LA police to find the killer. Enough time for Bobby to grow up and stabilize a little more. Enough time for the media and public to bury him even further down the list of interesting topics.

The thought of leaving niggled at Joe like candy tempting a child.

He trusted Rachel. Every nerve in his body cried out that she was someone upon whom he could absolutely depend. But it was no small thing that she held his and Bobby's immediate future in the palm of her hand.

Perhaps, he rationalized, this discovery was God's way of encouraging him to leave while he still could. Or perhaps it was Satan tempting him to break the hearts of three elderly women who had helped him even when they didn't know who he was.

As he pondered what to do, he wandered into Bobby's

bedroom and stood there, watching his son sleep. He did this every evening. Sometimes he checked on him several times during the night, reassuring himself that his son was still with him, still alive.

He could leave right now, in the middle of the night. The truck was running well. They could be hundreds of miles away before Rachel and the aunts even knew he was gone.

Bobby had kicked the covers off, and Joe bent to tuck them in more securely. There was nothing he wouldn't do for this child. Was it wise to risk staying here now that he had a way out? Wasn't protecting Bobby his top priority?

Rachel might decide, after all, to confide in one of her coworkers...or to make a few indiscreet phone calls to check further on the murder. Her logical cop's mind must be itching with the need to try to solve this mystery. Could he trust her enough to resist the pull of solving a crime? He wasn't sure. But one thing he *was* sure of—he couldn't risk Bobby.

The image of his son proudly holding that sack of hardware came to mind. "Am I a good helper?" Bobby had asked.

"The best," Joe whispered now, looking down on his son's sleeping form. "You are the best helper-boy I could ever hope for."

No, he could *not* allow Bobby to go through the trauma of another media circus. He had to keep Bobby safe—even if keeping him safe meant disappearing again.

Joe pulled the duffel bag out of Bobby's closet, opened the top dresser drawer, and lifted out a small stack of tiny underwear. Oddly enough, toward the back of the drawer and hidden beneath the underwear was a carefully folded piece of paper Joe had never seen before. Puzzled, he opened it.

His son had drawn a crude stick-figure house with smoke curling out of the chimney. It was a simple drawing typical of a four-year-old's concept of home. The house was purple and the smoke was yellow. In front of the house was a little boy holding hands with a man on one side. Four women held hands with the little boy on the other side. One of the women had a ponytail. The other three wore barely recognizable little prayer kapps. Everyone was smiling.

There was a sixth figure in the picture. Up in the sky where most children would have drawn a sun was a woman with long blond hair and wings. Much loving care had been put into coloring this woman. Joe knew in an instant that it was Grace. She, too, was smiling, as she looked down on Bobby and his purple house and stick-figure family.

His heart aching, Joe folded the paper with reverence and put it back beneath the tiny underwear. Bobby drew pictures all the time. Abraham's refrigerator was covered with Bobby's drawings. Every picture his son had ever made had been stuck under Joe's nose to admire. At least Joe had *thought* he had seen every picture Bobby had ever made.

But not this one.

This one was Bobby's secret, and it was a secret he knew he needed to allow his son to keep.

He slowly closed the top drawer, returned the duffel bag to the closet, and sat down on the edge of Bobby's bed.

The choice of whether or not to run had been taken away from him. Bobby was not a newborn infant who could be whisked away with no conscious memory of the people left behind. He had his own worries and grief and hopes and attachments that Joe had no business destroying.

The three aunts and Rachel had been good for his little boy. The stability of living here had been healing. The changes in his son had been dramatic.

He smoothed Bobby's tousled curls off his forehead and planted a light kiss there.

His son had drawn a picture of his family—and everyone,

including Bobby, was smiling. There was no way on God's green earth that he would destroy this bit of security to which his little boy clung.

"Whatever you do, Rachel," Joe whispered, "please don't betray us."

CHAPTER 19

After taking pictures of Stephanie's bruises and writing up a report with the few bits of information about "Mack" the girl had given her, Rachel took Stephanie to see the doctor.

"She's about seven months along," Dr. Harold Walters said. "And except for these bruises, she's strong and healthy. There's no reason she can't have a normal delivery."

The doctor moved the ultrasound wand over the girl's protruding belly while Rachel held onto her hand. "Ah. A little girl. And look at that!"

Rachel and Stephanie both stared at the screen where the doctor pointed. "What?" Rachel asked. She couldn't make heads or tails of the fetus—literally.

"She's sucking her thumb," Dr. Walters said, smiling. "I love it when they do that."

Stephanie was entranced. "A real baby." She tightened her grip on Rachel's hand. "I have a real baby inside of me." Her voice was awestruck.

"Well, it's definitely not a doll." The doctor chuckled. He wiped the gel off Stephanie's belly and began putting the instruments away while Rachel helped the girl climb off the table.

"I knew it was a baby," Stephanie said. "But it just didn't seem real until now."

"You have a little person inside of you that will be depending on you to take care of her," Dr. Walters said. "You'll have to grow up fast and make good decisions for both of you."

"Like what?"

"Like not going back to whoever gave you these." Dr. Walters touched a bruise on Stephanie's arm. "Like telling us who you are. I don't buy your amnesia story, Stephanie. I know that's big in soap operas, but it's pretty rare in the real world."

Stephanie shook her head. "I really can't remember."

The doctor wrote out a prescription and handed it to Rachel. "It's late in the pregnancy, but something is better than nothing. She needs to be taking these vitamins. And she needs to see me— or preferably her doctor at home—in a couple of weeks."

"Thanks, Doctor," Rachel said.

Dr. Walters waved her thanks away. "That's what I'm here for."

Stephanie was chatty after they left the doctor's office. She talked about the baby, possible names for the baby, her favorite rock groups, a boy back home she had liked before "Mack" came into the picture....

Then she said she was hungry. Rachel stopped at Beachy's and watched with amazement as Stephanie polished off a heaping plate of food that most truck drivers would have found daunting.

Rachel had no idea what she was going to do with the girl if she didn't break down and give her a name and an address. She had already checked all recent missing persons reports, and Stephanie didn't fit any of them. She hated to turn her over to Social Services —although that might eventually be her only option. Taking her in had been a stopgap measure. Not a permanent fix—although Stephanie seemed to be settling in for the long haul.

"I need to stop by and check on my aunts for a couple of minutes," Rachel said. "Are you okay with that?"

"Sure."

As they pulled into the farmhouse drive, Rachel saw a fresh sign at the end of the road. It read:

CAKES/PIES/COOKIES/BREAD

TODAY 8-2

HAITIAN ORPHANAGE FUND-RAISER

Rachel sighed. What *was* it with her aunts? They would rather work than eat. Of course, they seemed to enjoy both a great deal. Their idea of a perfect day was to have what they called "work frolics," which took the form of barn raisings or quilting bees combining communal labor with large amounts of food.

As Rachel and Stephanie got out of the car, Joe strode past, pushing a wheelbarrow mounded with dirt.

"Hey there." He set the wheelbarrow down. "Are you feeling better, Stephanie?"

"I'm having a little girl!" she said.

He turned to Rachel. "Is everything all right?"

"She's fine. The doctor prescribed vitamins."

"I'm glad everything is okay." He grasped the handles of the wheelbarrow. "Any luck in remembering your last name?"

"Sorry." The girl looked anything but.

"What does Bertha have you doing today?" Rachel was curious about the wheelbarrow's load of dirt.

"I decided to fill in some low places in the yard. It'll make it easier to mow come spring."

"You're staying until spring?" She tried not to show how pleased she felt at that news.

"We'll see." Joe shrugged. "I sure wouldn't mind."

"I see they have their sign up again."

"Buggies and cars have been coming all morning. Lydia's in her element. In fact, this evening I'm supposed to hitch up the buggy and go down to the IGA to purchase more supplies."

"What am I going to do with them?" She shook her head in mock frustration.

"I think your aunts are out of your control, Rachel."

"*Tell* me about it."

"I get the distinct impression that we're just along for the ride. Maybe Bertha too." He chuckled. "I think Lydia may be the one calling the shots this time."

"Can we go inside?" Stephanie pleaded. "Reading that sign made me hungry again."

Rachel was incredulous. "You just cleaned out Beachy's!"

Stephanie smoothed her hand over her belly and smiled like a sleek little cat. "I'm eating for two."

"I'll leave you women to sort that out," Joe said. "I'd better get back to work." Joe pushed the wheelbarrow to a dip in the front yard and began to shovel dirt.

His back was broad and the muscles beneath his T-shirt were outlined with sweat. He was so obviously an athlete, Rachel wondered that she hadn't ferreted out his secret long before.

"Is Joe your boyfriend?"

Rachel's head whipped around. She'd forgotten about Stephanie—who was watching her with interest.

"No."

Stephanie smiled knowingly. "You look like you wish he was."

217

"He's just a friend."

"Uh-huh. Take my word on it. That's how it starts."

Rachel laughed. "You're, what, fifteen? And you're giving me advice about relationships?"

"Face it, Rachel. The guy's a hunk."

Rachel smiled. In spite of everything, it was sort of fun having Stephanie around. Of course, she reminded herself, the girl must have family somewhere who were worried sick.

She headed toward the farmhouse with Stephanie trotting along beside her. "Do you *wish* he was your boyfriend?"

Rachel hesitated. She really didn't know what to say. How could she explain to Stephanie that no matter how much she wished things were different, Joe was entirely out of her league?

"He's a nice guy, Stephanie, but I don't think he's interested in me in that way."

"Rachel, Rachel, Rachel." Stephanie shook her head. "You're never going to get a guy with that attitude. You have to go after him before someone else beats you to it."

"You think?" Rachel stole one last glance at Joe as she entered the kitchen door.

Anna pulled back from the kitchen window when they came in. There was a small smudge on the window where she'd pressed her nose. A worry line creased her forehead. "Joe's digging."

"He's just filling in holes."

"My flowers?"

"I'm sure Joe won't hurt your flowers, Anna."

"Oh my!" Stephanie's voice was filled with awe. "Look at that!"

The table and shelves were spread with three kinds of pies, several dozen cookies, and four cakes. A small cash box sat on the counter. The kitchen smelled like a bakery.

"Lydia?" Rachel called.

Her aunt came rushing in, positioning a strip of double-sided Scotch tape to the inside of her prayer kapp.

"Why are you putting tape in that little hat?" Stephanie asked.

Lydia positioned the kapp on her head and pressed it down with the flat of her hand. "It helps keep it in place."

"She used to stick it on with straight pins," Rachel said.

Stephanie winced. "You're kidding."

"It is not as bad as you make it sound." Lydia shot Rachel a disapproving look. "We wove the pin through the kapp and a few strands of hair."

"The tape I bought you works well?" Rachel said.

"We appreciate your gift, Rachel. It does indeed work better than the pins." She looked at Stephanie. "And who is this?"

"A new friend." Rachel didn't want to get into the details yet. "She's staying with me for a little while. Her name is Stephanie, and this is my aunt, Lydia."

"Pleased to meet you," Stephanie said.

Lydia accepted Rachel's introduction and explanation at face value. Evidently, if Rachel wanted to have a pregnant teenager living with her, Lydia wouldn't question it. At least not while Stephanie was present.

"That pumpkin pie looks really, really good," Stephanie said. "I think I could eat the whole thing. Seriously."

"The whole thing?" Lydia's eyes gleamed. "Here, let me get you a fork and knife." She bustled about, sat the girl down at the table, and watched her dig in.

She stretched out her hand. "That will be four dollars and fifty cents," she informed Rachel.

"Lydia thought you might need sustenance."

Joe glanced up from his work. Rachel had three cookies and a glass of water with her.

"You must be her favorite. She's not charging *you*," she said.

Joe leaned his shovel against the wheelbarrow. "Thanks." He grabbed the glass and took a long swig of the water. "I did buy an apple pie from her earlier, if that makes you feel any better."

"I'm already missing the good old days when Lydia simply baked for the joy of watching me eat it."

"She *is* baking for the joy of it—the joy of purchasing material for those Haitian girls. Oh, you might want to know that they're also purchasing seed packets to fold into the cloth when they ship it. You wouldn't believe how much fun your aunts are having over that."

"I can imagine. They've always sponsored a child or two, but now that they've closed down the inn, they're really focusing on this project." She handed him the cookies. "You want these?"

"Lydia's sugar cookies? Absolutely."

"Anna saw your shovel and is concerned that you might dig up some of her flowers," Rachel said.

"Tell her not to worry." He licked a cookie crumb off his thumb. "My mom loved flowers. I know how to be careful."

He glanced over at a large maple tree in the backyard. A heavy wooden bench leaned against it.

"I could use a break," he said. "Want to sit a minute?"

"Sounds good." Rachel strolled over to the bench with him. "Although by the time I get back, I might owe Lydia a good chunk of my paycheck. I think Stephanie is capable of eating me *and* my aunts out of house and home."

"The little mother has an appetite, has she?"

"You could say that."

"So what's the news on our mystery girl?" Joe asked as they sat down.

"The doctor wasn't impressed with her amnesia story. And he says she's about seven months pregnant."

"Then you don't have a lot of time."

"No, but I doubt she can stick to her story much longer. Now that she's fed and rested, she's turning out to be quite a chatterbox. If I spend enough time with her, I think she'll slip up and I'll be able to figure it out."

Joe grinned. "Like you did with me?"

"You weren't easy."

"I'm flattered. Besides waiting for Stephanie to slip up, is there anything else we can do?"

"I don't know. I've checked her picture against all the runaways and missing persons' pictures."

"And?"

"Nothing."

"Fingerprints?"

"She's not in the system."

Joe relaxed against the bench. "Well, at least that's one good thing."

"I suppose."

"So." Joe stretched out his long legs. "You're sharing your house with a pregnant girl who can't—or won't—remember her name."

"She's mentioned a grandmother, so there must be someone who's worried about her."

"I hope so."

"In some ways, she's a really neat person. There must be someone in her life who helped her become that way."

"You're getting attached to her."

"She's talking about becoming a cop when she grows up."

"Ah. I'm sure she is. Being around you would make any girl want to be just like you."

"You think?" Rachel blushed. "I'd better be getting back." She stood up.

Joe grasped her wrist. "Stay for a minute."

Surprised, she sat down.

Joe didn't let loose of her wrist. "I want to ask you something."

"What is it?"

"One of the guys at the hardware store told me about a movie playing at the Quaker Theatre over in New Philadelphia that his son liked. I think Bobby would enjoy it too. It involves animated bugs. If you'll drive, I'll buy the tickets and the popcorn."

"I—I could do that."

"Meet me back here at six?"

"I don't know what to do about Stephanie."

"Bring her along, of course. Do you suppose she likes bug movies?"

Her lips quirked. "If there's popcorn and chocolate candy involved, she'll like it."

"It's a date. I'll see you tonight."

He felt a lifting of his spirits as he went back to work and she went in to collect Stephanie. *It isn't* really *a date,* he reminded himself. Real dates didn't usually involve bringing small boys and pregnant teenagers along.

Still, he found that he was looking forward to this evening very much.

An hour later, with the holes satisfactorily filled, Joe put away the wheelbarrow and shovel, rinsed off his hands at the pump, and went to the aunts' kitchen to collect Bobby—who had spent the afternoon alternately playing with his kitten and entertaining Lydia's customers with a running commentary on her baked goods.

As much as he loved his son, sitting inside a dimly lit house for an entire evening with only a dancing pickle for company was not his idea of a great evening. After several days of going to bed extremely early, a movie sounded *really* nice. Going with Rachel sounded even nicer. Now that he no longer had to hide his identity from her—now that they were friends—asking the pretty cop to accompany him to a kids' movie seemed an excellent way to spend the evening.

Except that she'd blushed when he'd asked her.

And she wasn't the kind of woman to blush easily.

As a cop, she had no doubt waded into scenes that would make some grown men faint. And yet she had blushed and stammered when he'd issued a friendly invitation to watch a bug movie with him and his son.

He didn't know whether to be worried or happy. Was there the remotest possibility that she might be interested in him?

What an intriguing thought. Rachel Troyer, all strength and loyalty, combined with a graceful beauty that could turn heads even in a no-nonsense cop's uniform. Strange, how she seemed utterly unaware of her attractiveness. He wanted to get to know her better. A lot better.

Would that be a mistake?

I've got your back, Joe.

Her words came back to him. She had meant them.

No, spending time with Rachel was *not* a mistake. In spite of the cloud hanging over him, in spite of all that had happened back in LA, he was going to allow himself to enjoy her company at the movies tonight.

———

Rachel was in her bedroom trying to decide what to wear when she heard retching coming from the bathroom. She rushed in to check on Stephanie.

"Are you okay?"

Stephanie's face was ashen, and her eyes were red and teary from the strain of being sick. "I thought morning sickness was supposed to happen only in the morning—but I never know *when* it's going to hit."

"I've heard that happens sometimes. Of course, maybe it's not morning sickness. Maybe it's all that food you ate today."

"I couldn't help it. I seem to be hungry all the time these days."

Rachel looked at her watch. It was 5:45. They needed to be leaving. She pulled a washcloth out of a drawer, wet it, and handed it to Stephanie, who was sitting on the floor beside the commode. "Maybe this will help."

Stephanie wiped her face, got up from the bathroom floor, rinsed out her mouth, and looked at Rachel.

"Would you care if I don't go to the movie with you? I don't feel so good."

"Are you feeling better now?"

"Yes."

"You won't be afraid to stay here by yourself?"

"I'll be fine."

"You sure?"

"Yeah. I'll just watch TV."

"I'll have my cell phone on me. Call me if you need me."

"You go on and see that bug movie, Rachel. And have fun with Joe."

"I will. But, sweetheart, I want you to be thinking seriously about what you're going to do. You could be giving birth within the next few weeks, and you need to be with your family when that happens. Staying here with me is not an option."

"I know. I just can't remember."

Rachel blew out a sigh. Deflated by Stephanie's illness and her lack of honesty, she silently finished getting ready.

Joe and Bobby were sitting on the front porch steps of the

daadi haus when she pulled up. Joe had showered and changed. Bobby, a pint-sized image of Joe, beamed up at her.

Joe stood. "Give Rachel your present, buddy."

Bobby brought his arm out from behind his back and presented Rachel with one late, wilted rose from the aunts' flower garden.

"Bobby seems to be under the impression that a gentleman should give flowers to a lady on their first date."

Rachel tried to ignore the feeling of pleasure the use of that word "date" gave her. Was that truly how Joe was viewing their evening together? Deep down, she hoped so.

She stooped to take the flower from Bobby's hand. The child was so innocent. So trusting. So easy to love. In fact, she already loved him.

"Thank you, Bobby," she said. "It's lovely."

"My mommy liked flowers."

Her heart turned over. "I'll bet she did."

"Where's Stephanie?"

"She's not feeling so good tonight."

"Oh?" Joe said, concerned. "Is everything all right?"

"She lost her supper before I left. It's either belated morning sickness or too much of Lydia's pie. I've got my cell phone on me and she promised to call if she needed something."

He glanced down at Bobby. "You ready to go see some bugs?"

"Uh-huh."

Joe looked at Rachel. "Are you ready to go see some bugs?"

Rachel tucked the rose into a buttonhole on her yellow cardigan. "Can't wait."

Bobby grasped her hand and smiled up at her. Then he reached for his father's hand, forming a solid link between her and Joe. As they walked toward the car, she had the feeling that her life was finally beginning.

CHAPTER 20

R achel hummed as she donned her work jeans the next morning. Today she was going to help start painting the farmhouse that Joe had scraped and prepared. Many of her Amish cousins were coming to help. Today was going to be an Amish work frolic—something her aunts had been looking forward to for weeks.

Best of all was that she would be working alongside Joe.

Even though her jeans were worn, they fit pretty well, and she was wearing a deep maroon sweatshirt with them. Then, surprising herself, she screwed in a pair of gold hoops and added a line of pale lipstick. Looking nice around Joe had begun to be a priority.

"You're lookin' good." Stephanie walked into the kitchen, rubbing her eyes. "Not wearing them ugly police pants today?"

Joe's T-shirt was stretched tight around Stephanie's middle. A pair of Rachel's jogging pants were rolled beneath her belly. If the girl stayed much longer, they'd need to do some serious shopping. But, of course, she wasn't going to be staying much longer. Yesterday Rachel had mentioned the possibility of contacting

Children's Services, thinking the threat of foster care might jog Stephanie's memory.

"I'm hungry. Are you fixing anything for breakfast?"

"Help yourself to whatever you want. I'm headed over to the farmhouse to help paint. I asked you last night if you wanted to come. Remember?"

Stephanie scratched her belly. "Watching people paint doesn't sound like fun to me. I'll hang out here and read some magazines or watch some TV."

"You sure?"

"Yeah. I might throw up again."

"Okay." Rachel felt a twinge of conscience. Stephanie seemed to be alone too much. But there was nothing she could do about it right now. She was looking forward to the day too much to stay home and babysit her.

Babysit. It worried her that Stephanie would be in charge of an infant in a few weeks.

Rachel shoved her concerns about Stephanie aside, finished packing her mother's old picnic basket with the muffins she had baked last night, and headed out the door. Nothing was going to keep her from enjoying today. She wasn't going to worry about anything except having a wonderful time with a good man and his sweet little boy.

She hummed along with the radio. It was a beautiful fall day, and all her windows were rolled down as she drove to the farm.

Her foot hit the brake when she saw a black news van parked in front of the daadi haus. A smaller white van was parked in the driveway...and a group of people milled about in the yard with microphones and cameras.

Bewildered-looking Amish, prepared for a workday, stayed huddled inside their buggies to avoid being photographed. She saw Anna peeking out of an upstairs window.

Heartsick, she parked her Mustang, climbed out, and began to elbow her way through the small crowd to the daadi haus's door.

"Coming through," she commanded.

As a cop, she was used to crowds opening up for her when she asked. Dressed in civilian clothes, her "cop's voice" was ineffective. The reporters turned on her with interest.

"Are you his girlfriend? A relative? Can you tell us anything at all about Micah Mattias? How long has he been here? Is it true he's been working as a handyman for Amish people? Is his son with him? Has the boy told you what he saw the night his mother was killed?"

Rachel realized that cameras were being trained on her and she tried to shield her face with her hand as she steadily worked her way onto Joe's porch.

"Joe! It's me!" she shouted, pounding on the door.

It opened a crack, and she angled her body inside. Once she was in, Joe closed it against the clamor of questions outside. As it clicked shut, she looked into eyes filled with anger.

He held Bobby in his arms. The little boy's head was buried in his neck, and he was crying. Joe's face was dark with fury.

"What happened?" Rachel asked.

"Perhaps *you* can tell *me*."

Rachel was surprised. Why was he angry with *her*?

"I don't understand," she said. "Why are they here? How did they find out?"

"What did you do, Rachel? Confide in a girlfriend? Mention it to some guy at work? Send an anonymous e-mail to a gossip magazine?"

"You think I—?" Her voice choked at the unfairness of the accusation. "You *know* I wouldn't—"

Joe cut her off with a slash of his hand. "You were the only one who knew. I *trusted you*." His jaw clenched. "Do you know the questions they tried to ask my little boy this morning when he innocently opened the door? Can you imagine what they threw at him? Did you even *think* about the two lives you were destroying when you told whoever it was you told? Or did you just want to be known as the girl cop who had discovered Micah Mattias's hiding place?"

"I *didn't.*"

"Get out, Rachel. I'll deal with these people. I've dealt with them before—but I never want to see you again."

He opened the door and practically shoved her outside. Rachel stumbled into the cacophony of questions and microphones.

"Did he confess to murdering his wife? How long has he been hiding here? What's your connection to him? Are you dating him? Did you have a relationship before his wife died? What are all these buggies doing here?"

Rachel pushed her way through the sea of bodies, so shocked by Joe's accusations that she could barely process anything that was happening. She saw the reporters' mouths move, but it was as though they were talking silently and in slow motion.

Amish buggies began to work their way back toward the road. The work frolic her aunts had looked forward to was ruined.

As she pulled away, she saw the curtains being yanked shut, one by one, in the downstairs windows of her aunts' house as a news photographer tried to point a camera inside. It had been decades since her aunts' curtains, one dark cloth panel per window, had been released from the single swag holding them back and positioned to block out the world.

How bewildered the three of them must feel right now.

She considered going inside and trying to explain to them what was happening, but it would take too much time. They would be all right for now. She had a higher priority.

In spite of her own hurt and her aunts' ruined work frolic, the main thing on her mind was how alone Joe must feel right now. And how afraid Bobby must be. His little-boy sobs still echoed in her heart.

She cast around in her mind for a clue as to who might have tipped off the press. The only person she could think of was Kim Whitfield. She'd been a fool to give Kim all that information…a fool for having confided in the girl about her suspicions concerning Joe. Obviously, Kim had done the research and figured it out. Unfortunately, she had also chosen to share her discovery with the world.

It was a five-minute drive to her house, her gun, her uniform, and her squad car.

She made it in three.

Stephanie was sitting at the kitchen table buttering a stack of toast when Rachel burst in.

"We need more bread," Stephanie said. Then she looked up. "You're home awful early. Did you forget something?"

Rachel took in the scene at a glance. In addition to the toast sitting on the table, there was a stack of magazines beside the plate.

She strode over to the table and scanned the top one. It was the most recent issue of the *People* magazines she had carried out of the library. And along with the others, it had been tucked away on the top shelf of her closet.

"Where did you get these?" she demanded.

"Your bedroom," Stephanie answered. "I was looking for some clothes—I thought maybe you'd have something that would fit." She took a bite of toast. "You don't have much for me to work with, you know. You should shop more, Rachel."

Rachel ignored Stephanie's rudeness and focused on the problem at hand. "How long have you had these?"

"What? These? They're just magazines."

In spite of Stephanie's attempt to look innocent, Rachel saw that she was hiding something.

"There are about thirty reporters camped out on Joe's front yard. Do you know anything about that?"

Stephanie turned the pages of the top magazine, her eyes cast down. "I might."

Rachel grasped Stephanie's jaw in her hand and forced her to look at her.

"*What* did you do?"

Stephanie wrenched her face away, scattering toast crumbs across the table. "I made a phone call. I got a baby girl inside of me, Rachel! You keep telling me I need to be thinking about how to take care of her."

"What does that have to do with Joe and Bobby?"

Stephanie opened the pages to a picture of Joe where he hadn't shaved for a couple of days. Although there was only a shadow of beard, it was enough to tip someone off if they looked hard enough.

"I was bored. Then I saw this stack of magazines in your bedroom. I *love People* magazine, but the only ones you had was of that baseball player everyone was talking about and trying to find. I knew right away it was Joe. I figured there might be some money in a good tip like that, so I called the *National Enquirer.* I was right. They were *very* interested."

"How did you even know how to get in touch with them?" She was appalled. The *National Enquirer?*

"Did you ever hear of the Internet, Rachel?" Stephanie rolled her eyes. "I surfed around on your computer. The *Enquirer* said they'd pay for 'good stories and juicy tips about celebrities.' I figured this was as good a story and as juicy a tip as I was ever going to get."

Unconcerned about the lives she'd just destroyed, Stephanie calmly slathered strawberry jam on her toast and took a bite.

There were a half dozen things Rachel wanted to say—but now was not the time. Instead, she abruptly left Stephanie to her toast and magazines and went into her bedroom to suit up. After a couple phone calls, she donned her uniform, loaded her gun and her utility belt, clipped it around her waist, grabbed her hat, and slammed out of the house.

Joe might never trust her again, but she could at least keep the press from beating down his door.

Bobby sat in the middle of his bed, sniffling, while Joe packed the duffel bag. In the bottom of the bag was some money he had gleaned from the books in Abraham's library.

Rifling through the old man's books had made him feel like a thief, but he knew that no matter what, he'd pay it back. With interest.

His plan was to wait out the rest of the day and then leave in the middle of the night while the reporters, hopefully, were half asleep.

Getting to his truck and then out on the road was going to be difficult. It was blocked by one of the news vans. He would have to drive through the yard. He had little hope of getting away undetected, but the least he could do was lead the newshounds away from the gentle women who had taken him in. The three aunts did not need to have this happen to them.

He ached to think of how their little work frolic had been destroyed—all because of him. They were undoubtedly disappointed. *He* was disappointed too.

Now he would never get to smooth fresh paint over the boards

232

he had so painstakingly prepared. He had looked forward to working alongside Eli's sons and the others. He had looked forward to sharing food and camaraderie at the long table he had helped set up in the backyard. Laughing. Talking. Working beside friends while his son tumbled about, playing with the other children.

Rachel and the newspeople had stolen this from him.

The only thing left to do now was to go back to LA, dragging a tail of reporters behind him. He would hole up at his house again. Give the interviews Henrietta would schedule. Find a good shrink for his son.

"It'll be all right, buddy." He tried to reassure his little boy in spite of his own heartbreak. "Daddy will take care of you. We'll have an adventure."

"Don't want 'venture." Bobby sniffed. "Want Anna and Lydia and Bertha and Rachel and Gracie."

"I know. We'll come back someday, after this is all over—when the people out in the yard go away."

"Those people are *bad*." Bobby curled into a ball, and his thumb went into his mouth.

"They aren't bad. They're just doing their job." Joe lifted his son onto his lap and wiped away the tears that streaked down his little cheeks.

He hated Rachel for what she'd done to them.

Outside Bobby's bedroom, he noticed a flashing colored light falling faintly on the hallway wall. He went to investigate. In the living room, blue-and-white flashing lights filtered through the new blinds he had installed.

He lifted one of the slats a fraction of an inch and quickly inhaled. Rachel had pulled her squad car directly onto his front lawn, parallel to the porch, blocking access to his house. She had changed into her uniform and was standing in front of the driver's door—her feet planted wide and a shotgun held loosely at her side. He couldn't hear what she was saying, but even from where he was watching, it was obvious that she had drawn an imaginary line in front of his house and was daring anyone to cross over it.

His heart turned over at the sight of her. She'd said she had his back. Now she was guarding his house. Could he have been wrong in accusing her of alerting them?

The reporters were slowly backing off the lawn, but they stopped at the aunts' property line. They still lined the road.

He didn't know who had called the media, but it hit him with full force that Rachel couldn't possibly have done so. It simply was not in her. The woman was no liar. If she said she had told no one —he knew she told the truth.

And he had shoved her out the door.

And she had come back to try to protect him anyway.

His heart ached with the sight of her, so valiant, so ready to do battle.

Except there was little she could do. He had dealt with publicity most of his adult life. The newspeople would never give up—not as long as there was a story. The fact that he had been able to slip away from them once had been nothing less than a miracle.

At that moment, he heard a knock at the back door. Probably another reporter—one who had been willing to make his way through the tangle of the aunts' rose garden. He opened the door a crack and was shocked to see Eli standing there with clothes draped over his arm.

"You are having druvvel—trouble—again?"

Joe pulled the old man inside. "Just a little."

"It is best you leave now, Rachel says." Eli shoved the clothing into his hands. "Today you become an Amishman—for a while."

Joe was dumbfounded. "I do?"

234

"Put these on. Both you and the boy. The hats too. We have much to do. Our Rachel has a plan."

Rachel's plan, whatever it was, *had* to be better than trying to shove his way out to the truck.

Eli watched out the blinds at the front window as Joe stripped and jerked on the Amish clothes. His fingers fumbled with the buttoned flap in front. Bobby, after being dressed in some of Eli's grandson's clothing, became fascinated with the image of himself in the mirror.

Eli looked Joe up and down and grinned. "My son's clothes are too short for you, but we have to fool those Englischers out there only for a little bit."

"What are we going to do?"

Eli peeked out at his horse and buggy. "We go to my house now."

"They'll see us."

"They will see two Amishmen who came for the work frolic and are disappointed that it was cancelled by the presence of rude Englisch reporters. Bobby, you will get behind the seat and hide like a good boy. Joe, put whatever bags you have in the back of the buggy with him. I will keep the flaps down so they will see little."

Joe positioned Bobby in the back and climbed in. With Rachel arguing with reporters and providing a distraction, Eli drove the buggy out from behind the house.

"Keep your head down, Bobby," Eli commanded. "Joe, hold the hat over your face."

Reporters tried to block the buggy.

"Out of my way! Go home! Go home!" Eli shouted. *"Ich huf seliau camera fleght zu schtickau!"*

It was the most Pennsylvania Dutch Joe had ever heard Eli speak. He had no idea what the old man had said, but the string of guttural German didn't sound at all like the gentle Amishman Joe thought he knew.

Even though they backed away, the reporters did try to snap pictures. Following Eli's cue, Joe covered his face with his hat—a frequent Amish response to the despised photographs—as they trotted down the road and toward the sanctuary of Eli's farm.

When they had gone a safe distance, Joe turned around. To his relief, he saw that they had not been followed. The reporters were still mistakenly back at the daadi haus, exchanging heated words with Rachel.

"What in the world did you say to them back there?" Joe asked.

"You don't want to know," Eli said. "I am ashamed. I lost control of my tongue."

"Was that cursing?"

"I did not curse, but I *did* tell them that I hoped their cameras would fly to pieces." Eli hung his head. "I considered mentioning the similarity between their faces and my billy goat's, but I restrained myself. It was a great temptation."

Joe roared with laughter and threw an arm around the old man's shoulders.

Eli looked stunned. He scooted to the far edge of his seat, putting as much space between himself and Joe as possible—apparently fearful that Joe might be overcome with an overwhelming Englisch need to hug.

As Eli brought the buggy to a stop in his own backyard, a silver blue Mustang pulled up. Rachel's car.

For a moment, Joe's heart leaped. He would get a chance to apologize. Then he realized that Rachel was still back at the daadi haus. A tall young woman with auburn hair, dressed in the uniform of a Sugarcreek cop, unfolded herself from the low-slung vehicle.

"My name is Kim Whitfield." She held out her hand. "I work with Rachel. You must be Joe."

"I am."

"Sorry about all that's happened today. Rachel asked me to pack her car for you. There's an untraceable cell phone and a car seat for Bobby. There's also enough money in the glove compartment to rent a room for a few nights. She advises you to go now, while she has the reporters distracted. Here are the keys. If you don't mind me saying so, there's a limit on how long they'll be content to take pictures of her. You'd better take off."

Wordlessly, Joe grabbed their duffel bag out of the buggy and threw it onto the Mustang's floor. As he buckled Bobby into the child's booster seat Rachel had never removed, Kim made one more comment.

"Rachel said to tell you it was Stephanie who called the press. The girl figured it out from some old magazines Rachel had in her closet that had you on the front cover. She said she'd appreciate it if you'd try to forgive her for being so stupid as to leave them there with a nosy teenager around."

"Tell her thanks, and I'll call her later."

"I'm sure she'd like that," Kim said.

Joe handed the two hats back to Eli. "I'll get your son's clothes back to you as soon as I can," he said.

"There is no hurry. We Amish do not lack for handmade clothing and hats." Eli smiled. "May Gott go with you, my friend."

"And with you, Eli."

With everything in him, he hoped this would not be the last time he ever saw the old man.

"Drive the speed limit and be careful," Kim reminded him. "Remember, you still don't have a driver's license. We don't want you to get picked up."

"I'll be careful," Joe said.

As he drove away, he found himself newly amazed at Rachel. Instead of dissolving into tears because of his angry words, as Grace would have done, she had quickly and efficiently gone into action to extricate him and his son from a bad situation.

His first impression of Rachel had been an accurate one. Rachel was indeed a fighter. The question he had to ask himself was— with a woman like that by his side, why in the world was he running?

CHAPTER 21

"Thanks, Aaron." Joe set his duffel bag on the floor and looked around at the hunting cabin. "This is...great."

"Are you sure?" Aaron shoved his glasses up the bridge of his nose, an action Joe remembered from college as a barometer of Aaron's nervousness.

Who *wouldn't* be nervous, with him and Bobby showing up out of the blue and asking for sanctuary?

His old college roommate had not inquired about, and Joe had been too tired to explain, the unusual clothing he and Bobby were wearing. That was typical of Aaron. He accepted everyone without question exactly as they were. Whether that was from compassion or disinterest, Joe had never decided. He supposed Aaron figured that if Joe felt the need to dress like an Amishman, there must be a reasonable explanation.

They had been close friends at one time, and college roommates for two years. Aaron had taken his Bible classes seriously.

Joe had not.

Aaron had tried to keep in touch, even after Joe's star on the pro baseball circuit had begun to rise.

Joe had not.

At the time, he'd had more exciting friends to hang out with than earnest old Aaron, who was stuck in West Virginia trying to eke out a living from a little gospel bookstore.

Aaron had contacted him directly after Grace's death, when the storm of public intrusion had been at its peak, and had once again offered Joe the use of the empty hunting cabin he had inherited from his grandfather, along with a solemn promise of privacy.

It was all that Aaron had to give, and he offered it freely.

Deep down, Joe realized he had been slowly working his way to Aaron ever since they'd left LA. His old nerdy friend and Aaron's wife, Deborah, were Christians down to the marrow of their bones. Because of this, Joe felt he could trust them.

Aaron's nervousness now took the form of taking his glasses off and polishing them furiously. "If I'd had any idea you were coming, I would have gotten it in better shape." He shoved the glasses back onto his nose.

"It's fine—just the way it is."

With cobwebs on the ceiling, mice droppings on the floor, and an abandoned bird's nest in the corner.

With nostalgia, Joe thought back to the clean, orderly daadi haus in which he had awakened with such hope only this morning.

"I'll come back tomorrow and help you get it in better shape," Aaron promised.

"Really, Aaron, it's fine." Joe tried to keep the exhaustion from his voice, but he was dead on his feet. "The only other thing I need from you is a promise that you won't tell anyone we're here."

"We won't." Aaron blinked a couple of times. "But wouldn't Bobby rather sleep at our house tonight? There's an extra cot in our little boy's room."

Bobby had cried half of the way here.

"I doubt he would be willing to do that," Joe said. "But thanks for asking."

"It can get pretty cold up here in October." Aaron rubbed his arms. "If you need it, there's wood stacked outside, some kindling in the box beside the fireplace, and dry matches in that jar on the mantelpiece."

As much as Joe appreciated what his friend was doing for him, feeling like a refugee was even more infuriating after experiencing the respite of the daadi haus and his small circle of Sugarcreek friends. He didn't want to be here.

He was running. Again.

He hated it.

He despised what fame had stolen from him and his family. It had come upon him one ball game at a time, one fan at a time. He hadn't awakened one morning suddenly being unable to shop for his own groceries without being accosted for autographs. Fame had grown slowly, the inconveniences offset by the riches he thought he had wanted.

Regaining his anonymity for these past few months had convinced him that the price fame had exacted wasn't worth it. Life as a regular guy was sweet in Sugarcreek. Having tasted that sweetness, all he really wanted now was the freedom to live in that small town, where a handful of people truly cared about him. *Him* —not the legend.

He had fantasized about coaching Bobby's little league team someday and having pizza with the other dads. He wanted to be able to go to a parent-teacher conference and have a teacher feel free to scold him, if necessary, over his child's behavior. He wanted to go to church and help pass communion without people whispering about him and pointing as he did so.

He wanted to be able to open the door to the daadi haus

without microphones and cameras being shoved into his and Bobby's faces.

And he wanted Rachel. Loyal, beautiful Rachel, who had helped him even after he accused her of lying and told her to get out of his life. He had only known her a few weeks, and yet being near her had already become necessary to his happiness.

He needed Aaron to leave now so he could sort it all out. There were decisions he needed to make about his future that would take time and stillness—and most of all, prayer. His father's weapon of choice.

"I'm really tired, Aaron," he said. "Can we talk in the morning?"

Aaron's troubled eyes filled with compassion. "I'll bring breakfast. There are plenty of clean blankets and sheets in a plastic box in the closet. We keep them there so the mice can't get into them."

"Thanks."

He closed and locked the door after his friend left and pulled Rachel's phone out of his pocket along with his own. He needed to call her and let her know he was okay.

But there were no bars on either phone. They were too far into the boonies to get a signal. No landline, either. He wouldn't be able to call her tonight.

It was astonishing how much that saddened him.

Bobby was huddled in the corner of an old couch. "I don't like it here, Daddy."

"Me either, son."

"Can we go back home now? I miss my kitty."

"It's late, buddy. Let's get some sleep. Things will look better in the morning."

Bobby stuck his thumb in his mouth and mumbled, "Can I thweep w' you?"

It felt like being hit in the stomach with a baseball bat, watching Bobby suck his thumb and revert to baby talk again. He had been so proud of the fact that his child finally felt secure enough to sleep in his own little room at the daadi haus.

Exhaustion, both physical and emotional, made Joe's limbs feel heavy. He was so tired of trying to protect his traumatized little boy and failing. He was so tired of trying to make decisions and finding out he'd been dead wrong.

"Yes, son." He sighed. "You can sleep with me."

Dear Rachel,

My amnesia is gone! I called my grandparents, and they came to get me. They said my cousin and her husband want to adopt my baby. My cousin can't have babies of her own, so I guess this will be a really nice Christmas present for them and I can still see my little girl whenever I want to. I can't wait to go back to school. I didn't think I would miss it, but I do. I want to graduate from high school. I'm thinking about becoming a cop when I grow up, just like you did.

Love,

Stephanie Anne Fowler

P.S. Please don't be mad at me.

"Her grandparents came for her?" Rachel laid the letter on the counter at the police station.

"They came in when she brought the letter, and I met them," Ed said. "Nice people. Worried about their granddaughter. They said to give you their thanks."

She smoothed a hand over the letter. It had been written on flowery stationary that Rachel had forgotten she possessed. The girl had also somehow managed to find a florid purple felt-tip with which to write. Typical. She wondered how many of her drawers Stephanie had dug through in order to come up with writing materials that fit her fifteen-year-old tastes.

In spite of the round, childish scrawl, Rachel was impressed with Stephanie's literacy. There was not one misspelling. The girl would do well in school. That thought gave her comfort.

She traced her finger over the lines of the letter. "Stephanie dots her i's with little hearts."

"She's a kid," Kim said. "Probably still believes in the tooth fairy."

"She certainly believed the fairy tale that 'Mack' told her," Ed said with disgust.

"Have you given up on finding him?"

"We have no real name, no make of car, no license number, no fingerprints, no destination—and Stephanie probably wouldn't testify against him even if we did manage to find him. There are a million guys out there just like Mack."

Kim picked up the letter and studied it. "I think it's interesting that she included her whole name."

"Why?"

"Unless I miss my guess, that little girl is hoping you'll find her. With all the information we have, it shouldn't take long."

"I might do that when I get over being 'mad' at her for selling out Joe. I have a feeling Stephanie might be an interesting person to know in a few years."

"You probably helped her more than you know."

"I hope so."

During the past few hours, Rachel had seen a side of Kim she had never expected. The volunteer had been an enormous help with getting Joe out of town. It occurred to her that Kim would make a fine police officer for their town someday—if and when there were any openings.

"Thanks for helping out today, Kim. I owe you one. Is there anything I can do for you in return?"

"Well," Kim said wistfully, "I've kind of been wondering. Do you suppose your aunt Lydia might ask me to come around for dinner sometime? I don't have any relatives around here and—"

"I'm sure of it," Rachel said. "But I'm giving you fair warning: bring some cash. There's this orphanage in Haiti that my aunts are involved with, and Lydia's cooking doesn't come cheap these days...."

"They're like two peas in a pod," Aaron said, watching Bobby and his son Davey build a tower out of Lincoln Logs. "I shouldn't be surprised, with only a month's difference in their ages."

"You'd almost think they were twins, except for the difference in hair coloring." Joe was enjoying the sight of his son so absorbed in play that Bobby seemed to be unaware that his dad was even in the room.

"Have you figured out what you're going to do?" Aaron asked.

"I have an idea," Joe said. "I don't know if it will work."

"Tell me."

"I've been thinking about something that Bertha, the old Amish lady I was telling you about, said. She told me that the way they deal with curious tourists is to simply go about their daily business. She says that when the tourists have looked their fill and asked all their questions, they lose interest. And visitors to Amish Country soon discover that the Plain people aren't so different after all."

"And you think that will work—for you?"

"It's the only thing I have left. It's either go completely public or live in some gated community for the rest of my life. Bobby deserves a normal childhood. I want to give it to him if I can. I think that childhood could happen in Sugarcreek."

"How can I help you, brother?" Aaron's eyes were filled with compassion.

"I need to go back and deal with things."

"Would you like us to keep Bobby while you do?"

"I don't think he would stay."

Aaron watched the boys play a few more moments. "Ask him."

Joe thought over Aaron's suggestion. Asking couldn't hurt. "Bobby? Come here. Daddy needs to talk to you."

Bobby's reluctance to come to his father was evident. He had the Lincoln Log project to complete. New puppies wriggled and whined in a basket in the corner. And there was a small homemade playground out back that he and his new friend had run to and from all morning. Aaron's place was packed with wonderful things for a child to enjoy, and Bobby was having the time of his life.

"What, Daddy?" He glanced back over his shoulder at his playmate.

"I'm thinking about going back to Sugarcreek for a few days. Do you want to come with me?"

"Right now?" he whined.

"Yes. Right now."

"Can't I play with Davey some more, Daddy, please?"

"You can if you want to. Would you like to stay here a few more days? Sleep in Davey's room? I need to leave and take care of some things."

That got Bobby's attention. "What things?"

"I'm going to try to make it so we can go back home and live in Sugarcreek forever."

"Will those people go away?"

"I'm going to talk to them and ask them not to do that anymore."

"Can Davey and his mommy and daddy come visit us?"

"Absolutely. And we'll come here." He glanced at his old friend. "Often."

"It's only a three-hour drive," Aaron said. "If he gets upset, we'll bring him to you."

"I'll call you every night, son."

"'kay." Bobby's attention was already wandering back to his little playmate and the litter of pups.

"I think that's a yes," Deborah commented and smiled.

"He'll regret it tonight when he realizes I'm gone."

"Aaron and I will deal with it," she said.

"I appreciate it," Joe said. "Things might get pretty intense in Sugarcreek for a while. I'd rather Bobby not be in the middle of it."

"He'll be safe here." Deborah put her arm around Aaron's waist. "You go do what you need to do, Joe."

"You've done so much for us already, my friends. I needed a place to rest and pray and think things through, and you gave me that."

"Brook Cherith," Aaron said.

"Excuse me?"

"My grandfather always called his hunting cabin 'Brook Cherith,' after the place where the prophet Elijah rested," Aaron said. "After which Elijah called upon the name of the Lord and overcame four hundred and fifty prophets of Baal."

"Prophets of Baal, huh? That's an encouraging thought," Joe said. "Pray for me, Aaron. If what I'm planning doesn't work, I'm all out of options."

CHAPTER 22

"We made Joe sleep outside in that one-room cabin," Bertha said. "With him used to mansions and fancy hotels. Goodness' sakes."

"He didn't mind," Rachel said for the hundredth time. "He was grateful for everything you did."

Her head was pounding with one of the worst headaches of her life. She was also just about as depressed as it was possible for her to get. It had been a week, and Joe had only made one quick call from a friend's house to let her know that he and Bobby were safe.

The press had left. Strangely enough, she had the distinct feeling they weren't upset in the least by Joe's sudden disappearance. It was his very elusiveness that made him such desirable prey.

She missed him. She missed Bobby. She missed her car. She even missed Stephanie.

Drained, she left her aunts to their never-ending speculations about Joe and his former life.

When she arrived home, she went into the bathroom to take some aspirin. Placing both hands on either side of the sink, she looked at herself in the mirror. There were dark circles under her eyes, and her cheeks looked hollow. She had barely slept since Joe and Bobby left.

Pictures of Joe's haunted eyes from the first night she met him kept pouring through her mind. She winced every time she remembered the belligerent attitude she gave him when he was new to town.

She also remembered watching Joe jump with feigned terror each time Anna played her little "boo" joke on him, recalled his never-ending patience with her aunts and his extraordinary love for his son. She replayed how they had sat together at church and how surprised she had been the first time she had heard him singing the old hymns with conviction and enjoyment.

Her favorite memory of all was of sitting beside Joe as they had laughed together at that bug movie—Bobby snuggled in her lap, Joe holding the popcorn. It had been one of the best evenings of her life.

Against her will, she had fallen head over heels in love with the man *and* his son even before she knew what the rest of the world did. Now she didn't know if he would ever come back to Sugarcreek. He couldn't keep running forever, could he?

That was the problem. As long as he felt he needed to go underground to protect Bobby, he might.

The thing she most wanted to do was climb back into bed, pull the covers over her head, and coast into oblivion—but she was pulling a double shift tonight. She hoped there was plenty of coffee at the station. She would need it.

As she drove to the station, a bottle green truck with jacked-up tires roared past. The Keim twins were at it again—still living their rumspringa to the fullest. She was sick to death of dealing with them and that ridiculous truck.

Flipping on her squad lights, she gave chase through town,

hoping to pull them over before they left the township limits—her jurisdiction. Unfortunately, they gunned the truck and tried to outrun her, hurtling down Route 93.

She was not in the mood for this. Those boys needed to be taught a lesson. Her worry about Joe and Bobby morphed into anger at the boys as she flipped the switch into a chattering siren.

They sped up.

She gritted her teeth and stomped on the accelerator, hoping there would be no buggies on the road.

Of course, in and around Sugarcreek, there were *always* buggies on the road. The boys knew this as well as she did. They had driven their share of buggies until they had gotten jobs at the Belden Brick Company and sunk their paycheck into the truck they were presently using to outrun her.

Surely they would know to watch for buggies.

Their truck was swerving back and forth on the road, and she began to suspect that whichever twin was driving was drunk. Her decision to chase them was looking less and less wise. At the speeds they were driving…

The slow-moving buggy didn't stand a chance.

The truck plowed into it, crushing it like a cardboard box. She saw a body fly out. The horse, locked into its traces and whinnying in alarm, fell into the ditch.

Before she could even completely stop her car, the truck had backed off the wreckage and was roaring down the highway again, swerving around the crumpled body in the road.

She jerked the radio mic to her mouth. "Accident on State Route 93, just south of town. I need an ambulance."

The familiar-looking horse was badly hurt, flailing its legs in the air—but she couldn't deal with that now. She had to find out if the person from the buggy was alive. Hopefully no traffic would come. The squad car with its flashing lights would be some protection. She didn't have time to set up flares until she found out…

Her legs buckled when she got close enough to identify the driver of the buggy.

"Dear God, no!" She fell to her knees beside him.

It was Eli, who had been like a second father to her.

He didn't respond. His legs lay at an unnatural angle. His face was gray. And there was blood seeping from a head wound.

She wanted to howl in fury, to shake her fists at the sky at the unfairness of yet another lethal confrontation between a buggy and a motorized vehicle.

But she neither howled nor shook her fist. Her training immediately kicked in. She pressed two fingers to Eli's throat while begging for his life.

"Father, please—not this man—please, Father…"

A faint, thready pulse quivered beneath her fingers. If the EMTs would get here fast enough, there was hope!

"Hold on, Eli," she sobbed. "Please hold on. Your family needs you. I need you."

Tears dripped down her cheeks and off her chin, wetting the black cloth of the old man's coat. She staunched the blood from the cut on his head the best she could while waiting for the life-saving siren of the ambulance, praying that no other cars would come around the curve and be going too fast to stop.

The ambulance arrived. Hands lifted her up and away from the old man—the old man who had comforted her the day she buried her father. A gurney appeared, and Eli was strapped in and rolled into the awaiting ambulance.

As though from a long distance, she heard a gunshot. Someone had put the broken and dying horse out of its misery. She glanced over and saw Ed shaking his head in regret as he holstered his gun.

Too many horses had died because of impatient drivers. Too many Amish people had been hurt for no other reason than trying to hold their families and churches together by using the slow-moving vehicles.

The crisis, for now, had been taken out of her hands. As though her body knew that nothing more was needed from it for now, it began to shake. Not from the cold of the overcast late October weather, but from nerves and regret and grief. The very marrow of her bones felt chilled.

Then she felt a broad chest behind her and arms that warmed hers, and she looked up, wondering who would dare to be holding her. Surely not Ed or one of the other police officers. They would never be that unprofessional.

At first she didn't recognize who the tall man was. His eyes were a startling cobalt blue, he was clean-shaven, and his hair was short and wavy. She had never seen this man before—except...

Except in pictures.

"Joe!" She clung to him, all reservations gone. "You came back!"

"Of course I came back," he said. "How could I not? This is my home."

She buried her face in his chest, remembered where she was, and let out a moan. "I don't think Eli is going to make it."

The daadi haus smelled musty and unwashed. Joe had departed in such a hurry that things had been left in disarray. It surprised him how much this bothered him as he walked through the rooms straightening bed linens, putting dirty clothes in the hamper, and opening windows.

This cottage didn't belong to him, and yet after painting and scrubbing and making it into a home, he felt more ownership of it than any place he had ever lived—including the mansion Grace had chosen and bought.

He retrieved a pair of Bobby's socks that were peeking out from beneath the bed. They were so small. He smoothed them out with his hand, feeling a tug in his heart at being separated from his little boy.

He hoped the reporters would come soon. He was anxious to put his new plan into place—a plan that involved never running again.

After he put the cottage into shape, he threw some tea bags into a pan of water and brought it to a boil. Then he stirred in some sugar.

He would not wait on someone like Stephanie to alert the media ever again. He would let them know exactly where he was, and when they arrived he would talk their ears off—hopefully until they were sick to death of him. He intended to talk until all the glamour and mystery had worn off. Until he had become, in their eyes, just an ordinary Joe, who was no longer newsworthy. He would talk to them nonstop until they and everyone else in the world was so bored with him that he could bring his son home to live in peace.

He was planning on becoming the most tedious ex-legendary baseball player on earth.

It was the one thing he had never tried.

While the tea cooled, he dialed a number on his cell phone. He needed to contact Henrietta. Now that he had decided to go public, there was no better person to put in charge of alerting the press.

"Henrietta Stiles." Her voice was as rich and smooth as smoked honey. "Business manager to the stars," she said with more drama than necessary. It was her trademark.

Her voice was enough to make a man pause. Her physical

appearance was not. Henrietta had the tenacity of a pit bull and the appearance of a fifties-style housewife—complete with pastel shirtwaist dresses and pearls. He and Grace had often wondered how Henrietta could be so successful, rubbing elbows with people who considered themselves the elite, without some upgrade in fashion rubbing off.

They had come to the conclusion that she was astute enough to deliberately dress like June Cleaver—making her the ultimate mother figure as she dealt with some of the most insecure people in the world.

"How are you doing, Henrietta?"

He heard a quick intake of breath. "Micah!"

It felt strange hearing himself called by his real name. In the past few months, he had *become* Joe Matthews. Micah Mattias was someone he didn't know anymore.

"Where are you?" Henrietta asked. "Are you and Bobby okay?"

"We are."

"Why haven't you called? It's been months! I've been so worried. And then the press found you and you disappeared again."

"I'm safe." He looked around at Abraham's cottage. "For now."

"Tell me where you are and I'll come get you."

It was tempting. Henrietta was, hands down, the most competent woman he had ever known. His wife would have been lost without her—the two of them had been together for years. Soon after his marriage, he had allowed Grace to talk him into letting Henrietta handle his business affairs. He had never regretted it.

"There's no need for you to come, Henrietta. I have a place to stay, and Bobby is fine. He has a kitty cat now."

"Where *are* you?" Her voice was insistent. "Hiding away like this isn't healthy."

"I'm back in Sugarcreek. I'm not hiding anymore." He let that sink in a moment. "But I want to go public again. I'd like to give some interviews. Can you arrange that for me?"

Henrietta lived and breathed public relations. Her ability as a publicist was famous.

He could almost hear the wheels spinning in her head. "Oh, absolutely."

He could picture her pulling a notepad and pen toward her and making notes in that heavy, spiky handwriting of hers.

"How about if I set up a phone interview with your old coach first?" she said. "Under the circumstances, there's a chance he'll take you back."

Joe flexed his right shoulder. It still hurt.

"Don't contact him," he said. "Just alert the media for now. Call whoever you want to contact. I'll talk to anyone. The sooner the better."

Henrietta's voice was unsure. "If you say so. What's going on, Micah?"

"Have there been any updates from the police on Grace's murder?"

"No. Nothing." Henrietta hesitated. "The news said you were working as a handyman for some Amish people?" Her voice rose in question as though she couldn't believe what she was saying.

"I am. It's a long story, Henrietta. Listen, I need for you to send me some ID. I need to have access to my bank accounts again."

"Can't you just come home? I'll reserve a flight immediately. You can be here within a few hours."

"I appreciate all that you've done over the years, Henrietta. But there's no 'home' for me to come back to. I want you to sell my house as soon as you can. Make sure you keep a nice commission for yourself."

"You want to sell the house?"

"Yes. I'm planning on staying here."

"Please, Micah—you aren't thinking straight. If you'd just come back for a few weeks, maybe we could—"

He didn't want to argue with her anymore. "I have to go, Henrietta."

He heard her voice take on the businesslike tone he was used to. "Tell me where you're staying."

He gave her the address.

"I'll make those calls now, Micah. Get braced for an onslaught."

"Thanks, Henrietta."

Before the news that he was no longer hiding hit the airwaves, there was one more phone call he needed to make.

The number had been written on a slip of paper, and he'd kept it in his wallet for years. The wallet was gone, along with the number, but the digits had been burned into his brain. His heart thudded against his chest as he dialed the number. He had no idea how this would turn out. He only knew that he needed to make this call. Now.

Sitting at the hospital while Eli struggled for every breath had shaken him to his core. There were no guarantees in this world that the people you loved would be here tomorrow. Each day was precious. Each *moment* was precious.

If it was within his power to do so, he was not going to allow one more day to slip by without inviting his father back into his life.

He didn't know if it was just his imagination, but the ringing on the line seemed faint and far away. An ocean away.

A voice as familiar as his own answered. Joe closed his eyes in disappointment. It was only an answering machine.

"It's Micah, Dad. I—I wanted to say that I'm sorry. About

everything. I'd appreciate it if you would call me back when you get a chance."

He gave his phone number and address and hung up. He'd made the first move. Would his father return his call?

With all his heart, he hoped so.

CHAPTER 23

E ven though he was unconscious, Rachel held onto Eli's work-roughened hand as though it were a lifeline. Both of his legs were in casts. Tubes snaked into and out of his body. Bandages wreathed his head, making it look twice its size.

"Your cousin Joseph would like to come in now to see his father, Rachel." A daughter-in-law of Eli's gently touched her shoulder. "He just arrived from Pennsylvania."

"Of course."

She reluctantly let go of Eli's hand and left the room as Eli's youngest son entered. The room was already filled with the maximum number of relatives the hospital allowed—all sitting vigil beside their patriarch's bed. It would be selfish of her to take up space any longer.

Several members of Eli's church sat quietly outside in the waiting room. Embedded within the Amish church members were the Keim twins, still dressed in their Englisch clothes but wearing hangdog expressions. Flanking them like battered bookends were their mother and father, who were pale and shaken but valiantly trying to absorb some of the great damage done by their unruly sons.

No fingers were being pointed, no accusations leveled. There would, of course, be no lawsuit brought against the boys—no matter how steep the hospital bill.

Unless she missed her guess, the Keim twins would be making their kneeling prayer of confession soon, accepting the rite of baptism that would ensure their place in the Amish church. Regardless of whether Eli lived or died, there would be no recriminations from the rest of the Amish population. Ever. Their shameful rumspringa would be forgiven and forgotten.

Nor would any Amish person blame her for chasing the Keim twins into Eli's buggy. They would bow, instead, to what they saw as the will of God. It was their way. One she respected enormously —and understood the least.

Of course, no one had to blame her for the accident. She was too busy blaming herself.

She felt out of place in her police uniform as she made her way from Eli's room and weaved through the quiet crowd to the exit. As much as she cherished her father's relatives, she was not Amish, and that created a polite but permanent and invisible barrier about which she could do nothing except go home and hope that Eli survived.

The twenty-minute drive from Union Hospital in New Philadelphia seemed to evaporate as she tried to absorb everything that had transpired during this long, long day that still wasn't over. Her horror over Eli's accident, the guilt she felt over giving chase to the vehicle that had plowed into Eli, the sudden appearance of Joe right at the moment she needed him most—it was all almost more than she could process.

It was, however, nice to have her beloved little Mustang back. The silver blue car purred along as though reveling in their reunion. There were few people whom she would ever have allowed access to her "baby," but Joe was one.

As she entered Sugarcreek, she decided to drive by the farmhouse to talk to her aunts. They would be terribly worried—and hungry for an update on Eli. As she pulled into their driveway, she was at first puzzled when she saw several vehicles in their yard. Then she noticed two news vans, and her heart sank.

So, Joe had gone through with his decision to talk at length with the media. She wasn't sure it was wise, but it wasn't her choice to make.

As she drove closer, she saw that Joe was sitting on the porch surrounded by reporters and cameras. And unless her eyes deceived her, half of them were holding glasses of iced tea.

She parked and walked toward the knot of reporters grouped around Joe. As she drew closer, it sounded like he was giving forth, in mind-numbing detail, about where he and Bobby had gone after he'd left LA.

"Well, then we drove through the Midwest for a while. Bobby really likes the barbecue in Oklahoma City. There's a restaurant there that does something with their sauce that's out of this world. But he didn't like the coleslaw. He's usually pretty good about eating his vegetables, but he hates cabbage. Especially when it's made into coleslaw. I can get him to eat cooked cabbage sometimes, though, if I put enough butter in it."

She caught his eye over the shoulder of one of the reporters. Joe winked.

That caught the attention of the reporter closest to him— whose eyes had begun to glaze over. "Is this your girlfriend?" he asked, perking up.

"Not yet," Joe said. "Although I think she has possibilities, don't you?"

The reporters looked her up and down. "So how did you two

meet?" one of them asked, obviously hoping for something juicier than Bobby's food preferences.

"That's a long story." Joe lifted a pitcher sitting on a small table beside him. "Here—let me refill your glasses while I tell you all about it."

Rachel bit her lip to keep from laughing as Joe launched into a lengthy recitation of his truck breaking down and their confrontation outside the cabin at her aunts' farm. As she backed away, she saw a reporter signal a cameraman, who then began to put away his equipment.

It seemed to be a good plan—so far. But after Joe finished boring the reporters, the fans would come. She didn't know how many or how long they would stay, and she wasn't sure it would be as easy for them to lose interest. But it appeared that Joe's plan was working in the meantime.

Suddenly there was a small commotion on her aunts' front porch. She saw Lydia and Anna struggling to carry a table outside. She jumped to help.

"What in the world are you doing, Lydia?"

Her aunt nodded toward the group of reporters. "I think they look *hungahrich*," she said. "Don't you?"

Rachel looked them over. "I *do* think they look hungry," she said solemnly.

Bertha limped out, carrying a large spackleware pot of coffee in one hand.

"I am thinking three dollars for a piece of pie with one cup of coffee," Lydia said. "Do you think that is too much?"

"For your genuine, homemade Amish pies?" Rachel surveyed the bored reporters. "Those are big-city people sitting there on Joe's porch. I'd charge 'em *six*."

Rachel was lying in bed, watching TV, when the phone rang.

"So how do you think they like me now?" Joe asked.

"I think you're going into the hall of fame as one of the biggest gasbags of all time."

Joe spluttered with laughter. "That's what I'm hoping."

"How's Bobby?"

"I just talked with him. Apparently in addition to a kitten, we'll be having a mixed-breed puppy coming to live with us."

"He's okay, then?"

"So far. Aaron's being a good fill-in dad while I'm gone. He was giving Bobby and Davey 'horsey-back' rides when I called. Bobby seemed impatient to get back to all the fun."

"I'm relieved to hear that."

"He asked about you."

She was surprised. "Really?"

"Uh-huh. He wanted to know if you and I were kissing yet. I told him no, but I would give it some consideration."

She heard a chuckle in his voice. She had no idea how to respond.

There was an awkward silence as the image of kissing filled her mind.

Joe cleared his throat. "Four-year-olds these days are a lot more precocious than I was at that age."

"Probably."

"All I wanted to think about was playing ball when I was a kid."

"I'm not surprised."

"I was pretty rough on you last week when I thought you had called the press. I still feel bad about it."

"You've already apologized." Rachel pulled herself higher up against the pillows. "Besides, I understood."

"I should have trusted you more."

"It's over, Joe. I've forgotten it. I would probably have reacted the same way."

"No, you would have faced them down from the beginning. You would never have run in the first place."

"I doubt that. I was taught at the academy that when faced with overwhelming odds and no backup, it's best to retreat. If I'd had Bobby to care for, I would probably have done exactly the same thing you did."

"Maybe." He cleared his throat. "When this whole thing is over, Rachel, I want to spend some serious time together."

"I'd like that."

"Sleep tight, Rachel."

"You too, Joe."

She hung up and stared at the phone. She cared so much about that man, she was almost afraid to hope this relationship could turn into anything deeper than a friendship.

Joe congratulated himself on having made the right decision this time. Even though he was missing Bobby terribly, he was certain he had made the right choice. He had laid himself bare, and other than a few die-hard fans who would probably show up on his doorstep in the next few weeks, he was counting on people eventually losing interest in him.

There would be other good ballplayers to take his place in the public eye. As for playing pro ball ever again, he knew that he simply didn't have it in him anymore. He had had a good run, but somewhere along the path he and Bobby had traveled together this past year, he had lost the desire to compete at that level, and he knew in his heart that he would never get it back.

What he had not taken into account in the beginning, after

Grace's death, was that the country, as a whole, had a short attention span. There would always be a breaking story to replace the
one that had gone stale. People would soon tire of a has-been
ballplayer who was no longer winning games. He should have realized that before starting out on this journey.

But had he not taken this journey, he would never have met
Rachel and her aunts. He would still be trying to get his arm back
in shape, hoping to eke out another season, instead of realizing
that it was a relief to step away from the intensity and pressure of
being a high-profile athlete.

Something good that had come from this last go-round with
the press was that the news had brought focus, once again, on
Grace's death and the fact that her killer was still at large. Several
mentions had been made about the reward he had posted for
information leading to her murderer. Unless he missed his guess,
the cops back home were getting an earful. Most of it useless
information, no doubt, but he was hopeful there might be some
small thing that would eventually lead to an arrest.

He knew he would never be completely at peace until Grace's
killer was behind bars.

He carried an empty plate to the sink and was rinsing it off
when he heard a knock at the door. He stiffened. It was dark
outside. Most people, at least those who had electricity, were at
home by now, watching television.

Pulling back the curtain, he saw an unfamiliar car. Assuming it
was a reporter or a fan, he waited, hoping they would go away. The
knocking continued. He opened the door a crack and was stunned
at what he saw.

Dr. Robert Mattias, dressed in a crumpled gray suit, stood on
his doorstep. Joe threw the door open wide.

"Dad!" he cried.

He found himself enveloped in a hug. "I booked a plane the

minute I heard your voice on the answering machine," his father said.

"Yeah," a familiar voice echoed from behind his father, "he couldn't wait."

His brother, Darren.

Joe wasn't thrilled to see his brother, but he was determined not to let Darren's presence spoil his reunion with their father.

"Bring the suitcases in, son," his father said, "and we'll all get caught up."

Darren sauntered back to the car.

"I can't believe you're here," Joe said. "I never dreamed you would just pick up and come."

"I've wanted to make amends since Grace's death. I saw it in the papers. Yes, even in Africa we get news. But then you disappeared and I had no idea how to contact you."

"I almost called you a dozen times. It's been so hard, Dad."

"I know."

"I understand now—"

"It was wrong of me to—" His father spoke at exactly the same time.

"You first," Joe said.

His father nodded. "Yes, I'll go first. I am the one most in need of apologizing. It was wrong of me to ask you to give up something you loved so much. I did it for selfish reasons. I knew that once you started playing pro ball, you'd never come back to us. And with your mother gone, I could hardly bear to have you so far away. Once you made your decision, I was so hurt that I just clammed up. Your mother would say it was my hardheaded Mattias blood coming out."

"You weren't entirely wrong to try to stop me, Dad. I got into some weird stuff for a while."

"But you stopped. I've read everything about you I could find."

"I had to clean up my act once Bobby was born. When I held that little boy in my arms, I knew I had to grow up and be a real father to him. I could no longer spend my life partying."

"Come on, now. You did more than just party. You saved three villages from drought with the wells you paid to have drilled." Robert put his hand on Joe's shoulder. "You sent truckloads of food when some of my people were starving."

"You weren't supposed to know."

"Your brother told me."

"I asked him not to."

"Darren isn't good about keeping secrets—unless they're his own." His dad craned his neck to peer over Joe's shoulder. "Where is this grandson I've been longing to meet?"

"With friends, for now."

Joe explained the situation to his father as he led him into the home. He decided he would put Darren in Bobby's room for the night. His dad he would give the other twin bed in his own room. There was so much he wanted to tell his father, preferably without Darren listening. They could talk long into the night and make up for lost time.

"Ten years we went without speaking," Joe said two hours later. His hands were laced behind his head as he lay in bed, staring up at the darkened ceiling.

"Your mother would not have been pleased."

"She would have knocked our heads together. I miss her."

"As do I."

"I loved Grace, but she wasn't like Mom."

"I'm sorry I never met her."

"You would have liked her. Beneath the makeup and the glamour, she was just a little girl playing dress-up. But she was a good mother to Bobby and supportive of me. She wanted me to contact you and apologize. I wish I had."

"Me too."

Somehow that answer rankled. His father could have just as easily contacted him. "I didn't disown you, Dad. It was the other way around, remember?"

"You were always my son. I never stopped loving you. I had nothing against you playing ball—except for it taking you away from us and from God—but I was terrified of the kind of lifestyle you started living. I was afraid it would destroy you."

"It almost did."

"The only weapons I had to fight with were my prayers and the threat of withdrawing from our relationship. You were my prodigal son, and I had to let you go. Remember that story? It used to be one of your favorites."

Joe turned on his side, facing his father. "I wasn't quite down to eating pig slop, but I was pretty close when the Troyer sisters took me in."

"I'm grateful they didn't let it come to that."

"I remember how the father ran to greet his prodigal son when he saw him from afar off. Now that I have Bobby, I can understand how that father must have felt."

"Then you must know how I felt when you called."

"You came running to me."

"Yes. I came running to you."

"Even though I'd broken your heart."

"No. Because I knew *your* heart was broken."

Joe absorbed that. "How long can you stay, Dad?"

There was a long silence.

"How long would you like for me to stay?" his dad asked.

"Forever?"

His father chuckled in the darkness. "We'll see."

"Dad?"

"Yes."

"Can you see the stars out that window?"

"I can. Did you make them?"

"Nope." Joe grinned. "I didn't make them."

"Me neither. I wonder who did."

"God?" Joe said the same thing he'd said so many years ago. Only this time, he knew there was nothing childish about his answer.

"Do you suppose He made them so that a father and son could look into the sky and know how much God loves them?"

"There's no 'suppose' about it, Dad." Joe felt the same warmth and security in his father's presence that he had known as a small child. "I'm absolutely certain of it."

CHAPTER 24

The husky whisper came in the middle of the night.

"You're next." A sarcastic, muffled voice drifted from the telephone.

Rachel, half asleep, rolled over to check her caller ID. It was blocked. "Who is this?"

"Your worst nightmare."

What movie did the caller get that *from?* she wondered. She checked the illuminated alarm clock. It was 2 a.m.

"What do you want?" She lay back against her pillows and yawned. Ugly calls in the middle of the night weren't the norm, but she'd gotten a few in her career. It went with the territory. She had arrested some real jerks in her time. Some liked to make phone calls when they got out of jail—and usually while stoned or drunk.

The next sentence made her sit straight up.

"Stay away from Micah," the disguised voice said. "This is a warning."

A chill went down her spine. Was this the voice of Grace's killer?

"What do you want?" Rachel gripped the receiver tighter.

"You heard me. Stay away from Micah."

The caller hung up.

Well. She tried to shake it off but knew she would be getting no more sleep that night. Perhaps she would go to the hospital and check on Eli. One of the good things about being a cop was that even though it was after hours, she knew they would let her in.

The morning sun was unusually bright, but Joe and his father had lain awake so long talking, he was too sleepy to get out of bed and close the blinds. He pulled a pillow over his face to block out the sunlight.

Wait a minute. Had he slept through milking Eli's cows? He sat upright, trying to get his bearings. He glanced at the clock—only 4 a.m. Something was terribly wrong. The light streaming through his window was not the sun—it was an inferno.

The aunts' farmhouse was on fire!

He jumped out of bed, shook his father awake, and pounded on his brother's door—yelling at Darren to get up and get out. As his father called the fire department, Joe ran outside, wearing only shorts and a T-shirt.

The fire was worse than he could have imagined. The whole back of the house was aflame, the blackened bones of the structure visible through the fire.

Were the aunts still inside?

The heat was so intense that he had to shield his face with his arm as he ran toward the burning house.

He heard a muffled scream and looked up. There, inside a front upstairs window, were two figures, one of whom was struggling to open the window.

He leaped onto the banister and muscled his way onto the

270

porch roof, using a metal trellis for a toehold. Once on the roof, he ripped his T-shirt over his head and made his way to the window. Lydia's face was ashen in the moonlight as she clawed at the window, trying to open it. The sound of a house going up in flames crackled all around him. Anna had gone blank-faced at the danger, unable to deal with or process what to do.

He wound his T-shirt around his arm and elbow. Lydia, seeing what he intended to do, put her arms around Anna and took a step backward. Joe shattered the double panes of glass with his padded elbow. Shielding his hands the best he could with the cloth, he ripped the remaining shards of glass away.

"Take her!" Lydia shouted, helping her sister through the window first.

Joe held Anna around the waist as he led her to the edge of the roof. The metal roof was slick with dew, but their bare feet gave them some traction.

"Over here!" his father called. His face peered over the roof near the trellis. "I found a ladder. Give her to me."

Joe's dad wasn't young but he was still a powerful man, and Joe was grateful his father was there. Briefly, he wondered why his brother wasn't helping.

He had no idea how frightened Anna was or what this experience might do to her weak heart. He took her face in his two hands and looked her in the eyes.

"My father will help you down the ladder. You can trust him. Okay?"

She gulped. "'kay."

"You'll need to turn backward. When you get to the edge, I'll be holding onto you."

Obediently she did as he asked, but she was awkward and afraid. She clung to him, terrified to step backward onto the ladder. It felt like it took forever to get her turned around with her feet on the top rung. Most of her weight was still supported by him.

She was heavier than he had expected, or perhaps it was the awkward position he was in. He felt the tendons in his bad shoulder protest as he helped her step one rung at a time down into his father's waiting arms.

"She's safe!" his dad called from the ground.

Joe had no time to rejoice. He glanced back to check Lydia's progress. She had managed to climb out of the window and was now crawling on all fours toward him, inching her way to the ladder. Behind her, he saw flames beginning to eat at the walls of the bedroom from which she and Anna had escaped. The metal roof beneath him was growing warm, and he knew they had only moments before their flesh would be seared.

"Hurry, Lydia!" he called.

"I am." Her voice quavered.

By the light of the blaze, he could see her nightgown-covered knees slipping on the slick metal as her arthritic fingers scrabbled for a hold on the seams.

He sat down and scooted backward, to where she trembled with pain and fear.

"It's okay," he crooned as he took her into his arms. "I've got you."

The flames were now licking at the windowsill, and the metal roof had heated to a point that it was starting to burn his skin. So much adrenaline was coursing through his body that it felt as though the old woman weighed nearly nothing, as he inched down the roof with her in his arms.

As he helped her onto the top rung of the ladder, she nearly slipped from his grasp. He lurched forward, tightening his grip on her as she screamed out in fear. Joe followed that scream by an agonized groan of his own, as a feeling of torn muscle sent a shock of pain through his arm. His throat choked in protest at the smoke billowing around him. He smelled the stink of burning hair, not registering the fact that it was his own.

"I've got her, son. Now you get down off of there!"

He didn't have time for Lydia to make her way down the ladder. He felt the heat against the soles of his feet. Letting himself down until his feet touched the banister turned into an awkward half tumble as he tried to lower himself off the porch with only one good arm.

His father enveloped him in a hug the moment Joe fell to the ground.

"I have to get Bertha!" He shook off his father's embrace and ran toward the door.

"Son!" his father shouted. "Stop!"

He couldn't stop. He had to get to her. Covering his face the best he could, he fought his way through the heat near the front door. Bertha's bedroom was on the first floor, but with her leg in a cast, he didn't know if she could get out by herself.

"Joe!" A voice shouted his name and he felt a body slam into his —a firm, strong body that hit him so hard it knocked him sprawling. His head hit the ground. He was awakened a moment later by someone dragging him backward as the black skeleton of the house collapsed in on itself, sending flying embers high into the air.

A sickness curled in his belly, and he began to retch at the sight. Within seconds, still on his hands and knees, he felt a cool hand holding his forehead and another patting his back.

"Here," his father said, handing him a clean handkerchief. "You always did get an upset stomach when something bad happened."

Joe shakily got to his feet. Rachel was standing next to him, and he realized it was her hand that he'd felt on his forehead. And Rachel who had tackled him.

"Why did you stop me?" he said. "I was trying to get Bertha out."

"Bertha's fine," Rachel said. "She was out before you ever climbed onto that roof. I had to knock you down to keep you from trying to rescue a person who was already safe."

"She's okay, then?"

"Her modesty is shaken—she's not used to being seen in her nightgown—but she's physically unharmed."

"Thank God."

"Amen." Rachel looked him up and down. "I wish I could say the same for you, Joe. The pain hasn't kicked in yet, I'm sure, but you're messed up."

"I don't care—as long as your aunts are safe."

Rachel threw a light blanket around his shoulders. "I'm beginning to think Bertha was right about you being an angel. If it weren't for you, I don't know what would have happened to Lydia and Anna."

"How did you get here so fast?" he asked.

"I went to the hospital to check on Eli. I saw the flames on my way back."

"How is he?"

"He's going to make it, Joe." Tears of gratitude welled in her eyes. "Eli's going to live."

The Sugarcreek Fire Department had already arrived and were drenching the daadi haus, saving it from the flames.

The farmhouse was gone.

Joe knew he could not begin to fathom the grief the sisters must be feeling right now. They had grown up in this house. Everything they owned, everything they loved, had gone up in smoke.

Bertha, so long the guardian of this special place, must be utterly crushed.

"Well." He heard her familiar voice behind him. "We will no longer have need to paint the haus."

She stood behind him, leaning on her walker and gazing at the fire. Her face was inscrutable, but tears were streaming down her face.

"I'm so sorry, Bertha," Joe said. "Are you okay?"

"Of course I am." She scoffed. "It is just boards and bricks. It is worldly to grieve over such things."

"I suppose insurance will help replace it," he mused.

Bertha was silent.

His father cleared his throat. "I don't believe the Amish carry insurance."

"What?" Joe was incredulous.

"Gott will provide," Bertha said.

It was still two hours before dawn. Everyone was gathered around a kerosene lamp on Joe's kitchen table.

The fire chief had broken the news to them as gently as possible. Anna looked on with wide, solemn eyes, clutching and unclutching the green tablecloth Lydia had so happily spread over Joe's table what now seemed ages ago.

"It was arson?" Lydia was aghast.

"There was an empty gasoline can and some charred rags behind the farmhouse. Do you have anyone mad enough at you or your church to want to burn the place down?" the fire chief asked.

"Is this possible?" Bertha said.

"The state fire marshal will do an investigation, but it looks pretty cut-and-dried to me. Are you ladies okay?"

"I am okay," Bertha said. "My sisters are okay. The person who set the fire—is not so okay, I think."

"He certainly won't be if we find him," the fire chief muttered. "He won't be okay at all."

The theory of the fire having been deliberately set validated Joe's deepest suspicions. In his heart, from the moment he'd seen the blaze, he had suspected that this was not an accident.

He knew that somehow, someway, this house had been destroyed because of him.

"Where's Darren?" he asked his dad.

"I don't know. He wasn't in Bobby's room when I went to wake him after I called the fire department."

"Darren always liked playing with fire."

"Your brother would never do this."

Joe did not reply. There were many things Darren had done that their father had never known about.

"Tell me about this brother." The fire chief looked at them with interest.

"You can talk to him yourself," Joe's father said. "He'll be home soon. I'm sure he had nothing to do with it."

It was a hard thing, Joe decided, having a brother he didn't trust.

"Who would want to hurt us?" Bertha's eyes were haunted. "We have done nothing wrong to anyone."

Bertha, so stolid, so strong, looked shrunken and old for the first time Joe could remember. Even a broken leg had not taken her down so far.

"I need to get the three of you home," Rachel said. "You can stay at my house for as long as you want."

"There's no need for that," Joe said. "Dad and I can move into one of the cabins, and the aunts can have the daadi haus."

"No." Bertha rallied, showing some spirit. "We will not take your home from you. We will go with Rachel." Her face fell. "It will not be so bad."

Rachel looked hurt. "Not so bad?"

"This is all because of me." Joe clenched his fists in front of him on the table. "If I hadn't come back, this would never have happened."

"You don't know that," Rachel said.

"I *did* know! I knew better than any of you what kind of things, and people, follow me. It was naive to think I could somehow carve out a normal life."

Rachel laid her hand over his. "We'll find whoever did this, Joe; I give you my word."

"You just do that, Rachel." He covered her hand with his own. "Whoever this person is, whatever grievance they think they have against me—and the people who care about me—you find them. And when you do, unless you want a homicide on your hands, you'd better keep me away from them." He gritted his teeth. "Because I'm not running anymore."

"Joe…"

He rose from the table. "I have cows to milk."

CHAPTER 25

J oe heard a *thump* against the front door a few hours later and
went to pick up the local *Times-Reporter* newspaper. He sat
on the daadi-haus steps in the early dawn, trying to ignore
the sad sight of the smoking ashes of the Troyer sisters' home. And
trying to ignore the pain in his shoulder and the bandages on his
arms and feet.

The picture of the fire covered half of the front page, orange
blazes against a dark morning sky. There he was, huddled in a
blanket. He was sick of seeing himself splattered all over newspapers and magazines.

He was furious at himself. He should never have tried to settle
in and make a life here. All he had managed to do was bring pain
and destruction to the very people who had helped him.

"Do you want some company?" Rachel sat down close beside
him. He had been so engrossed in reliving the nightmare, he hadn't
even noticed her walking around from the back of the house.

"No. I don't need company."

He heard her quick intake of breath at his hurtful statement. He laid aside the newspaper and took her hand in his. "What I need is a friend."

"Me too." She sighed and relaxed against him. "My aunts left my home this morning. They are not going to be staying with me after all."

"Why not?"

"Bertha was on the phone a little bit ago, making arrangements with one of Eli's sons—for the three of them to live in Eli's home while he's in the hospital. I overheard her say that she is not comfortable staying in my house."

"That must have stung. What, exactly, made her uncomfortable?"

"It was my own fault. They were acting so lost when we got home, I thought it might be good to get their minds focused on something besides the fire."

"What did you do, Rachel?"

"I found a program on the Discovery Channel called Planet Earth. It's a nature program. There is nothing the least bit risqué or questionable about it. Wonderful cinematography. Very educational. They were fascinated."

"Doesn't seem like a bad thing to do."

"Obviously you aren't an elderly Amish woman. As Bertha put it, 'We are used to our ways.' I guess she was afraid I was going to corrupt them with electricity and TV if they stayed."

"I'm so sorry."

She shrugged and looked away. "No matter how close I feel to them, no matter how much I know they love me, there is always a barrier between us simply because I am not Amish. Being Amish is very, very important to them, Joe. It is as though it is embedded in their DNA. It is not just another religion. It is, in their eyes, the only true religion."

"I thought Bertha left the church for many years. Why is she so strictly Amish now?"

"Because she's Bertha." Rachel smiled ruefully. "She made a vow to observe the Ordnung, and she meant it."

He put an arm around her. "Any word about Eli this morning?"

"Yes. He's a little better. I'm going to go see him again when I leave here." She fidgeted with a button on her shirt cuffs.

"What's wrong, Rachel?"

"You were pretty shook up last night, and you were hurt. I didn't want to add to all your worries—but you need to know something. I got a threatening phone call shortly before the farmhouse caught fire."

Joe tightened his grip. "Who was it?"

"The caller disguised the voice. I don't even know if it was a man or a woman. But I was warned to stay away from you."

"You're kidding!"

"I wish I were."

"Why didn't you tell the fire chief last night?"

"I did. He knows and so does Ed. There was nothing you could do about it last night, and I wanted you to get some rest if you could."

"Between the arson and that phone call," Joe said grimly, "the killer could be right here in town."

"True. Or some nut job who wants to scare us for the sheer thrill of it."

"Grace knew the person she let in, Rachel. Remember? She turned the security system off."

"I know." Her voice suddenly became nonchalant. "By the way, did your brother ever come home?"

"You don't have to pretend. I'm starting to be suspicious of Darren myself. He's inside sleeping now. Said he had a stomachache and drove to the Wal-Mart in New Philadelphia for some

Pepto-Bismol. In the middle of the night. He said he ha
to wake us up. He acted shocked about the fire too. Dad bo...

"Should I bring him in for questioning?"

"Not yet."

"Why?"

"I want to watch him and see what he does. I used to know him better than anyone. Besides, I've barely gotten my dad back. I'd like to enjoy him for a few days without putting him in the position of having to defend his youngest son."

"The Amish are going to start rebuilding in a couple days."

"The ashes haven't cooled!"

"They work fast. They love my aunts. And they haven't had a work frolic for quite awhile."

"How will your aunts pay for it? I mean, even if the labor is donated, materials to rebuild a house aren't cheap."

"An Amish assessor will figure out how much the materials will cost, and then my aunts will need to come up with 20 percent of that. Everyone else in the church district will be assessed one dollar for every thousand they own—whether for land or possessions or livestock. That money will go into a fund to pay for the other 80 percent of the materials. Of course the labor is always free."

"That fund—is that something they contribute to every month or year or what?"

"No, only when there is a fire or tornado or other kind of disaster. Some years they pay nothing. Some years they are assessed several times. The Amish take care of their own. It's a good system. It takes care of the problem in such a way that no one is required to give more than they can afford, and no one gets rich off the profits."

They both looked up as a news van drove into the yard. It was closely followed by two more.

"It's starting again," Rachel said.

"It never really stopped." His shoulders drooped, and he hung his head. "I am so sick of this."

"Do you want me to do something? Make this whole farm a crime scene or something? Rope it off with tape?"

"No. Let them take their pictures. Let them ask their questions. At least I got Eli's cows milked before they showed up."

"You know his sons will take care of those cows, don't you?"

"I asked permission from his sons to do it. It was the one thing I could offer. Eli has so much family that I would only be in the way in the hospital, but I love that old man, and it makes me feel better to have something I can do."

"Even if it means getting up at four in the morning?"

"Eli would do it for me."

"Yes, he would."

"You'd better leave, Rachel," Joe said, "unless you want to see yourself on the front cover of every magazine at the checkout counter this week."

"You'll be okay? Here alone?"

"He won't be alone," a deep voice behind them said. "I'll be here with him."

"Dad." Joe was pleased. "I thought you were sleeping."

"Not anymore." His father watched as newspeople began to pile out of the vans. "In fact, I'm wide-awake and ready to tangle. Why don't you go back inside, try to get some shut-eye, and let me deal with these people?"

"I don't know, Dad. You aren't used to this."

"I'm not used to crowds? Come on, son. You know me better than that."

"What'll you say to them?"

"Well"—a huge grin spread across his father's face—"I thought perhaps these good people would enjoy hearing one of my sermons. Or several. Depends on how long they intend to stay. I might as well give them a good taste of the gospel while I'm here. You go on in and get some rest."

"I've missed you, Dad."

As Rachel got into her car, Joe slipped inside the daadi haus, leaving his father to deal with the media. It felt amazing to be able to leave things in his father's capable hands once more. He smiled as he heard his dad greeting the newspeople with enthusiasm and warmth. Dr. Robert Matthias was in his element, and those people had no earthly idea what they were in for.

CHAPTER 26

The bulldozer arrived to clear away the debris. The Amish workmen came and started getting ready to create a new foundation.

Joe was hurrying to wash the dishes after his father's and brother's early breakfasts. He knew his father would love watching the work frolic.

Darren, on the other hand, was morose and distant, quick with sarcasm. Joe felt Darren's eyes following him everywhere. He didn't know if his brother was dealing with a guilty conscience or sizing him up for another hit for money.

As the crowds of fans and media came and went, as he and his father dealt with their curiosity and questions the best they could, Joe kept an ever-vigilant eye out for someone he recognized. Someone out of place. Someone Grace might have allowed access into the house late at night. So far, he'd seen no sign of anyone he recognized...

Except for his brother.

He hadn't told Rachel that Darren had also been fond of crank phone calls back when they were in boarding school.

He wanted time to think things through first. After all, he only had one brother.

Darren had always been jealous of him, he knew that. He had even envied him Grace—he knew that too. And he could envision Darren setting a fire. But was he capable of murder? Joe didn't believe so. On the other hand, he had lived long enough to know that there was a dark side to everyone, including himself. It was simply darker in some people than in others.

"Son, can you come in here for a moment?"

Joe wiped his hands on a dish towel and went into Abraham's study. His dad was seated at the big desk with several books opened in front of him.

"Do you need something, Dad?"

His father glanced at him. "Have you looked at any of these books?"

"A couple."

"Did you take any off the top shelves?"

"Why do you ask?"

"Is Darren in the house?"

"No." Joe sat on the edge of the desk.

"It appears that Abraham had a significant stash secreted in his books."

Joe looked at the heavy books lining the wall of shelves. "I know."

"You knew about this?"

"Yes. I took some of it when I thought I'd disappear again for a while."

"But you put it back?"

"Every penny."

His dad drummed his fingers on the desk. "Do you know how much there is?"

"I never went through all the books. I only took what I thought I'd need."

Robert leaned back in his chair and stared at the ceiling. "Books don't burn well—too compressed. Of all the places Abraham could have hidden his money, these old books were probably one of the safest places he could have chosen. Do the sisters know about this?"

"Things have happened so fast since I got back, what with Eli's accident and then the fire, I haven't had the privacy to tell them."

"Don't you suppose it might help them with the building supplies you mentioned they would need?"

"Of course. I was planning on helping out as well—once Henrietta sends me the paperwork so I can have access to my accounts again. But I have a question, Dad. Why did you ask me if Darren was here before you told me about your discovery?"

His father looked down at the floor. "I've learned not to trust your brother completely. It pains me to say it, but something is not quite right with him these days."

"It always was. You just didn't want to see it." Joe picked up a book and absently rifled through it, not wanting to look his father in the eyes. "Darren told me he was in Africa with you the night Grace died. Is that true?"

SLAM!

Both Joe and Robert started at the sound of the front door slamming shut.

"What was that?" his dad asked.

Joe rose, went to the front door, and looked out to see his brother striding away from the cottage. He came back to the study.

"That was Darren."

"Do you think he heard what we were saying?"

"I'd say there was a good chance."

A car engine started. Through the window, Joe saw his father's rental car speed away. "Actually, Dad, I'd say there was an excellent chance he heard us."

"What a terrible thing for him to hear," Robert said, "his own father admitting that he doesn't trust him."

"If the shoe fits…"

"There's no way he would have hurt your wife."

"Was he with you, Dad?"

"He may have some problems, but he would never hurt someone."

"You aren't answering me. Was he *with* you?"

His father dropped his eyes. "Darren just happened to be in the States the week Grace died. He was scheduled to leave out on a plane that very night."

"What airport?"

His father hesitated. "LA."

"LA! Did he make the flight?"

"He was late. He missed it and had to take another one."

Joe slammed his fist on the table. "Dad, why didn't you *tell* me?"

"Because I knew you would think the worst, and I absolutely knew that Darren would never hurt a fly. There was no way I was going to shed suspicion on my own son."

"You were wrong to keep it from me, Dad."

"No, I wasn't." A steely glint came into his father's eyes. "There is no way your brother is guilty of Grace's murder. No way!"

"He's your son. You're prejudiced."

"I wasn't so prejudiced that I couldn't see *your* faults and try to make *you* face them."

Joe gritted his teeth. "I guess we'll have to wait and see whether Darren decides to come back. Maybe then we can find out the truth."

"He'll be back. He's probably just driving around, blowing off steam."

"He might be a killer, Dad. I need to talk to Rachel about this."

"Knock, knock," a throaty feminine voice called from the living room. "Is anyone home?"

Joe and his father glanced at each other.

"Looks like you have company. If you don't mind, I think I'll go outside and see if I can get your brother on his cell phone," his dad said.

"Good idea."

Henrietta Stiles walked into the study just after Joe's father exited. She immediately gave Joe a kiss on the cheek. "Surprise!"

Past Henrietta's shoulder, he saw Rachel standing in the doorway. There was a strange expression on Rachel's face that he couldn't read. He raised his eyebrow in a question.

Rachel shrugged. "I found her wandering around town, asking how to find you."

"Thanks," he said. "What in the world are you doing here, Henrietta?"

She leaned away from him but grasped his hands. "I saw the story about your friends' house burning, and I wanted to help. You're quite the hero back in LA for rescuing those poor old Amishwomen, by the way."

"That's nice of you, but—"

"Some of our friends insisted on donating money to help the poor old things rebuild. Is it true they somehow manage to live without electricity?"

"Yes, actually, it's—"

"I can't begin to imagine. No television. No Internet. How do they survive? I'd be bored to tears."

"Life here is—"

"Oh, and Joe, your house is all ready and waiting for you. I had a bit of redecorating done while you were away. I thought it might help to take away some of the bad memories if things looked slightly different when you and Bobby got back."

"I appreciate that, Henrietta. You're a good friend."

Henrietta began describe, in detail, the changes she had made to his home. He wasn't surprised. She had always loved to decorate. She and Grace had spent hours together picking out fabrics and colors for their homes.

Henrietta's chatty voice turned into background noise as he drifted out of the conversation, allowing himself to ponder his father's revelation. The few times Darren had visited their home, Grace had told Joe that his brother gave her the creeps. Even though Joe knew Darren had admired her beauty, like everyone else in the world, he had never acted comfortable around Grace. But he had always been fond of Bobby.

Fond enough to protect his little nephew from the sight of his own mother's death?

It fit. And it was plausible that Grace, although she didn't like his brother, might have opened the door to him even if it was late at night.

"Earth to Micah!" Henrietta laughed and waved a hand in front of his eyes.

He shook his head and tried to concentrate on what she was saying. "I'm sorry. I guess I got sidetracked there for a minute. You were saying, Henrietta?"

"I could help with the rebuilding. As you know, I'm extremely good at organizing people and events."

"Thanks, Henrietta, but I'm pretty sure the Amish have everything under control. They've done this sort of thing for hundreds of years."

"But I can stay and watch, right?"

"If you want."

His mind was still filled to overflowing with suspicions of his brother. "Rachel, could I talk with you a minute?"

Henrietta let out a small huff and opened a thin, red, leather briefcase. "I declare. I haven't seen you for months, I've traveled two thousand miles to get here, we have business to discuss, and that's all you have to say to me?"

"I'm sorry, Henrietta. I just need to talk with Rachel for a minute."

"Oh, the two of you can talk anytime." She pulled folders out of the briefcase. "There are so many things we need to go over. You need to sign some papers. I insist that you pay attention."

Outside, he heard the roar of a bulldozer and the *clip-clop* of horse hooves. More Amish workers were arriving.

"Go ahead, Joe," Rachel said. "You aren't needed outside. Whatever you want to tell me can wait." She ran her hands down her uniform. "I worked the night shift last night, and I'm feeling grungy. I think I'll go home and change. I'll be back in a few minutes to help. We can talk then, Joe."

"His name isn't 'Joe,'" Henrietta said irritably. "His name is *Micah*."

"Right." Rachel strolled out to the porch.

The papers he signed were a blur. He obediently put his signature wherever Henrietta pointed. Hopefully he would have access to his accounts and a provisional driver's license in a short while.

As soon as he finished the paperwork, Henrietta accompanied him outside as he tried to find Rachel in the sea of people. Cars and buggies and news vans lined the road on either side as far as one could see. Photographers were trying to take pictures of Amish workers as those workers held hats to their faces.

"Is that man on the bulldozer *Amish?*" Henrietta's voice was incredulous.

He glanced in the direction she was pointing. Sure enough, the bulldozer operator was dressed in suspenders and wore a black flat-brimmed hat along with an Amish-style beard.

"From what Bertha told me, that guy has wanted to operate a bulldozer from the time he was three years old and he watched a bulldozer operator his father had hired build a farm pond."

"Uh, *excuse* me—but I thought the Amish drove those little buggies."

"They do, to go someplace. This guy hires a driver who isn't Amish to haul his heavy equipment to each location, and then he and his son do the work. They don't use it to travel anywhere. It's a tool to them."

"This place is crazy." Henrietta shook her head in disbelief. "You need to come back to LA, where people are normal."

He would have liked to debate that particular issue of "normalcy" with her, but it didn't matter enough to discuss it. Nothing mattered right now except that he needed to talk to Rachel about the fact that Darren might have been in LA the night Grace was killed. It broke his heart, but the coincidence was too great to ignore.

At that moment, Darren pulled into the driveway and got out of the car. He took one long look at Joe and then turned away, but not before Joe saw that his brother's eyes were red—as though he had been weeping. Darren started into the daadi haus just as two Amishwomen came barreling out, apparently already in the process of setting up for the worker's lunch. They were barefoot and chattering between themselves.

Joe saw their mouths move, but sound had ceased for him. All he could think about was getting to his brother and shaking the truth out of him.

Like a sleepwalker, he waded through the crowd and followed Darren into the house. When he got inside, Darren had already pulled a glass out of the cupboard and was standing by the kitchen sink, gulping water.

His father was sitting at the table, looking pale and shaken.

Darren turned around, looked his brother straight in the eyes, and said, "I didn't do it."

Joe gritted his teeth. "You were there."

"Joe," his father said. "Please…"

"Yes. I was there."

"You…" Joe made a lunge for his brother.

His father half rose as though to intervene, but Darren side-stepped him.

"I didn't kill her."

Joe's fists were clenched, aching to connect with his brother's face. "Then who *did*?"

"I don't know. When I got there, she was already gone, so I went to find Bobby." Darren's hand trembled as he drew another glass of water.

"You're the one who—"

"I'm the one who put out the juice boxes and the snacks and made sure he couldn't get out of his room."

"There were no fingerprints."

"I watch TV. I know how these things work. I used my hand-kerchief and shirtsleeves. I didn't leave any prints."

"If you didn't kill her, why didn't you get him out of there? Why didn't you call the police?"

"Me? Call the police? The no-account brother showing up minutes after Grace was murdered? What are the chances? There's no way I could have proved I didn't do it."

"You left my son in that house alone!"

"He was asleep, but he was never alone. I sat outside your house in my car all night, watching and wishing that my big-shot brother would come home."

"You were there when I arrived?"

"Yes, but you didn't see me. As soon as you came home, I left. You didn't notice my rental car parked behind the house. I got lucky. Those houses are so big, no one bothers to look outside."

"Why did you even go there in the first place?"

"There's this business idea I had—a sure thing. I hoped you were good for one last hit."

"Who killed her, Darren?"

"I don't know. If I did, I'd tell you. Grace was always kind to me, even though I could tell she didn't like me. She was a good person. She didn't deserve that."

"How long had she been gone when you got there?"

"I don't know. I knew something was wrong when I saw the front door ajar. I knocked and called for Grace, but when no one came, I let myself in. I heard the back door slam as I walked into the living room. I think my sudden appearance might have saved Bobby's life." Darren laughed mirthlessly. "Actually, I might have accidentally done something right for a change."

Joe glanced at their father. He seemed frozen into position, waiting for his sons to work things out.

Joe then stared at Darren as he sifted through everything his brother had told him. There was a tiny muscle at the side of Darren's eye that twitched whenever he was lying. He'd never told his younger brother of his discovery, because he knew Darren would find a way to control it if he knew. Joe had won a lot of clandestine poker games when they were kids because of that tell-tale twitch.

It wasn't there.

His brother was telling the truth.

CHAPTER 27

Rachel pulled her keys out of her pocket as she made her way to her Mustang. As she unlocked it, Henrietta caught up with her. "Do you mind if I tag along?" she said.

Rachel was surprised. "Why?"

"I came straight here from the airport. To tell the truth, after all those hours in a plane, I'm worn out and my head is splitting. I didn't want to bother Micah for a place to lie down and rest. He seems a little stressed with all these people. I know it's a lot to ask, but I'd appreciate a chance to slip away and have a cup of tea or something. To get my bearings and get over this headache."

"Sure." Rachel was a little puzzled by the woman's request, but some people were pushier than others. Perhaps this was the way people in LA acted. "Hop in."

"What a cute little bungalow," Henrietta gushed when they arrived at her home.

"It's okay, I guess." Rachel unlocked the front door and tossed her keys onto the counter. "Can I get you anything?"

Henrietta was busy looking around and didn't answer. "What?"

"Would you like something to drink? You mentioned needing a cup of tea? I have aspirin and Tylenol."

There was a distant look in Henrietta's eyes, as though she were thinking about something far away. She shook herself, focused on Rachel, and smiled. "I have my own pain medication in my purse, but I'd love a cup of tea, please. I'm parched."

"Sure." Rachel went into the kitchen, microwaved a cup of tea, and brought it out to Henrietta, who was now seated on the couch and leafing through one of the *People* magazines from the library.

"There's sugar in the canister in the kitchen and milk in the fridge," Rachel said, handing her the cup.

"Thank you," Henrietta replied. "This is fine just as it is." She waved her hand at the magazines she had fanned across the table. "This is all so sad. Grace was such a wonderful person."

It occurred to Rachel that Henrietta could fill in a lot of questions for her, things that had been niggling at her ever since she'd discovered who Joe was. She sat down in the chair across from her. "Did you know Grace well?"

"I'd say so. I was her business manager, and I also took care of her public relations. I took Grace on as a client when she was just starting out. We went through several movie projects together. Grace was very talented." Henrietta sipped her drink. "She put her movie career on the back burner when she was pregnant with Bobby. After he was born, she never quite got it going again."

"Do you have any suspicions as to who killed her?"

Henrietta sighed. "The police questioned me about that over and over. I told them I could think of no one who had anything against either of them. Micah and Grace were the perfect couple. I couldn't imagine anyone wanting to hurt them. In my opinion, it was a random break-in. Some crazed killer. The police have pretty much come to the same conclusion."

"Well," Rachel said doubtfully, "things like that do happen. When it's a stranger, it's so much harder to solve."

Privately, Rachel doubted that was truly the conclusion the cops had come to.

"If you'll excuse me," Rachel said, "I'll go change now. I need to get back and help my aunts set up for the midday meal. Do you mind if I take the time to shower?"

"Of course not. I'll be fine here. You take all the time you need. It's so nice to be in a comfortable living room instead of crowded into a plane. Thanks, Rachel."

"There are sandwich things in the fridge if you want to eat," Rachel said. "Help yourself."

"I'm fine. Enjoy your shower."

Rachel closed the bedroom door, dropped her clothes into the laundry basket, laid her gun and cell phone on the bedside table, and turned on the shower in the small, adjoining bathroom. As usual, she left the bathroom door open in order to hear the bedside phone if it rang. Soon steam began to rise and fog the clear glass of her shower stall.

She was shampooing her hair when she heard her bedroom door open and shut. She froze. "Henrietta, is that you?"

"Yes, dear. Micah called and asked you to call him back as soon as you get out of the shower."

Rachel relaxed. "Thanks." Funny, she hadn't heard the phone ring. But then, she had probably had soap suds in her ears. She leaned her head back to rinse out the shampoo.

"Are you and Micah dating?" Henrietta called from the bedroom.

Henrietta's voice interrupted Rachel's thoughts. The woman was going to talk to her even while she showered? How rude. Oh well. Some people couldn't stand to be alone. "No, Henrietta. Not really."

296

"But you'd like to, right? He's so good-looking, and I think he likes you."

Rachel squeezed a dollop of conditioner into her palm and began to work it through her hair.

"We're just friends," Rachel said. No way was she going to confide her feelings for Joe to this woman.

"Really *good* friends, right?"

This was starting to get weird. Rachel rinsed her hair, turned off the shower, pulled her bathrobe down from where she had draped it over the top of the shower stall, and pulled the belt tight.

Then she walked out of the bathroom and into her bedroom.

Henrietta was wearing long calf-skin gloves. She smiled at her pleasantly while pointing Rachel's own 9mm semiautomatic Beretta directly at her navel.

"You didn't answer me. I said, you and Micah are really *good* friends, right?"

Rachel's mind raced, taking inventory of her situation. Except for the robe, she was naked, vulnerable. There was nothing at hand she could use for a weapon.

"I know." Henrietta sighed dramatically. "This must feel so strange. You're usually the one holding the gun, aren't you, dear?"

"What do you want, Henrietta?"

"Isn't it obvious?"

"Not to me."

"I want Micah, of course."

Everything fell into place. "You're the one—"

Henrietta's smile spread across her face, reminding Rachel of a deranged-looking hyena she had once seen at a zoo. Henrietta raised the hand not holding the gun, palm out. "Guilty as charged."

Weird suddenly wasn't a strong enough word for how Rachel felt. Henrietta sat there in her pearl necklace, bright smile, and flowery housedress. All she needed was high heels to finish out the image of the perfect fifties' housewife.

Oh yes, and to lose the gloves and gun.

Keep her talking, Rachel thought, as she stood dripping on the bath mat with her wet hair streaming down her back. *Keep her talking.*

"I don't understand, Henrietta. I thought you liked Grace."

Henrietta got that faraway look in her eyes again. "Oh yes, I liked Grace. *Everyone* liked Grace. From the time we were kids, everyone liked Grace."

"You were children together?"

"Grace spent time in a foster home while her folks were going through a bad patch. I was living in the same house."

"Joe never mentioned that." Rachel crept forward half an inch.

"Micah didn't know. Grace was embarrassed about her past." She frowned. "She was ashamed of how we met."

"I'm sorry," Rachel said, creeping closer. "That must have been tough."

"Oh, you're sorry? I'm sure your heart is just breaking."

"What happened in that home, Henrietta?" She knew there were foster homes that were havens of love and kindness. There were others that were houses of horror. She was betting on Henrietta and Grace having lived in the latter.

The other woman's eyes lost their focus for a moment, as her thoughts turned inward. "I took care of her," Henrietta said. "She was so little and pretty, and our foster father was not...a good man."

"I'm sorry you had to experience that, Henrietta."

Henrietta shook herself and came away from the dark place she'd gone. Now her eyes looked straight at Rachel, and they were deadly.

"She owed me."

"Is that why she took you on as a business manager? To give you a start?"

Henrietta threw back her head and laughed. "My dear, it was me who made her into who *she* was." Her eyes narrowed. "I *invented* her."

"What are you talking about?" Rachel moved forward another quarter-inch. If she could keep her talking until she could get close...

"Grace had the beauty. She even had the talent. I had the brains and the drive. Do you think a girl gets to be a runner-up in the Miss Texas pageant without someone backing her? It was me who worked two jobs to pay for those clothes, me who researched and trained her. Grace might have been the one actually walking down the runway, but it was *me* who belonged up there. I was the one who did all the work."

"But what about Joe?"

"Don't call him that." Henrietta's voice was peevish. "His name is *Micah*. A man like him could never answer to a name as common as *Joe*."

"All right." Rachel resisted the temptation to argue with her. "What about Micah?"

"It was Micah and me who were soul mates. Always. From the moment I laid eyes on him, I knew he was meant for me. The problem was, he was so besotted with Grace's beauty, he could barely see me for looking at her. I finally realized that I would have to get her out of the way if he was ever going to notice what he was missing with me."

"But what about Bobby? Don't you feel bad about taking his mother away from him?"

Henrietta's face clouded. "I'll be a better mother to Bobby than she ever was. I'll be a *real* mother once Micah and I are married."

"Have you talked to that little boy?" Rachel crept another quarter-inch closer. "Have you seen how much he misses her? How often he mentions his mommy?"

Henrietta closed her eyes and rolled her shoulders, as though the strain of holding the gun was creating too much tension. "He'll get over it."

As she said that, the gun's nose pointed toward the floor for a split second. That quickly, Rachel considered leaping toward Henrietta and forcing the gun out of her hand. But Henrietta immediately jerked the gun up and pointed it at Rachel's heart—as though she had read Rachel's mind.

"I will pull the trigger." The woman's voice was as matter-of-fact as if she were discussing a sale on panty hose. Rachel felt goose bumps rising on her skin—not from being cold, but from the knowledge that however homely Henrietta looked and no matter what sacrifices she may have made for Grace in the past, the woman had gone completely and utterly mad.

And she was obsessed with Micah.

Rachel was in mortal danger, and she knew it. Unless she thought of something fast, these would be her last moments on earth. A deep sadness engulfed her. There was so much more she wanted to do and see…so many unfulfilled plans and hopes.

In that instant, she resolved that if she got out of this alive, she would never again hold back from living her life. She would no longer allow police work to consume her. She would even find out if there was a chance Joe could ever love her, and if she found that he could—she would hold onto that love with both hands for the rest of her life.

But first, she had to survive. Her only hope was to keep this crazy lady talking until Henrietta's attention faded or Rachel could get a few steps closer. She had the skill to disarm someone, but not from eight feet away.

"Is that the reason you locked Bobby in his room? To keep him safe until Micah got home?"

Henrietta's face clouded over. "That wasn't me. That was Micah's brother. He let himself in the front door before I could complete my plans."

Rachel wondered if Joe knew.

"And what were those plans, Henrietta?"

"Why, that I would find the body, of course. I would heroically rescue Micah's little boy from that awful, awful scene. No one would ever suspect little 'ol June Cleaver—me." Then she cackled.

It was eerie. There was no other word for the sound. It raised the hair on the back of Rachel's neck. "What are you planning to do with me, Henrietta? You can't shoot me in cold blood. People saw you leave with me. I have neighbors who will hear and report a gunshot."

Henrietta smiled condescendingly, as though Rachel had told a mildly funny joke. "Oh, *I'm* not going to shoot you, dear." Her eyes narrowed and her voice deepened. "At least it will never appear like I did."

"What are you talking about?"

"You're going to commit suicide, of course. By your own hand, with your own gun. Cops do it all the time. Pressures of the job, you know. I'll tell them that I tried to stop you but you were totally depressed by the fact that Micah had rejected you. They'll believe me. I'm a very good actress, you know. I took the same acting classes Grace did."

"Of course."

She cocked an eyebrow. "Don't use that sarcastic tone of voice with me, Rachel. I don't like it."

"But I don't understand, Henrietta. Why me?"

"Because Micah is in love with you, dear. I can see it in his eyes and in the way he looks at you. I know every expression, every nuance of his face. I can read him like a book. I have a Ph.D. in Micah Mattias. I've only misread him one time."

"When was that?"

"I didn't anticipate his disappearing with Bobby. I've been trying to find him for months now. He covered his tracks very well. But then, he would. I was proud of the way he avoided the press and everyone else—even though it was quite naughty of him to not even tell *me* where he was going." Henrietta changed the gun from one hand to the other.

That was a good sign. Her arm was getting tired. Fully loaded, the Beretta weighed two and a half pounds, which didn't sound like much until one tried to hold and point it for an extended period of time. Rachel decided she would be ready to leap the next time Henrietta traded hands. *If* she traded hands.

There was, in Rachel's opinion, an excellent chance that she was not going to survive this day. Henrietta's mental illness, or evil, or obsession, or whatever was wrong with her, made her completely unpredictable.

Again she fell back on her plan to keep Henrietta talking. Since most women loved to talk about the man they loved, she decided to go with the subject closest to Henrietta's heart.

"When did you first meet Micah?"

"Grace kept telling me about this ballplayer." Henrietta's expression softened. "Finally we met. He was magnificent. I knew at that moment that we were destined to be together."

"What's the age difference between the two of you, anyway?"

Henrietta stiffened. "Age doesn't matter between soul mates."

"How old are you, fifty?"

Henrietta gasped. "That's none of your business."

"Sorry, but I'm pretty good at guessing people's ages. You look like you're at least fifteen years older than Micah."

Henrietta's mouth flattened. "I'm forty-one. Not that it's any of your business. You won't be around to tell anyone."

Henrietta was so indignant that she didn't hear what Rachel was hearing—which was why Rachel was baiting her, getting her angry, distracting her. Rachel heard the sound of crunching gravel outside her home.

CHAPTER 28

"Your phone," his dad said.

Joe had been so involved in studying his brother and dealing with the information his brother had just revealed that he hadn't felt the cell phone buzzing in his pocket.

He jerked it out, annoyed at the interruption but fearful that it might be Aaron calling about Bobby.

"Hello!"

"This is Grant."

The private detective he had hired? The one Henrietta had quit paying? Why was *he* calling?

"What do you need, Grant? I'm kind of in the middle of something here."

"Is Henrietta there?"

"Not at the moment. She was, though."

"I just did something illegal."

"What's that?"

"I don't have a warrant or anything, and no chance of getting one either, but I found a place near her home where I could see into her upstairs bedroom."

"Why?"

"She's been acting a little strange lately. Call it a hunch."

"What did you see?"

"Pictures of you."

"Of course you did. She was my business manager. She did PR for me."

"Henrietta did PR for a lot of people, including Grace. Yours was the only face I saw—all over her walls. These weren't PR photos. They were private snapshots, enlarged. Looked like she'd been snapping away for years."

"What are you trying to say?"

"How long has Henrietta been there in Sugarcreek?"

"She arrived today. Showed up at my house a little while ago."

"Wrong. She flew out of LA several days ago. She's been registered at a hotel in Millersburg for a week—well before that fire I read about."

"Before?"

"The woman is obsessed with you. I think she would do anything to get you to come back to LA."

"You think she could have set the fire?"

"I don't know, Micah, but there was only one other picture on the wall with yours."

"I don't know if I want to hear this."

"It was a picture of that place where you've been staying—that Amish inn."

Joe was afraid he knew what was coming next. "And?"

"She had slashed it to pieces."

Joe's heart felt as if it dropped to the floor.

"Where is she now, Joe?"

"I—I don't know."

"You'd better find her, fast. I've been suspicious of Henrietta for a while now. I think there's something really wrong with the woman. Might be smart if you got to that lady cop the papers all say you've been seeing, before Henrietta does."

Joe snapped the phone shut and looked around, wild-eyed. "Where's Henrietta?"

"What's wrong?" his father said.

"I don't have time to explain."

Darren looked at him with interest. "It was Henrietta, wasn't it?"

"Yes."

"I saw her climb into a blue Mustang with that girl-cop about twenty minutes ago."

"I have to go." Joe rushed toward the door.

"Not without me," his brother replied as he ran behind him.

As Joe started his truck, he called Rachel's home. The phone rang and rang. Then he tried her cell phone. No answer there either. Sick with fear, he called Ed and alerted him as to what was happening. He sprayed gravel leaving the farm, praying that the scene he would find at Rachel's wouldn't be a carbon copy of what he'd stumbled upon in his own home in LA.

Rachel heard a small *click* as someone let themselves into the front door. She hadn't bothered to lock it when they'd come in, so it could be anyone—and at this point, *anyone* would be welcome.

Except…

Anna poked her head inside the door. "Rachel? Lydia wants to know…"

Rachel groaned inwardly. *Anyone* except Anna.

Anna's eyes went wide at the sight of Henrietta holding the gun on Rachel. She swallowed and bravely persevered with her task of giving Rachel the message. "Lydia says to ask you if..." Anna lost her train of thought. "Are you playing a game, Rachel?"

"No, sweetheart," Rachel said. "This is no game. Let her go, Henrietta. She has no part in this."

Henrietta scooted back against the head of the bed and aimed the gun at both of them. It put her about three feet farther away, which was, in some ways, a good thing. Most civilians didn't realize that handguns were a lot harder to aim than TV shows would have them believe. An extra three feet improved Anna's survival by a fraction.

"Who are *you*?" Henrietta demanded, motioning Anna into the center of the room with her gun.

"I'm Anna Troyer. Are you Rachel's friend?"

Henrietta let out a mirthless laugh. "No, dear. I'm not Rachel's friend. I'm Micah's friend. A very good friend."

Anna frowned. "Who is Micah?"

"Joe," Rachel said. "She's a friend of Joe's."

Anna's face cleared. "Oh. Joe's nice." She smiled at Henrietta as though she'd discovered a new person to love.

Rachel considered the lamp beside the bed. The base was metal and heavy. If she could get to the lamp while Henrietta was distracted by Anna, she would at least have a potential weapon in hand. She started to creep closer.

"Stay where you are." Henrietta trained the gun on her once more. "Don't move. I have to think."

Rachel stopped. "You'll never get away with it, Henrietta."

"Is she gonna shoot us, Rachel?" Anna's voice quavered. Rachel's stomach turned over at the sound. No one had a sunnier disposition than Anna. No one expected the best of people as much as Anna did. No one was kinder or loved deeper. To have her beloved childlike aunt enduring a face-to-face confrontation with such evil was torture, and she was helpless to protect her.

Anna looked at Rachel for direction. "Will the bad woman get mad if I pray?"

"I don't know." Rachel looked straight at Henrietta. "What do you say, Henrietta? Will the bad woman get mad if Anna prays?"

"The two of you are giving me a headache. I have to think." Henrietta rubbed her forehead with one hand. "She can pray as much as she wants. It's not going to do her or you any good."

"Go ahead, Anna," Rachel said.

Henrietta exchanged hands with the gun again, but she was too far away for Rachel to take advantage of the momentary lapse.

Rachel caught Anna's eye and nodded. "Out loud, Anna."

"Out loud?"

"Yes, Anna."

Anna swallowed and closed her eyes tight. "Gott, don't let the bad woman shoot us. But if she does, make her shoot me and not Rachel. People need Rachel. People don't need me so much."

You have no idea, dearheart, Rachel thought. *You have no idea how much we need you.* She gritted her teeth. If she came out of this situation alive, she would never forgive Henrietta for putting Anna through this.

The phone began to ring on the bedside table. "Shall I get that?" Rachel asked.

"Touch it and you die," Henrietta growled.

After four rings, the answering machine kicked on. Whoever was on the other line didn't leave a message. A second later, the cell phone on Rachel's dresser began to buzz. The three women waited in a frozen tableau until it stopped.

"Someone's looking for me," Rachel said. "You have to give this up, Henrietta. Anything you do to us will only make things worse for you."

"I'm not giving anything up."

"What is taking you so long?" Lydia marched into the bedroom and saw Anna and Rachel. Then she saw Henrietta sitting on the bed, holding the gun. "Oh my goodness…"

"What *is* this, Rachel?" Henrietta exploded. "Your home, or Grand Central Station?"

"It isn't usually like this." In spite of the danger of the situation, Rachel smiled inwardly at the sound of frustration in Henrietta's voice. "I live a quiet life."

"It's going to get a lot quieter here in a few minutes," Henrietta threatened.

"She wants to shoot us," Anna confided to Lydia.

Lydia gasped and put her hand over her mouth.

"Shut up. Just shut up. All of you!" Henrietta rubbed her right temple furiously.

Good, Rachel thought. *The more distractions, the better.* Rachel watched her like a cat watched a mouse, ready to pounce the second she let down her guard.

And then it came. Henrietta shifted the gun to her left hand. Rachel had already noted that she was right-handed. And for one —brief—split second, Henrietta closed her eyes.

Rachel leaped, grabbing Henrietta's weaker hand—the one holding the gun—and forced it straight up, causing it to go off. A bullet embedded itself in the ceiling.

Henrietta tried to wrench the gun down for a second shot, but Rachel slammed the woman's hand against the sharp wooden edge of the bed's headboard until she heard the gun clatter to the floor behind the bed.

Now *this* was something Rachel was trained for. There was no way she was going to get away from her now.

Unfortunately, Henrietta was wiry and stronger than her appearance would indicate. She grabbed Rachel by her wet hair and snapped her head back. Rachel gritted her teeth and ignored the pain as she grappled with the woman.

Henrietta seemed to be filled with almost superhuman strength. She hit Rachel in the face, causing her nose to explode with pain. Flashbacks of the fight that put her in the hospital came flooding back.

Still, she managed to hold on through the pain, as Henrietta's legs thrashed wildly. Then the struggle ended abruptly, as both Anna and Lydia sat down on Henrietta's legs.

Later, Rachel wished she'd had a picture of that moment when the fight went out of Henrietta. Rachel had one knee pinning Henrietta's left arm to the bed. Her own left hand was clutching Henrietta's hair, and her right hand was pressing Henrietta's right arm against the mattress.

Lydia and Anna, their prayer kapps askew, had kept Henrietta's legs still and were panting as if they had run a marathon.

Rachel was almost afraid to move, for fear that Henrietta would start fighting again.

The front door opened and closed. "What is going on in here?" She heard Bertha's voice calling from the living room. "What is taking so long?"

"We're in here, Bertha," Rachel called, making sure she didn't release her hold.

"I send you two in to find Lydia's purse, and—" Bertha stopped dead in her tracks.

"There are handcuffs in my utility belt on the peg in the foyer, Bertha. Would you get them for me?"

Bertha retrieved Rachel's handcuffs and carried them in, pinched between two fingers and held out at arm's length, as though she might be bitten.

Rachel quickly secured Henrietta with the handcuffs and allowed herself to relax slightly. There was no way the woman could get away now.

She stood up and retied her robe while Henrietta glared at her from the bed.

Rachel gave her belt an extra-hard yank. "You messed with the wrong posse, sister."

Anna, breathing hard, got up from the bed and stared Henrietta directly in the eye. "Boo!" she said.

Then they heard the sound of two vehicles sliding into her driveway. Her front door flew open and Joe and his brother burst in, closely followed by Ed.

The men took in the situation at a glance. Ed yanked Henrietta to her feet.

"Micah," Henrietta pleaded, "don't let them do this to me. I only did it for you. Everything was always for you."

"You were Grace's friend," Joe said.

"But…"

Her protests rose to a wail as Ed led her out to the squad car.

"I was so afraid…" In spite of all the people still in the room, Joe pulled Rachel into his arms and began to rain kisses all over her face. "I was so afraid we would be too late."

They were interrupted by a small voice.

"I was very brave too." Anna sounded as though she were about to cry.

"Yes, you were!" Joe released Rachel and gathered Anna into a non-Amish type of hug. "I'm sure you were very brave." Anna didn't seem to mind the hug in the least.

"Actually," Rachel said, "Anna and Lydia saved my life."

He glanced at Bertha. "How did the three of you get here, anyway?"

"Eli's son Adam brought us to retrieve Lydia's purse," Bertha said. "He dropped us off when we saw Rachel's car here. We thought she could bring us back to the frolic."

"Thank God you came when you did."

311

"Exactly." Bertha smiled. "Gott's timing is always perfect."

"It's over, Joe." Rachel retrieved her gun from behind the bed. "We finally know for sure who the killer is."

A long, drawn-out sigh of relief escaped him, as though he had been holding his breath for a very long time. "All I need now is to go get my son."

Rachel smiled. "Well, then, go get him, Joe. We've missed him too!"

CHAPTER 29

"I sat on the bad woman's feet and—"

"I couldn't have done it without you, Anna. You guys were awesome," Rachel said as they sat together in Eli's farmhouse. She knew that Anna would tell her part in this story over and over, just as they had heard the details of Anna's one trip to the beach a hundred times.

Rachel didn't mind. She was so grateful that all of them were alive.

Anna's face was flushed and excited by her part in the capture. "And I prayed goot too."

"I'm proud of you, Anna."

"Anybody home?" Joe called.

He had Bobby by the hand as he entered through the kitchen door. She had never seen such a welcome sight in her life.

"Bobby!" Anna squealed.

The little boy ran to each of them in turn, giving hugs to all four women. Rachel savored the smell of his baby-fine hair and the feel of his chubby arms. She had missed this child more than she had ever dreamed possible.

313

"Can I see my kitty now?" Bobby asked.

Anna held out her hand. "Let's go."

Joe sat down at the table beside Rachel. "Did Henrietta confess to setting the fire yet?"

Lydia brought a coffeepot to the table and poured cups for Joe and Rachel.

Rachel took hers and blew on it. "Ed says she confessed to everything. She figured if your job as handyman went up in flames, you would be forced to go back to LA."

"How was she able to walk around Sugarcreek without me seeing her? I'd have recognized her."

"She hadn't helped Grace become an actress for nothing. Ed found several disguises when they went to her hotel room."

"I never suspected. Not once," Joe said. "I saw her all the time back home. She was a little eccentric, but I never guessed there was anything wrong. I should have paid closer attention. Grace would still be alive if I had paid closer attention."

"I doubt it," Rachel said. "Henrietta is a good actress. She had everyone fooled, not just you."

"I know, but—"

"A good person tends to trust people, Joe."

There was a knock on the door, and Lydia went to answer it. She came back with Joe's father and brother.

"*Told* you I didn't do it," Darren said.

Joe rose from the table and put his arm around his brother. "This is the man who watched over my son."

"What I think," Lydia said, with a sparkle in her eyes, "is that we all need to celebrate with a nice piece of apple pie."

Rachel reached for her purse.

"No, this one is on me," Lydia said. "We have already shipped enough material to keep the Haitian girls busy for quite awhile. I made this one for Bobby's homecoming. It's his favorite."

"And mine," Joe's father said. "The boy takes after me, don't you think, Lydia? He has my eyes and mouth. I'm thinking he might become a preacher someday."

"Dad," Joe said. "Don't start."

"Or a baseball player. Or whatever he wants to be," Robert amended. "As long as he serves the Lord with his life. Now, about that pie..."

Later, when his father and brother had gone back to the daadi haus and Bobby was happily playing with Anna, Joe rose and put his cup in the sink. "Let's go outside awhile, Rachel. It's nice out tonight."

"I'd like that."

They sat down on the porch swing together.

"I told Bobby that you had captured the woman who took his mommy from us." Joe rested his arm along the back of the swing. "You're quite a heroine to him now."

"I don't want to be a heroine to him."

"Why not?"

Rachel hesitated. Yesterday, while staring down the barrel of Henrietta's gun, she had resolved that if she ever got out of the situation alive, she would grab onto life with both hands and never let go.

"To tell the truth..." Rachel knew she was taking a great risk, but she was not someone who played games. Never had been. Never would be. Joe would either accept her as she was—a straight-talking small-town cop whose only beauty regimen was soap and water—or he wouldn't accept her at all.

"I don't want to be his hero. I'd rather be..." She swallowed hard. "His mom."

315

Joe glanced at her, startled. Then his arm dropped to his side and he stared straight ahead as silence descended.

She tried not to care. She had spoken the truth. She had no control over what he would choose to do.

"So..." Joe seemed to be at a loss for words.

She pressed forward. "I love that little boy with all my heart."

"That's great, but—how do you feel about his father?"

"That's easy. I would walk over hot coals for him."

"Even if he's a washed-up, over-the-hill baseball player? I think my shoulder has had about all the abuse it can take. I'll never be able to play ball on a professional level again."

He actually thought that was important to her? No matter what happened next, she was determined to put all her cards on the table.

"I would take you any way I could get you, Joe. I love you. I have for a long time."

Joe didn't respond immediately. Instead, he stared up at the full moon hanging just above the treetops.

"I don't know what's ahead of me, Rachel. I have things I need to take care of back home. Business things. Considering what Henrietta did to our family, I'm suspecting she might not have taken care of us financially after all. I need to check the records and see what she's done. I used to be a rich man. Now I have no idea if there's anything left."

Her heart plummeted. He was bringing up Henrietta and finances on the heels of her telling him that she loved him?

So much for putting her cards on the table. She couldn't help it if she wasn't movie-star beautiful. She couldn't help it if she was just a small-town cop. She had reached for a dream, and it was out of her reach. Unwilling to embarrass herself any further, she rose to depart.

"No." He grabbed the back of her shirt and pulled her back down beside him. "Don't walk away from me."

"Why? I figured this conversation was over."

"It isn't. We have more to talk about."

"Like what?"

"Like Grace."

So he wanted to talk about Grace. A movie star. The Marilyn Monroe look-alike. A woman he had loved enough to marry. She wished she had never begun this conversation.

"Okay. What is it you want to say?"

"You need to know that I was never a perfect husband, but I *was* faithful to her. Even when I was on the road. Always."

She swallowed. This was something she had wondered about but never would have asked.

"You must have loved her a great deal."

"I did." He took her hand in his and intertwined their fingers. "But living with Grace was a lot like living with a beautiful, vain child who needed constant attention. She was adorable and charming, and I was the envy of all of my male friends, but…"

Rachel was afraid to stir, wondering what Joe was about to say.

"It isn't easy for me to say this—it feels disloyal—but…I love you, Rachel. I love your heart, your loyalty, your wholeness. I love your spirit. I love the fact that you took in an abused teenager without giving it a second thought. I love the way you try to protect your aunts. I love the fact that you faced down the news media and made it possible for me to get my son away. I love the fact that I've never heard an untrue word come from your lips. I am proud of who you are, what you do, and your strength and courage. And frankly, I think you are the most beautiful woman I have ever known, but…"

"But?" Rachel was almost dizzy from trying to process so many wonderful things all strung together at once, but she knew she didn't like the sound of that word.

"I'm not eaten up with pride like some men, but I *do* have some." His voice was low and intense. "From the moment you knew who I was, you've tried to protect me. You even took out Henrietta for me. I have to get back to LA, figure out where I stand, and decide who I am now that I can no longer play baseball. Maybe then I can begin to feel worthy of you. I'll come back as soon as I can to court you properly—but I need to feel like a man while I'm doing it."

Court her? Worthy of her?

"Oh, you do that, Joe." Rachel felt herself grinning wildly in the darkness. Her spirit and hopes and dreams were rising as high as the moon. "You just go back to LA and—"

Her words and thoughts were snatched away as Joe covered her mouth with the warmth of his own.

EPILOGUE

Anna clutched a bouquet of yellow rosebuds against her chest as she haltingly walked down the aisle, trying to keep time to the music. Bobby, solemn as the ring bearer, held her hand as they made progress to the front of the Englisch church.

She was taking her maid-of-honor responsibilities very, very seriously.

The beautician she had visited with Rachel this morning had washed and conditioned her hair until it felt as light and fragrant as spun sugar. It had been wound it into a lovely bun and secured with hairpins. A stiffly starched, formal black prayer kapp sat on her head, complementing the brand-new navy dress Lydia had made for her.

Rachel had given her a maid-of-honor gift of the most wonderful perfume all wrapped up in a pretty package. It smelled just like wild honeysuckle. A smidgen was behind her ears right now!

She felt beautiful today. Almost like a bride herself, as she walked down the aisle, taking her time, savoring every second of being the center of attention. This was the best day of her life, except maybe for the morning she had walked the beach in Florida and gathered seashells.

Life was good again, even though her home had burned down and things had been very, very scary and confusing for a while.

Her family was getting bigger, and this thrilled her. More people to love!

After the wedding, Joe and Rachel and Bobby were going to be living in Rachel's house until they could build a new one on property next to the farm. They said she could walk over and visit as much as she wanted. She couldn't wait!

Joe's daett was living in the daadi haus. He was ready to retire and wanted to be near his son and grandson. She had heard Joe tell Bertha that he knew his father wouldn't like retirement and would probably be working with some local church before the year was out. Bertha said she understood completely.

Anna thought Joe's daett was nice. He always looked her in the eyes and talked with her patiently even though she knew her tongue was clumsy sometimes and her words didn't always come out quite right. He even liked her "boo!" joke and never acted tired of it.

The announcement of Joe and Rachel's engagement hadn't surprised her one bit. She saw a lot more than people thought. She had known for a long time that Rachel thought Joe was handsome. It was written all over her face. It was why Rachel had been so grouchy for so long—because she didn't want to like Joe so much.

Darren was Joe's best man. She was happy to see the two brothers getting along so well. That was the way a family was meant to be.

The president of a local community college had come by and offered Joe a coaching job. Joe had been very happy about that. He had swung Rachel around and around in his joy. Lydia and Bertha had turned their heads in embarrassment, but Anna had liked watching all that happiness.

There weren't as many newspeople camped out on their property anymore. Joe was pleased, but Lydia was disappointed. She had found another sewing machine she wanted to send to the orphanage in Haiti. Lydia had made a lot of money selling those pies and cookies to the newspeople.

And best of all, they now had a brand-new house just like the one they had had before the fire. Only this one had three bathrooms. Two were upstairs! Bertha had been able to pay for the building materials with the money Joe had found hidden in Daett's books.

Rachel had shocked everyone when she announced that she was going to be working only part-time with the police department. She said it was because she wanted to help Lydia and Bertha start up the Sugar Haus Inn again. Anna had overheard Rachel telling Joe, "If you can't lick 'em, join 'em." Joe had laughed.

She thought maybe Rachel was a little bit tired of being a policewoman all the time.

Anna was happy they were going to have guests at the Inn again. Kim Whitfield was going to take Rachel's full-time position at the police station. Anna thought Kim was nice. Lydia had been giving Kim cooking lessons.

Someone waved at her from the audience. Distracted, she stopped in the middle of the aisle and concentrated hard on figuring out who that person was. Suddenly she recognized her. Stephanie! Only now Stephanie didn't have a big belly anymore, and she was with some people Anna had never seen.

Oh! A tiny pink bundle was in Stephanie's arms! Anna hadn't seen the baby yet, but she knew Stephanie had named the little girl Rachel Jo, after the two people who had rescued her.

Anna temporarily forgot her important responsibilities and

wandered over to the side of the aisle with Bobby still in tow. Stephanie obligingly held up the baby so she could see it. Anna let loose of Bobby's hand just long enough to touch the baby's little cheek. It was as silky as a rose petal.

"She's *pretty*," she whispered.

"I'll let you hold her after the wedding," Stephanie promised. Anna's bubble of happiness rose higher in anticipation. Babies were even nicer to hold than kittens.

She smiled at the people on both sides of the aisle as she continued her walk. Everyone smiled back.

Many townspeople who had watched the story of Joe and Rachel unfold had come to the wedding. Even Anna's cousins had arrived in their many buggies and filled up the remaining pews.

As Anna and Bobby neared the front of the church, Joe greeted her with a grin and a wink. He was dressed in a black tuxedo and was by far the handsomest man Anna had ever seen. She decided he was probably the nicest also, except perhaps his daett, who stood beside him holding his Bible, ready to say the words that would marry Joe and Rachel.

Things, in her opinion, had turned out very well.

The music stopped when Anna arrived at the front. She carefully toed to the tape Rachel had put down during the rehearsal, the spot where she was supposed to stand.

She turned around. The new music began, and now it was Rachel's turn to come up the aisle. She had chosen a lacy white dress that made her look like a princess instead of a police officer. Her shiny brown hair was all in curls.

And the very best thing of all on this big, big day was that down the aisle, still limping from his terrible wreck, Eli walked slowly right beside Rachel. Anna had known that Rachel wished Eli could walk her down the aisle—but no one had thought that Eli would be well enough to do so.

Thrilled, Anna clapped her hands in happiness. Someone else took up her clapping, and then the entire crowd was on its feet, drowning out the wedding music with thunderous applause.

Eli acknowledged the applause with a dignified nod of his head before solemnly handing Rachel over to Joe. Tears were streaming down Rachel's cheeks, but she was smiling.

Anna checked Joe's face. He wasn't crying, but his expression told her that he was thinking Rachel looked like a princess, too, as he stepped forward and gave her his arm.

Joe's daett opened his Bible to a passage Joe and Rachel had chosen. They said they knew it was an odd scripture to use for a wedding, but they wanted it to be the theme for this one—as well as the theme for their future life together.

Clearing his voice, Joe's daett read, "'Be not forgetful to entertain strangers: for thereby some have entertained angels unawares.'"

LOVE'S JOURNEY IN SUGARCREEK: RACHEL'S RESCUE (BOOK 2) - SAMPLE

Joe's car crawled forward at the blinding speed of four miles an hour. The black Amish buggy in front of him swayed from side to side as the horse labored up the steep hill.

Even though it would take only a couple of seconds to pass the slow-moving buggy, he could not risk doing so. The chances of meeting another car were too great. The roads in Tuscarawas County, Ohio were hilly, curvy, and increasingly unsafe for the Amish buggies that stubbornly shared them with their impatient non-Amish neighbors and the sometimes careless tourists who flooded the countryside each spring.

Even though he had lived here for nearly two years, he still marveled at a belief system so strong that it caused a people to put themselves and their children at risk rather than succumb to the temptation of owning a motorized vehicle.

He just didn't get it. A car would have protective air bags and seatbelts and a steel frame. A buggy had nothing to protect its occupants except the too-easily crushed wood. To him, the choice was a no-brainer. To them, it was a matter of faith. If it was God's will that they make it home safely, they would. If it was God's will that they endure a tragic accident, then that was to be accepted as well.

It was a fatalistic mentality, but one they had held onto for generations. He respected his wife's Amish relatives, but he did not understand them. All he knew was that he was determined never to be the cause of the pitiful wreckage he'd seen too many times while traveling these roads.

Yes, it took a lot of patience to live in Amish country but it was worth it. He would gladly trade time plodding behind a buggy in this beautiful countryside, versus getting stuck in L.A. traffic, an experience which had once been a daily routine for him. And so he followed the black buggy at a snail's pace even though he was jittering with the desire to see his family.

He made the time pass a little more quickly by flirting with three adorable children peeking out at him from the back of the buggy. Joe waved and one ruddy-cheeked boy about his little son's age shyly waved back. The boy's two smaller sisters, both with white-blonde curls escaping from miniscule black bonnets, followed their big brother's example.

Joe made the peace sign, which they copied—the little girls putting one hand over their mouths while they giggled. Then he waggled his fingers on the steering wheel and they waggled their fingers, enjoying the game of mimicking the silly Englischman in the car behind them.

He gave them the live-long-and-prosper Vulcan hand sign from Star Trek. That was a momentary challenge to them, but they soon mastered it and exhibited their new skill to him with shy smiles. The children appeared to be about a year apart. Stair step children. Common among the Amish.

It wouldn't be long now. He was almost home. The flight to Columbus from L.A. and the two-hour drive from the airport to

Sugarcreek was almost at an end. He couldn't wait to find out what wonders had happened while he was gone.

It seemed like there was constantly something new and exciting for his son, Bobby, to experience and excitedly share with him. New piglets? New kittens? Pears ripe for picking growing in the old orchard behind the Sugar Haus barn? Life was a constant source of wonder to a small boy spending much of his time on a working farm.

Not only did Bobby have Rachel's Amish aunts' farm to explore, he was also welcome at Eli's, a cousin who owned the small dairy farm next door. Eli had raised many fine sons and did not seem to mind answering a six-year-old's stream of questions. Eli, who was a widower, seemed to welcome Bobby's constant chatter.

There were many things Joe regretted in his life, but choosing to raise his son within the loving circle of Rachel and her Amish relatives was not one of them.

During his recent stay in L.A., his longing to get back to Ohio had become so strong it surprised even him. His west coast friends could tease him about living in fly-over country all they wanted but he didn't care. He knew where he belonged and best of all, he knew to whom he belonged.

In spite of the troubles he had discovered in California, the feeling of getting closer to the farm where the people he loved most in the world awaited him, was intoxicating.

The horse and buggy topped the hill and Joe saw a straight stretch in front of him with no other cars coming. He carefully pulled around the buggy, giving it a wide berth so as not to frighten the horse, and then he sped up as much as was safe on this road. It was hard to hold back. He had been gone three whole weeks, and those three weeks had felt like an eternity.

So many memories washed over him as he approached his

hometown of Sugarcreek. Right there was the tree where his truck had broken down. A few minutes later he passed the shop where his truck had been towed for repairs.

Larry Johnson, dressed in stained gray coveralls and with a red kerchief sticking out of his back pocket was pondering the engine beneath the hood of an ancient Ford truck when Joe drove past. Larry glanced up, saw him, and waved. They were friends now, but he remembered the look of suspicion Larry had given him when he asked for a deposit on the truck parts and Joe discovered that his wallet had been stolen.

Of course, the look of suspicion that Larry had given him was nothing compared to the flinty-eyed stare with which Rachel, the beautiful Sugarcreek cop, had lacerated him when she discovered that he was penniless and staying with her three elderly Old Order Amish aunts in their farmhouse bed and breakfast.

Nope, he had definitely not impressed her. A rough-looking stranger. Dressed like he'd crawled out of a dumpster. No ID. No money. He'd been as determined not to let anyone know his identity as she was to discover it. It had been quite a clash of wills, until Rachel learned his true identity…and became his greatest ally.

Those weeks of hiding from the media, unable to access his bank account or to cash in on his fame, struggling to keep his son safe--had taught him a great deal about the priorities of life.

Many people spent their lives wishing for fame and fortune. Too many of them believed that the only thing standing between them and a perfect life was to have plenty of money and admiration. He had experienced both and knew first-hand that it wasn't all it was cracked up to be. His own experience was that fame and fortune did little except put a target on your back….and on the back of those you loved.

Yes, it took patience and grace to live in Ohio Amish country. Especially when sharing the road with slow-moving buggies, but that patience and grace was always returned. He loved Tuscarawas County and the eccentric and loving people who lived here.

If he had his way, he would never leave again. The only problem now, after what he had learned in Los Angeles, was finding a way to stay.

AUTHOR'S NOTE

Although I have attempted to describe the Sugarcreek area and its culture as accurately as possible, this is a complete work of fiction. No individual in this story is based on any person, living or dead, and I did not intentionally represent any real Sugarcreek police officer or their work.

A huge thank-you to: Joyanne and Clay Ham, owners of Oak Haven Bed and Breakfast in Sugarcreek—for creating a lovely home away from home. Bev Keller, editor of *The Budget*—for permission to include the story about the compassion of her Amish neighbors. Les Troyer, linguist, Bible translator, world traveler, and columnist for *The Budget*—for insights into growing up in an Amish household. Former Sugarcreek police officer Jennifer Lowery—for answering questions about law enforcement in Sugarcreek. Freeman and Rhoda Mullet, owners of The Gospel Shop bookstore in Sugarcreek—for a warm welcome and their enthusiasm for this project. Lowell and Diana Youngen of the Alpine Hills Museum—for the use of their rare copy of the history of Sugarcreek. Connie Troyer—for her excellent editing skills. The staff of Summerside Press—for their ongoing encouragement and support. Sandra Bishop, agent and friend—for her professionalism and hard work. Emilie Richards, gifted author and friend—without whom I would still be shoving unfinished manuscripts beneath my bed. Kay Stockham, Jane Hillal, and Jillian Kent, sisters of the pen—from whom I have learned so much about the craft of writing. My family, who patiently endured listening to way too much information about Sugarcreek. And most of all, a heartfelt thanks to the Amish families of Sugarcreek, who asked not to be named but who honored me with the gift of their friendship.

-Serena

ALSO BY SERENA B. MILLER

LOVE'S JOURNEY IN SUGARCREEK SERIES

- The Sugar Haus Inn (Book 1)
- Rachel's Rescue (Book 2)
- Love Rekindled (Book 3)
- Bertha's Resolve (Book 4)

LOVE'S JOURNEY ON MANITOULIN ISLAND SERIES

- Moriah's Lighthouse (Book 1)
- Moriah's Fortress (Book 2)
- Moriah's Stronghold (Book 3)
- Eliza's Lighthouse (Book 4)

MICHIGAN NORTHWOODS HISTORICAL ROMANCE

- The Measure of Katie Calloway (Book 1)
- Under a Blackberry Moon (Book 2)
- A Promise to Love (Book 3)

UNCOMMON GRACE SERIES

- An Uncommon Grace (Book 1)
- Hidden Mercies (Book 2)
- Fearless Hope (Book 3)

ALSO BY SERENA B. MILLER

THE DOREEN SIZEMORE ADVENTURES

- Murder On The Texas Eagle (Book 1)
- Murder At The Buckstaff Bathhouse (Book 2)
- Murder At Slippery Slop Youth Camp (Book 3)
- Murder On The Mississippi Queen (Book 4)
- Murder On The Mystery Mansion (Book 5)
- The Accidental Adventures of Doreen Sizemore (5 Book Collection)

UNCATEGORIZED

- A Way of Escape
- More Than Happy: The Wisdom of Amish Parenting

Sugarcreek, Ohio

THERE IS NO PLACE ON EARTH QUITE LIKE SUGARCREEK, OHIO.

It was settled in the early 1800s by German and Swiss immigrants and is proud of being known as the Little Switzerland of Ohio. During the Swiss Festival, one can listen to booming harmonies of giant alphorns or see inhabitants in authentic Swiss costumes dance enthusiastic polkas in a downtown that resembles an Alpine village.

The area is also home to a thriving Amish community. Buggies trot alongside cars on every road. *The Budget*, a Sugarcreek newspaper established in 1890, publishes a national edition that includes dozens of detailed letters written by Amish and Mennonite correspondents, or "scribes," from all over the world.

A feeling of simplicity and abundance permeates the surrounding countryside blanketed with acres of soybeans and cornfields. Neatly kept dairy farms dot the rolling landscape, providing milk for local, world-class, family-run cheese factories. Thriving home businesses advertise with homemade signs. The largest family-owned brick-making factory in the United States is also situated there. Beachy's Country Chalet serves sumptuous food with generous portions—but not on Sunday! The Lord's Day is reserved for worship and family, two things dear to the hearts of the inhabitants of Sugarcreek, Ohio.

-Serena

ABOUT THE AUTHOR

Best Selling author, Serena B. Miller, has won numerous awards, including the RITA and the CAROL. A movie, Love Finds You in Sugarcreek, was based on the first of her Love's Journey in Sugarcreek series, and won the coveted Templeton Epiphany award. Another movie based on her novel, An Uncommon Grace, recently aired on the Hallmark channel. She lives in southern Ohio in a house that her husband and three sons built. It has a wraparound porch where she writes most of her books. Her mixed-breed rescue dog, Bonnie, keeps her company while chasing deer out of the yard whenever the mood strikes. Her Manitoulin Island series is a labor of love based on many visits to the beautiful island.

For More Information, Please visit
serenabmiller.com

facebook.com/AuthorSerenaMiller
twitter.com/Serenabmiller
instagram.com/serenabmiller